PRAISE FOR

A JUST DETERMINATION

"A page-turning thriller that captures you at the beginning and shocks you at the surprise twist in the ending."

—Capt. David E. Meadows, USN,
author of The Sixth Fleet and Joint Task Force series

"Reading like a melding of Robert Heinlein's *Space Cadet* and Bentz Plageman's *The Steel Cocoon*, Hemry explores gallantry, honor, duty, and patriotism—as well as their opposites—in a book where both the court scenes and the space-chase scenes are page-turners."

—Steve Miller, coauthor of
the award-winning Liaden Universe® series

"Bravo! [A] clean, tight, precisely crafted story. I had a hard time putting it down, and was sorry when it was over."

—Stephen L. Burns,
author of *Call from a Distant Shore*

"A trim novel and a promising series start by an author who obviously knows what he is writing about." —*Starlog*

"Hemry keeps it fascinating with a well-designed background and characters that seem very real."

—*Philadelphia Weekly Press*

"Incredible insight into life on an outer space vessel as if John G. Hemry served on one."

—Harriet Klausner of *Midwest Book Review*

continued . . .

BURDEN OF PROOF

☆ ☆ ☆ ☆ ☆

John G. Hemry

ACE BOOKS, NEW YORK

This is a work of fiction. Names, characters, places, and incidents either are the product of the author's imagination or are used fictitiously, and any resemblance to actual persons, living or dead, business establishments, events, or locales is entirely coincidental.

BURDEN OF PROOF

An Ace Book / published by arrangement with
the author

PRINTING HISTORY
Ace mass market edition / March 2004

ISBN: 0-441-01147-0

ACE®
Ace Books are published by The Berkley Publishing Group,
a division of Penguin Group (USA) Inc.,
375 Hudson Street, New York, New York 10014.
ACE and the "A" design
are trademarks belonging to Penguin Group (USA) Inc.

PRINTED IN THE UNITED STATES OF AMERICA

10   9   8   7   6   5   4   3   2   1

*To Thelma Durnan,
whose heart has been big enough to include
not only her husband, children, and grandchildren,
but also dozens of midshipmen far from home
who will always remember her as
"Mom-away-from-Mom."*

*For S,
as always.*

ACKNOWLEDGMENTS

I am indebted to my editor, Anne Sowards, for her valuable support and editing, and to my agent, Joshua Blimes, for his inspired suggestions and assistance.

"The burden of proof to establish the guilt of the accused is upon the government."

RULE 920
RULES FOR COURTS-MARTIAL
MANUAL FOR COURTS-MARTIAL, UNITED STATES

CHAPTER ONE

☆　☆　☆　☆　☆

"**O**KAY, Kris. I've got it." Paul Sinclair, his left hand locked firmly onto the nearest tie-down, saluted Lieutenant Junior Grade Denaldo with his right.

Kris Denaldo saluted him back, her happiness at coming off watch duty clear. "I stand relieved." Raising her voice so it carried through the bridge, Kris called out, "This is Lieutenant Junior Grade Denaldo. Mr. Sinclair has the conn."

"This is Ensign—" Paul bit off the next sentence required by the ritual of relieving the watch as the enlisted watchstanders grinned at his mistake. "Correction. This is *Lieutenant Junior Grade* Sinclair. I have the conn."

Kris, laughing, tapped one of the silver bars adorning Paul's uniform in place of the gold ensign insignia he'd worn until a short time ago. "When I got promoted, I didn't forget it so quickly."

"We can't all be as good as you, Kris."

Denaldo laughed again at Paul's sarcasm as she unstrapped herself from the chair at the Junior Officer of the Deck's duty station. "That doesn't mean you can't try." Grinning, she pulled herself to the hatch and off the bridge.

Paul strapped himself in, checking once again the status

displays whose light provided much of the illumination on the darkened bridge. Scores of status lights shone a soft, comforting green from their positions on the several other watch stations that helped crowd the bridge of the USS *Michaelson*. Pipes, cables, and ducts ran across the overhead in a controlled riot of vital wiring and ventilation. Despite the responsibilities he'd just assumed, Paul still felt comforted by surroundings that had become familiar in the months since he'd reported aboard the ship.

The straps holding him into the seat, on the other hand, weren't so comfortable. Paul jerked at one tight band, trying to ease a tensioner locked into a setting that had been appropriate for Kris Denaldo's smaller frame. His pull brought forth a loop of slack, which snapped quickly back into a slightly less oppressive state. "Are they ever going to fix these?"

Lieutenant Carl Meadows, seated not far from Paul at the Officer of the Deck watch station, shrugged as he fiddled with one of his own straps. "I doubt it. In any case, it beats floating around in zero gravity."

"Floating I don't mind. It's those sudden accelerations that I worry about." Paul focused on the large maneuvering display, with its view of the outside. Beginning just off the *Michaelson*'s port bow, the Milky Way formed a brilliant banner against the blackness of space. Innumerable other unblinking points of light hung everywhere, marking countless stars, distant galaxies, and all the other luminous objects the universe held. Somewhere off the ship's starboard quarter, Paul knew, a bright blue-and-white disc marked the planet Earth, which the USS *Michaelson* was currently headed away from at a velocity measured in kilometers per second. Despite that speed, her crew would experience weightlessness until the *Michaelson*'s main drive or thrusters were lit off again. In an emergency, those might be fired without warning, and since the force of the drives would send unsecured objects and sailors flying painfully into the nearest bulkheads, experienced space travelers followed the ancient seafaring rule of "one hand for the sailor and one hand for the ship." Or, in this case, "keep your straps tight."

"It's not the acceleration that hurts," Carl reminded Paul. "It's the sudden stops when you hit something. So, now you've attained the exalted rank of lieutenant jg. Are you drunk with power, yet?"

"Give me a break. I just got the jg bars pinned on half an hour ago."

"So? You're not an ensign, anymore. You're no longer at the bottom of the officer totem pole."

"That *does* feel good."

Carl leaned back, scanning the maneuvering screen. "Looks like smooth sailing this watch. Except for that skunk passing near our operating sector."

Paul nodded. "Yeah. Kris told me he'd been hanging around." For reasons lost in the mists of the past, unknown ship contacts were referred to by the Navy as "skunks," a terminology carried into the Space Navy. "All we're getting from him is a generic scientific mission identifier. What do you suppose he's up to?"

"Hopefully, nothing. He's the only spacecraft anywhere close to us, except the range safety ship." Another Navy ship, its blue symbol shining clearly on the maneuvering display, had entered the area ahead of the *Michaelson* to ensure no one had wandered into restricted space. "That skunk could mess up this weapons test if he doesn't stay clear." Carl checked another screen, scrolling through information, then tapped an internal communications key. "Hey, Combat."

"Combat, aye," the Combat Information Center watch officer answered immediately.

"How are you reading the telemetry from the target?"

"Five by five, good buddy."

Carl chuckled. "Good to hear. Thanks." He leaned back and highlighted a symbol on the display that represented their target. "It's a fine day for blowing holes in things. Okay, everything's ready for the test firing. We've got forty-five minutes to go. I figure that means the Captain and the XO will show up in about half an hour."

"I bow to your wisdom. I'll try to look professional about that time."

"You do that. Me, I'm almost gone."

"Don't rub it in. Did you hear who your relief is, yet?"

"Yeah." Carl rubbed his chin with one hand. "Lieutenant Scott Silver."

"Silver? Why do I know that name?"

"Maybe because he's Naval Academy, like you. Or maybe because his daddy is Vice Admiral Silver."

"Oh." Paul scratched his head, frowning in thought. "Yeah, I remember now. There was a guy named Silver a couple of classes ahead of me at the Academy. That must have been him."

"You only had one guy named Silver at the Academy?"

"Naw." Paul glanced back at the enlisted watchstanders to ensure they weren't listening, then lowered his voice a little more. "He took five years to graduate. Academic problems."

"A hold back? They allow those at the Academy? I thought they just kicked out people who couldn't hack it."

"Most, they do. They grant a few waivers. Word was Silver got taken care of because he was an admiral's boy."

"Nice." Carl's tone gave the word full sarcastic force. "For him, anyway. Was he a jerk?"

"No, I never heard that. He got an extragood deal, but he seemed fairly popular. Maybe he was just too laid-back for the Academy."

"Huh. Well, maybe he turned out okay. It wouldn't be the first time someone grew into responsibility, and Admiral Silver's supposed to have all his ducks in a row, so maybe his son's okay. I'm not going to judge the guy before he gets here."

Paul laughed. "What do you care? You're leaving, heading for the paradise of shore duty, where they actually let you go home at night instead of making you work some more."

"Hey, I earned it. Three years on the *Merry Mike* is about two years, eleven months too long."

"Tell me about it."

"Buck up. You've got less than two years left, now."

"The first year was bad enough." The first Captain of the *Michaelson* Paul had encountered was Peter Wakeman, a frustrated and impulsive officer who had caused innumerable headaches for his crew and ultimately ordered the mistaken destruction of another ship. The resulting court-martial had turned on Paul's testimony about the ambiguous orders the *Michaelson* had been operating under, testimony Paul had reluctantly concluded he had a moral and professional duty to volunteer.

"That was *your* fault," Carl observed. "Okay, not entirely. But any baggage you picked up from Wakeman's court-martial came from your own freely reached decisions."

Paul smiled. "Part of that baggage is Jen."

"Well, if you complain about *that*, you'd really be a cretin."

"Jealous?"

"Not at all. Jen Shen would have me for breakfast. I prefer my girlfriends a little less, um . . ."

"Careful."

"Dynamic?"

Paul laughed. "Jen's dynamic all right. Also dynamite. I hope her ship's in when we get back."

"If you want to date another space warfare officer you have to be used to a lot of good-byes."

"We know that. So far the hellos have more than made up for the good-byes."

"Please. We're under zero gravity right now, and my stomach's already a little queasy. Speaking of which, do you think our new Captain has his space legs yet?"

Paul changed his smile to a look of mock disapproval. "My own struggles to get my stomach to accept zero g and occasional acceleration are recent enough that I don't make fun of anyone else going through that."

"You've got a point there. It's hard to believe Captain Gonzalez is leaving us already. We always knew she'd have a short tour as commanding officer since she was a fill-in for the job after Wakeman got relieved for cause, but I'd miss her if I wasn't leaving, too."

Paul snorted. "After Wakeman, anybody could look good. But Gonzalez has been okay. And there'll be some continuity in command since we'll still have Kwan as executive officer."

Carl rolled his eyes. "You lucky dogs. But he's not all that bad. Depending on which Kwan you happen to get."

"Even Good Kwan is no Herdez."

"Ha! You're the only one on this ship who'd say that as if you missed Herdez."

"She was a good XO!"

"No question. Also so tough she could've been tossed out an airlock naked and climbed back in an hour later no worse for wear. They only made one Herdez, Paul, then they broke the mold before any more could be generated by accident. Of course Kwan's not Herdez. I give thanks for that every day. You should, too."

Paul smiled to avoid answering. Commander Gwen Herdez had been incredibly demanding and a perfectionist as the ship's executive officer, but she'd also been so thoroughly professional and fair that Paul had ended up admiring her. *It's like that old saying about what doesn't kill me makes me strong. I learned a lot from Herdez.* "Do you know anything about the new Captain?"

"Hayes?" Carl shrugged. "Nope. He's been real quiet." Hayes had been on the ship for the last week, turning over responsibilities with Captain Gonzalez and observing the crew's performance underway. "But I don't think he misses much."

"I've noticed that. You think he's just kind of hanging around, then you notice his eyes are following everything real close."

"Speaking of following stuff." Carl pulled up the checklist for the firing test. "What exactly is a pulse-phased laser, anyway?"

"I heard the contractors who installed it talking. Apparently it shifts color randomly to counteract protective filters."

Carl looked unhappy. "It's a blinding weapon?"

"Just against ship sensors."

"That's the only way it *can* be used, or that's the only way it's *supposed* to be used?"

"I don't know." Paul looked at the checklist. "This doesn't say."

"Of course it doesn't. Well, there's a lot of stuff on board that could be misused. I guess this is one more."

"Yeah. At least it's not a weapon of mass destruction."

"Did you ever think you'd be grateful for that?" Carl indicated the checklist. "Let's get going on this."

A few minutes later, Commander Kwan, the ship's Executive Officer, entered the bridge, pulling himself over to the seats occupied by Carl and Paul. "How's it going, guys?"

Paul caught Carl's surreptitious wink. *I guess this time we got Good Kwan. I won't complain.* "Doing fine, XO. Just running down the final checklist for the test firing."

"No problems, I take it?"

"No, sir. There's one unidentified spacecraft in the vicinity, but he's outside our operating area."

"Okay! Keep up the good work." For a moment, Kwan scanned the panels where data on the *Michaelson*'s systems overlay displays showing space around them. Smooth arcs traced the paths of every spacecraft being tracked by the *Michaelson*, while a series of lines outlined the sector of space where the weapons test would take place. "Paul, what's the maximum effective range on this new phased laser?"

"One moment, XO." Paul called up the test-firing plan and looked for the weapon's data section.

Kwan frowned, his good nature vanished in an instant. "Mr. Sinclair, you mean you don't have that information memorized?"

Paul felt a chill that had nothing to do with the temperature on the bridge. *Uh-oh. I'm "Mr. Sinclair" now instead of "Paul."* "It's right here, sir. The maximum range is—"

"Mr. Sinclair, if the Captain asks you that question, or anything else pertaining to this test or the weapon, she isn't going to want to wait while you look things up. Is that clear?"

Paul didn't bother looking to Carl for help. He'd screwed

this up all by himself, and nothing Carl could do would divert attention from that. *You'd think I'd know better by now. If Herdez had still been here, I'm sure I'd have memorized that stuff already. But she's not, and I knew I was making jg, and I just got a little sloppy. Stupid. stupid, stupid. At least I know enough not to try any lame excuses. There's only one thing I can say that won't make things worse.* "Yes, sir."

Kwan pointed to the data Paul had called up. "The Captain will be up here soon. I'd recommend you start memorizing that real fast."

"Yes, sir."

"I'm going down to check with Weapons Division and the contractor personnel. I'll be back in a few minutes."

"Yes, sir." Paul watched the XO leave the bridge, then rapped his forehead with one fist. "Maybe I ought to be busted back to ensign."

"That'd be one for the record books," Carl noted. "Ensign to jg to ensign within a few hours."

"I can't believe I slacked off like that. Just because Herdez isn't still here doesn't mean I still don't have the same responsibilities. Getting careless could literally cost somebody's life."

Carl pretended astonishment. "I never thought of that."

"Oh, go to hell. Can you keep an eye on things while I speed-memorize this stuff?"

"First you insult me, then you ask for favors. You're a born space warfare officer, Paul. Go to it. I'll scream if something's about to blow up. And don't be too hard on yourself. *I've* still got a lot to learn, and I've been doing this longer than you."

Paul ran through the test-firing plan quickly, using his Academy-honed last-minute cramming skills to commit as much of it as possible to memory in the shortest possible time. He glanced up occasionally, feeling guilty at being absorbed in the task while he should be attending to his duties as Junior Officer of the Deck, but the bridge remained quiet, nothing breaking the routine of a normal watch.

The bosun mate of the watch brought himself to attention

as Captain Gonzalez entered the bridge followed closely by Captain Hayes. "Captain's on the bridge!"

Paul thumbed off the test-firing plan, converting his screen to a maneuvering display, while breathing a silent prayer that everything he'd packed in would remain in his memory until the test was over.

Carl pivoted to face the Captain. "Ma'am, all preparations for the test firing are proceeding on schedule. The range safety ship has reported all clear within our operating area."

"Very well." Captain Gonzalez pulled herself into her chair on the starboard side of the bridge, buckled her harness with the automatic habit of any spacefarer, then leaned back in her chair, putting her feet up on the display panel before her. "Nothing of concern, then, Mr. Meadows?"

"Only one thing to watch, ma'am. We still have that skunk hanging around the edge of the operating area."

Gonzalez eyed her own display, then shook her head. "Yes, we do. He's outside the area, but I don't like having him that close."

"He's about sixty degrees to starboard of our firing vector, ma'am. Well clear."

"Is he within range of the test weapon?"

Carl didn't have to check. "He will be when we're at the designated firing point, yes, ma'am."

"Then let's move his butt. Tell comms to send him a 'get-out-of-here, restricted area' message. Medium heat version, for now."

"Yes, ma'am." A few minutes passed while Carl passed on the order to the communications personnel, and the standard scripted message went out directed to the skunk. "He should be getting it about now."

Paul nodded with satisfaction. "We're seeing an aspect change. He's maneuvering to head away."

"Yeah." Carl's expression went from casual to concerned as he scanned the readout. "Something doesn't look right."

Captain Gonzalez raised an eyebrow and checked her own screen. "What's wrong, Carl?"

"I don't know, yet, Captain. Something about the way

that guy's moving makes me wonder which way he's pointing."

Commander Kwan had returned to the bridge, unnoticed by Paul, and now pulled himself close to Carl, squinting at the display. "You don't think he's going to leave the area?"

"Sir, he just looks funny to me."

Gonzalez glanced over to where Captain Hayes had hooked himself to a tie-down near her chair. "Lieutenant Meadows is one of our most experienced watch officers. Sometimes an experienced sailor can spot things your instruments can't."

Hayes nodded. "Just like back on Earth."

"Yup. Mr. Meadows, is there—"

Carl interrupted as his display flashed. "He's lighting off his main drive, Captain."

Paul slapped his console. "Look at that vector! He's headed in, not out. You were right, Carl. What's he up to?"

"Beats me. Captain, request permission to order the range safety ship to intercept that guy."

"Granted. We can't do the test shot with him there. Have comms send a high-heat version of the get-out-of-here message to that idiot."

The range safety ship, positioned closer to the intruder than the *Michaelson*, boosted onto an intercept course with the unknown spacecraft. A moment later, a green spacecraft identification symbol blossomed on the *Michaelson*'s display where the skunk had previously been represented by a yellow "unknown" symbol. "He's finally broadcasting a specific ship code. Ah, hell. He's Greenspace."

"Greenspace." Gonzalez shook her head in disgust. "That figures. No wonder they're messing with our test firing."

Captain Hayes indicated the glowing symbol. "Do they interfere with a lot of test firings?"

"They interfere with anything they can. Anything they think is about the 'militarization' or 'economic exploitation' of space. Hell, humans *came* up here to exploit space economically, and once we started doing that some people wanted to fight over who got to exploit what, which is why the Navy's here."

Hayes smiled humorlessly. "So, basically they interfere with everything."

"If they can. But spacecraft are expensive, and we're watching for them, so they don't get too many places. Unfortunately, they got to this one."

"I see. If they enter an operating area like this, do they fall under our jurisdiction, or do we need to call in civil authorities to arrest them?"

Gonzalez waved toward Paul. "Ensign . . . pardon me, *Lieutenant Junior Grade* Sinclair there is your collateral duty ship's legal officer. He will provide you with all appropriate guidance in such situations. Correct, Mr. Sinclair?"

Paul nodded, acutely aware he was the object of two captains' attention. "Yes, ma'am."

"And such guidance in this case would be . . . ?"

It's a good thing I checked the rules on that subject before we got underway for this test shot. At least I've learned something since I was a new ensign. "We're authorized to make arrests and seize property if the protesters enter a posted restricted area and disregard instructions to leave." *And . . .* "We're to notify civil authorities and turn over the protesters and property as soon as, uh, reasonably feasible."

"Very well. If we end up needing to know just what 'reasonably feasible' means, we'll get back to you, Mr. Sinclair." Captain Gonzalez motioned to Carl. "Lieutenant Meadows, did the Greenspacers acknowledge our latest warning to leave?"

Carl double-checked his panel, then shook his head. "No, ma'am. No reply."

"Then have comms tell that ship to get out of here *now*, or we will intercept and seize it. Make sure they know there'll be no more warnings."

"Aye, aye, ma'am." Carl bent to the task, but halted as an alarm sounded. "What the hell? That Greenspace ship is launching something."

"A lot of somethings," Paul added. "What are those?"

Gonzalez was chewing on a thumbnail. "Since that's a Greenspace ship, at least we can be reasonably sure they're not weapons. I want a quick ID on those things."

Paul and Carl exchanged a quick glance. When ships' Captains said "I want," their crews knew they'd better satisfy the request. Commander Kwan wedged between them, his expression and voice harsh. "Let's get that ID for the Captain. Now."

As if we needed the XO telling us that, and as if leaning on us will get the Captain a faster answer. Bad Kwan strikes again, but then he might still be ticked off at me for screwing up earlier. Biting his lip to help hide his reaction, Paul tapped in commands that upped the priority on a target ID. The *Michaelson*'s targeting system beeped a moment later, calling attention to its identification of the objects. Paul stared at it. "They're short-range emergency escape pods."

"Escape pods?" Gonzalez checked the ID herself, as did Commander Kwan.

"There's nothing wrong with that ship," Paul insisted.

"I'm sure there isn't." Gonzalez looked seriously out of sorts. "But they've just sown a dozen of those pods through our firing area. It'll take us and the range safety ship so long to round them up that we'll have to postpone the test firing."

"Sweet," Commander Kwan muttered. "Maybe we should just leave them."

"Wish we could, George, but those short-range pods have real limited life-support capability. If we don't pick them up within a few hours, those protesters will be dead meat, and letting them die because of their own stupidity will make *us* look real bad. Go figure. I've got to give them credit for thinking of this." Gonzalez unbuckled her harness and swung out of her chair. "I'll go get on a private line to the Commodore and let her know what happened. Lieutenant Meadows, plot intercepts to those pods. Tell the range safety ship I'd appreciate it if she seized that mother ship."

"Aye, aye, ma'am. Best-speed intercepts on the pods?"

"Naw. We've got to postpone the firing anyway. Make sure we take a while to get to those pods. Not too long, but long enough to make 'em sweat on whether their life support'll hold out."

Carl grinned. "Aye, aye, ma'am."

The bosun mate of the watch stiffened to attention again

as Gonzalez and Hayes exited through the hatch. "Captain's left the bridge!"

Commander Kwan pointed at Carl. "Keep me informed."

"Yes, sir."

Paul glanced at Carl after Kwan left. "Not exactly the nice, routine event you were looking forward to."

Carl shrugged in an exaggerated fashion as he worked on the intercept plan. "No. But that's okay. This is kinda fun. Maybe I can meet our 'visitors' when we haul them aboard. 'Welcome to the USS *Michaelson*. We hope you have a pleasant stay in the two-meter-square compartment we're going to cram you all into.'"

Paul chuckled despite the stress of recent events. "Thanks for mentioning that. I'd better give the Sheriff a heads-up." He quickly paged the ship's master-at-arms. "Hey, Sheriff. We're going to have some hippie peacemongers coming aboard." Paul vaguely knew "hippies" had been a group of some sort back in the twentieth century, but the term had long ago entered the permanent vocabulary of the military to describe any particularly unmilitary appearance or anti-military civilians.

"Once again you have made my day, sir." Master-at-Arms First Class Ivan Sharpe, the *Michaelson*'s onboard law enforcement professional, didn't sound thrilled.

"Happy to oblige. You've got . . ." Paul checked the maneuvering plan Carl was finalizing. "About two hours before we haul in the first one. The rest will dribble in over the next couple hours after that."

"They'll be prisoners?"

"Until we turn them over to the civilian cops on Franklin Station, yeah."

"Fine. I'll set them up in our finest minimal living standards compartments."

"By the book, Sheriff. These Greenspace guys love publicity. We don't want to give them any bones to gnaw on."

"Ah, shucks, there goes my idea for feeding 'em."

"Once you've worked it up, give me a rundown on your plans for confining them until we reach Franklin. I'll brief the XO after that."

"How many hippie peaceniks are we talking, sir?"

Paul checked the number of escape pods, each of which was automatically broadcasting the number of people on board. "Looks like twenty."

"Twenty? What am I gonna do with that many hippies?"

"I'm sure an experienced cop and highly qualified petty officer such as yourself will find a solution."

"Gee, thanks, Mr. Sinclair. Maybe I can stuff 'em into some of the officer staterooms."

"Can't use mine, Sheriff. The starboard ensign locker is already crammed full."

"What a shame. Speaking of ensigns, are the rumors I hear correct, that you are now a Lieutenant Junior Grade in the United States Navy?"

"That's so, Sheriff. I've been promoted. Any word on whether you're going to make Chief Petty Officer this year?"

"No, sir. But if I do, I'll know it was all due to your inspired leadership, sir."

"I'm glad you appreciate that, Sheriff. See you later."

"Aye, aye, sir."

Carl grunted with satisfaction. "My, that looks purty." On his navigational display, a smooth curve arced from the *Michaelson*'s current path, aimed at intercepting the nearest of the Greenspace pods. From there, shorter curves leapt from point to point, painting intercept courses to where the other pods would be when the *Michaelson* reached them. "We should be able to nab those pods on the fly, if their grapple sites are up to specifications."

Paul studied Carl's work. "That's nice. Hey, maybe we ought to make sure the ship's gig is ready to launch, just in case we miss a pickup on one of the pods."

"An excellent idea. I'm glad I thought of it."

"That's funny, you don't look like Sam Yarrow."

Carl grinned. Lieutenant Junior Grade "Smilin' Sam" Yarrow had a well-earned reputation among the other officers. "Okay, I'll admit you thought of it. Just don't compare me to Sam." He tapped a communications circuit. "Captain, this is the officer of the deck. I have a plan worked out for picking up the pods for your approval. I'd also recommend having the gig ready to launch in case we have a problem with any pickups."

Gonzalez's voice came back over the circuit. "Shoot me a copy of your plan, Carl. Okay, got it. Wait." A couple of minutes passed while Carl and Paul waited silently. One of the lessons Paul hadn't needed reinforcing was the foolishness of bantering on the bridge when the Captain might be listening in. "Very well, Mr. Meadows. Execute your plan as you prepared it, and notify the First Lieutenant to get the gig ready."

"Aye, aye, ma'am. Execute the plan as prepared and ready the gig." Carl switched circuits. "Hey, Ensign Diego. Are you home?"

"Uh, yeah."

"This is Carl Meadows on the bridge. Have I got a deal for you."

"Carl, I'm working on updating my division's training records—"

"Not anymore. The Captain wants the gig crewed up and ready to go while we're hauling in those Greenspace escape pods."

"What Greenspace escape pods?"

"Oh, Randy. Being that out of touch with recent events is no way to make lieutenant junior grade. Let me know when the gig's ready." Carl swung and pointed to the bosun mate of the watch. "Broadcast a maneuvering warning when we hit the ten-minute mark. Which is about forty seconds from now. Also order the gig crew to stations."

The bosun stiffened into a semblance of attention. "Aye, aye, sir. Maneuvering warning at the ten-minute mark, and crew the gig." Carl spent the next few seconds sending a copy of the maneuvering plan to the XO, then the bosun opened the all-hands broadcast circuit and shrilled his bosun's pipe in the age-old naval call to attention. "All hands prepare for maneuvering in ten minutes. Secure all objects and materials. Undertake no task that cannot be completed prior to maneuvering. Gig crew to duty stations. I say again, gig crew to duty stations."

Paul admired the arcs of the maneuvering plan again. "Are we going to do this manually?"

Carl's eyebrows shot up. "Manually? Hell, no. We'll let the ship handle it. There's too much mass and momentum involved to risk a screwup on these maneuvers."

Paul hid his disappointment, nodding in response to Carl's order. He'd seen Lieutenant Tweed, the officer of the deck he'd first trained under, use manual control to make the *Michaelson* dance like a horse under a skilled rider. *Someday, I want to learn to do that half as well as she could. But Carl's probably right. Right now, we've got the lives of those Greenspacers riding on whether we execute these maneuvers correctly.*

The bosun mate repeated his warning at the five-minute point. A moment later, Ensign Diego called in. "The ship's gig is crewed and ready."

"How's its fuel state?"

"Uh . . ." Carl winked at Paul as the pause lengthened. After a few more seconds, Diego came on again. "Three-quarters of maximum."

"That *might* be enough, but it'd be a good idea to get the gig's fuel topped off as soon as you can."

"Yeah. Okay. How long will we be standing by?"

Carl checked his plan before replying. "About four hours, assuming nothing unexpected happens."

"Four hours? Man, I've *got* to get those training plans reviewed—"

"Randy, Randy, Randy. First off, complaining on this circuit is a bad idea because either the CO or XO might well be listening in to see how our preparations for the pod pickups are going, and neither of them is going to be sympathetic to your problem. Secondly, you can link your data pad to your divisional training records via the status panel in the gig's dock. Just make sure you're paying enough attention to what's going on with the pickups that you'll be able to jump into action if we need to order the gig launched."

"Oh, uh, okay."

Carl shook his head, then looked at Paul. "Now you see where ensigns get their reputations."

Paul snorted. "I've had plenty of painful personal experience on that score. Give Randy Diego a break He's only been aboard about a month."

"True. Let's hope he's learned enough by now to pay attention to good advice." The bosun's three-minute warning interrupted whatever else Carl might have said.

Paul once again checked the straps securing him to his watch chair, then glanced back to ensure that the enlisted watchstanders were properly strapped in as well. "Looks like we're ready to go."

"Yup. Since you've got the conn, go ahead and authorize the maneuver for the ship."

"Authorizing the maneuver, aye." Paul carefully depressed two buttons in sequence, telling the *Michaelson*'s computers to carry out the preplanned maneuver when the countdown hit zero. "Maneuver authorized." It had taken a while for Paul to get used to the standard Navy practices of repeating back orders and stating information everyone should already know, but he'd soon learned how important both routines were to ensuring orders had been properly understood and that everyone actually knew all that they needed to know.

The two-minute and one-minute warnings passed, then Paul watched the final seconds count down. After long periods spent without maneuvering, any change of course and speed brought some excitement, as well as extra stresses on the bodies of the *Michaelson*'s crew.

"Executing ordered maneuver," the *Michaelson*'s voice announced. A moment later, Paul felt his body strain against his straps as the maneuvering thrusters pushed the *Michaelson*'s megatons of mass down and over to a new heading. With the ship swinging toward the proper heading, Paul's back slammed into his chair as the ship's main drive cut in, pushing the ship onto the proper vector to intercept the first escape pod. Paul watched the gravity meter climb swiftly to more than twice Earth's normal gravity under the force of the main drives, then switched his gaze to the main display, where the arc of the *Michaelson*'s actual course smoothly dropped toward the new course laid out by Carl. The main

drive cut off, causing Paul's stomach to lurch as zero gravity abruptly returned, then his body hit the straps again as
more thrusters fired to halt the ship's bow on the proper
heading.

"Sweet," Carl muttered, eyeing the perfect joining of actual track with the planned course. "How're you doing?"

"Nauseated and bruised."

"Welcome to the glamorous Space Navy. It's not just a
job, it's physical and mental abuse." Carl checked the display again. "One hour, fifty minutes to intercept of the first
pod. Hey, did we notify the bosun mates we'd be needing
the grapnels?"

The bosun mate of the watch cleared his throat. "Beggin'
your pardon, sir, I took the liberty of passin' that word."

"Thanks, Bosun." Carl shook his head and smiled ruefully. "Imagine if we'd been bearing down on that pod and
suddenly realized the grapnels weren't ready. So many ways
to mess up, Paul. I can't say I'll miss it all that much."

The hour and fifty minutes dragged slowly onward as the
Michaelson steadily headed toward the point where she'd
intercept the track of the first Greenspace pod. About fifteen
minutes prior to the intercept, the XO came onto the bridge,
scanned the displays silently, then pulled himself into his
chair and strapped in. Five minutes after that, the bosun
once again called out, "Captain's on the bridge!" as Gonzalez and Hayes entered as well.

Carl tapped his panel to bring up direct communications
with the bosun mates operating the grapnels. "We've got a
fast passing speed on this intercept. Are you tracking the
pod?"

"Yes, sir." The voice was recognizable as that of the leading chief bosun mate, personally supervising her sailors during this evolution. "Those pods have reinforced grapnel
points. We should bring off the snatch fine, unless he tries
moving at the last minute. It'll bruise him up a little, of
course."

"That's a real shame, Boats." Carl turned toward Gonzalez. "Captain, the grapnels are ready."

Gonzalez nodded almost absently, her eyes on the display

where the pod symbol and that of the *Michaelson* steadily closed on each other. "Very well."

Hayes leaned forward as well. "Officer of the Deck, is the First Lieutenant supervising the grapnels?"

"No, sir. He's in charge of the gig, so he's standing by there. The leading bosun chief is at the grapnel station."

"I see. Thank you."

Carl raised an eyebrow toward Paul, who made a noncommittal expression back. It was impossible to tell whether Captain Hayes approved of the situation or not. Which was how it should be, since Gonzalez remained the Captain of the *Michaelson*, but it left Paul and Carl wondering what Hayes might do, what things he might change, when he assumed command in the near future.

The *Michaelson*'s maneuvering system spoke to the bridge. "Closest Point of Approach to Contact Alpha Charlie One 100.2 meters in four minutes, thirty seconds. Recommend maneuvering to open CPA."

CPA stood for Closest Point of Approach, and one hundred meters at the speed the *Michaelson* was traveling meant they'd pass very close indeed. But that was their intention. Paul tapped a switch to acknowledge the information and recommendation, then hit another command to keep the *Michaelson* from automatically continuing to recommend opening the distance to the pod.

"CPA to Contact Alpha Charlie One is 99.6 meters in two minutes, two seconds."

Carl faced the Captain again. "Request permission to launch grapnel when ready."

"Permission granted."

"Boats, launch grapnel when ready."

"Launch when ready, aye, sir. Standing by."

They could have turned off the *Michaelson*'s announcements completely, but most officers preferred letting them be spoken to reduce possible misreading of displays. "CPA to Contact Alpha Charlie One is 99.1 meters in fifty-three seconds."

Moments later, an alert signified the launching of a grapnel to intercept the pod. Technically, the launch was simply

a matter of letting the *Michaelson*'s fire control system cal-
culate the launch time and direction. In practice, experienced bosuns always let their instincts time the launch. On
the bridge close-in displays, a representation of the grapnel
snaked out toward the oncoming pod. The end of the grapnel merged with the pod symbol, then the *Michaelson*
lurched slightly as the ship absorbed the pod's momentum
and mass, seizing the pod like a catcher snagging a ball in
midflight. Carl tapped his communications panel. "How's
the strain, Boats?"

"A little heavy, but she's okay, sir. A few more seconds,
and I'll start reeling in our catch."

"Our first catch, Boats."

Paul tapped his own control. "Boats, is Petty Officer
Sharpe down there?"

"Yes, sir. Along with all his deputies. We got a nice little
reception waiting for our guests."

Paul grinned. "Be nice, Boats. Use minimal force necessary to maintain control."

"Heck, sir, I never use excessive force." The bosun mate
at the back of the bridge coughed suddenly, his face reflecting disbelief at the statement.

"Never?" Carl asked.

"Well, hardly ever, sir. We got a firm grip on the pod, sir.
Starting retraction sequence. What'll I do with the pod once
I get the dirtbags out?"

Carl frowned, then glanced at Captain Gonzalez, who
frowned and looked at Paul. "Mr. Sinclair, is there any fleet
legal guidance on that?"

Paul swallowed. "Ma'am, I'll have to check."

"Do that. It's not like any of the rest of us thought of it
before now."

Paul called up his legal references, hastily conducting a
series of searches while trying not to notice how the pod was
being reeled in closer every second. "Captain, the general
rule is that an escape pod belongs to the originating ship or
ship owner and should be either held for their retrieval or
left with a beacon for eventual pickup."

Gonzalez rubbed her chin. "That's the general rule, huh? But we just seized that ship."

"Yes, ma'am. The guidance on seizure of ships violating restricted areas says we should hold them for whatever disposition is decided upon by fleet command."

"It sounds like you're telling me we have to drag those things along with us, Paul."

"Yes, ma'am, I think so."

"We can't just leave them with a beacon?"

"No, ma'am. I'm reading between the lines here, but I guess there's concern that if they're left, the Greenspacers might be able to swoop in with another ship and recover them before another of our ships can do the job."

"Well, hell." Gonzalez threw up her hands. "Thank you, Mr. Sinclair. Mr. Meadows, inform the Chief Bosun that we'll need to bring all the pods along. I'd appreciate any recommendations she might have for doing that."

"Yes, ma'am."

A few minutes later, the Chief Bosun called the bridge. "Mr. Meadows, Petty Officer Sharpe's got our, uh, guests in hand. I've got just enough room in this here airlock to cram in two pods. The after lock can hold two more, then the starboard locks can hold another four. That'll leave four, which I think I can shove in with the ship's gig."

Captain Gonzalez rubbed her forehead this time. "Boats, are those pods going to damage the locks or the gig?"

"I can't swear they won't, ma'am. But I'll tie them down good, and pack stuff around them. That's the best I can come up with."

"Very well. Let me know when the ship can maneuver again."

"You can do that, now, Cap'n. We've got this pod snugged in."

"Thank you, Boats. Mr. Meadows, let's go."

"Aye, aye, ma'am." Carl motioned to Paul, who activated the next maneuver.

Once again thrusters fired, then main drive, then thrusters. Paul took a deep breath and tensed his abdominal muscles, trying to stretch his body where it had been jerked around. The next pod loomed only fifteen minutes away on their current intercept course and speed. "Boats, the next pickup's coming up fast."

"Understood, sir. I'm tracking it."

The second catch went smoothly as well, followed by another maneuver to head for an intercept with the third pod. Despite having his body jerked around by the firing of the thrusters and drive, Paul couldn't help admiring the way the *Michaelson* moved smoothly along each trajectory before altering course to the next. *I wonder why making the* Michaelson *dance feels so good? And these clean pickups feel good. too. At least these Greenspacers gave us an excuse for some fun.*

CHAPTER TWO

☆ ☆ ☆ ☆ ☆

O N the third pickup, as the *Michaelson* swung in less than two minutes from intercept, the escape pod suddenly fired its own thrusters, jinking off at an angle. "What the hell is that moron doing?" Carl seethed.

Captain Gonzalez made an angry face as well. "Being a pain in the butt. I guess they're trying to complicate our pickups just to screw up things a little longer."

Carl tapped his panel. "Boats, can you still get that pod?"

"Negative, sir. It's heading off too fast, now. Even if I managed to get latched on, the line'd part for sure under the strain."

"Understood. Captain, recommend launching the gig to recover this pod and continuing on ourselves to the fourth."

Gonzalez nodded. "Very well. Get the gig going. And work up a message to broadcast to the pods that if they keep playing games, we might not be able to get them all recovered before their life support gives out."

"Aye, aye, sir. Ensign Diego, launch the gig and recover the pod designated Contact Alpha Charlie Three."

Ensign Diego sounded startled when he replied. "Yes, sir."

Paul breathed a silent prayer that Diego had been smart enough to follow Carl's advice and remain aware of what was happening. *If he's been buried in his training records, Diego might be dangerously disoriented until he gets himself up to speed. I hope there's a good helm driving that gig.* "Do you want me to draft the warning to the pods, Carl?"

"No, I'll do that. Tell the ship to head to intercept the fourth pod."

"Head for the fourth pod, aye." Paul ordered the maneuver, wincing as the latest thruster firing pushed his straps against a bruise caused by an earlier firing. *Okay, that particular part of sailing around nabbing these guys isn't fun.*

The thrusters fired again briefly to counteract the launch of the ship's gig. A moment later, Carl pointed to his display. "What d'you think, Paul? Give me a sanity check on this statement before I run it by the Captain."

"Sure." Paul read quickly. *To all escape pods. Be advised that you have limited life support. We are attempting to recover your pods, but if you maneuver away from us when we attempt recovery, we may not be able to bring in all the pods before some suffer from life-support failure. I repeat, any measures you take to avoid or complicate recovery may result in the deaths of some individuals in some of the pods.* "Can I suggest adding something?"

"That's why I asked you to read it."

"Sorry. Okay, I'd add something along the lines of 'Anyone who complicates and delays the recovery of their and other pods will be held criminally liable for any deaths that occur as a result.'"

Carl looked surprised. "We can do that?"

"We won't. Civilian law enforcement types can, though. And I'm betting the Captain will want to threaten these people with more than guilty consciences."

"Okay. Thanks." Carl rapidly added the sentence, then transmitted the message to the Captain's display. "Captain, I've got a draft warning for your approval."

"Thank you." Gonzalez read intently, then nodded. "Looks good. Go with it."

"Yes, ma'am. Sending message to the pods now." Carl

keyed an emergency broadcast circuit reserved for search-and-rescue functions, one which he knew the escape pods would automatically monitor, and repeated the statement slowly, then set the communications system to retransmit the warning at ten-minute intervals.

The fourth and fifth pods were nabbed and reeled in by the time the *Michaelson*'s gig had caught up with and snagged the third pod. The *Michaelson*'s thrusters and drive rolled and shoved the ship onto her intercept course with the sixth pod while the bridge watch began concentrating on keeping their breakfasts down. The fairly rapid series of accelerations, vector changes, and abrupt returns to zero gravity had even the most veteran crew members feeling increasingly queasy. Paul made another unsuccessful attempt to adjust his harness straps so they'd hold him firmly and not aggravate any existing bruises, wondering once again why the Navy couldn't seem to design comfortable harness systems. Rumor had it that if aircraft aviators back on Earth rejected a harness as substandard, it got sent to a spaceship.

"*Michaelson*, this is the gig. We have secured the pod. Request scheduled course and speed activity so we can plan an intercept."

Carl made a slapping forehead gesture, then quickly sent the requested data. "This is the *Michaelson*. Our current course and speed projections are attached to this transmission."

"Roger. We copy full transmission. Preparing intercept plan. Request advise disposition of pod."

Carl glanced at Captain Gonzalez. "Ma'am?"

Gonzalez gave him an arch look in reply. "When's the gig going to get back to us?"

"Uh, I'll find out, Captain." Carl checked with the gig, waiting with visible impatience until the reply came. "They project intercept in forty-five minutes, halfway between our pickup of pods eight and nine."

"Good. Ask the bosun where he'll want that pod at that time."

"Yes, ma'am." Carl looked cross as he called the bosun and got the reply, then sent the instructions on to the gig.

Paul leaned close to him and spoke in a whisper. "What's the matter?"

"What's the matter?" Carl muttered back. "I should've realized the bosun needed that information before the Captain asked me for it. At least Gonzalez was nice about it, but she could've burned me, and I wouldn't have had any grounds to complain."

Paul nodded. *There are so many details to handle in such a short time. It's a good thing we've got multiple people watching everything.* "Coming up on the sixth pod." The first couple of pod intercepts had been exciting, but by now the process was beginning to feel tedious. Paul's mind drifted a bit as he imagined his upcoming reunion with Jen, but he jerked himself back to full attention. *This is still dangerous. I've got to stay sharp.*

Six, then seven, then eight. As the *Michaelson* was pushing over to her intercept with escape pod number nine, the ship's gig called in. "We are closing on you at this time. Request further instructions."

Paul glanced at Carl. "They had quite a stern chase to catch up with us."

"Yeah. I'm sure they burned a hunk of fuel doing it."

"Did Randy top off the gig before they launched?"

Carl indicated his readouts with one extended finger. "Nope."

"Oh, man."

As the acceleration eased again, Carl pivoted his chair to face the Captain. "Ma'am, the gig has the pod and requests further instructions."

"So I understand, Mr. Meadows." Captain Gonzalez pondered the question for a moment. "What's the gig's fuel state?"

Carl rechecked his remote readouts on the gig. "I read 51 percent fuel remaining, ma'am."

"Fifty-one percent? How can it be that low already?" Gonzalez thumbed a communications switch. "Gig, this is Captain Gonzalez. Confirm your current fuel state."

Ensign Diego's voice held a hint of worry when he replied. "The gig is at 51 percent fuel, ma'am."

"How'd you get down to 51 percent this quickly? Is there a problem with a fuel tank?"

"Uh, no, ma'am. We, uh, launched at 75 percent—"

"You didn't launch with one hundred percent fuel?"

"N-no, ma'am."

Gonzalez glowered at her display, her face reddening, the fingers of one hand drumming on her chair arm. "Mr. Meadows, order the gig to come back aboard. Have the Chief Bosun Mate personally supervise getting the gig and the escape pod secured inside the dock. Mr. Diego, in the future you are to *ensure* the gig's fuel is topped off prior to launch so that I have the option to use it as needed instead of bringing it back almost immediately. Is that *clearly* understood, Mr. Diego?"

"Y-yes, ma'am."

"It had better be."

Carl turned toward Paul and let a flash of exasperation show on his face.

Paul nodded briefly back. *Carl had told Randy to fuel up the gig. Randy didn't listen, probably because he'd stayed focused on getting his training records reviewed. Now Randy's in the Captain's doghouse, and the Captain is probably looking for someone else to screw up so she can rip their head off. I hope Carl and I don't run into any more problems until Gonzalez calms down again.*

Fortunately for Paul, Carl, the rest of the bridge watch, and any other sailor within Captain Gonzalez's sight and hearing, no further problems hampered the recovery of the remaining pods. Whether cowed by the warning the *Michaelson* had sent out, or simply exercising an uncommon degree of common sense, the demonstrators avoided any other maneuvering, so their pods could be snapped up in tense but problem-free intercepts.

"Knock it off!" Carl gave the enlisted watchstanders a hard look to accompany his order, and both ceased their conversation instantly.

Paul raised an eyebrow at Carl. "They weren't that loud," he noted in a whisper.

Carl frowned, then nodded. "No, they weren't. I'm a little on edge."

"Me, too. We sit here for half an hour, then for a few minutes everything's tense as we grab a pod, then we get beat up by the ship maneuvering and get to wait a while again. I'll be real happy when we either get that last pod or our watch reliefs get here."

"They're here, Paul." Carl hooked a thumb toward one corner of the bridge.

Paul glanced that way, surprised to see Lieutenant Diem and Ensign Gabriel attached to tie-downs there. He checked the time, shocked to discover he was already past due for relief. *Heck. I've been so wrapped up in each stage of this I lost track of how long we've been chasing these damn pods.* "Why haven't they relieved us?"

"In the middle of this goat rope? I wouldn't want to take over under those conditions, and neither would you. We'll finish this out, then they'll relieve us."

Paul nodded reluctantly. "I guess that's true. What if we'd only been halfway through snagging the pods when our relief time rolled around?"

"We weren't. Different situation. Don't get locked into fixed procedures, Paul. If everything could be handled by formulas, they'd have a couple of robots doing our job." Carl paused, his expression thoughtful. "Of course, my robot would be a lot better than your robot."

"And prone to delusional thinking. Okay, we're about to snag the last pod."

Carl tapped his communications panel. "Boats, any problems with stowing this last pod?"

"No, sir. It'll fit. The gig's not going anywhere else 'til we off-load these pods, though."

"Understand the gig's penned in by the pods in the dock. Thanks, Boats. Here comes number twelve."

Another pass, another lurch, and *Michaelson* had the last pod in tow. Carl gazed upward thankfully. "Mission accomplished. Captain, we have the last pod in tow."

Captain Gonzalez nodded shortly. "So I see. Notify me when the pod is secured."

"Aye, aye, ma'am."

Lieutenant Diem stole a glance at Captain Gonzalez, still stewing in her chair, then unlatched himself, quickly swung over to Carl, and spoke in a low voice. "What's with the CO? She looks ready to chew some serious butt."

"It's a long story, starting with the Greenspacers screwing up the test firing. Just be real careful around her for a while."

"You don't have to tell me twice." Diem watched intently as the last escape pod was hauled in toward its resting place in the gig dock.

After several more minutes, the Chief Bosun called the bridge. "All pods secured, sir. Request permission to secure the gig and grapnel details."

Carl looked toward Captain Gonzalez, but before he could repeat the question she nodded sharply. "Permission granted."

Carl echoed the command. "Boats, permission granted."

He gestured to the bosun mate of the watch, who sketched a salute, keyed his all-hands circuit, then blew a wail on his pipe to get the crew's attention. "Secure the gig and grapnel details. I say again, secure the gig and grapnel details."

Lieutenant Diem looked from Carl to Gonzalez. "What do we do now?"

"Good question." Carl gave the glowering Captain a look out of the corner of his eyes. "I really don't want to do this, but I have to."

"I can ask . . ."

"No. It's still my job." Turning to face the Captain, Carl spoke with careful precision. "Captain Gonzalez, request further instructions."

Gonzalez took a moment to reply. "Prepare a course back to Franklin Station. Standard speed. Hold off executing it until I get confirmation from the Commodore, but I expect we'll need to drop off our 'guests' and wait for the test firing to be rescheduled." She turned a hard face toward Carl, then made a visible effort to relax. "Well done, Mr. Meadows. You and your bridge team handled things well." Ripping her harness loose, Captain Gonzalez pulled herself off the bridge.

"Captain's off the bridge!" The bosun of the watch made the announcement as Captain Hayes, his face betraying no emotion, followed in Gonzalez's wake.

Carl Meadows inhaled deeply, then exhaled with relief. "I still live. Can you cook up that course for the Captain?"

"Piece of cake," Diem assured him. "What else you got?"

Carl and Paul quickly filled in their reliefs on other information, then Gabriel offered Paul a salute. "I relieve you, sir."

Paul returned the salute gratefully. "I stand relieved." Raising his voice once more, he announced the change. "On the bridge, this is Ens—" *Dammit.* "Lieutenant Junior Grade Sinclair. Ensign Gabriel has the watch and the conn."

"This is Ensign Gabriel, I have the conn." Gabriel lowered her voice and made an apologetic face. "Sorry we relieved you guys so late."

"It's not your fault. Taking over in the middle of picking up those pods would've been asking for trouble, and the Captain might've raised hell if you'd tried."

"Thanks, Paul. Hey, congrats on the promotion."

"Thanks back at you. There's hope for everybody, I guess."

Gabriel laughed. "I think you earned it."

Paul looked over at Carl, who'd also been relieved of the watch but was spending a few minutes unwinding by chatting with Lieutenant Diem. Paul waved at the other officers. "Later, guys." He pulled himself wearily off the bridge, using the easily reached handholds in the overhead. *Before I got to a real ship, I used to worry about getting stuck in the middle of a big compartment with no way to reach a handhold. I never stopped to think that there isn't any reason at all to have big, empty compartments on spacecraft. They'd be just a waste of space inside the hull.* He floated for a moment outside the bridge hatch, eyes closed, feeling the tension from being on watch slowly draining from his muscles.

I wonder how the Greenspacers are behaving? Aw, geez. That's my job, too. Got to get going. Reaching for another handhold, Paul hastened down to the gig's dock, where the Greenspacers were still being held in a tight bunch by the presence of a menacing-looking Master-at-Arms Ivan Sharpe and his six deputy masters-at-arms. Paul paused as he got his first look at the Greenspacers, most of whom were grinning like kids who'd gotten away with a clever stunt. *They do look like hippies.* "Any problems, Sheriff?"

Sharpe kept his eyes on the Greenspacers as he shook his head. "No, sir."

Paul saw he'd become the center of attention for the Greenspacers. One, a tall man with a beard who carried himself like some sort of secular saint, moved forward slightly before halting as Sharpe and his nearest deputy made warning gestures. "Are you in authority here?"

"I'm the ship's legal officer." *Which has been nothing but a pain in the neck since I got assigned that extra job the day I reported aboard this ship. Why did I have to have had a two-week gap in my orders which somebody decided to fill by sending me to the ship's legal officer course? Being the Combat Information Center Officer is more than enough work without needing to deal with all the junk being legal officer tosses my way.*

The Saint looked at Paul sternly. "We expect to be released immediately. This detention is unlawful."

"No, sir, it is not. United States law authorizes us to take you into custody if you deliberately violate a restricted area."

An intense-looking woman laughed harshly. "Space is free!"

"You'll have to discuss that with the United Nations, ma'am. Now, if you'll—"

The Saint raised a demanding palm. "We will not tolerate being held by military forces. This is a violation of our human rights."

Paul glanced at Sheriff Sharpe, whose expression made it obvious what he thought of the Saint's human rights, then addressed the group. "You would have all died if we hadn't rescued you. It's our duty to rescue humans in distress in space. Our humanitarian duty." Some of the Greenspacers glowered back, while others smiled as if they were sharing a joke with Paul. "You will be held in protective custody until we can turn you over to civil law enforcement authority."

"You're jailing us?"

"No, sir. A warship is a dangerous place. Even a misplaced hand could cause serious repercussions. For your own protection, you'll be kept in two compartments, one for the men and one for the women."

The intense woman laughed again. "We're all equals! We've no need for your archaic cultural codes."

"Ma'am, I regret to inform you that your needs are not this ship's priority. You will follow Petty Officer First Class Sharpe as he leads you to the compartments. Anyone who attempts to damage the ship or leave the group will be dealt with as necessary to ensure the safety of everyone on board." The last sentence of Paul's statement had been boilerplated in fleet guidance for handling situations like this. It simplified Paul's task and helped ensure he wouldn't say something potentially embarrassing or illegal.

Fortunately for all concerned, the Greenspacers followed Sharpe quietly. Some of the protesters obviously lacked much experience in space, having difficulty moving smoothly through the cramped passageways of the *Michaelson* in zero gravity. Paul had to suppress a couple of smiles as Greenspacers bumped painfully off pipes, wiring, cabling conduits, and other equipment lining the sides and overhead of the passageway.

As the Greenspacer men were shepherded into their compartment, grumbling over the tight quarters in the tiny crew recreation room, which had been commandeered for their confinement, the Saint looked back toward Paul and smiled once more, this time triumphantly. "This shows the difference between us and militaristic fascists such as yourself. We don't believe in criminalizing peaceful acts of protest, or confining those who care only for the well-being of others."

Paul fought down his first biting reply, then smiled back.

"That's your interpretation, sir. I think the difference between us is that every once in a while I'm willing to consider the possibility that I might be wrong." He swung around to leave, catching a wide grin on Sharpe's face as he did so. "Let me know when they're snugged down, Sheriff."

"Aye, aye, sir. May I make a suggestion, sir?"

"By all means."

Sharpe indicated the alarm panel next to the hatch leading into the temporary prison. "I wouldn't count on those, sir. Sometimes people figure out ways to mess with automated controls and alarms, and we've no idea what skills these prisoners might have. I want to put my deputy masters-at-arms on watch outside these compartments."

Paul paused to consider the suggestion. The Sheriff's deputies weren't masters-at-arms by specialty. They were petty officers from other ratings, such as fire control technicians, gunners mates, and bosun mates, who'd volunteered for the extra responsibility. Putting them on a watch here would take them away from their primary duties, and make at least a few of their division officers and department heads unhappy. But Sharpe's suggestion made sense. Paul had a vision of Greenspacers with unknown skills and idealistic foolishness loose within the ship for even a few minutes, and had to fight down a shudder. "Do it, Sheriff."

"Aye, aye, sir. I'm sure the XO will approve."

Paul cocked an eyebrow at Sharpe, then smiled. It'd been one of the smoother means of proffering advice he'd received from enlisted sailors since joining the Navy. "I'm sure he will, too. I'll brief the XO right away, so if anyone complains, refer them to me, so I can refer them to the XO."

Sharpe's reply sounded perfectly serious. "Excellent idea, sir."

"Thanks. If you need me after that, I'm going to get some coffee."

"Another excellent idea, sir."

"Yeah, I'm full of them today."

The XO agreed immediately to the wisdom of using Sharpe's deputies to ensure the Greenspacers didn't wreak any havoc on board, leaving Paul a few minutes to unwind.

He headed for the wardroom, squeezing back against the sides of the passageways to let those on more urgent errands pass, then swung through the hatch into the relative haven of the *Michaelson*'s small wardroom. The chair normally occupied by Commander Steve Sykes, the *Michaelson*'s Supply officer, sat uncharacteristically empty. However, Lieutenant Sindh was strapped into a seat at the small wardroom table, holding a drink the Navy hopefully labeled "Near East Tea" but sailors referred to as "Nastea," and staring contemplatively into space.

Paul grabbed some coffee and strapped himself into another chair. "Hey, Sonya."

Lieutenant Sindh focused on Paul, then raised her own drink in a mock toast. "Are our new passengers taken care of?"

"For the time being at least. They shouldn't be able to screw up anything else before we off-load them." Paul shook his head. "It's kinda strange."

"What?"

"Well, I saw those Greenspacers, and I'm thinking, 'Get a haircut, for pity's sake. Stand up straight, get a shave, and get your clothes neatened up.' I mean, they did look like hippies to me, but when I stand back and think about it, I realize I used to look a lot like that."

Sindh grinned widely. "Ah. Culture shock."

"I've been around civilians since I entered the Navy."

"But not recently. When's the last time you were home?"

Paul only had to think a moment. "After graduation from the Academy. I haven't been back since I got orders to space duty. You know how hard it is to get a shuttle home, especially when we have so little time available to take leave."

"Uh-huh." Sindh leaned back, a meaningless gesture in zero gravity yet one that every human still attempted out of habit. "*I've* been back. Let me tell you, it's tough. My little brother, I thought he looked like some sleazy thug. He wasn't. He was just a typical teenage civilian. And my parents . . ." She laughed this time.

"What about your parents?"

"They thought I was insane."

Paul eyed her to see if Sindh was serious. "Why?"

Instead of answering directly, Sindh pointed to the drink in Paul's hand. "Are you going to put that down?"

He frowned down at the coffee. "I'll dispose of it when I'm finished."

"And until then you'll either keep one hand on it or clip it to your belt. Right?"

"Of course! If I just left it sitting, it'd be a missile hazard when the ship maneuvered."

Lieutenant Sindh laughed again. "Okay. Right. So I go home after being in space for close to two years. And I'm neat. I'm really, really, *really* neat. Just like you are, now. I don't leave *anything* lying around, because it might be a missile hazard, or float off and get stuck in something important. We all do that because it's an essential part of the survival skills up here, and it's drilled into us as habit. But at home . . . my parents were just thrilled at first. 'She's neat! She cleans up her room!' " Sindh grinned, wickedly this time. "My little brother thought I'd been taken over by an alien life-form. Before I left for the Navy we had a contest once over who had the oldest piece of forgotten food in their room. I won. Do you want to know how old it was?"

"Uh, no, thanks."

"I don't blame you. Anyway, my parents are happy as clams. For the first twenty-four hours or so. Then it starts to worry them that if Mother puts down a drink, five seconds later I'm securing it in the dishwasher. Like the house is ever going to accelerate unexpectedly and make it a hazard. But I can't help it. They worried about me for maybe another twenty-four hours, then they called a psych to see if the Navy had fried my brain."

Paul laughed with her this time, assured by Sindh's tone that the story didn't have an ugly ending. "What'd the psych say?"

" 'Don't worry,' she said. They know all about this. Psychs even have a name for it now. Learned Work Pattern Universality Syndrome or something like that. The psych reassured my parents that I was still at least technically sane, and the best way to cope was by keeping everything put away so I wouldn't get all twitchy around them."

"Wow." Paul contemplated his coffee for a moment. "Is everybody like that?"

"What do you mean by 'everybody'? All of us in the Space Navy? Pretty much. Just look around sometime. Oh, that reminds me of another thing that drove my parents crazy. I kept grabbing on tight to anything solid within reach."

"Sure you did. That's just common sense." Paul caught himself. "I see what you mean. It's common sense in a spacecraft."

Lieutenant Sindh sighed. "There are all sorts of things like that. There always is between military and civilian, you know, but us being in space for so long makes the differences even bigger. We adopt habits that are necessary up here but unnecessary down there, and all we see for months on end is each other."

"I guess the way I saw the Greenspacers' clothes is an example of that."

"Yes. And the hair. You, me, and everybody else up here keeps their hair short because they don't need long tresses floating into their eyes every five seconds, or long loose hairs drifting through their living quarters. But my mother wailed when she saw my short hair! 'Your hair was so long and beautiful!' Yes, it was. So what? I've got nice legs, too, if I say so myself, but I don't wear skirts up here, either, for what I hope are obvious reasons."

Paul briefly contemplated the vision of female sailors drifting through zero gravity in skirts, then shook his head to dispel the vision. "That'd be, uh, distracting."

"As well as embarrassing and impractical. Paul, you have to realize the way you see things, the way you do things, has changed. It changes for everybody who joins the military, and doubly so for everybody who serves in space." Sindh tilted her head as if examining Paul. "Which, in my opinion, made your decision to have a serious relationship with Jen Shen a good one."

"Since you know Jen, you'll understand a lot of it was her decision, and I was happy to go along with it."

Sindh grinned widely again. "That's Jen, all right. But, you see, you two can understand each other because of your shared experiences. You've both served on warships, both spent months in space, both dealt with similar situations. An outsider will wonder why you never let go of your drinks. But neither of you will ever question the other about it."

"No, I guess we wouldn't. But there's still friction between us sometimes."

"I'm simply shocked, Paul. Friction with Jen? Nice, quiet, compliant Jen?"

Paul couldn't help laughing. "You must know another Jen."

"Not I. Ah, our missing command presence has arrived." Sindh raised her drink in another toast as Commander Sykes swung inside the wardroom, somehow seeming to amble even while floating in zero gravity.

Sykes grabbed a coffee in passing, then settled into his seat before casting a jaundiced eye toward Sindh. "My good Lieutenant Sindh, please do not use the word 'command' when speaking of me. I am a limited duty officer. I command nothing but my little empire of ship's supplies and spare parts." Sykes smiled gently. "Without which, of course, you combatant line officers would all quickly perish."

Paul gestured for Sykes's attention. "Suppo, speaking of supplies, we're going to need to feed those Greenspacers."

"I suppose we are." Sykes took a slow drink, his face thoughtful. "I have just the thing. We have a quantity of emergency battle rations which are due to expire in a few months."

Both Sindh and Paul failed to stop automatic expressions of revulsion. Sindh shook her head in evident disbelief. "Emergency battle rations? You can feed those to civilians?"

Sykes shrugged. "Why not?"

"I'd imagine there's some sort of inhumane treatment provision of the law that prohibits it."

"There's nothing of the kind, dear lady. Is there, Mr. Sinclair?"

Paul shook his head. "None that I know of. But, Suppo, those rations are really rank."

"Nonsense. The Navy has assured me the rations have been pronounced tasty, nutritious, and downright yummy by selected service personnel chosen to taste test them."

"I've always wondered who those selected personnel are, and where they are now. I'd love to have some words with them on their definition of 'tasty.' "

"They're probably in some sort of witness protection program, safely hidden from their vengeful service mates. No, I believe this is an excellent means to dispose of our soon-to-expire rations and keep our guests fed at the same time. Whatever their drawbacks in terms of taste, smell, texture, and similar issues, the battle rations are compact, nutritious, and produce no crumbs or sticky remnants. If our guests try to protest by, say, hurling their rations against the bulkhead, no harm will be done."

"They might dent the bulkheads," Paul suggested. "Do you really dislike the Greenspacers that much, Suppo?"

"Dislike them? Not at all. I believe any society needs those who are willing to question assumptions and challenge our beliefs. I also believe any society that feels unable to tolerate their mere presence, as opposed to outlawing unsafe acts on their part, has problems beyond those the protesters highlight. No, the use of the battle rations is purely a matter of pragmatics. After all, Mr. Sinclair, I'd feed *you* those rations if necessary, even though I confess a slight fondness for your touching youthful naïveté."

"Thanks."

The bosun's whistle wailed across the all-hands circuit. "All hands prepare for maneuvering in ten minutes."

Sindh glanced at Paul as the bosun continued her recital. "Any idea where we're going?"

"Back to Franklin is my guess. That's what the Captain was talking about when I left the bridge, and we have to off-load all those escape pods and our Greenspace guests."

"We'll be back early? What a shame."

Paul turned at the sound of someone else entering the wardroom, and found himself meeting the eyes of the chief engineer. Commander Mae Destin, as usual, wore a cloak of melancholy like an extra uniform. No one on board knew if the melancholy had been born of personal or professional tragedy, and Commander Destin had apparently never confided in anyone in the five months she'd been on board the *Michaelson*. This time, though, her bearing also displayed exasperation. "Sinclair. Just the officer I was looking for."

Paul quickly searched his brain for any action or inaction that might have ticked off the Chief Engineer. "Ma'am?"

"I've just been informed by my main propulsion assistant that one of her petty officers is no longer available to stand watches in Engineering because he's been reassigned to watches as a deputy master-at-arms. By order of a certain Mr. Sinclair."

Paul tried to keep from wincing. Bypassing the chain of command tended really to aggravate those officers who'd been bypassed, especially if the offender was also junior to those who'd been bypassed. "Ma'am, the XO approved the assignment of the deputy masters-at-arms to guard duty." *Thank you, Sheriff, for tipping me off to brief the XO right away.* "It's to ensure the Greenspacers don't get loose."

Commander Destin twisted her mouth. "Did the XO tell you not to bother informing the department heads and division officers whose personnel were affected by this decision?"

Ouch. And here I am sitting in the wardroom instead of working when Destin asked me that. I couldn't have screwed this up worse if I tried. "No, ma'am. I regret failing to inform all those officers as soon as possible."

"I would appreciate it," Destin stated with heavy sarcasm, "if in the future you didn't fail to let me know about actions impacting on my personnel."

"Yes, ma'am."

"*Thank* you, Mr. Sinclair."

Commander Destin swung out the hatch, leaving the wardroom temporarily silent. Paul glanced at Lieutenant Sindh and made a helpless gesture. "Oops."

Sindh flashed another smile. "Don't forget, Paul. For all you've learned, and believe me you have learned a great deal since you came aboard, there is still much to learn."

"I've already been reminded of that a couple of times today. I think I'll go run down some officers and brief them on the deputy masters-at-arms issue."

"Good idea. Make sure you're at a tie-down when the final maneuvering warning sounds."

"You don't have to warn me. I'm a psycho Space Navy type like you, remember? Besides, I've already got my full quota of bruises for today. I don't want a concussion on top of those." Paul unstrapped, then offered a salute to Commander Sykes. "By your leave, sir."

Sykes gave Paul a sidelong look. "You don't need *my* permission to get to work, young man. *I'm* not in your chain of command like the good lieutenant sitting over there."

"I know, Suppo. I just made the gesture as a sign of my deep respect for you."

Sindh snorted into her drink, continuing to laugh as she cleaned up the mess. Sykes cocked an eyebrow at Paul and shook his head. "I'll assume you're serious, of course, since otherwise I'd have to believe you were mocking your elders. John Paul Jones never would've stood for that kind of behavior in junior officers."

Sindh finally got her laughter under control. "How can you be sure, sir? Did you know John Paul Jones?"

Sykes smiled. "Of course. Quite a bright young lad. Now, *he* listened to my advice. Except the part about getting tasks started on time. One day he ended up in a battle and partway through it hadn't even begun to fight yet." Sykes sighed and took another drink. "But it turned out all right in the end. As things will for you, young Sinclair, if you learn from your mistakes instead of repeating them."

"Believe me, Suppo, I intend continuing to do just that." Paul left, pulling himself rapidly through the ship. He had six officers to run down, including the main propulsion assistant who already knew Paul had shafted her. But he had formally to advise even that officer, because he owed it to her.

Most of the officers grumbled mildly but took the news in stride. Personnel were often pulled off for extra duties with little or no notice. Lieutenant Kilgary, the Main Propulsion Assistant, even joked that she was usually the one borrowing other division's personnel.

But, then there was Lieutenant Junior Grade Sam Yarrow. "Sam, I wanted to tell you that Petty Officer Geraldo has been assigned by the XO to watches on the compartments holding the Greenspacers until we get rid of them."

Yarrow glowered back. "I need Geraldo."

"Sam, he's a deputy master-at-arms, and the XO—"

"He won't be any longer. I'm pulling him out of that."

Paul glanced over at Chief Hadasa, Yarrow's senior petty officer, who was attempting to appear unaware of the dispute between officers being played out in front of him. "Sam, Geraldo has to make a request to be pulled off the deputy master-at-arms duties, and the XO has to approve it." *So why don't you stop making a major issue out of this in front of your chief? What are you trying to prove here?*

"We'll see what my department head says about you drafting people out of her department."

"I've already talked to her, Sam." *And Commander Destin wasn't happy at all, but I'm not about to tell Sam Yarrow that right now.*

Yarrow seemed to be trying to find something else to say, then shifted his glare to Chief Hadasa. "Chief, what's the story on these maintenance records? What's with these discrepancies?"

Paul backed out of the hatchway. *And good-bye to you, too, Sam. First he picks a fight with me in front of an enlisted sailor, now he's chewing out his chief in front of me. Did Yarrow go to some sort of antileadership school?*

The starboard ensign locker, so named because it held four junior officers and their meager belongings crammed into every available square centimeter of space, offered a brief refuge. Paul pulled himself to his tiny desk, strapped in, then called up the personnel records for the enlisted sailors assigned to his division. *I need to have performance evaluations done on all my sailors in four more days. And the XO's screening every evaluation with software designed to detect cut-and-paste copying, so every evaluation has to contain original wording. It'd be easy if I didn't have a hundred other things to worry about.*

He'd barely begun writing when a hand rapped on the hatch. "Paul?" Lieutenant Mike Bristol, the *Michaelson*'s junior supply officer, leaned partway into the ensign locker. "Suppo told me to let you know the feeding schedule for the Greenspacers is all taken care of. They'll get three squares a day until we off-load them."

"I thought they were getting soon-to-expire battle rations."

"They are. Those are sort of square." Bristol spread his hands apologetically. "The Navy says it'll feed people. It doesn't say how *well* it'll feed them. Say, do you know why Randy's in a snit?"

Paul rolled his eyes. "Ensign lessons. Carl warned him to get the gig's fuel topped off, but he didn't, so the Captain took a bite out of Randy."

"Oh. Randy owns the gig?"

"Yeah. It comes with him being First Lieutenant."

"Oh," Bristol repeated, then looked puzzled. "Paul, why is he the 'First Lieutenant'? Randy's one of the most junior officers on board, and he's not even a lieutenant, come to think of it."

Paul grinned. "Ancient history, Mike. Back in the days when ships had sails, the guy in charge of the deck stuff, that is the sails and the rigging, was really important. They assigned the job to the most senior lieutenant on the ship, so he was literally the First Lieutenant in terms of rank. Since then, the importance of deck stuff has gone way down. It's still important, of course, but it's not nearly as important as it used to be in sailing days. But we still call the guy in charge of it the First Lieutenant."

"That makes absolutely no sense, Paul. Why not change the name to reflect the way the job's changed?"

Paul shrugged. "Because this is the U.S. Navy, and that's the way we've always done it, and that's the way we'll always by God do it until hell freezes over and forces us to change. How long have you been in the Navy, Mike?"

Bristol grinned as well. "Longer than you, but my Navy isn't the same as the one you nutcase line officers live in. I'm not saying everything in the supply system makes sense—"

"You'd better not try to claim that."

"—but it seems saner than some of the stuff you guys do. So is Randy going to catch major hell for this mistake?"

"Naw. It annoyed the Captain, which isn't good, but it's not like Randy blew a hole in the hull."

"He won't be charged with some offense, then?"

Paul looked closely at Mike to see if he was serious. *I guess he is serious. And as legal officer I'm the logical guy to ask.* "No. Technically you could charge Randy with something like failure to obey a standing general order, or if you really wanted to nail him, hit him with improperly hazarding a vessel. But nobody's going to do that because nothing serious happened, it wasn't that big an error, and Randy's not a habitual screwup. Randy got chewed out for making the Captain unhappy, and that'll be all there is to it."

"I get it. No real punishment, then."

"What are they going to do to him? Cut his hair short and make him stand watches in the middle of the night?"

Bristol smiled wider, recognizing the irony of equating normal Navy requirements with punishment. "Or maybe assign him to a warship and send him out for a long patrol?"

"And then send his girlfriend out on another patrol as soon as he gets back."

"You're kidding. Jen's ship is taking off right after we return to Franklin?"

"Yeah. We've got about a week together, then the *Maury*'s heading off on a mission. I don't know how long, but it'll be a few months, at least."

"It sounds like a conspiracy," Bristol joked.

"I'd believe that, too, if I thought the Navy could manage a conspiracy like that without creating a book-length operations order that everybody and their brother would know about." The ensign locker's communicator buzzed rapidly in the tone pattern which meant the XO was calling. Paul made an "uh-oh" face to Mike as he answered. "Lieutenant Junior Grade Sinclair, sir."

"Paul, get up to the Captain's cabin. She wants you to brief Captain Hayes on ongoing ship legal matters."

"Aye, aye, sir. I'm on my way." Paul unstrapped and swung out of his chair. "Sorry, Mike. Gotta go. Duty calls."

"Better you than me."

CHAPTER THREE

☆ ☆ ☆ ☆ ☆

HALFWAY to Captain Gonzalez's cabin, Paul got another call from the XO diverting him to the wardroom. When he poked his head in, he saw Captain Hayes and Commander Sykes conversing casually. "Captain Hayes, sir? I'm supposed to brief you on ship's legal matters."

Hayes nodded, then smiled at Sykes. "It's good seeing you again, Steve. Let's talk again tonight."

"Certainly, sir."

"Gwen Herdez sends her respects. Apparently the supply officers she's dealing with ashore aren't nearly so, uh, creative as you are."

Paul felt uncomfortable hearing senior officers bantering together on a first-name basis. He could never think of the ship's old XO as "Gwen." She'd always be Herdez to him.

Sykes feigned regret. "Alas, my talents are somewhat unique." He waved toward Paul. "Have you met Lieutenant Junior Grade Sinclair, sir?"

Hayes smiled politely at Paul. "Not one-on-one, though I could have sworn he was Ensign Sinclair this morning."

"He was indeed, sir. I credit my own example with his meteoric rise in rank."

Hayes laughed. "I'm sure. See you around." As Sykes exited, Hayes gestured Paul to another seat. "Quite a bit of action on the bridge today, wasn't there?"

Paul made a small smile. He knew so little about Hayes so far. *I need to be very careful how I talk to him. Not too casual, but not too stiff. I wish I was sure how to do that. The last thing I want is to poison his opinion of me the first week he's on board. This is the guy who's literally going to be controlling my life for the next couple of years.* "Yes, sir."

"You seemed to handle things okay."

"Thank you, sir. Carl Meadows and I are a good team."

Hayes nodded again. "It sure looks like it. Too bad Lieutenant Meadows is leaving us. Who'll be your underway officer of the deck after that?"

"I don't know, sir."

"How close are you to qualifying to stand watch as OOD yourself?" asked Hayes, using the Navy's abbreviation for officer of the deck.

Paul took a brief moment to form his reply as he ran down a mental list of what needed to be done. "I almost have that section of my Open Space Warfare officer qualifications completed, sir."

"You've been on board a year?"

"About fifteen months, sir."

"Hmmm." It was hard to tell what Hayes thought about that. "Okay. Tell me about the legal stuff. Your chief master-at-arms is Petty Officer Sharpe?"

"Yes, sir."

"What do you think of him?"

"He's an excellent master-at-arms and petty officer, sir. I can always depend upon his advice."

"Hmmm." Captain Hayes grinned. "I guess Ivan Sharpe hasn't changed. Say hi to him for me."

"Yes, sir." *He knows Sharpe? Then he just asked my opinion to see what my judgment was like. I wish the Sheriff had given me a heads-up on that little item. What else does he already know?*

"Anything major I should know about in the legal area?"

"No, sir, nothing major. No ongoing investigations or anything like that."

"How often do you talk to the JAGs on Franklin?"

Paul paused to think. The military lawyers on Franklin Station, usually called "JAGs" after the initials for the Judge Advocate General's Corps, were only called upon for serious legal matters. "Not too often, sir. Every once in a while I have a question whose answer isn't too clear from the Manual for Courts-Martial or the Judge Advocate General's Manual, and then I check with them."

"Are the ship's copies of the MCM and the JAGMAN up to date?"

"Yes, sir."

"Do you like being legal officer, Paul?"

Paul hesitated while he thought about that. *I don't hate the job, but it's not my favorite pastime, either.* "It's a big responsibility, sir."

"As big as your line officer responsibilities?"

Paul didn't have to look to know that Hayes was watching him intently. "Yes and no, sir. I mean, no one's going to die because I slack off legal officer duties, like they could if I messed up while on watch, but mistakes on my part as legal officer could hurt the careers of any sailor on board."

Hayes smiled tightly. "Not to mention *my* career, Mr. Sinclair."

"Yes, sir."

"And yours."

"Yes, sir."

"Keep on top of things. I don't want to be bit by anything because we failed to cross a 't' or dot an 'i' on some legal requirement."

"Yes, sir."

"Thanks, Paul. You're the Combat Information Center officer as your primary job, right?"

"Yes, sir."

"I'll have a separate session with you and the rest of the Operations Department. We'll go over that stuff then." As Paul unstrapped and rose from his chair, Hayes smiled again. "Commander Herdez sends her greetings to you as well."

She did? "Thank you, sir."

"Apparently you impressed Commander Herdez. That's not easy to do."

What do I say in response to that? "Yes, sir."

"Are you doing as well as she'd expect?"

That one was easy, if Paul was going to answer it honestly. "I'm trying, sir."

"But not always succeeding? Don't worry. You gave the right answer. If you'd told me you *were* doing that well, I'd figure you for a liar."

Paul hung in the passageway outside the wardroom for a minute, one hand on the nearest tie-down and the other rubbing his forehead. *Did that go well? I wish I knew. It's nice Herdez told him something good about me, but that might mean Hayes now expects me to be the greatest junior officer since John Paul Jones. Well, so far this has been one hell of a day. I wonder what else—*

The bosun's pipe sounded on the all-hands circuit. "Lieutenant Junior Grade Sinclair, your presence is requested in the executive officer's stateroom."

I had to ask. The XO's stateroom wasn't far from the wardroom, so Paul made it there within a couple of minutes. Paul knocked, waited for the XO to call out an invitation to enter, then pulled himself inside. "You need me, sir?"

Commander Kwan gave Paul a sour look. "The prisoners insist upon talking to an officer. Is that right, by the way? Are they prisoners?"

"Detainees, sir."

"Fine. The detainees insist on talking to an officer. The Captain doesn't want to do it, and I don't want to do it. Guess who that leaves, Mr. Sinclair?"

"Uh, sir, if it's a food or berthing issue, Commander Sykes—"

"Doesn't want to talk to them, either. No, this sounds like another job for the ship's legal officer. Have fun."

"Yes, sir." Paul tried not to sigh heavily as he turned to go.

"Oh, Sinclair, make damned sure you don't promise them *anything*."

"Aye, aye, sir." Paul headed toward the temporary confinement areas, trying not to get too angry over the XO's parting instruction. *Does he think I'm an idiot? Ever since I've been on this ship I've been dealing with people making unreasonable demands on me. These Greenspacers ought to be easy compared to that.*

Petty Officer Williams was standing watch outside the confinement area, her deputy master-at-arms patch in place to signify her status. Paul took a moment to wonder how even in zero gravity sailors found ways to lounge against bulkheads. Williams noticed him, brought herself mostly to attention, and sketched a salute. "Good afternoon, sir."

"Not for me." Paul's answer brought a grin to Williams's face. "I understand our guests want to talk to an officer."

"That's right, sir. They've been banging on the hatch and calling on the intercom every few minutes."

"Okay. Pop the hatch, and let's see what's up."

Paul and Williams both stood back, ready for any tricks the Greenspacers might have cooked up, as the hatch automatically released and swung open. But it revealed only the detainees hanging in the compartment, looking toward them expectantly. Paul came forward, stopping at the hatch. "I understand you wish to speak to an officer."

The secular Saint nodded. "We wish to speak to the Captain, to be precise."

"I'm sorry, but the Captain is very busy. What do want to say?"

"We want to speak to the Captain."

"The Captain is busy. I'll listen to whatever you have to say."

The Saint eyed Paul for a long moment, then apparently decided that Paul could keep up the back-and-forth as long as the Saint could. "Our accommodations do not meet legal requirements for prison facilities. Are you familiar with those requirements?"

Not familiar enough to know precisely how many square meters of space each prisoner is supposed to have, but I

*know these compartments don't meet whatever standard
that is. Come to think of it, the sailors' berthing compartments on this ship probably don't meet those standards.* Outwardly, Paul simply nodded. "These are not prison facilities.
They are temporary accommodations, so they don't have to
meet prison standards."

"We are prisoners!"

"No, sir, you are not. You are being temporarily detained
until you can be transferred to civil law enforcement authorities. You are being kept in these compartments in order
to ensure your own safety."

"Surely you don't expect us to believe that."

"I can't control what you believe, sir, nor do I want to try.
I'm simply answering your question. Is there anything
else?"

The Saint held up a blocky-looking, fibrous mass. "Is this
supposed to be food?"

"Yes, sir. Those are emergency rations. They meet all nu-
tritional requirements."

"We demand to be fed as well as the crew of this ship!"

Paul pointed to the ration. "Sir, the crew's eaten those in
the past and surely will again. I've eaten those. But I'll pass
your complaint on to the ship's supply officer." Over the
next few minutes, complaints were registered again regarding the size of the compartment the detainees occupied, the
fact they were detained at all, the food, the lack of means to
occupy their time, the food, the quality of the bedding
they'd been issued, the food, the ventilation, and the food.
Paul fended off each complaint until the Saint ran out of
steam, then watched thankfully as Petty Officer Williams re-
sealed the hatch. The intercom next to the hatch almost immediately erupted into a babble of insults.

Williams looked at Paul, her face hopeful. "Can I disable
the intercom, sir?"

"No. We have to hear what they're up to."

"Damn."

"I hear you, but make sure that intercom stays on."

"Yes, sir."

Paul pulled himself along a series of passageways and

ladders, ducking objects that protruded down from the overhead and flattening himself in the narrow passages to pass other crew members, and on into the wardroom, where the junior officer dinner shift had already begun. "Hey, Suppo," he called to Commander Sykes, the senior officer assigned to provide adult leadership to the junior officers during this meal shift. "The detainees don't like the food."

Carl Meadows examined the mysterious meat in his meal. "My heart bleeds. What were they expecting? And what *is* this stuff, Suppo?"

Sykes beamed back at him. "Syrian beef stew, Mr. Meadows."

"They didn't use a real Syrian in it, did they?"

"I don't think so. But you know the rule, Mr. Meadows. If you can't recognize something you're eating, don't ask what it is. As for you, Mr. Sinclair, I trust you soothed the irate detainees."

"Suppo, there ain't enough soothing here or on Earth to convince someone that those emergency rations are decent food." Paul paused at his seat. "Request permission to join the mess, sir."

Sykes waved one hand grandly. "By all means. Permission granted."

Paul strapped in, eyed his own meal dubiously, then focused back on Sykes. "They also complained about their quarters, their bedding, and their lack of entertainment."

Lieutenant Sindh raised her eyebrows. "Lack of entertainment?"

"Yeah, you know. Reading material, games, videos."

Sindh smothered a laugh. "Commander Sykes," she advised with exaggerated solemnity, "you may be in danger of losing one of your stars in the *Space Accommodations Guide*."

"Really?" Sykes shrugged. "Ah, well, I probably only had one star to begin with. Mr. Sinclair, I shall see what I can provide our guests in the way of entertainment."

"You're kidding." Paul glanced around, seeing the other junior officers also watching the Supply Officer with surprised faces. "Why? We don't owe them a good time."

"Ah, Mr. Sinclair, this isn't about what's good for them, it's about what's good for us. If our guests have nothing to occupy their minds and time, what will they do?"

Kris Denaldo answered the question. "Think and talk and think some more."

"Yes, indeed. And what will they be thinking and talking about?"

"How to make life more difficult for us?"

"Bravo, Ms. Denaldo. I see lieutenant's bars in your future. Perhaps long in your future, but surely someday."

"Thanks." Kris bowed in her seat while the other junior officers applauded her. "So you'll hand them enough stuff to divert their attentions from plotting."

"Exactly. Idle hands and all that." Whatever else Sykes might have been intending to say was cut off by Captain Gonzalez sticking her head through the hatchway.

"Attention on deck!" Lieutenant Sindh called out, but before the officers could unstrap, Gonzalez waved them back.

"Carry on," she advised. "Commander Sykes. This Syrian beef stew we had tonight. You're not going to serve it again, are you?"

"Ah, well, ma'am, we do have some more on board—"

"Commander Sykes. You're *not* going to serve it again, *are you?*"

"Uh, no, ma'am. I wouldn't dream of it."

"Good. Captain Hayes and I are of one mind on this issue, just in case you were planning on using it after the change of command." Gonzalez smiled briefly around the wardroom, then departed.

Sykes shrugged again. "I try. I try."

Paul grinned. "Cheer up, Suppo. Now you don't have to worry about being sued for libel by the Syrians. Hey, has anybody heard when we'll be back at Franklin?"

Kris gave Paul an arch look. "Oh, eager to get back to port, Paul? Could it be the USS *Maury* is in port there now?"

"She could be."

"Ha! As if you don't know. I'm sure you're heartbroken at seeing Jen again a day early. Count yourself lucky the Captain didn't listen to the department heads."

"Why? What'd they want?"

Kris rolled her eyes. "They suggested we drop off the Greenspacers, then conduct some extra underway drills instead of docking. The XO thought that was a good idea, too. Fortunately, the Captain reminded them we had to drop off the contractors, who are on board for the weapons test we didn't get to conduct, and their contract calls for in-port offload except in emergencies."

Carl Meadows shook his head. "Gah. What do they do to people's brains when they get promoted to commander? No offense, Suppo."

Commander Sykes smiled. "None taken."

"I'm just glad their evil plans were foiled. I never thought I'd be this grateful to a contractor."

"Speaking of people awaiting us in port," Kris added, "I saw some administrative messages. A certain Lieutenant Silver is there, no doubt eager to relieve Carl of his many burdens."

Carl smiled broadly. "My relief is at hand. That news is almost enough to make this meal taste good."

Commander Sykes smiled back. "Indeed?"

"I said 'almost,' Suppo."

Paul had barely left the wardroom after the meal when his data pad buzzed urgently. He checked the page, then gritted his teeth. *Garcia wants to see me. Right away. Great. The perfect cap to this day, no doubt. I wonder if I offended the universe yesterday?*

"You needed to see me, sir?" Commander Garcia, Paul's department head, looked up with a frown deeper than his habitual bad humor. *Uh-oh. Now what?*

"I need the personnel evaluations for all the enlisted in your division."

"Yes, sir. They'll be to you by Thursday."

"I need them *tomorrow*. Tomorrow *morning*."

Paul stared at Garcia, trying to imagine where he'd find time to get the evaluations done that quickly. "Sir? Tomorrow morning? But—"

"*Tomorrow morning*." Garcia unbent enough to add an explanation. "Because the test firing was postponed, we're heading back to Franklin Station. That leaves a hole in our operating schedule. The XO wants the evaluations done through the department head level before we get to Franklin so everyone can concentrate on preparing for heading out for the rescheduled test firing."

Oh, great. He's *got a hole in* his *schedule, so I have to spend the next twelve hours straight writing like a madman, in addition to little things like standing watches and taking care of my other duties. Thanks for thinking of us, XO.* "Yes, sir." It wasn't Garcia's fault, so there wasn't any sense in complaining to him. *Not that complaining about stuff to Garcia ever makes much sense.*

"Where's Ensign Taylor?"

Ensign Taylor had been assigned as the ship's Electronic Materials officer when she reported aboard. For some reason, perhaps because much of Taylor's work supported Paul's job as Combat Information Center officer, Garcia had decided Taylor worked for Paul. "I don't know, sir."

"Make sure she gets her evals in on time." Garcia turned away in obvious dismissal.

Paul fought down an impulse to make a rude face at Garcia's back. *Taylor's a mustang, for crying out loud. Former enlisted, worked her way up the ranks, has been in the Navy almost as long as I've been alive, and* I'm *supposed to ride herd on her. Yeah, that makes sense.*

Paul pulled himself rapidly back toward his stateroom, paging Taylor as he did so to pass on the new deadline for the evaluations. Taylor's response came almost immediately, and included a few obscenities Paul hadn't heard before. *I wonder if I should ask her what those mean? That'd probably be a bad idea.*

Kris Denaldo dodged to one side and looked alarmed as Paul darted past. "What's up, Paul? You look like general quarters is about to be called."

"Close enough. You didn't hear? The XO wants the enlisted evals done before we get back to Franklin. Mine are due in tomorrow morning. I'll bet you'll soon get word yours are, too."

"Oh, no. I've got the midwatch! I was about to grab a few hours of sleep before I go back on watch at midnight."

"It's going to be a long night, Kris. I'd lay in some extra coffee if I was you."

"Yeah. Thanks for the heads-up." Denaldo reversed her own course and hurried back toward the Port Ensign Locker as Paul continued toward his own stateroom.

Ensign Diego was watching a movie on his desk display when Paul swung in. The video was some old war movie, apparently set during the twentieth century. On screen, a grizzled warhorse of an officer glared at a motley collection of soldiers and announced "Reveille tomorrow morning is at 0600" as his soldiers groaned.

Diego laughed. "How come *they* get to sleep in?"

"They must be on holiday routine," Paul replied. "Unlike us. Bad news, Randy. Be advised the enlisted evaluations in my department, and probably yours as well, will be due tomorrow morning. I'd get to work writing if I was you."

Diego looked horrified. "Tomorrow morning? Why are our department heads doing that to us?"

"The XO wants it that way."

"But I thought our department heads were supposed to look out for us."

Oh, man. Was I ever that naive? "Let me pass on some wisdom, Randy. I got told this right after I reported on board. Officers in the Space Navy tend to fall into three categories. There's the exiles, guys who think they've been unjustly consigned to isolated duty in which they've little chance to maneuver for promotion. So the exiles tend to ride their subordinates hard in hope of somehow gaining favorable recognition for themselves. Then there's the survivors, officers who are merely trying to endure their tours without killing themselves or anyone else. They're usually relatively easygoing for Space Warfare officers, but I imagine you can already guess there aren't that many survivors at department head level and above."

Randy Diego grimaced. "Yeah. I haven't met any I'd call easygoing. Except for Commander Sykes."

"He's a special case. Finally, there are the idealists, who

believe in human destiny in space and are willing to put up with extra hardships to help accomplish that, even if it doesn't necessarily enhance their careers. Paul didn't say that he'd been pegged as an idealist early on by his then-fellow-ensign Jen Shen. "Now, my department head, Commander Garcia, is very definitely an exile, which doesn't make life for me any easier and means Garcia's number one priority is looking good. Trying to talk the XO out of some new deadline the XO dreamed up is no way to look good. What about your department head?"

"Commander Nimitz? Uh, I think he'd be an idealist."

"Okay, so would an idealist, willing to undergo hardships himself, beg off the XO's new deadline so you can get a halfway-decent night's sleep?"

Randy slumped for a moment, then with a flurry of curses shut off the movie and pulled up his own evaluation files. The compartment stayed silent after that, except for the sporadic sounds of Paul and Randy working.

Kris Denaldo rapped on the hatch coaming and leaned in. "Got word on the XO's anti-cut-and-paste program. As long as you make sure at least every fourth word varies, even by one letter, it'll give you a clean bill of health."

"Really?" Paul looked at his work and grinned. "Oh, that'll make things go a lot faster. How'd you find out, Kris?"

"I ran into Senior Chief Kowalski, and he happened to mention it."

"God bless him." Senior Chiefs weren't technically fonts of all knowledge, but they were close enough that smart officers tried to work well with them.

"Later."

Kris vanished, followed a moment later by a red-faced Sam Yarrow. "What'd Denaldo want?" he asked the compartment in general.

Paul debated not answering for a moment, then decided that keeping silent would be acting too much like Sam. "She'd just talked to the Senior Chief, who said—"

"I haven't got time for whatever the Senior Chief told

Kris Denaldo." Yarrow strapped into his chair and called up his own evaluation files.

Paul raised one eyebrow, then glanced at Randy Diego, who favored Yarrow with a "screw you" look. Paul smiled, shrugged, and went back to work as Randy smiled in turn.

Hours later, Paul closed his files out and blinked at the time display. *I have to go on watch again at 0400, which means getting on the bridge by 0330 to turn over with Kris, which means getting up no later than 0300. Hey, I might get three hours sleep tonight. What a deal. I sure hope tomorrow—* Paul checked the time again, seeing it was past midnight, and corrected himself. *I sure hope today's better than yesterday.*

ABOUT twenty-four hours later, Paul stood beside Sheriff Sharpe as the Greenspacers were herded off of the USS *Michaelson* by a bevy of security personnel. Some of the *Michaelson*'s crew gawked at the protesters, while others like Sharpe eyed them disdainfully. The Saint offered Paul a fierce grin in passing then called out, "Until next time!"

Sharpe blew out a breath. "Looks like you made a friend, sir."

"Yeah. Do we get some kind of receipt for turning these guys over in one piece with no bruises?"

"They got bruises, sir. We maneuvered some after picking 'em up, remember?"

"Oh, yeah."

"But I got the receipt, sir. We're clear."

"Great. I'll tell the XO." Paul sensed someone nearby and turned to see Captain Gonzalez there. "Good evening, ma'am."

"Good evening, Paul." Gonzalez watched as the Greenspacers were marched away. "Never a dull moment, eh?"

"No, ma'am."

"Can you believe I'll miss it? Even this kind of nonsense. There's no other job like it."

"I won't argue with that, ma'am."

Gonzalez grinned. "I believe you have a visitor, Mr. Sinclair."

Paul followed her gaze, then smiled himself. Jen was a little hard to spot in the crowd on the pier since many of the others there were taller than her. She smiled brightly when their eyes met, walked to the USS *Michaelson*'s brow, saluted the national flag at the aft end of the *Michaelson*, then saluted Ensign Gabriel, who was officer of the deck in port at the moment. "Request permission to come aboard."

"Permission granted."

Jen saluted Captain Gonzalez as well. "Good evening, ma'am."

"Good evening, Ms. Shen. Nice to see you again. I'll leave you two alone." With an indulgent smile, Gonzalez left the quarterdeck.

Jen grinned, then looked at Paul. "Hey, sailor. New in town?"

Paul smiled wider. "Yup, and looking for a good time. You know of any prospects?"

"I'm not busy tonight."

"Unfortunately, I am."

Jen made a face. "Duty?"

"Yep. I can't leave the ship. Can I interest you in a wardroom meal and a flick afterward?"

"Be still my heart. Okay. Hey, what's this?" Jen pointed at the silver bars on Paul's collar. "You got promoted!"

"You don't have to sound so surprised."

"I'm not. Your name showed up on the promotion list a while back. But it's still cool. We'll have to celebrate."

Paul ached to hug Jen, but with them both in uniform and him on duty, that would violate a number of regulations regarding public displays of affection. As if reading his mind, Jen reached out to squeeze his arm.

Petty Officer Sharpe cleared his throat. "My work here is done, sir. Request permission to get on with my life."

Paul returned Sharpe's salute. "Permission granted, Sheriff. Have fun."

"Thank you, sir." Sharpe flashed a grin. "You kids be good tonight."

"You don't have to worry about busting us. We both know the regs about no hanky-panky on ships."

Jen gave Sharpe an arch look. "Heck, Petty Officer Sharpe, I can't even kiss this guy. Do you know how hard it is not to do that?"

"Not ever having had the urge to kiss him, ma'am, I can't say I do."

"That's a relief." With another grin, Sharpe left the quarterdeck. "Paul, how *do* you put up with that guy?"

"The Sheriff? He's respectful when he should be, he never crosses the line into being too familiar, and he really knows his job."

"Works for me." They headed for the wardroom. "So, what's tomorrow look like on the good ship *Merry Mike*?"

Paul paused outside the wardroom hatch. "Change of command ceremony. After that, rumor says we'll get early liberty."

"Ohhhh, good deal."

"Then tomorrow night Carl's got his farewell laid on at Fogarty's. You'll be there, right?"

"I wouldn't miss it." Jen stared down the passageway. "It's funny. The *Michaelson* stays the same ship. It was my home for more days, weeks, and months at a stretch than I care to remember, a place I knew like the back of my hand. But as the people I knew on board transfer off she's slowly becoming a place I don't belong. I belong on some past version of the *Merry Mike*— one crewed by the memories of officers and enlisted who have gone on to other assignments. I wonder if this is how a ghost feels?"

Jen stood silent for a few moments, leaving Paul to think through her words. *I don't understand. I guess because I'm seeing the changes happen one by one, and they don't impact on me the way seeing a bunch at once would. Or maybe because the* Michaelson *is still home for me, all too often twenty-four/seven. I wonder what'll it feel like to watch her leave port, knowing I don't belong on board anymore?* He glanced at Jen's face, then reached out to squeeze her shoulder. "You feel real to me."

"Watch it, sailor. You're going to need that hand someday." But Jen grinned to remove any hint of real threat from her words. "Life goes on. Whether we like it or not."

"Yeah. Speaking of which, are you coming to our change of command?"

"Sorry. No can do. I served less than forty-eight hours under Gonzalez, so I can't convince my department head to let me go. But I'll bolt from the *Maury* the instant liberty call goes down. How's your new Captain look? Is he another Wakeman?"

"Hell, no." Paul couldn't hide his reaction to the thought. "Hayes seems okay. Of course, he hasn't taken over, yet." As an observer, Hayes had been bound to follow the way Gonzalez wanted to run the ship. As Captain, Hayes would be able to change things to suit himself.

"Speaking of captains, we're meeting for dinner on Thursday."

"Gee, Jen, that's three days from now, right before your own ship leaves. Are you sure it's a good idea to plan for that?"

"Excuse me, Paul. I didn't say 'can we meet.' I said we *are* meeting."

"What's so important about dinner that night?"

"The *Mahan* is in port. Long-term refit."

"Uh, yeah. So?"

"So that means her captain is in port, too." Jen paused, eyeing Paul as he looked baffled. "Captain Kay Shen."

"Captain Shen? Your father?"

"The only one I know of."

"Captain Shen?"

"You already said that."

"Your father."

"Oh, for heaven's sake. Look, I'll be at the *Michaelson* by 1730 that night to make sure you look decent. We'll be dining on the *Mahan* as guests of the Captain, so you'll need to break out your service dress. Mine's fresh-pressed. How's yours?"

"Uh . . ."

"Wadded up in the back of a drawer? Probably. We've got a couple of days to see what we can do with it. Although

I don't know what you were planning to wear to the change of command. Are you okay?"

"Yes, I'm fine."

"You're not worried about meeting my father, are you?"

"What's he like? You've never said much about him."

"He's my father. Don't worry. It's no big deal."

Jen walked into the wardroom, exchanging greetings with the other officers there whom she knew, while Paul hung back for a moment. *No big deal? Give me a break. Her father's the Captain of the* Mahan? *Life just keeps getting more complicated.*

CHAPTER FOUR

☆ ☆ ☆ ☆ ☆

THERE wasn't any one place on the *Michaelson* even remotely big enough for the entire crew to gather, so the
change-of-command ceremony took place in a special hall
on Franklin Station that existed for just such functions. With
the exception of a skeleton duty section remaining behind
on the *Michaelson* to watch over the ship, every other officer and enlisted was gathered in the hall, the sailors ranked
by their divisions, the divisions grouped into their departments, and the officers in charge of each standing out in
front of their division or department. Chief Imari, the leading chief petty officer for Paul's Combat Information Center
division, walked down the ranks of sailors in their unit, trying to form them into straight lines, align the ranks front to
back, and correct any sailor whose idea of standing at attention didn't conform to Navy standards.

Grumbling under her breath, Chief Imari came up to Paul
and saluted. "OI Division assembled and accounted for, sir,"
she reported, using the shipboard designation for the unit.

Paul returned the salute, feeling stiff in his formal dress
uniform. "Thanks, Chief. They look pretty good."

Imari glanced back at them. "For sailors, I guess. Just be

glad there aren't any Marines around to make them look bad. And that they don't have to march anywhere." She shook her head. "Sailors don't march worth a damn, sir."

"I know." Paul remembered being a midshipman at the Naval Academy, where slightly sloppy marching was often considered a sign of distinction. Army cadets at West Point or Air Force cadets at Colorado Springs marched in perfect formations. But Navy midshipmen were above all that, except when the officers and senior enlisted training them cracked down. Paul turned his head and spoke in a clear but low voice. "OI Division, puh-rade rest!" With a slightly ragged movement, the sailors went from the erect posture of attention to the slightly more relaxed position of parade rest, their legs spread slightly and their arms crossed behind them, with their hands overlapping at the base of their spines.

Commander Garcia walked rapidly across the front of the divisions in his department, glaring at each unit in turn. Apparently finding no problems he could hammer anyone for, Garcia took his proper position in front of the rest, his back stiff even at parade rest in an attempt to look very, very professional.

Paul and the rest of the crew waited. Aside from an occasional scuffing sound or a brief cough, everyone remained silent. The minutes crawled, and Paul let his mind wander. At least at parade rest individuals could maintain their stance for long periods without cramping anything, but inexperienced sailors could still pass out if they held themselves too tightly. Paul, with years of Academy experience of standing around at parade rest waiting for something to happen, didn't have any problem, but after a long enough time he came to attention, pivoted 180 degrees, and checked over his division carefully to see if anyone looked about to fall over. No one did, so Paul pivoted to face front again and resumed his parade rest stance.

Finally, a door at the back of the hall opened, and Commander Kwan strode briskly to the front and center of the room. "Attention on deck!" he snapped.

The crew of the *Michaelson* came to attention, not with

the crisp snap Marines would have easily achieved, but with a slightly drawn-out rustle of uniforms. Kwan eyed them narrowly, then turned to face the door through which he'd entered. "Post the colors." From somewhere, the "Star-Spangled Banner" began playing. "Hand salute."

Paul brought his right arm up, his hand flat, the index finger against his right temple. If his sailors had been carrying rifles, they'd have been ordered to present arms, but since they didn't have rifles, they stayed at attention. Three sailors entered, the front one carrying at a slight angle a short flagpole from which a brilliant American flag hung, the other two behind him with the flags of the U.S. Navy and the U.S. Marine Corps. The honor guard marched slowly across the hall to the front center, placed the flags into stands awaiting them, then stepped back and saluted as well. The music continued for a few more seconds, while Paul recited the words in his head.

Silence fell for a moment. "Two," Commander Kwan called out, and all those saluting brought their arms back down to their sides. Kwan saluted again as Captain Gonzalez and Captain Hayes started to enter.

A bosun mate standing at the door piped a full wail. Six other sailors, arranged three to a side on either side of the door, came to attention, fulfilling the ancient role of sideboys. Some of the "sideboys" were women, of course, but in the change-of-command ceremony they retained the name given back when ships traveled under sail and were built of wood. Another sailor bonged a bell four times in pairs of two bongs and announced "USS *Michaelson*, arriving" as Gonzalez passed through. Hayes was heralded with the announcement "Captain, United States Navy, arriving." The captains returned Kwan's salute, and Kwan marched to stand to one side.

Gonzalez let her gaze wander over the crew for a moment. "Parade rest." Another prolonged shuffle followed. "I am here today for one of the most painful tasks any officer must face, the need to say farewell to a ship and a crew who have served me and their nation well. My superiors tell me I'm leaving the *Michaelson* with a good record, that while I was in command the ship performed well, and her crew performed better. But I know the only reason I look good to my superiors now is because of the crew I had the honor to lead for the past year. I thank you. I could talk at length about your sacrifices, about the deeds you accomplished, about how well you met every challenge. But I'm not a big talker, as you know. I hope I have nonetheless offered praise each time it was merited to each of you who merited it. Now, rather than hold you in formation for an extended period while I reminisce about the good old days and go over my career day by day, I will cease this speech and let my actions, and yours, speak for me."

Captain Gonzalez pulled out her orders, but stopped as Senior Chief Kowalski stepped forth, carrying a large object. "Ma'am, with the compliments of the crew of the USS *Michaelson*."

Gonzalez smiled slightly and took the object, then carefully pulled off its wrapping. A gleaming model of the USS *Michaelson* emerged, its football shape shone to a high polish instead of the vision-defying dullness of the real ship. Captain Gonzalez's face lit up. "Thank you. This will be the center of my love-me wall, I promise. Thank you very much."

Paul found himself smiling as well. A "love-me wall" was the slang for the place where a sailor hung up all the pictures, plaques, and medals acquired in the course of a career. Paul's own "love-me wall" (if he'd a wall to use that way) would be very sparse at the moment, limited to his Academy diploma and his ensign bars. He imagined Gonzalez's wall, made up of the achievements and assignments of more than twenty years in the Navy, with the model of the *Michaelson* shining in the middle. It felt nice to think about.

Kowalski went back to his position, and Gonzalez returned her attention to her orders, reading them aloud as tradition required. She went through the boilerplate in every set of orders, to the heart of these. "When relieved as commanding officer, USS *Michaelson*, proceed to duty on staff, Joint Chiefs of Staff, Pentagon, Washington D.C." Gonzalez licked her lips, her eyes lowered, then stepped back.

Captain Hayes stepped forward and held up his orders. Paul watched, barely listening, until Hayes reached the important part. ". . . Proceed port in which USS *Michaelson* (CLE(S)-3) may be, upon arrival assume duties as commanding officer."

Commander Kwan pivoted to face the crew. "Attention on deck!"

Captain Hayes faced Gonzalez and saluted. "I relieve you, ma'am."

Captain Gonzalez returned the salute. "I stand relieved."

Instead of leaving at that point, Captain Gonzalez faced the crew again. "With Captain Hayes's kind permission, I have been allowed to issue one more order to the crew of the USS *Michaelson*. Early liberty shall be granted today, commencing immediately upon the completion of this ceremony." A brief murmur of excitement rose up, quickly quelled as officers and chiefs turned their heads and glowered back at the enlisted ranks.

The two captains headed for the door. As Gonzalez departed through the channel between the sideboys, the bosun piped again, and the bell bonged four more tunes. "Captain, United States Navy, departing." A moment later, Hayes followed. "USS *Michaelson*, departing." The *Michaelson*, and her crew, had a new master.

Commander Kwan faced the crew again. "Officers and crew of the USS *Michaelson*, you are dismissed except for those members of the duty section present."

Paul relaxed, taking a deep breath and letting it out as a babble of voices arose around him and the neat ranks started to dissolve into their component sailors. "Chief, they're all yours."

Chief Imari saluted him with a grin. "Only for a moment, Mr. Sinclair. OI Division, duty section personnel return to the ship. *Directly* to the ship. All the rest of you are dismissed until expiration of liberty at 0700 tomorrow."

Paul started walking back to the ship himself. He didn't really have anyplace else to go for a while, and there was still plenty of work to catch up on.

But he still found himself leaving the *Michaelson* as soon

as he could reasonably head for the *Maury*, docked one section over from his own ship. The *Maury* and the *Michaelson* were sister ships, part of the same class of spacecraft built from the same plans. Yet there were subtle differences to the *Maury*'s quarterdeck, the results of years of minor changes. A fitting that on the *Michaelson* shone with polished metal, on the *Maury* revealed nothing but a smooth coat of paint. The *Maury*'s bell had been set perhaps a half meter to one side of where the *Michaelson*'s bell rested. Paul stood on the brow leading to the *Maury*'s quarterdeck, saluted aft to the national flag, then saluted the officer of the deck. "Request permission to come aboard."

The *Maury*'s ensign returned the salute. "Granted. What can I do for you, sir?"

Sir? Oh, yeah, I'm not an ensign anymore. "I'm here to see Lieutenant Junior Grade Shen. Personal business," Paul added, to ensure the ensign wouldn't put too much priority on getting Jen to the quarterdeck.

"Lieutenant Shen? Oh." The ensign grinned. "You're Lieutenant Sinclair?"

Paul turned to make his name tag fully visible. "Right."

"I'll let her know you're here."

Jen popped out onto the quarterdeck a few minutes later. "You're early."

"We got early liberty, just like I said we might."

"And you spent it working until you could come over here."

"Uh . . ." *How did she know?*

"Give me a couple of minutes. Want to come inside?"

Paul hesitated. *Inside her ship? Why does that feel strange?* "Okay."

Jen led the way through passageways whose small differences jarred with their overall familiarity before stopping at her stateroom hatch. "Why don't you wait out here for appearances' sake?"

"Why'd I come in if I was going to wait outside?"

"You'll survive." She went inside.

Paul heard her talking to her roommate as he waited.

Some sailors came by, giving him curious looks, then a lieutenant who frowned slightly. "Can I help you?"

"No, thanks, sir. I'm just waiting for Je— I mean, Ms. Shen."

"Oh." The lieutenant smiled. "She's taken, you know."

Jen popped out at that moment. "Hey, Gord. Have you met Paul?"

"Oh, this is The Paul." The Lieutenant laughed, emphasizing the capital he gave the "The." "Nice to meet you."

"Thanks. Same."

Jen gave Paul's arm a tug. "Let's go before something else breaks, and the XO tells me to stay aboard all night trying to fix it. See you tomorrow, Gord." They went back out to the quarterdeck, requested permission to go ashore, and saluted the national flag as they left. Jen glanced at Paul after a few moments of silence. "What's up?"

"Nothing. Well, it felt funny back there."

"What? What felt funny?"

"That ensign obviously knew about me, and so did the Lieutenant, and I realized there was a wardroom over on your ship that knew about us, even though I'd never met most of them. It felt a little strange, that's all. I mean, on top of being on a ship that's so much like the *Merry Mike* but isn't the *Mike*, you know?"

"I know. You never quite get used to it. I stop by the *Michaelson* and see something different from the *Maury* and sometimes can't figure out which ship I'm on. Then I see officers I never met during my time on her. It's like seeing strangers living in your home." Jen laughed. "I never thought I'd refer to the *Merry Mike* as home, even in a figure of speech."

They walked all the way, but bars tended to locate themselves near the sailors they served, so in less than half an hour, Paul was flopping down into a chair in Fogarty's, where the officers from the *Michaelson* normally hung out during too-rare in-port periods. Jen sat next to him, then hoisted her drink toward Carl. "To Lieutenant Carl Meadows. Farewell! May the road rise to meet you, yada, yada, yada."

Everyone laughed and drank to the toast, then Jen sighed and shook her head. "I still can't believe you're leaving the *Merry Mike*, Carl. She won't be the same without you."

Carl grinned. "And she hasn't been the same without you, Jen. I hope you don't begrudge my impending freedom."

"Hell, no. Where's your relief, by the way?"

"I know that." Mike Bristol waved in the general direction of the *Michaelson*. "He showed up about noon. With most of the crew gone on early liberty, they just checked him in and told him to come back tomorrow."

"Lucky timing," Carl observed. "The clock stops ticking on his leave, but he doesn't actually have to go to work until tomorrow. Ah, well, it doesn't matter to me. Lieutenant Silver's life will overlap only briefly with my own, then we shall part like, uh . . ."

"Ships in the night?"

"Yeah. Same with Captain Hayes, of course. He might be one fine Captain, or he might turn out to be a screamer but *I* won't have to worry about it."

"We will," Paul observed.

"Whatever. He won't be as bad as Wakeman was."

"I hope. I don't need to go through that sort of thing again."

Kris Denaldo raised her glass. "Amen. None of us need to. But if worse comes to worst, we can count on Paul to make a glorious moral stand and set everything right."

Paul winced as everyone else laughed. "I think I've had enough of that for one career."

Ensign Diego leaned closer. "That must have been something. Having your Captain court-martialed."

Carl stood up and struck a dramatic pose. "I was there, young ensigns. I was there when Paul Sinclair made his famous charge into the very teeth of the military legal system. Forward, Paul Sinclair! Nobly he rode. Lawyers to the right of him, lawyers to the left of him, judges in front of him, volleyed and thundered with verbs and adjectives and really hard legal-type questions. But Paul rode on, plucking the fruits of victory from the very jaws of defeat, and came forth again unscathed, his new lady fair at his side."

Jen stuck her tongue out at Carl. "You're just jealous."

Paul assumed a puzzled expression. " 'Plucking the fruits of victory from the very jaws of defeat?' What the heck does that mean?"

Carl grinned. "Who says it has to mean anything? It's poetry."

"It is not. Nothing rhymed."

"It's, uh, free verse poetry."

"You don't even know what that is."

"Do you?"

"Uh . . ."

"Then how do you know it's not?" Carl bowed triumphantly to acknowledge applause from several of those present. "Who needs another drink?"

The evening wore on with everyone recounting favorite stories about Carl Meadows's time on the *Michaelson*. After they ran out of real stories, they started inventing new ones that had Carl involved in various heroic and frequently obscene exploits. Captain Hayes stopped by, not in uniform, and offered Carl a handshake along with regrets he'd be leaving the ship soon. Everyone then toasted the new Captain, who begged off after two rounds.

At some point, Paul and Jen found themselves alone with Carl, at a point where gaiety had subsided, and weariness had set in. Paul noticed Carl gazing somberly at nothing in particular. "You okay?"

Carl shrugged. "I guess. Worn-out's more like it. I'm glad I'm leaving the ship before I got bled too dry. I've never been Mister A-Number-One Supersailor to begin with, but I've been feeling tired with everything more often these days."

Paul nodded. "I could tell something was bothering you."

"I haven't been acting any different. Have I?"

"You've ridden a couple of the new ensigns pretty hard. That's not like you."

Carl frowned down at his drink. "No," he finally admitted, "it's not. I guess I feel sort of bad leaving them. You know, it's like we're wise elders trying to teach them and protect them."

"Wis*er* elders, maybe."

"I won't argue that. But I'm leaving. Those new ensigns, and the *Merry Mike*, they'll be on their own without me. Maybe I'm trying to teach them as much as I can as fast as I can."

Paul thought about it for a little while. "You still feel responsible. For whatever happens after you leave."

"Paul, the *Mike*'s my first ship. I've spent three years dedicated to that demanding bitch, three years of almost constantly being aboard, three years of seeing her bulkheads and passageways and learning every little quirk of her equipment. Three years working with people like you, sharing our life on her twenty-four hours a day for months on end sometimes. I can't just walk away from that. Ever."

Jen nodded, her face solemn. "She's in your blood, Carl. You'll never shake her, or the space she sails in."

Carl eyed her skeptically. "How'd you get so wise about this?"

"I've watched my dad go from ship to ship. The one he usually tells stories about is the first. And I split-toured to the *Maury*, so I felt the same thing already."

"Great." Carl drained his drink. "It's like some curse that's going to follow me the rest of my life. If I have to have a woman haunting my dreams, why'd she have to be the *Merry Mike*?"

"Hey, first kiss, first love, first ship. Sailors don't forget them, no matter how old they get."

Carl sighed, watching some ensigns a few tables over laugh among themselves. "Do you guys ever listen to old music? The classics? I was skimming the ship's library and I heard this really ancient song where this young guy was singing about how he hoped he'd die before he got old."

"Sounds inspiring."

"Yeah, really uplifting. But I don't think it was really about aging. It was about getting old inside. Do you ever worry that someday you'll wake and find out you've become a senior officer?"

Paul smiled quizzically. "I thought we all *wanted* to be promoted."

"I'm not talking about being promoted. I'm talking about becoming a senior officer."

"Oh. You mean one of those guys whose civilian clothes are twenty or thirty years out-of-date, and gets real nervous every time they have to leave a ship or a base and actually interact with people who aren't also senior officers?"

"Yeah. You know the type."

Jen shrugged. "I don't see it happening to me."

"I guess not. You're more likely to turn into another Herdez."

"Bite your tongue. What do you think you'll turn into, Carl?"

"Oh, I know what I'll turn into, assuming I get promoted that far. When I grow up I wanna be Commander Sykes. How about you, Paul? Who do you wanna be?"

"I don't know. I guess I haven't thought about it all that much." He looked over at Jen. "I guess it won't matter as long as Jen's with me."

Jen rolled her eyes. "Oh, barf."

Carl nodded. "My sentiments exactly. Remember the good old days? About a year ago? Cruising the bars for chicks—"

Jen's eyebrows shot up. "I don't recall cruising for chicks."

"Or studs, as the case may be. Playing darts and drinking beer until the sun came up—"

"The sun's always up in this orbital location."

"Then staggering back to the ship to get screamed at by our department heads while Commander Herdez plotted to get a standard day expanded to twenty-five hours so we could work that much longer. Ah, the good old days. Now, you two are practically domesticated. I bet Jen's starting to cook and knit and stuff."

"You lose. I get drinks sometimes, and I punch buttons on a microwave if we're at a self-service place."

Paul nodded. "But she does both of those real well. I always said there's nothing like a home-microwaved meal."

Jen eyed Paul suspiciously. "The ice you're skating on is getting thinner every moment. If you wanted to marry a cook, you had plenty of other choices."

Paul laughed. "I guess, but . . . did you say marry?"

Carl looked toward Jen. "I heard the word 'marry.' "

Jen shook her head. "Not from me you didn't."

"Did the other Jen Shen say it?"

"No, and neither did this one. You're both victims of wishful thinking."

"I don't want to marry you. Paul does."

"I do?"

Jen glared at him. "You *don't?*"

"I didn't say that."

Carl laughed. "Okay. So far Jen and Paul have both not said they want to get married. Anybody else want to not say it?" He stopped laughing when he noticed their discomfort. "Hey, lighten up, you two. Somebody's tongue slipped. Big deal."

Paul looked back sourly. "This from the guy who's worried about being haunted by the *Michaelson.*"

"Exactly. And I have a really snappy comeback to that. I just can't think of it at the moment." Carl glanced at his empty drink. "Well, there's the problem. Excuse me while I take on more fuel." He stood up, wobbled slightly, then grimaced with discomfort. "Maybe I ought to pump bilges, too. Pardon me while I use the head." Carl set off on a slightly weaving course toward the bar's rest rooms.

Jen tapped Paul's hand. "Let's go talk."

"Jen, I didn't mean—"

"I know. But I need to walk around a bit, and I could use a break from the noise in here."

They left the bar, strolling out onto the wide passageway that served as the station's main street. It was late enough that few people were about, and all the benches along the walkway were empty. Paul and Jen picked one out of line of sight of the bar entrance, then sat silently for a little while.

"Are you okay?" Paul finally asked.

"Uh-huh." She leaned against him, her head resting on his shoulder. "I'm going to miss Carl."

"Me, too. It's like you said. We'll always be tied to the *Michaelson*, but we'll really be tied to *our Michaelson*, with the people we knew and the places we went. Ten years from now, I'm sure if I visited her, I'd feel like a stranger."

"You can't go home again. Who said that?"

"I don't remember." They were quiet again for a while. Paul felt Jen leaning against him, realizing how good it felt, not simply to be touching her but to be part of her life. *What the hell am I waiting for? Do I really think anything else even half this good will ever come along for me?* "Uh, Jen?"

"What?"

"*Will* you marry me?"

She raised her head from his shoulder, then turned slowly, eyeing him. "Just how drunk are you?"

"Not all that much. I mean it."

"Sure you do."

"Dammit, Jen—"

"Okay, okay. You mean it. And I'm just drunk enough to consider saying 'yes.' "

"Really?"

"I said 'consider,' Paul." Jen buried her face in her hands. "Aw, hell. It's not supposed to be like this. I'm sorry. But why now, Paul?"

"I've been thinking about it. Haven't you?"

"Of course I have. But my ship's heading out for three months underway in a few days. I'm not sure this is a good time. I'm not sure we wouldn't be rushing into something because we were afraid instead of because we were happy."

Paul took her shoulders so he could look straight into her eyes. "Jen, I *know* I want to be with you. The only thing I'm afraid of is losing you, of not knowing you'll be there, with me, always."

"That's what you say now. What about in five years or so, when we're maybe stationed on opposite ends of the solar system, so far apart we can't even carry on a conversation because of light-speed lag? When you're surrounded by sweet young ladies with sugary dispositions whose idea of heaven would be to spend the rest of their living days gazing adoringly at you? Are you still going to think abrasive, outspoken Jen Shen is the end-all and be-all at that point?"

"Jen, if I wanted a sweet young lady with a sugary disposition, I wouldn't have been attracted to you from the start." Jen tried to glower but ended up smiling. "We were friends long before we got serious, remember?"

"You were just desperate. You'd have been friends with a spiny-backed lobster if it'd been willing to spend time listening to you."

"Maybe, but you're nicer to look at than any spiny-backed lobster would have been."

"Not by much."

"Jen, you're beautiful."

"You're so delusional." Jen shook her head, looking away. "Paul, things have been going pretty well between us. But this isn't exactly a normal life. We see each other for brief stretches when both of our ships happen to be in port, and we always have stuff to talk about because we're living the same lives as crew members on warships. What about once that's over? When we've both got different jobs?"

Paul spread his hands. "Jen, I really think we'll always have plenty to talk about."

"And what if spending lots of time together makes us crazy? What if after six months of being there for each other every day, we're ready to choke each other?"

"The only way we'll know the answer to that is to try. Maybe we will need extra space for ourselves, but that's not hard."

"Not hard? Have you seen the size of married living quarters on this station? We'll be bumping into each other every time we turn around."

"I like bumping into you."

"Stop it! We really need to think about this, Paul. Need to think about whether there's more to you and me together than just lust and someone convenient to talk to. Don't say it. I know some people get married for those reasons. I won't. I'd rather you left me than stay with me just because you were afraid you'd never find anyone else to share a bed with you."

Paul shook his head. "That's not what I'm thinking, and I hope you aren't, either. What are you saying? That you're not happy? That if your ship gets back and I'm not waiting on the pier, and instead you get a note from me saying that I've found someone else and it's over between us, that you'd be fine with that, Jen?"

"No, I wouldn't be fine with that. I love you. So I'd hunt you down and rip your lungs out. But wouldn't you prefer getting that kind of treatment from an ex-girlfriend instead of an ex-fiancée?"

"I'll have to think about that."

"You've got three months to think about it. And so do I."

Paul felt his jaw tightening as he stared at the deck. "This wasn't how I expected things to happen, either."

"You mean just now or in general? I'm sorry, Paul. I know you're this big-time romantic who deep down believes in true love and dreams of happily-ever-afters, but that doesn't really happen. You haven't got Cinderella. You've got me."

"I'm not exactly Prince Charming, either."

"No, but you'll do." Jen giggled as Paul gave her a sour look. "Sorry. And I do love you for who you are. Really. But tell me something honestly. If you're afraid to wait three months for an answer, or maybe longer, doesn't that mean you're really not all that sure of things? What's the rush?"

"We've been dating for about a year, now."

"Not in real time, Paul. Add up the times my ship's been out and your ship's been out or we've been on duty and couldn't see each other and you probably have only a couple of months of actually being together."

"Jen, I don't want to lose you."

"No, you don't want to *risk* losing me. Right?" She came close to him, looking straight into his eyes. "Be the guy I fell for, and I won't go anywhere. Okay, I'll go wherever my ship goes, but I'll always come back."

"So will I."

"Then what's the problem? Don't answer. I know. We're both not absolutely sure if that's always going to be true. Probably we never will be. But this isn't a decision I have to make tonight. That's Jen speaking, not Cinderella. If you love me, you'll respect my reasons."

"How could I respect and love you and not respect your reasons?" Paul threw up his hands. "Very well, Lieutenant Shen. I will stand by for further instructions."

"You will not. You will live and think and take time to decide something important to both of us. Just like me. Problem?"

"No problem." He kissed her, the gesture lingering. "What have I gotten myself into?"

"You knew who I was when you volunteered for this relationship, sailor. Come on. Let's get back inside before somebody notices we're both missing and thinks we're, like, involved or something."

They went back inside Fogarty's and had a few more drinks. Then Carl got maudlin again, and they all had a few more drinks. Then Carl cheered up, and they all had a few more drinks. Eventually, closing time came around, Fogarty's staff threw them out, and the ragged remnants of Carl Meadows's farewell party staggered back to the *Michaelson*, pausing only to drop Jen off at the quarterdeck of the *Maury*.

The next morning, the strung-out survivors of the farewell discovered to their horror that a no-notice "fast cruise" had been scheduled so that Captain Hayes could evaluate how well the crew handled a variety of situations. A fast cruise involved pretending the ship was underway instead of actually getting underway, but otherwise involved plenty of stress, plenty of demanding work, and plenty of alarms sounding to simulate emergencies.

Paul, like the other members of the farewell, was still sobering up when the emergency drills began. His hangover building rapidly, Paul gripped his command console in the Combat Information Center so hard his hands turned white under the pressure as the strident clamor of the general quarters alarm pounded repeatedly into his brain. He imagined his face looked just as pale as his hands at the moment. The alarm finally halted, replaced by an amplified voice booming details of the "emergency" they were to practice dealing with.

"Paul?" The voice over the comm circuit was a pained whisper.

"Yeah. Kris?"

"I think so. I'm in incredible pain."

"Me too."

"I'm going to kill Carl."

"He didn't know they'd have all these drills today."

"I don't care. When I feel this bad, someone has to die. And I can't very well threaten to kill the Captain."

"No. That always looks bad. How's Mike Bristol?"

"Last I saw, he was pretending to be alive. He wasn't too convincing, though."

"How about Carl?"

Her answer was forestalled by another urgent announcement. "This is a drill! All hands brace for collision!" A moment later, the piercing squeal of the collision alarm drove daggers into Paul's head. The alarm finally halted, leaving Paul staring cross-eyed at his console as a follow-on announcement heralded the next phase of the drill. "This is a drill. Collision has resulted in decompression of all compartments on 01 level. I say again, collision has resulted in decompression of all compartments on 01 level. All personnel on 01 level assessed dead from decompression. Damage control parties prepare to reenter 01 level and reestablish airtight boundaries."

Paul glanced up as Chief Imari tossed aside her headset. "You heard the announcement, folks. We're all dead."

I'm dead? "Really?"

Chief Imari looked at Paul, failed to conceal her reaction at his appearance, then shook her head. "No, sir. It's just part of the drill."

"Okay."

"Do you need some aspirin, sir?"

"How many have you got?"

Paul and the rest of the sailors in CIC spent the next hour lying on the deck pretending to be dead as survival-suited investigators, then Damage Control teams, picked their way across the compartment. An occasional snore testified to some of the sailors taking advantage of the opportunity.

Chief Imari's aspirin slowly brought Paul's pain level down to a tolerable level, and he managed to catch a few minutes of sleep himself.

All good things, of course, come to an end. "All hands secure from collision drill. Stand by for next event."

Chief Imari stood, stretched and roared at the sailors sprawled around CIC. "You heard the word! On your feet, you useless gaggle of neutrons."

Paul replaced his own headset, then called up the chief on a private circuit. "Neutrons, Chief?"

"Yes, sir, Mr. Sinclair. Neutrons got practically no mass."

It took Paul's still-hungover brain a moment to get it. "They're lightweights."

"Yes, sir."

"Thanks for the aspirin. I notice they've run drills in engineering, weapons, and damage control so far. I bet we're next."

"I wouldn't be surprised, sir."

General quarters sounded once more, the bongs somehow penetrating the calming aspirin to hammer at Paul's head again. "This is a drill! Multiple contacts inbound."

Paul's console lit up with close to a hundred unknown contact markers, each on a different path and each radiating different information that had to be evaluated in order to guess at its identity. *Oh, this is going to be ugly.* "All right, everybody. I want a threat evaluation for all contacts based on current trajectories, then threat IDs for all contacts, then a threat hierarchy based on trajectory and probable ID. Don't depend on the targeting and tracking systems to get all that automatically. They're sure to have thrown in some curves that'll confuse the automated systems."

"You heard the lieutenant!" Chief Imari added, then she quickly divided up the tasks among the operations specialists.

The next fifteen minutes passed in a blur of activity. Paul tried to monitor everything his sailors were doing without trying to do their jobs for them. With all the information at his fingertips, it was entirely too easy to focus on the details of one small part of the job instead of keeping an eye on the big picture.

A majority of the contacts had been assigned identification when Operations Specialist Second Class Kaji called in. "Chief? I've got something funny here."

"Show me. Give the lieutenant a copy, too."

Paul frowned as his display focused on a small segment of the incoming contacts. "What's up, Kaji?"

"Sir, right here." Kaji highlighted an almost invisible contact. "It's very faint."

"What do you think, Chief?"

"I'd call it a system echo off the stronger contacts, sir. Except this is a simulation, and they don't show echoes because the sims assume the systems work perfectly."

"Then what is it?"

Petty Officer Kaji spoke up. "It could be a warship, sir. With all masking systems operational."

Something clicked in Paul's memory. "It's a Pile On Maneuver."

Chief Imari sounded puzzled. "A what?"

"A Pile On Maneuver. It's a theoretical plan I got briefed on in one of my classes at the Academy. You shove a lot of debris toward your objective, then hide your own approach inside the apparently natural shower of space objects."

"Sir, how the hell would you get so much junk flying on the trajectories you need? That sounds cool in theory, but it doesn't sound very practical."

"That's why it's still a theoretical plan, Chief. But simulations don't have to worry about real-world practical considerations. I think Kaji's spotted the joker in this deck. Good job."

"Real good," Chief Imari agreed.

Paul tagged the faint contact with a "possible warship, identity unknown" symbol, then called the bridge to verbally pass the information as well. The drill spun on for another thirty minutes of frantic activity before the screens displayed an "exercise completed" message. While Paul was still wondering how they'd done, the command circuit sounded with the voice of Captain Hayes. "Good job, Combat. You nailed that one."

Paul grinned at Chief Imari, who offered back a thumbs-up, while the enlisted trackers exchanged high fives.

After another hour of hearing drills being run elsewhere on the ship, the euphoria of doing well had faded for Paul. *Man, there's so much else I could be doing right now, but I don't dare try in case Kwan or Garcia is checking our terminals to see what we're up to. How long are we going to have to stay at general quarters?*

His headset sounded again. "Paul? Kris."

"Here. You sound better."

"I had to either get better or die. Thank God for aspirin. Have you seen Lieutenant Silver?"

"Who?"

"Lieutenant Silver. He's Carl Meadows's relief, remember?"

"Oh, yeah. No, I haven't seen him. Why would he be up here?"

"I don't know. But he's not anyplace else. Surely he reported on board this morning."

"Why not try the quarterdeck? It's still crewed."

A brief pause followed. "Duh. I guess my brain's not working all that well, yet. Wait one." Paul waited, a task made easier by the fact he had nothing else he could do at the moment. "Okay. Chief Hadasa is officer of the deck in port. Lieutenant Silver showed up about half an hour after the fast cruise started. Since the brow'd been sealed except for emergencies, they had to tell him to leave and come back later."

Paul found himself laughing. "Lieutenant Silver certainly has a remarkable sense of timing."

"You can say that again. At this rate, he and Carl may never meet. See you at lunch. If general quarters is secured by then. Maybe we'll have to eat battle rations at our combat stations."

"Ugh. Good thing Sykes got rid of the oldest rations."

"Do you really think that'll make any difference in how they taste? Later."

A weary half hour later, the bosun mate passed the welcome word to secure from general quarters. A small cheer erupted in Combat. Paul took off his headset, rubbed one ear where the headset had rubbed it, then looked around at his division. "Good job, people."

Chief Imari nodded. "Thank you, sir. Now that drills are over we can get back to work." The other enlisted groaned at her words. "But I guess we can let 'em eat lunch first."

"Careful, Chief. You'll spoil them." A chorus of playful protests followed Paul as he headed for his own stateroom. He wasn't sure how he looked after hurriedly throwing on his uniform that morning, but he couldn't imagine it was all that great. *I'd better make sure I look halfway decent before I run into Kwan or Hayes.*

CHAPTER FIVE

☆ ☆ ☆ ☆ ☆

"Hey, Paul!"

Paul turned, puzzled by the hail since he didn't recognize the voice. A tall, lanky lieutenant stood at the other end of the passageway, Carl Meadows at his side. Carl beckoned, and Paul walked toward them. "This is Lieutenant Silver, Paul."

"Hi." Silver flashed a big smile and extended his hand. "Call me Scott. You're another ring-knocker from the Academy, right?"

"Yup. Nice to see you, Scott."

"Oh, I bet you're not half as happy to see me as Carl was. It seemed like I couldn't get on this ship!"

Carl nodded. "It's a real short turnover. We only have a couple of days left."

"But I was Auxiliaries officer on the *Rickover*, so I can handle the turnover for Main Propulsion Assistant quickly."

Paul gave Carl a puzzled look. "Main Propulsion Assistant? But you're the Weapons and Fire Control officer."

Carl spread his hands. "It's a rolling turnover. Lieutenant Kilgary's taking over my job, and Scott Silver's taking over Kilgary's job."

"Kilgary's going to Weapons? Why?"

"Colleen's afraid of being typecast in engineering and being forced to serve in that type of assignment her entire career, so she wants to get experience in another area. She's too late, if you ask me, but I understand why she's doing it."

"Yeah." Paul didn't know Colleen Kilgary all that well because their duty sections and watch patterns rarely crossed. *But I'm sure she'll do great as Carl's replacement, and having her on board after Scott takes over her job will mean he has a source of knowledge to draw on. It should be a win-win situation for everybody.* "Is she going to replace you as my underway officer of the deck?"

"Nope," Silver replied with another smile. "That'll be me. Carl tells me you're a great junior officer of the deck, so I'm looking forward to it."

Carl checked his watch. "Let's get going, Scott. I need to get you to engineering and pick up Colleen to pass on my stuff to her."

"Sure. See you around, Paul." Paul watched them go, then mentally shrugged. *He seems okay. Friendly, that's for sure. And if he's been on the* Rickover, *he ought to be familiar with how the* Michaelson *handles as well, so I shouldn't have problems with him as my officer of the deck. I hate to see Carl go, but this could be a lot worse.*

Paul, busy with his own work, saw little more of either Carl or Scott Silver before he received a page from the quarterdeck. *Jen's here?* He glanced at the clock. *It's only 1700. She's the one who's early this time.*

Jen gave his uniform a critical going-over. "Did you actually get this pressed?"

"Yeah."

"I guess you're okay."

"Thanks. I haven't had a uniform inspection this tough since I left the Academy."

"Ha-ha. Forgive me for wanting you to look decent. Ready to head for the *Mahan?*"

Two docks over this time, and another quarterdeck very similar but not exactly the same as the *Michaelson's.* A very sharp-looking officer of the deck welcomed them aboard, then a very sharp-looking ensign escorted them to the Captain's quarters.

Jen rapped on the hatch. "Lieutenant Shen reporting as ordered."

Captain Shen looked up from his desk. "At least you follow orders now that you're in the Navy, Jen. This is Sinclair?"

"Yes. May I present Lieutenant Junior Grade Paul Sinclair."

Kay Shen squinted at Paul. "Pleased to meet you. I thought I might have to wear my sunglasses to this little get-together."

"Sir?"

"Jen keeps talking about this knight in shining armor of hers. I figured I'd need my sunglasses to cut down on the glare."

Paul smiled politely, unsure how to respond, and trying to figure out why Jen and her father were acting so formal with each other.

"Well, let's eat." Captain Shen led the way back to the *Mahan*'s wardroom, where a small group of officers awaited. After a dizzyingly fast round of introductions, Paul found himself seated opposite Jen, unable to be sure of the names of anyone else at the table except Captain Shen himself. The meal passed quickly as well, with only occasional small talk and a few questions to Paul about his operational experiences on the *Michaelson*. Before he knew it, Captain Shen was rising, everyone else was following suit, and he was once again walking with Jen back to the Captain's stateroom.

Captain Shen sat in the one chair, waving Paul and Jen to the small couch against one bulkhead. Paul sat a little stiffly, unable to relax.

Kay Shen smiled briefly at Paul. "You're an Academy graduate."

"Yes, sir." Jen's body, next to his, felt tense.

Captain Shen leaned back, raising one eyebrow at Paul. "I looked up your record. You weren't the anchorman, but you didn't distinguish yourself in class rank, either."

Jen's voice carried an edge. "Dad . . ."

"Okay, okay. Somebody's got to be in the middle. So, Mr. Sinclair, do you have any plans about making my daughter an honest woman?"

"Dad! I don't require some male keeper to make me an honest woman."

"Oh. You don't want him."

"I didn't say that."

Captain Shen glanced at Paul again. "I take it you two aren't sharing quarters, yet."

"Dad!"

"No, sir. We're both still assigned to ships."

Captain Shen nodded. "Different ships, fortunately. Good thing you had Gwen Herdez riding herd on you when you were both on the *Michaelson*."

"You know Commander Herdez, sir?"

"I had the pleasure of serving with her once. Hard as nails."

"She has high standards, sir."

"Damn straight." Captain Shen smiled once again, the expression coming and going rapidly. "So does my daughter. She's never held on to a man this long before. They usually got the boot pretty quick."

"Dad, if you don't—"

"Mind you, they all deserved to get the boot, because they didn't deserve her. Apparently she feels differently about you."

"I'm a very lucky man, sir."

Jen covered her eyes with one hand. "Oh, please."

"Good people tend to make their own luck. Are you good enough for Jen?"

"I'm doing my best."

"We'll see if your best is good enough."

Jen spoke sharply. "I'll be the judge of that."

"Sure, Jen. Where's your next assignment? Any word yet?"

"I've got six more months on the *Maury*, Dad. I've got my dream sheet in with the detailers telling them what assignments I really want, but no responses from them."

"Nothing too odd about that. Am I correct in assuming you two have matching dream sheets?"

"Yes. We want assignments close to each other and know we need to make sure our detailers know that. I'm not an ensign anymore, Dad."

"Heck, no. You're a lieutenant junior grade! Practically an admiral. Let me lay it on the line. As long as you're not officially hitched the detailers are real unlikely to worry about sending you to the same general area on your next assignment."

"We know that, Dad."

"I assume there's no plans to rush into marriage to try to ensure you get similar orders?"

Jen's look of annoyance deepened. "There won't be any rushing into anything."

"Well, that's a relief. What are your career plans, Mr. Sinclair?"

Paul tensed some more. The question was outwardly run-of-the-mill, yet in professional terms the career plans of an officer told you a lot about him or her, for better or worse. "I've put in for shore duty on Franklin Station, sir. Preferably in the operations branch, but I'm willing to look at other options."

"Hmmm. Space officers tend to rotate to Franklin for shore duty, so I'm sure you'll get that. What about afterward?"

"I'm going to evaluate options when my next orders come up, sir."

Captain Shen looked skeptical. "That's not exactly long-term planning. Are you going to make the Navy a career?"

"That option's still open, sir."

"Options are all very well, but it's necessary to make decisions at some point."

Paul made a small gesture that stopped Jen's next eruption. "Sir, I'm fully capable of making decisions. I'm just awaiting some more experience before making decisions that don't need to be made now."

"The proof's in the pudding, young man."

This time Jen ignored Paul's attempt to handle the issue

himself. "Dad, Paul has proven his ability to make tough decisions. He doesn't need any criticism from you on that score."

"I take it you're referring to his testimony in his former captain's court-martial. Carrying out Commander Herdez's instructions—"

"Sir," Paul interrupted, hearing his voice carry an edge of anger, which he tamped down. "Commander Herdez gave me no 'instructions' on that matter. The decision was mine." He'd never boasted about it, but he couldn't bear having such a difficult, soul-wrenching decision casually dismissed.

"Really?" Captain Shen let the noncommittal reply hang for a moment. "Not a good moment for the Navy, in any event."

"I'm not happy it happened, sir."

"You're still the collateral duty legal officer on your ship?"

"Yes, sir."

"Aspire to be a lawyer, eh?"

"No, sir."

"I understand you had a run-in with Greenspacers recently. Tell me about it."

Paul recited the events surrounding the canceled test firing, but couldn't shake the feeling that he was reporting to a superior instead of sharing information with a fellow officer. *Boy, am I glad I don't work for this guy. No offense, Jen. Not that I'm ever likely to tell you that.*

Paul's report over, Captain Shen appeared ready to interrogate him in other areas, but Jen ostentatiously brought her wristwatch up. "I'm sorry, but I need to get back to the ship. Are you ready, Paul?"

"Sure." Trying his best to conceal his relief, Paul stood and offered Captain Shen his respects, then stood outside the stateroom while Jen said good-bye. Within a few minutes, they were off the *Mahan*.

Jen walked rapidly, her mouth tight. "Well," Paul finally offered, "that was fun."

She looked at him skeptically, then tried to smile. "No, it wasn't. You did well, though."

"What was that all about?"

Jen led the way over to one side, where a large screen portrayed an image of space outside the base. She leaned against the bulkhead, her head turned so she could look at the field of stars displayed there. "My dad's been in the Navy a long time, and he's been commanding ships for years now. I sometimes think he's forgotten there's another world, one where his word isn't law and people don't jump to carry out his orders. Instead, he acts like he expects everyone and every place to acknowledge him as the Captain." She smiled ruefully. "He usually gets disappointed when he tries, though."

Paul leaned against the bulkhead on the opposite side of the display. "Sorry, Jen."

"It's not your fault. But since he's my dad, he's sort of the baggage I bring to this relationship. I was hoping he'd be better tonight. He's not a bad person. Just tough and smart and demanding."

"Tough, smart, and demanding sounds familiar."

"Yeah, I come by it honestly."

"How's your mother handle it?"

Jen looked down at the deck, her expression hidden. "Mom died six years ago."

"Oh, geez, Jen. I'm so sorry." *No wonder she never talked about her mother. And with us being based up here and working constantly I never wondered about it. Family seems very far away, except when they come riding in with their own ship like Jen's dad did.*

"It's not something I talk about. Maybe someday. But Dad got harder after Mom died. Maybe she'd always softened his rough edges, maybe that's how he grieves. I don't know. He doesn't talk about it, either."

"That's a helluva big elephant in the room whenever you meet, though, isn't it?"

Jen looked up, smiling wanly now. "Sure is. But that's how we both handle it."

"I won't bring it up again, Jen. But if you're ever ready to talk, I'm ready to listen."

"Thanks, but don't hold your breath. It's not going to happen tomorrow, I'll guarantee, even if my ship wasn't leaving in the morning." She looked back at the stars for a moment, then reached down, unzipped one pocket, and fished in it until her hand surfaced with a rectangular, plastic, coded room key. "I got us a room."

"Are you sure you're up for that tonight?"

"Very sure. I'm tired of the universe, Paul. It's too complicated. At this moment, I just want to go somewhere private where you and I can forget about everything except each other for a while."

"I'd like that, too. Lead on, my lady."

"I have no intention of being a lady tonight."

They began walking. Aware of the weary moodiness in her, Paul felt an urge to drape his arm over Jen's shoulders and hold her tight. But they were in uniform, and the passageways of Franklin Station still held plenty of personnel attending to personal and professional errands, so such a public display of affection between officers would be unprofessional and improper. Jen looked over at him, and as if reading his mind, reached her near hand toward Paul and pantomimed squeezing Paul's hand. Then her hand dropped, and the two officers walked on with a half meter of space separating them.

PAUL sat in Combat on the *Michaelson* the next morning, watching his display report every detail as the *Maury* undocked and headed away from Franklin Naval Station. The symbol representing the *Maury* stayed bright as she accelerated outward, the distance between her and Franklin opening with dizzying speed. *I wish I could at least send Jen a letter, and maybe get some back. But ships on patrol don't send or receive anything but important operational messages. Mail receipt and sending would pose too big a risk of betraying the ship's location. So, farewell for now, Jen. For the next three months. I'll only be talking to you in my mind.*

Two hours later, Paul and the other junior officers gathered on the quarterdeck for Carl Meadows's final departure from the ship. The officers lined up as sideboys as Carl entered the quarterdeck with a seabag of personal belongings draped over one shoulder. Carl insisted on shaking everyone's hand, then stepped back, looked around for a moment at the ship, faced the officer of the deck in port, and saluted. "Request permission to leave the ship."

"Permission granted."

As Carl started through the ranks of his fellow junior officers, Lieutenant Sindh called out, "Hand salute!" They all saluted in unison, holding the gesture as Carl brought his own hand up, maintaining his return salute as he walked past their ranks. The bosun mate of the watch trilled attention on his pipe, bonged the ship's bell twice, then announced "Lieutenant, United States Navy, departing."

Carl pivoted after he'd cleared the *Michaelson*'s brow so he could face aft and salute the flag. Then he turned, smiling a bit wistfully. "See you guys around. Take it easy."

Lieutenant Sindh called out, "Two!" Everyone dropped their salute and waved to Carl as he walked away. Within a few moments, most of the junior officers had hastened off to work, leaving Paul and Kris Denaldo watching the dwindling form of Carl until it disappeared around a turn.

Kris slapped Paul on the back. "Come on. You and I've got work to do."

"I'm going to miss that guy, Kris."

"Yeah. It's hard when a friend leaves. I hated to see Jen go, but at least she's nearby, and I still see her every once in a while."

"I guess I'd better get used to it."

"You won't. You saw how torn up Gonzalez was to leave."

"It's a screwy way to live, Kris."

"You volunteered for it."

"You sound like Jen. Reminding me of my mistakes."

Kris laughed and headed back into the ship. Paul took one more look toward where Carl had disappeared, then followed her. *Two good-byes in one morning. At least Jen's coming back.* Unless an accident happened, unless Jen fell prey to the many ways a sailor could die in the course of "routine" duties. Paul's mind shied away from the possibility, though not before he realized Jen would have the same fears for him. *We understand each other's work. That's a good thing. It can also be a bad thing, I guess.*

Four days later, the *Michaelson* herself prepared to get underway again. The contractors were aboard, the pulse-phased laser appeared to be working properly, and this time two range safety ships would accompany the *Michaelson* to ensure another Greenspace trick didn't interrupt the test firing.

Paul twisted around from his chair on the bridge, looking for Lieutenant Silver. *Where's Scott? He should already be up here and helping get through the checklist for getting underway.* Paul focused back on the checklist, reviewing the next item.

Barely twenty minutes prior to the scheduled time for getting underway, Scott Silver came onto the bridge and strapped into his chair. "Hey, Paul. Sorry I'm late. Really sorry. Had some engineering issues, you know?"

"Uh, yeah." *It's not his fault if something tied him down until now. And engineering problems are the sort of thing that might keep us from getting underway at all.*

"How's the checklist coming?" Silver took a look at it, nodded, and smiled. "Great. Really good work. It's almost done. I can see why Carl Meadows said you were a great partner on a watch team."

"Thanks. There's a couple more items—"

"Right. Can you handle them while I get up to speed on your bridge arrangement?"

Paul nodded back, trying not to reveal any reluctance since the request seemed reasonable. Unused to handling all the checklist items by himself, Paul went through the last few items as fast as he could and still be certain they'd been done properly.

He'd just finished when Commander Kwan arrived on the bridge, looked around carefully, then focused on Scott Silver. "How's preparations for getting underway going?"

Silver smiled confidently. "The checklist's just been completed, sir. We're ready to go."

"Good work, Scott. Notify the Captain. He should up here any moment now."

Silver gestured to Paul. "Let the Captain know, okay?"

Paul bit back his first reply. *You could've let Kwan know I did the checklist instead of taking credit for it yourself. And why can't you call the Captain?* But Silver was the officer of the deck, which meant he had every right to delegate tasks to Paul. "Captain, this is Lieutenant Junior Grade Sinclair, the junior officer of the deck. All departments report readiness for getting underway."

"Thanks. I'll be right there."

A few moments later the bosun mate of the watch called out "Captain's on the bridge!"

Scott Silver pivoted his chair to face Captain Hayes. "Sir, the ship is ready to get underway."

"Thank you." Hayes eyed Silver carefully. "Do you feel familiar enough with the ship to get her underway?"

Silver looked regretful. "I think so, sir, but in a close maneuvering situation like this . . ."

Captain Hayes switched his gaze to Paul. "Lieutenant Sinclair, why don't you get the ship underway today?"

"Aye, aye, sir." *Am I going to do everything up here this watch? It makes sense, I guess. Scott hasn't been underway on the* Michaelson, *yet, which makes me the better-qualified one for conning her away from the station.* Paul took a couple of deep, calming breaths, exhaling slowly, as he studied the close-in maneuvering display and ran through the procedure for getting underway. *It's basically simple. I release the ship from the station, pushing her up and away, while the centrifugal force inherited from the station's rotation also pushes her up. I have to make sure the* Michaelson *doesn't drift too far to the side and smash into another dock before I get her clear of the station. And I have to avoid running into anything else.*

The status panel for the ship's automated maneuvering system glowed a happy green at every point. Paul saw Scott Silver's eyes were focused there. Sensing his gaze, Scott looked at Paul, then nodded at the automated system panel. "That'll do it for you."

"No, it won't. We never take the ship out on automatic. That system isn't foolproof. No system is. And if it fails, we need to know how to do the job ourselves."

Silver shrugged. "Okay."

Easy for you to say. They let the Rickover *leave port on auto? Never mind. Can't think about that now.* "Captain, all departments report they are ready for getting underway. We have received clearance from station control to get underway."

Captain Hayes nodded, his eyes on his own display. "Very well, Mr. Sinclair. Get the ship underway."

"Aye, aye, sir." Paul licked his lips and swallowed, trying to ensure his voice would sound smooth and confident. "Bosun, pass the word to all hands to prepare to get underway. Quarterdeck, seal quarterdeck access and retract the brow."

"Seal quarterdeck and retract brow, aye," the petty officer of watch echoed in a routine designed to ensure he had heard the order correctly. "Quarterdeck reports it is sealed. Station has retracted brow. All seals confirmed tight."

Paul checked his display, mentally lining up his commands and surreptitiously using his fingers to remember numbers and sequences. "Take in Lines Two and Three. Take in Line Four."

"Take in Lines Two, Three, and Four, aye." Some of the grapples holding the *Michaelson* tight against the station let go, allowing the *Michaelson*'s lines to float free. The ship reeled in the lines smoothly, ensuring they wouldn't flail about and damage either the ship or the station. "Lines Two, Three, and Four secure."

Paul checked his display again, rehearsing the next order in his head, acutely aware that Captain Hayes was monitoring every step of the process. "Port thrusters all ahead one-third. Let out Lines . . . One and Five."

"Port thrusters all ahead one third, aye," the helmsman echoed the command. Paul felt a kick as the thrusters began shoving at the *Michaelson*'s mass. Combined with the gradual loosening of her ties to the station, the fluctuating forces made the feeling of gravity on board shift as well, causing Paul's stomach to react as if they were on a thrill ride and introducing a dangerous distraction.

"Let out lines One and Five, aye," the petty officer of the watch responded.

Michaelson's mass accelerated ponderously away from the station, the two lines still tethering her to Franklin paying out slowly, the computers controlling their tension compensating for the acceleration as well as the inherited centrifugal force pushing the *Michaelson* out and to the side. Paul glanced at the emergency jettison panel. If one of the line computers failed, he'd have to hit the right switch as quickly as possible to cut the line and keep it from pulling on the ship and the station in a potentially disastrous way. The authorities on Franklin didn't like having to retrieve drifting lines, but they really hated mistightened lines pulling a ship and the station back into uncontrolled contact.

Paul watched, trying to follow the advice of his first officer of the deck and feel the ship's movement instead of just watching the displays. He stole another glance to the side, where Captain Hayes was watching his display with every appearance of calm interest. "Stand by to let go all lines."

"Standing by."

Another moment. Feel the ship. Watch the displays. Factor in the delay between giving an order and when it's carried out. "Let go all lines."

"Let go all lines, aye, sir. All lines let go."

The bosun mate of the watch sounded his pipe. "Underway! Shift colors!" Instead of physically lowering the bow and stern flags, then raising a flag to the mainmast as seagoing ships did, the bosun on the *Michaelson* pressed a control to change her broadcast identity code to show the ship was no longer tethered to another object with a fixed orbit.

Paul sat rigid, barely aware of a pain in his lower back from tense muscles held tight so he could watch his displays closely. The maneuvering screen showed the *Michaelson* moving at a gradually increasing pace out and away from the station, her projected course a flattened curve. Up ahead, no other ships or objects were visible, leaving the *Michaelson*'s intended course clear.

"Say again, sir?"

Damn! I said that too softly. I know better. Project command presence and say your orders loud and clear, dammit! "Port thrusters all ahead two-thirds. Main drive all ahead one-third."

"Port thrusters all ahead two-thirds, aye. Main drive all ahead one-third, aye."

Paul tried not to look toward Captain Hayes again, wondering how he'd reacted to Paul's miscommunicated command. A moment later, the *Michaelson*'s main drive kicked in, slamming Paul back against his seat. As the maneuvering thrusters pushed the *Michaelson* farther away from the station, the main drive shoved her forward, creating a new projected course leading over and away from the station. He briefly flashed on another training memory, when he'd wondered why the ships didn't just use their thrusters to pivot around so they could accelerate directly away from the station. Carl had given him an I-can't-believe-you-asked-me-that look, then pointed out that doing such a maneuver would direct the main drive's exhaust straight at the station. That'd be a bad thing, Carl had added with a grin. *Man, I wish Carl was still up here.*

On the maneuvering display, the *Michaelson*'s course rose toward a projected path set by the station traffic monitors. *Feel the ship. Feel the ship.* "Secure port thrusters. Main drive all ahead two-thirds."

"Port thrusters secure, aye, main drive all ahead two-thirds, aye."

Smooth. Not exact. But smooth. "Quartermaster. What's your recommendation?"

"Recommend course two zero zero degrees absolute, up two zero degrees, sir."

Paul looked toward the Captain. Hayes nodded judiciously without being asked. "Very well," Paul acknowledged. "Helm, come to course two zero zero degrees absolute, up two zero degrees."

"Come to course two zero zero degrees absolute, up two zero degrees, aye, sir."

Paul let out a breath he didn't know he'd been holding. *Something else. Oh. yeah.* "Captain, request permission to secure from getting underway."

Hayes nodded again. "Permission granted."

Paul called back to the petty officer of the watch. "Pass the word to secure from getting underway."

"Aye, sir." Keying the all-hands circuit, the petty officer called out the announcement. "All hands, secure from getting underway. The ship remains in maneuvering status. All hands exercise caution in moving about."

USS *Michaelson* shuddered as the helm orders caused thrusters around her hull to fire, killing drift in one direction, then bringing her bow around toward the desired course before firing again. Her mass responding to the thrust, the *Michaelson* ponderously steadied onto the planned trajectory. The desired course and the actual course displayed on the maneuvering screens merged into one curving path, then as the thrusters shut off their absence made itself felt as all sense of gravity disappeared. Paul's stomach lurched in an all-too-familiar fashion, but he fought it down with the ease of long practice.

Scott Silver tapped his controls. "I guess you trust the automated maneuvering system when you're clear of the station."

"That's right." Paul pointed at the display. "There's a lot more room for error if something goes wrong out here."

"Whatever."

Captain Hayes unstrapped, pulling himself from his chair gingerly in the new zero-gravity conditions. "Good job, Mr. Sinclair."

"Thank you, sir."

Hayes cupped one hand to his ear as if straining to hear Paul's reply.

"Thank you, sir!"

Hayes nodded, then headed for the hatch.

"Captain's off the bridge!"

Paul smiled to himself. *Captain Hayes chewed me out for*

*not speaking loud enough when I gave that one order, but he
did it without chewing me out. He just made his point.* Paul
heard a chuckle and looked over at Scott Silver, who was
laughing at him. *What right do you have to laugh about
that? You were just baggage up here this time.*

Apparently oblivious to Paul's soured mood, Silver chat-
ted through the rest of the watch, telling sea stories about
being at the Academy and his experiences since then. If Paul
hadn't been so ticked off at Silver, he might have found the
stories charming. Instead, he found himself questioning
some of what he was hearing.

The arrival of Lieutenant Diem and Ensign Gabriel to assume the watch was a bigger relief than usual. Partway
through the turnover, Paul realized that right after he discussed each important item with Gabriel, Silver would discuss the same item with Diem. The realization that Silver
appeared to be depending on Paul to keep track of important
details did nothing to improve Paul's mood. He rushed
through the last stage of the turnover, then bolted the bridge
as quickly as propriety would allow so he wouldn't have to
leave along with Silver.

Once inside his own stateroom, Paul pulled up his division's training records. He knew from experience that Commander Garcia usually did checks of training records soon
after an underway period started, though Paul had never figured out if Garcia did that because he was bored or because
he expected his division officers to have neglected their duties amid the hassles of getting underway. *Speaking of Garcia, he's the senior watch officer. Several months back he
scrambled watch sections to keep us from "getting too comfortable." Commander, please, please, please scramble the
watch sections again, so I don't have to spend hour upon
endless hour up on the bridge with Scott Silver!*

Sam Yarrow came in, strapped into his seat, then eyed
Paul. "What's eating you?"

"Who says anything's eating me?"

"The way your back's rigid and your ears are red and
you're pounding the keys on your data terminal."

Paul willed himself to relax, then tried to smile. "I guess

I'm just tense. It was a rough morning. I conned the ship out of the dock."

"So? You've done that before."

"Yeah, but the new Captain was watching me, and I had a new officer of the deck. It made things a bit more stressful."

"If you say so. What's that guy Silver like on the bridge anyway?"

Paul didn't have to fake his smile now. *Sam, do you really think I haven't learned not to spill my guts to you? If I said one word remotely critical of Silver, you'd be telling Silver and half the rest of the ship about it within the hour, and making me sound like I'd labeled Silver a hopeless incompetent.* "I can't tell, yet."

"That's not exactly a ringing endorsement."

"Because I don't have enough experience with Silver. That's all. I'm not going to evaluate someone based on a single time standing watch with him."

"It sounds like he didn't do too good."

Stop fishing, Sam. "I didn't hear any complaints." Which was true. Paul closed out his files. "Sorry, I've got a meeting."

Garcia didn't scramble the watch teams. Lieutenant Sindh began to develop a deepening frown as she waited for Scott Silver to arrive, always late, on the bridge to relieve her. Acting unaware of Sindh's disapproval, Silver always had an apology and an explanation for his lateness. Paul found himself begrudging duties on the bridge as Silver routinely assumed everything would be done by Paul as his assistant.

The test firing went smoothly. Either the *Michaelson*'s two escorts or the inability to replace the ship Greenspace had used last time meant no one interfered with the test. Paul, not on watch on the bridge, sat in Combat watching the *Michaelson*'s combat systems track the target, then engage it with the new weapon. The phased-pulse laser scored direct hits on the target, as it should have since the target had a beacon attached and was traveling on a fixed trajectory. The contractors smiled and pronounced the weapon a success. Whether it would work in a real combat situation was another matter altogether, of course.

CAPTAIN'S Mast, also known as Non-Judicial Punishment, also known as NJP in the initials-addicted military. The first Captain's Mast for Captain Hayes, meaning the first time the officers and crew would see him directly deal out discipline to those accused of relatively minor infractions against rules and regulations.

Paul stood at attention against one bulkhead of the crew's mess, having locked a hand onto a nearby tie-down both for safety and so he could keep his feet from drifting up into the middle of the proceedings. Next to him stood the ship's highest-ranking enlisted sailor, Senior Chief Petty Officer Kowalski. Kowalski nodded in greeting. "Another fine day underway, Mr. Sinclair."

"Underway's the only way." Paul gave the expected reply, only his tone betraying the expected irony in the statement. "How many have we got today, Sheriff?"

On the other side of the compartment, Master-at-Arms First Class Ivan Sharpe stood next to the hatch, ready to usher in those sailors who would face the Captain. He raised three fingers in response to Paul's question. "Slow day, sir."

"Fine with me."

Senior Chief Kowalski looked toward the hatch. "Everybody here?"

Sharpe leaned out to confirm, then nodded. "All present and accounted for, Senior Chief."

"In that case Petty Officer Sharpe, please notify the Captain we are in readiness for Mast."

"Will do, Senior Chief."

Paul knew it would take a few minutes for Sharpe to reach the Captain's cabin and return with Captain Hayes. He wondered again how Hayes would handle the Mast cases, and whether he'd ask more questions of Paul than either of his two prior Captains had done. Since Captain's Mast was nonjudicial, it wasn't really a legal proceeding, but the rules for it were still set forth in legal guidance like the Judge Advocate General's Manual. Still, most Mast cases dealt with routine offenses, so Captains rarely had to ask questions about procedures, and since no lawyers were present for Mast, they couldn't confuse the issues either.

Sharpe arrived back at the hatch and leaned in to yell, "Attention on deck!" Paul and Senior Chief Kowalski stiffened to attention.

Captain Hayes entered, his movements in free fall still a bit tentative, then looked at both Kowalski and Paul in acknowledgment of their presence. "At ease."

Paul and the Senior Chief relaxed into parade rest, though with their hands locked onto tie-downs instead of clasped together behind them.

Hayes looked toward Petty Officer Sharpe. "Bring in the first case."

"Aye, aye, sir. Seaman Haggerty."

A small procession entered the compartment. Seaman Haggerty, his uniform trim and neat, came to stand at attention directly before the Captain. Ensign Diego, Haggerty's division officer, came next and took up a position along the bulkhead opposite Paul, followed by Chief Petty Officer Bidden.

Hayes checked his charge sheet. "Seaman Haggerty. You are charged with violating Article 89 of the Uniform Code of Military Justice, Disrespect toward a Superior Commissioned Officer." He glanced toward Ensign Diego. "Are you the superior commissioned officer in question?"

Randy Diego nodded nervously, but his voice came out firmly. "Yes, sir."

"Tell me what happened, Mr. Diego."

"Sir, we were putting together a work detail. I had orders from my department head to get some materiel stowed away safely that night. Chief Bidden and I called the division together and told them we'd be working past liberty call to make sure it was done. There was some grumbling, Captain. I didn't mind that. But Seaman Haggerty came up and asked to be excused on account of a social engagement. I told him no, that everybody'd be working. At that point Seaman Haggerty turned away and said he couldn't believe he had to listen to orders from a, uh, 'snot-nosed kid.'"

Captain Hayes looked toward Chief Bidden. "Chief, did you hear that statement?"

Bidden nodded. "Yes, sir. Loud and clear. I told Haggerty he'd better express regret for that statement and do it then, but he had a head of steam up, I guess, and wouldn't."

"I see." Hayes centered his gaze on Seaman Haggerty. "What do you have to say?"

"Sir, I, uh, got a little worked up. I know I shouldn't have said what I did."

"It's a little late to admit to that, Seaman Haggerty. Do you have anything else to say?"

Haggerty looked momentarily desperate. "I . . . No, sir. I'm just real sorry. I'd take it back now in a heartbeat, Captain. I do want to apologize to Mr. Diego. Honest."

Hayes looked back toward Randy Diego. "Ensign Diego, what kind of sailor is Seaman Haggerty?"

"Captain, he's been a pretty good performer before this. I'd expected him to make petty officer third class soon. But I couldn't let this go by."

Hayes nodded. "That's right. Chef, do you have anything to add?"

Chief Bidden shook his head. "No, sir. Mr. Diego summed it up right. Haggerty's been a good sailor. He ain't talking, but I think he was looking forward to seeing a girl, and he let something other than his brain do the thinking that day."

"I see." Hayes eyed Seaman Haggerty. "Do you understand the gravity of your offense, Seaman Haggerty?"

"Yes, sir. Yes, sir, I do."

"Ensign Diego talked about you possibly making third class soon. How happy would you be if someone junior to you then responded to your orders by insulting you?"

"I wouldn't like it, Captain."

Hayes frowned down at the charge sheet for a moment. "I'd be fully justified in throwing the book at you for this, but your division officer and chief both say you've been a good sailor, and this incident was an aberration. Even then, though, I can't let it pass. Speaking so disrespectfully of an officer to his face cannot be tolerated." Hayes paused. "I'm going to order you to be fined half of one month's pay. And reduced in rate one pay grade." Haggerty flinched. "Suspended for six months." Haggerty brightened, then quailed again as Captain Hayes raised a hand in admonishment. "If you screw up again, you'll be a seaman apprentice, not a petty officer third class. Understood?"

"Yes, sir. That won't be a problem, sir. I promise."

"Good. Dismissed."

Haggerty looked toward Petty Officer Sharpe in some confusion. Sharpe hooked a finger to tell him to leave. Ensign Diego and Chief Bidden followed.

Paul nodded to himself. *That wasn't an easy case, but Hayes seemed to find the right balance between discipline and mercy. Haggerty's going to miss that pay, so he didn't get off free, but he's got a chance to beat the rest of the penalty if he keeps his nose clean.*

Hayes shook his head and glanced at Senior Chief Kowalski. "Let's hope that got Haggerty's attention. Next case."

Sharpe called out the next name. "Petty Officer Second Class Gadell."

Gadell came in, standing at attention before Captain Hayes, as Lieutenant Silver and Chief Asher followed.

Hayes looked at his charge sheet. "Petty Officer Gadell. You are charged with violating Article 134, Disorderly Conduct, Drunkenness. Lieutenant Silver, what does this charge concern?"

Instead of answering, Silver indicated Chief Asher. "The Chief knows the details, Captain."

Hayes frowned slightly and looked toward Chief Asher. "Well, Chief?"

"Sir, Petty Officer Gadell, she came back from liberty three sheets to the wind, if you know what I mean. Came into the berthing compartment after taps, raising hell and making noise. Everybody told her to shut up, but she just kept it up. So's I had to get involved. But she wouldn't listen to me, either. We had to tie her in her bunk. It was real bad, and everybody in the division was real unhappy. If we let Gadell get away with that kind of thing, others would think they could, too. So we had to do something, sir."

"Thank you, Chief. Petty Officer Gadell, what do you have to say?"

Petty Officer Gadell bit her lip before replying. "Captain, the charge is true. I drank too much. Lost control, and did some stupid stuff."

"You're not denying the charge at all? You aren't claiming any mitigating circumstances?"

"No, Captain. No, sir. I did it. I'm real sorry I did, but that's no excuse."

Hayes nodded, his expression thoughtful now. "Lieutenant Silver, what's Petty Officer Gadell's record like?"

Once again, Silver indicated Chief Asher instead of replying himself. Captain Hayes frowned a bit deeper this time.

Chief Asher looked unhappy. "Captain, Petty Officer Gadell's a real good performer. This isn't like her. I wouldn't have brought charges except she did this in front of the whole division. I count on sailors like her to be real good examples."

"And usually she's a good example?"

"Yes, sir. Normally, Gadell's a real fine sailor."

Hayes looked back at Gadell. "All right, Petty Officer Gadell. Getting so drunk you couldn't control what you were doing wasn't very smart, was it?"

"No, sir."

"Are you going to do it again?"

"No, sir!"

"You've got two things in your favor. The first is that your chief says you're a good sailor, and this isn't typical of you. The second is that you've accepted responsibility for what you did and didn't try to justify it. I can't let you off, because you do owe the rest of your division for causing all that disruption. But given your record and your attitude, I'm going to keep it light. Thirty days restriction to the ship. Don't let it happen again. Dismissed."

Petty Officer Gadell couldn't mask her happy surprise

before she left. As Lieutenant Silver began to follow her and
Chief Asher out, Captain Hayes beckoned him over. Hayes
spoke in a low voice, but Paul could still barely make it out.
"Next time you have a sailor up here, Mr. Silver, make sure
you familiarize yourself with that sailor's record."

Silver, taken aback, nodded several times. "Yes, sir."

Petty Officer Sharpe waited until Lieutenant Silver had
left before calling in the last case. "Seaman Apprentice Alvarez!"

Alvarez entered, her uniform looking good only relative
to Alvarez's usual appearance, and stood before the Captain.
Lieutenant Sindh and Chief Thomas took their positions opposite Paul, with Sindh giving Paul a brief eye contact that
spoke volumes. Paul fought down a sour grin. *Alvarez. She
was at the first Captain's Mast I attended on this ship, and
she's been pretty much a regular since then. I wonder what
she did this time?* A third person, Corpsman Second Class
Kim, entered and stood near Chief Thomas.

Captain Hayes consulted his charge sheet. "Seaman Alvarez. You are charged with violating Article 112a of the
Uniform Code of Military Justice, Wrongful Use of Controlled Substances, and Article 115, Malingering. What's the
story, Lieutenant Sindh?"

Sindh nodded toward Alvarez. "Captain, as you know,
the urinals on the ship are equipped with automatic drug-
testing monitors and identify anybody using them who has
drugs in their system. One such system notified us that Seaman Apprentice Alvarez popped positive for a synthetic
drug known as Blue Sky, which is on the list of controlled
substances."

"I see. What about the malingering charge?"

"After she was confronted on the positive drug detection,
Seaman Apprentice Alvarez declared herself to be in great
pain, claiming someone must have spiked her food with a
drug that was now causing severe reactions. She was taken
to sick bay, thoroughly tested, and placed under observation
for twenty-four hours. The duty corpsman reported Seaman
Apprentice Alvarez displayed no bodily stress indicators
that would have been consistent with pain, nor did she show

any other detectable signs of physical stress aside from her own declarations. Moreover, Seaman Apprentice Alvarez's descriptions of her suffering were not consistent. It was the duty corpsman's official assessment that Seaman Apprentice Alvarez had faked being ill."

Hayes bent a stern face toward Alvarez. "What do you have to say to the charges?"

Alvarez licked her lips and put a pleading expression on her face. "Captain, sir, it's not true. I don't know why that thing said I'd been using drugs, 'cause I don't. No, sir. That'd be unprofessional, sir. Those things malfunction, sir. I know that's true."

Hayes looked toward Corpsman Kim. "What's your assessment?"

Kim cleared his throat. "Captain, those automated testers do give false positives every once in a while. But as part of the tests I ran when Seaman Apprentice Alvarez said she was sick, I checked for drugs, of course. I got a clean positive on Blue Sky. There's no doubt it was in her system."

Alvarez shook her head. "Sir, somebody must have put it in something. I don't even know what that Blue stuff is."

Hayes's face stayed hard. "And what about the malingering charge? What do you say about that?"

"Captain, sir, I was terrible sick. I couldn't do nothing but hurt. I don't care what them machines say, I know when I'm hurting. I wouldn't fake that, sir. I know the rest of the sailors in my division are counting on me, sir."

Hayes looked back to Lieutenant Sindh. "What kind of sailor is Seaman Apprentice Alvarez?"

Sindh let her eyes rest on Alvarez. "Captain, she's a frequent source of problems. She requires constant supervision, her work is substandard, and her attitude is usually borderline insubordinate. Alvarez is a detriment to my division."

Hayes looked at Chief Thomas. "Chief?"

Thomas inclined her head toward Lieutenant Sindh. "Captain, I agree with the lieutenant, except I think maybe she could've been a bit harsher in her assessment of Alvarez."

The corners of Hayes's lips twitched upward in a momentary smile. "I see. I also see from Seaman Apprentice Alvarez's record that she's been a frequent visitor to Captain's Masts." He speared Alvarez with a look. "I don't need sailors like you on my ship. The first thing I'm going to do is reduce you in rate to seaman recruit, fine you one-half of your pay for three months, and order you restricted to the ship for the next ninety days. The second thing I'm going to do is get you off this ship. Senior Chief Kowalski."

Kowalski straightened to attention. "Yes, sir."

"You will work with the executive officer to find a way to get Seaman Recruit Alvarez transferred off of this ship as soon as possible, with a recommendation she be separated from the Navy with an administrative discharge." Hayes pointed a rigid forefinger at Alvarez. "You listen to me. If you pull any other stunts on board the *Michaelson* before I get rid of you, you'll be facing a court-martial and a bad conduct discharge. Is that clear?"

Alvarez's mouth worked silently for a moment. "Y-yes, sir."

"Dismissed."

Alvarez turned and left. Lieutenant Sindh, grinning widely, followed. As Chief Thomas left, she and Ivan Sharpe exchanged a high five. Sharpe saw Captain Hayes give him a stern look and quickly came back to attention, but still smiled. "That was the last one, Captain," Sharpe announced.

"You saved the best for last, huh? Why is Alvarez still aboard this ship?"

Sharpe looked at Senior Chief Kowalski, who shrugged. "Captain, if we were allowed to kill dirtballs, then Alvarez would've been stuffed into a launch tube a long time ago. But she's been able to convince people she could turn around."

"People?"

"Uh, your predecessors, sir."

"I see. Senior Chief, I hate losing a sailor, even one with a bad reputation, as long as I have reason to believe that sailor can be brought around. Nothing about Alvarez made me believe she'd ever get her act together."

"No, sir. God knows Lieutenant Sindh and Chief Thomas have tried, sir."

"Well, they'll have one less distraction soon. Let me know how we can get rid of her, Senior Chief, and how soon. Dismissed." Hayes nodded again to Paul, then headed for the hatch.

Sharpe yelled, "Attention on deck!" then grinned at Paul after the Captain had left. "Oh, it's a beautiful day, sir."

Senior Chief Kowalski smiled, too. "Alvarez hasn't left, yet. You keep an eye on her. I wouldn't mind booting her out with a bad conduct discharge."

"Me, neither, Senior Chief. Ah, Mr. Sinclair, I've been waiting for this day. Begging your pardon, sir, but if you were a woman I'd kiss you."

Paul laughed. "Then I'm glad I'm not." He left as well, heading for the wardroom in search of coffee. He found Mike Bristol and Lieutenant Sindh already there. "Well," Paul noted as he strapped into a chair, "Scott Silver appears to have accomplished the difficult task of looking worse than Randy Diego."

Lieutenant Sindh smiled. "It's nice to see Lieutenant Silver accomplish *something*."

Mike Bristol frowned in puzzlement, looking from Paul to Sindh. "What's wrong with Scott?"

Sindh took a drink before replying. "He's an ass."

"He seems like a great guy to me."

"That's because you don't have to depend upon him to do anything."

"Really?" Mike looked at Paul.

"Yeah. You think Scott's a great guy?" Paul shook his head. "He acts nice enough, I guess, but he lets other people carry the load."

"Huh." Mike Bristol scratched his head for a moment. "Most everybody likes him."

Lieutenant Sindh grimaced. "I'm certain Commander Kwan loves him, as no doubt does his department head, Commander Destin. However, to my knowledge neither of those officers has suffered as a result of Lieutenant Silver's avoidance of responsibilities."

"He's messed over both you guys?"

"Frequently and with apparent lack of remorse."

"Huh," Bristol repeated. "How come you guys haven't been complaining openly?"

Paul shrugged. "You don't do that. Who wants to be Sam Yarrow?"

"Why not? I mean, if the guy isn't doing his job, shouldn't someone know?"

Sindh and Paul exchanged glances. Paul shook his head again. "It's hard, Mike. You're not supposed to bilge people."

"Bilge?"

"Uh, the bilge is where trash ends up on a seagoing ship. It's a general term for bad stuff."

"It sounds like Scott's bilging *you*."

"You could say that."

Bristol scratched his head again. "I guess this is one of those fraternity of long-suffering line officers things, isn't it?"

"Well, yeah."

Lieutenant Sindh finished her coffee. "Consider, Mike. If the officers are running around dumping on each other, working relationships go to hell. The crew picks up on it, and problems such as insubordination become commonplace. Why respect an officer who isn't respected by his or her peers? In short order, you could have an actually hazardous situation on board, one in which accidents can occur because of ill feelings and bad discipline."

"But aren't your working relationships with Scott already bad?"

"Yes, but that's not the same as dysfunctional. I understand what Scott will do. Or, rather, not do. I can do my job understanding that. Paul can do his job. Introducing actual hostility on both sides into the situation would generate problems with carrying out our duties."

Paul nodded. *I hadn't thought it through quite like that, but she's right.* "That's why most of us ignore Sam Yarrow.

If we took him really seriously, that would hurt us all. Besides, Sam tries to make himself look good by making everybody else look bad. We don't want to have that kind of reputation."

"Okay, if you guys say so." Bristol checked the time and hurriedly unstrapped. "Gotta go."

Paul looked at Sindh after Mike Bristol left. "Are we doing the right thing?"

"What else can we do, Paul? Scott's professional behavior, or lack thereof, places an extra burden upon us. It doesn't translate into a danger to anyone."

"What if it does?"

She sat silent for a moment. "We must watch carefully. You know the truth, Paul. Mr. Silver is very popular with some of his superiors, at least, as well as many of the junior officers. Any complaints against him must be well justified and documented, or they will likely be ignored."

"You're being evaluated against him! He could end up ranking higher than you because all he does is try to impress his superiors and make everybody else like him."

"Neither the Navy nor life is fair, Paul." Sindh unstrapped and pulled herself out of her seat. "Come, Paul. We've both plenty of work to do. Letting Mr. Silver's faults distract us from that will only compound our problems."

When you're right, you're right. Paul followed her out.

A day later, they were back at Franklin. They'd be heading out again on Monday for more tests, and Paul had duty that weekend, so he had to stay on board the ship instead of taking a break enjoying what diversions Franklin Naval Station offered. Not that it mattered with Jen's ship gone for another two and a half months.

CHAPTER SIX

☆　☆　☆　☆　☆

DUTY days normally dragged, but weekend duty days were worse. Most of the crew were off the ship pursuing entertainment or simply some degree of freedom, leaving the duty section to stand watches and contemplate the ability of the Navy to turn even a Saturday into tedious drudgery. Paul yawned and checked his watch. *Almost time for eight o'clock reports. I guess I'll wander out to the quarterdeck.* He left his stateroom, moving with casual ease through the quiet passageway.

From somewhere, a muffled boom vibrated through the hull. Paul stopped, frowning down at the deck. *What the hell was that? Was it on board us or something that happened on the station?*

A moment later, the rapid ringing of the ship's bell over the all-hands speakers shattered the calm. "Fire, fire, fire! Fire in compartment 2-110-3-Echo, Forward Engineering. This is not a drill!"

The alarm began repeating as Paul broke into a run, ducking through two hatchways and out onto the quarterdeck, where Chief Imari was standing the watch as officer of the deck in port. "How bad is it?"

Chief Imari, her face pale, shook her head. "We don't know. Damage Control Central lost some sensors in Forward Engineering when that explosion went off—"

"That was an explosion?"

"Yes, sir. Apparently, it ruptured the fuel lines near the compartment. Somehow, the stuff ignited. We've got a high-intensity fire going and—" A shrill tone sounded, and Chief Imari stabbed a finger at the comm panel. "This is the officer of the deck."

The petty officer in Damage Control Central spoke rapidly and with an edge of panic. "Chief? This is DC Central. The fire suppression systems ain't working."

"Say again. Calm down. Speak slowly."

"Uh, yes, Chief. I tried to activate the fire suppression systems in Forward Engineering. They're off-line."

"How can they be off-line? Shouldn't the fire have triggered them automatically?"

"I dunno why they ain't working, Chief. And I dunno why they didn't trigger on auto. I tried a manual start, and nothing's happening."

Paul became aware that Lieutenant Silver, hastily adjusting his clothing, had appeared on the quarterdeck as well. "What's going on?"

"Explosion and fire in Forward Engineering," Paul summarized quickly. "Fire suppression systems aren't working."

Chief Imari was speaking again with forceful calm. "Is Forward Engineering isolated?"

"Yes, Chief," DC Central answered quickly. "All vent ducts, piping, hatches, and other accesses are sealed."

Lieutenant Silver grinned. "Then it should burn itself out pretty fast. No oxygen."

Chief Imari twisted her lips, then glanced at Paul, who shook his head. "No. The fuel supplies its own oxidizer. It'll burn as long as there's fuel."

"Then, uh, we need to dump the fuel. Get rid of it."

Chief Imari answered directly this time. "No, sir. Dumping fuel is prohibited in the vicinity of the station at any time. Dumping burning fuel is out of the question."

Paul leaned forward to speak to DC Central. "This is

Lieutenant Sinclair. Can we pump the fuel into another tank?"

"Negative, sir. Not with it burning on one end. If that fire raced up the transfer lines, the whole ship might blow. That fire's gotta be out, first."

Paul stepped back, looking around. It had been scant moments since the alarm sounded, yet it already felt like hours were being wasted. He focused on Lieutenant Silver, who was chewing his lip and staring at the nearest bulkhead. "What do we do?" Silver looked back but said nothing.

"Sir." Chief Imari gestured with one finger, pointing toward where Forward Engineering lay. "There's only thing to do. Put that fire out the old-fashioned way. The duty damage control party is forming up near Forward Engineering. They'll have to go in and knock that fire down."

Silver nodded quickly. "Yes. Sounds good. Get 'em in there."

DC Central spoke again. "Quarterdeck! The Damage Control team leader hasn't reported in. They've got everybody else."

"Damn!" Chief Imari snarled. "That's Chief Asher. You'd think he'd have been the first one there since that's his equipment in Forward Engineering . . ." Her voice trailed off, and she stared at Paul. "That's his gear in Forward Engineering."

"Oh, hell. He might have been in there? DC Central, has anyone seen Chief Asher?"

"Negative, sir. That team needs a leader, sir, and it needs it now. Those fire temperatures will cause damage to the surrounding bulkheads if they last long enough."

Paul glanced quickly around. *Silver's the command duty officer. He can't go to the scene because he has to coordinate the entire effort. Chief Imari is the officer of the deck, and Silver's primary assistant right now. That leaves me.* "I'll go." Silver was staring at the bulkhead again. "Scott? I'll go. Okay?"

"What?"

"I'll go lead the Damage Control team. You're in charge here. I need your approval. Is that okay?"

"Uh . . . yeah. Okay."

Paul spun on one heel and dashed toward Forward Engineering. He took ladders at a reckless pace, hurling himself down the steps, and ducking through hatches. One shoulder slammed against a hatch as he went through, and Paul moderated his pace just enough to maintain his balance. *The last thing anybody needs is for me to knock myself out right now.* Memories from his damage control training swarmed chaotically through his mind, merging into a stream of images of smoke, heat, water and torn metal.

The Damage Control team, an even dozen sailors, looked around as Paul pulled himself into the compartment. "Who's the assistant team leader?"

A small brunette held up her hand. "Me, sir. Petty Officer Santiago. You comin' in with us?"

"Yeah. I hope you got a spare survival suit."

"If we don't, you ain't comin', sir. But we got the Chief's. Any idea where he is, sir?"

Paul paused just a moment as he pulled himself into the suit. "He might be in there."

"*Dios.*" Santiago hastened to aid Paul's donning of the suit.

Paul activated the suit systems and watched data pop up on his faceplate display. The suit's air exchanger kicked in, blowing fresh air against his face. Everything seemed to be working properly, so he activated the local communications circuit. "Santiago. How'd you recommend taking this fire down?"

"Uh, sir, if it was me, I'd go in with both hoses on full spray, as fine a fog as we can put out. We can't smother that crap, so we gotta cool it enough that the fresh fuel comin' in stops ignitin'. That's what I'd do."

Paul nodded. The suit hindered the gesture a bit, being bulky enough to protect the wearer for a while against the extremes of space and hazards such as fires, but hopefully flexible enough to allow any necessary movement. "Then that's what we'll do. Get the hoses laid out and ready to go."

"Sir." A hull tech waved one hand. "That fuel's corrosive as hell."

"Right. Our suits should be able to handle it." *I remember that from my training. At least, they're supposed to be able to handle it.* "Everybody double-check the seals on your suits."

"Buddy check!" Santiago snapped, quickly running her hands over the seaman next to her while he did the same to her. "You, too, sir." Paul held still while Santiago's hands pressed across his arms, back, and legs. A ridiculous thought, that having Petty Officer Santiago pawing him would normally be a violation of a couple of articles of the Uniform Code of Military Justice, sped through his mind even as he knew that neither her actions nor his reactions were focused on anything but staying alive. "You're good, sir."

"Thanks." Paul forced himself to scroll carefully through communication options until he found the right one. "DC Central?"

"DC Central, aye."

"This is Lieutenant Sinclair. We're going to go into Forward Engineering with two hoses on full spray and attempt to cool the fuel down below its ignition temperature. I'll need all the fresh water you can provide to those hoses."

"Roger. Understand you need water maintained to the hoses. I'll notify the station to keep it coming."

Paul glanced at the hatch to Forward Engineering, which was beginning to glow noticeably. *Man, when we pop that we better be careful . . oh, geez.* "Santiago. Get the hatch into this space sealed. When we open up Forward Engineering it's going to flood this compartment with junk. DC Central, make sure all accesses and ventilation to this compartment are sealed."

"Roger. All accesses sealed, vents secured."

The low background hum of vent fans, a constant presence on the ship, cut off abruptly. Two sailors turned and made thumbs-up gestures from the other hatch. "It's tight, sir."

"Okay, um . . . who's lead hose?"

Santiago crouched and hefted the hose. "That's me, sir.

Uh, I'd recommend you not stand right in front of that hatch when we pop it, Mr. Sinclair."

Paul suddenly realized he was indeed standing right in front of the hatch, like the hero of some action-packed but stupid movie. He hastily moved back and to the side. "Thanks, Santiago. Okay, charge the hoses." The limp lengths of the hoses suddenly bulged into tight cylinders as water under high pressure surged into them. Petty Officer Santiago on one hose and a big male bosun mate on the other held their nozzles firmly as they jerked in response to the tightening hoses like eager horses fighting their bridles. The rest of the sailors formed up to help control and carry the hoses, except for two who stood back to help feed the hoses through the hatch once the others went in. "DC Central, Quarterdeck, this is Lieutenant Sinclair. We're popping the hatch to Forward Engineering."

The two hull technicians in the team punched the automated opener, and after getting no response hauled out tools, placed them in the manual opening slots, then pulled hard. The hatch resisted for a moment, then blew open so fast one of the hull techs barely avoided getting smashed. The hatch slammed back against the bulkhead, its interior surface a pitted, smoking ruin, then the entire Damage Control team staggered as a firestorm of heat and smoke fountaned out through the hatch opening. Paul caught himself, leaning into the eruption and watching the telltales on his faceplate blink rapid warnings. *If we hadn't been suited up when that hit, we'd have been fried instantly.*

Both hoses lit off, hurling out a high-velocity mist of fine droplets of water against the heat and smoke. Water mist flashed to steam, stealing heat from the fire, and beat back the smoke. "Fuel shouldn't be making that kinda smoke!" one of the hull techs shouted.

Paul watched the black-and-gray mass, then shook his head. "It's not the fuel making that. It's everything else in that compartment burning." Insulation, computers, wiring, plastic, and maybe at least one human. "And don't yell on the circuit."

"Aye, aye, sir."

"Advance when you're ready, Santiago."

"Advance when ready, aye, sir." Santiago began duck-walking forward, staying low beneath the hottest air and moving the nozzle in a tight circular pattern that opened a hole in the inferno for her advance. The backup hose paused while Santiago cleared the hatch, then followed, its spray covering and cooling Santiago as well as beating back the fire and smoke. Paul waited until about half the Damage Control team had entered, then pushed in himself.

His vision vanished so suddenly Paul almost panicked. Then he spotted the telltales still glowing on his faceplate and realized he hadn't gone blind, but that the smoke was so dense it had cut off sight completely. Paul's arms flailed out in search of contact with some surface, one hand brushing against something he grabbed on to like a liferaft.

"Who the hell—? Oh, Mr. Sinclair. Just a sec." A hand grasped his wrist just above where Paul's own hand was locked onto someone's shoulder, then guided Paul's hand to a taut, rounded surface he recognized as one of the hoses. "You okay, now, sir?"

"Yeah. Thanks." *Control your breathing. Don't hyperventilate. Don't let the team hear you sounding scared.* Paul became aware the hose wasn't moving. Peering ahead, he thought he could vaguely make out swirls in the smoke that must mark the fog nozzles at work, spraying a so-far-futile barrage against the firestorm. *Okay. Think. Remember your damage control training. When fighting a fire, aim at the base of the flames, not the flames themselves. If we can get to where the fuel's coming in, we can cool it there and stop the fire at its source.* "DC Central, this is Lieutenant Sinclair. We've got zero visibility in here. And I mean zero. We need guidance to the likely source of the fuel leak."

"Roger, sir. Providing virtual guidance now."

Glowing lines sprang to life on his faceplate, outlining the equipment, catwalks, and bulkheads Paul would have been able to see if not for the smoke. He turned his head, watching the lines shift to show another part of the compartment. it resembled nothing so much as a first-person perspective video game, though the graphics were far more primitive and the stakes much higher than in any game Paul had ever played. "Santiago. Everybody else. Have you got the virtual guidance?" A chorus of affirmative replies followed. "That arrow should point toward the location where the fuel leak is coming in. Head that way."

"Aye, sir." The hose began moving slowly and jerkily under Paul's hand, and he followed along, crouching low against the heat. The virtual guidance showed they were traversing a catwalk along the upper portion of the compartment.

"Damn!" The hose jerked, then steadied.

"Santiago! You okay?"

"Yessir. So far. The damned catwalk's half–blown away up here. I almost dropped through. I can make it along the bulkhead, though. I think."

"Roger. Be careful. Hose team, hold tight so that if Santiago drops we can pull her back." Paul scowled at the virtual guidance, which showed an intact catwalk running all the way along the bulkhead. *No, wait. Of course it shows an intact catwalk.* "Everybody, this guidance only shows what things looked like before the explosion and fire. They don't know what kind of damage might have happened, so it's not reflected on the guidance. Step carefully."

"Now you tell us," somebody muttered.

Paul found himself suddenly grinning widely at the gibe as he inched along through blinding black clouds of smoke shot through with gray swirls, feeling ahead with one hand while the other rested on the hose. He knew the smile was too wide, too tight to be natural. Waves of heat surged against him, so that even through the suit's protection he felt the warmth. A fine mist of what might be fuel droplets lay across his faceplate for a moment, then flashed away in another burst of heat. An indicator on his face shield blinked urgently, warning of estimated time remaining until the suit systems failed under the stress of the heat. *God, I'm scared.*

"I'm across," Santiago reported. "Come one at a time. I don't trust what's left of that catwalk."

Paul checked the time, shocked to see only minutes had

elapsed since they'd entered Forward Engineering. "Santiago, are you still in the lead?"

"Yes, sir."

"Do you see any sign of the leak?"

"No, si— Son of a bitch!"

"Santiago! What happened?"

"I found that leak, sir. Jesus. It's like a torch. Burned me through the suit."

Paul felt a chill at odds with the inferno around them. "It penetrated your suit?" He began trying to plan how to get Santiago out of the compartment as quickly as possible in zero visibility across a damaged catwalk with a fire raging, before the hole in her suit allowed the toxic fuel, smoke, and heat to kill her.

"No, sir. It did not. I think my arm's kinda boiled."

Paul exhaled heavily, not aware until then that he'd been holding his breath. "Can you still use it?"

"Yes, sir. I'm aiming my fog at the base of the leak. Okay?"

"Exactly right. Make sure the other hose keeps you cool."

"Yes, sir."

"Lieutenant Sinclair? This is Chief Imari. We've got damage control parties sent from the *Midway* and the *Belleau Wood* standing by to assist. Should I send them down to you?"

Paul looked around, as if he could judge the situation visually, then raised his hand in an instinctive and futile gesture to wipe sweat from his brow. "No. I don't know how we'd get them in here without sacrificing another compartment to the smoke and heat, and I don't know how'd we employ them in here. I can only get one or two people right up at the leak that's feeding the fire."

"Could they come at it from another angle, sir?"

Good question, but Paul dismissed it almost instantly. "I don't know, so I wouldn't recommend trying. There's damage in here. This catwalk we're on is half-gone. I have no idea what things are like on the other side of the leak."

"Understood. No assistance to be sent in at this time. With your permission, I'll send the *Midway* team down to begin rigging a temporary airlock outside the compartment you entered Forward Engineering from, and hold the *Belleau Wood* people in reserve."

Of course. They'd need to get out once all this was over. Or before it was over, if things went really bad. "Thanks, Chief. That's a great idea." Paul began inching forward again, running one hand over the hose, then over a sailor. "Who's that?"

"Lieutenant Sinclair."

"Oh. The damaged part's right ahead, sir. Stay close to the bulkhead."

"Thanks." Paul edged as close to the bulkhead as he could, watching the telltales on his suit display warning of the heat radiating from that surface. He stepped slowly and carefully, feeling the catwalk quivering under his feet. It sagged alarmingly under his weight at one point, leaving him wishing he was as light as Petty Officer Santiago, but on the next step the catwalk felt firmer. A few feet farther on, and Paul's exploring hand encountered another sailor. "Santiago?"

"Uh, no, sir. Petty Officer Yousef. Backup hose."

The big bosun mate, then. "Probably the only time you've ever been confused with Santiago, isn't it?"

"You got that, sir. She's right in front of me."

Paul slid forward even more cautiously, half-afraid of being partly boiled himself and half-afraid of shoving Santiago back into the torch that had already injured her. The fog from Yousef's hose cooled the air around him, beating back some of the smoke as well, so he actually caught a glimpse of Santiago's suit just before his hand reached her. "Santiago, it's Sinclair. Where's the torch?"

"I'm aimed right at it, sir."

Paul moved sideways around her, keeping as close to Santiago as possible without bumping into her. He felt heat beating at the side nearest the fuel leak and realized Santiago had been fronting that heat for several minutes, now. "How are you doing?"

"I'm okay, sir. I can hold out a bit longer. How much do we have to cool that fuel before it stops flamin'?"

"Uh . . . I don't know." Paul studied his suit's telltales. "It is cooling."

"Yeah. Real slow. Maybe I should go solid stream? Break it up?"

"No!" Paul had a vision of a solid column of water hitting the flaming fuel and casting it in all directions like a bomb. "Just keep cooling the base. DC Central, can you copy my suit readings?"

"Affirmative, sir."

"Are we getting anywhere close to cooling down that fuel enough?"

"Sir, I think so, but—"

"Wait." On Paul's telltales, the torch heat readings had suddenly plunged, then jerked up again. "What was that?"

"It flickered, sir. You're getting there."

Santiago hunched forward a little more. "Santiago! Don't get too close!"

"I'm gonna put this bastard out, sir. Don't worry. I can handle this."

"Yousef! Get a little closer to Santiago! Cover her."

"Yes, sir." The fog from the backup hose thickened a bit as Yousef followed Paul's orders.

Another plunge in torch temperature, another climb, then two more plunges in quick succession. "You're getting it, Santiago." A final plunge, and it stayed lower. It took Paul a moment to realize that drop in temperature was still far too high. "Keep your hose on it, Santiago. Yousef, get up here and train your hose directly on the leak as well. I need a patch up here!"

"Aye, sir. Patch coming." Moments later, two suits came past, feeling their way over Paul, Santiago, and Yousef, then vanishing into the murk. "Son of a bitch."

"What?" Paul leaned forward as if that would help him see.

"Sorry, sir. That's one nasty hole, and I'm getting fuel all over me feeling it out. Hey, Tatyana, gimme the half meter square patch and get a brace ready." Silence followed for a few moments, except for an occasional grunt. "Yeah. Gimme the end of the brace . . . okay, it's set. I'll hold it while you tension it." In his mind's eye, Paul could see the other hull technician spinning the tensioner on the brace, lengthening it until it held the patch firmly in place. "Okay. Lemme kick it. Yeah. That's tight. I got some patching goo around the edge and it seems to be holding. Looks like we got that leak, sir."

"Great. Thanks. DC Central, you copy?"

"Affirmative. We've begun draining fuel from that tank. Are there still flames elsewhere in the compartment? We've lost all sensors."

Paul tried to imagine how bad it had been to kill every sensor m Forward Engineering, then slowly looked around, watching his suit's telltales shift as the temperatures he faced varied. "I think there's still some burning going on. We'll try to knock it down. Is there any way you can get the smoke pumped out of here so we can see what we're doing?"

"Not yet, sir. Based upon your suit readings the stuff in there is too thick to run through our ship purifiers without clogging them. We've got a mass air purifier heading this way, but it's still a few minutes out. Then they'll have to run the suction tube down to you and hook it up."

"Great. Santiago, Yousef, everybody else. Let's head for the hottest spot and try to break the fire up."

"Aye, aye, sir." Santiago moved about a meter, then stopped. "What the— *Madre de Dios*."

"Santiago? What's the problem?"

"I . . . I think I maybe found Chief Asher, sir."

Paul eased up beside her, then bent slowly through the still-dense smoke until an object lying on the deck suddenly came into view less than an inch from his faceplate shield. He jerked back at the sight, fighting down a tight feeling in his throat.

"You think that's him, sir?"

"It . . . it could be." Maybe a leg, maybe an arm. Heat and corrosive fuel, perhaps on top of whatever damage the explosion had done, had left very little to tell for sure. *Don't throw up. Don't throw up. Think about something else.*

"Lieutenant Sinclair?"

"Yeah!" The reply was too shrill, too stressed. Paul forced himself to speak more calmly. "Yes. Who's this?"

"Lieutenant Candon, off the *Midway*. We've almost got an airlock rigged. May I respectfully suggest you pull your team back and let one of the other damage control teams handle mop-up?"

Paul licked his lips, fighting down what he knew was an irrational urge to ignore Candon's advice. But Santiago had been injured, he recalled with a guilty start, and everyone was exhausted from the heat. He checked the blinking warning against suit failure. Putting out the torch had eliminated the firestorm, but the heat was still intense enough to keep the warning fluctuating around perhaps a half hour's time remaining before suit systems might start being overwhelmed. It would take them a good portion of that time just to exit the compartment. "Yes. I think that's a good idea. Uh, we've got fuel on our suits."

"I understand you have fuel on your suits. We've set up a washdown system inside the airlock. Wait one." Paul waited for a moment, one hand on Santiago's shoulder and the other on Yousef's. "The air rig tube is here. They're mating it to the vent now. You should have some visibility by the time you get back this way."

"Understand air venting will start soon. Chief Imari? Is Lieutenant Silver still up there?" Paul found himself frowning as he asked the question, only now realizing he'd heard nothing from Silver since leaving the quarterdeck.

"Yes, sir, he is."

"Does he know our status and that we plan on pulling out now?"

"Yes, sir."

Paul waited again, but nothing more followed. *I guess he's okay with it, then.* "All right, everybody, change of plans. Somebody else will cool down those hot spots. We're out of here. Fall back slowly to the hatch." The catwalk quivered some more as Paul made his way back, first Yousef, then Santiago coming after him, their nozzles still trained toward the strongest sources of heat. *There is going to be one major effort required to get all that water recovered so it can be reused.*

Conserving water was something of a mania on spacecraft, so pumping out so much seemed almost sinful. But as one of Paul's instructors had advised, plain old water was also the best heat sink in the universe. Nothing beat it for cooling down a fire. *You do what you have to do.*

Reaching the hatch out of Forward Engineering offered little apparent change in conditions, but a major psychological boost. As he groped his way onward, Paul finally noticed a thinning in the gloom. Smoke visibly rushed away from him, moving toward the same bulkhead the Damage Control party was headed toward. By the time they reached the outer hatch, they could see it, as well as the nearby vent sucking up the smoke and routing it toward the air purifier, where the particles making up that smoke would all be scrubbed out. "Lieutenant Candon? We're at the hatch."

"Roger. Go ahead and open it. The temporary airlock should hold six sailors at a time. How are your suits holding up?"

"They'll last." The automatic openers still worked here, swinging the hatch smoothly open. The Damage Control team members surged toward the opening, but Paul blocked them with an outstretched arm. "We won't all fit at once. Santiago, you first. I'll count off the next ones until the lock's full. Keep your suits sealed until they wash the fuel off you."

The wait seemed interminable as the first group went through washdown, then exited. When Candon finally gave the word for the next group, Paul sent them one at a time until only he was left. Judging enough space remained, he crowded in, unwilling to remain alone in the outer compartment with the hatchway into Forward Engineering gaping behind him. Paul looked back before closing the hatch. The smoke had cleared enough that he could see partway into Forward Engineering. Black soot covered every surface, except where some still glowed with heat. The familiar shapes of equipment, ladders and piping had all been bent and warped from the heat, melting into odd shapes. In the aftermath of the fire, Forward Engineering seemed to resemble a Salvador Dali painting of hell.

Lieutenant Candon wasn't suited up herself. As Paul exited, she waved her own team forward. "Chief, do what the *Michaelson*'s DC Central orders. Let me know if there's any problems." She turned to Paul and shook her head. "Looks like it's pretty bad."

"It is." Paul slumped against the nearest bulkhead, suddenly intensely thirsty.

Another figure was before him, this one with medical insignia on the collar. "Lieutenant Sinclair? I'm *Midway*'s duty medical officer. I understand there was a sailor in the compartment? Did you find him?"

Paul looked away. "Yeah. We . . . think so."

"You think so? Oh." The doctor grimaced. "Beyond help, then. Are any of your team hurt?"

"Yes. Santiago, get over here and let the doc check your arm."

Santiago grinned with obviously false cheer. "It's okay, sir. I don't need no sick call."

"You told me the fire boiled your arm."

"It's better now, Mr. Sinclair. Really."

The doctor moved toward her, smiling reassuringly. "Can I have a look, anyway?"

Santiago looked around like a trapped animal, then slowly peeled back her suit to reveal a swollen, red arm. "Doc, I ain't gonna need no shots, am I?"

Paul found himself desperately fighting down laughter, afraid it might sound hysterical. Petty Officer Santiago, who'd led the way into a deadly fire, gone face-to-face with its source, and insisted on fighting it even after being injured, was afraid of getting a shot.

Lieutenant Candon came over to Paul again. "I can take over here. You look pretty used up."

Paul hesitated, his tiredness and thirst warring with his sense of responsibility. "No. Thanks. But I better stay here. She's my ship."

"Understood. Can I get you anything?"

"Have you got any water?"

Candon laughed. "You just used up about ten years' worth of an entire ship's water allotments! And you want more?"

Paul winced. "Hey, that's not funny."

"Yeah, it is. But you're in luck. We brought some of *Midway*'s finest bottled water with us. Have a liter."

Paul was raising the bottle to his lips when he noticed one of his Damage Control party staring at it. *Oh, hell.* "Lieutenant Candon, do you have enough water for my sailors here?"

"Sure thing. Come 'n' get it, you guys." While Candon passed out bottles to the eager sailors, Paul finally drank, not lowering his own bottle until it was empty. "You need another?"

"No, thanks." Paul glanced up as someone came down the ladder. "Kris. You're not on duty."

"Paul, you idiot, when there's an emergency everyone's on duty. They passed an emergency recall for the crew. I got back a few minutes ago, and the Captain told me to get down here and relieve you on the scene." Kris looked at Lieutenant Candon with a worried frown. As a lieutenant junior grade, she was outranked by Candon.

But Lieutenant Candon just shook her head and smiled. "It's your ship. My orders are to render all requested assistance. At your service, ma'am."

"Looks like you're doing everything we need at the moment. Paul, take a hike. You look like ten kilometers of bad road."

"I wish everybody would stop telling me how bad I look," Paul mumbled. "Where am I supposed to go?"

"I don't know. The Captain didn't say. I wouldn't leave the ship, though."

Paul glared at her. "Duh."

"I was joking, Lieutenant Junior Grade Sinclair. Go somewhere and sit down, for heaven's sake."

"Okay, okay." Paul straightened and smiled toward his Damage Control team. "Thanks, you guys. You did a great job. Petty Officer Yousef? I'd appreciate it if you got me a list of everyone who's in this team."

"No problem, Mr. Sinclair." Yousef grinned. "It's been real, sir. And it's been nice. But it ain't been real nice."

"You can say that again." Paul saluted Kris. "I stand relieved."

She flipped a quick salute back. "I've got it. Get out of here before that doc tosses you into sick bay."

Paul pulled himself up the ladder, then paused, looking around. *Where do I go?* He eventually decided on the quarterdeck. Standing in one of the hatches leading out onto the quarterdeck, he leaned outward enough to see Lieutenant Silver talking animatedly to the XO, smiles alternating with a studiously serious expression. Feeling a sudden desire to be alone, Paul pulled back and headed down toward his stateroom, then at the last moment turned into the wardroom instead in hopes of finding hot coffee.

The coffee wasn't fresh but it was hot. Paul hunched forward in his seat, drinking slowly, looking up only when he heard the hatch open, then jumping to his feet. "Captain."

Hayes gestured Paul back to his seat. "Sit down. You've had a rough night. The fire's out."

"Yessir. The source, anyway. There were still a few hot spots in Forward Engineering when I left." The words suddenly sounded wrong, as if he'd abandoned his duty station.

But Hayes simply nodded. "The team from the *Midway* is cooling them down now. Franklin Station authorities are going nuts over all the water we just used."

Paul looked down. "Sorry, sir."

"Do you think I'm complaining? We're already pumping it out of Forward Engineering and back to the station recycling tanks. Do you have any idea how the fire started?"

Paul looked up again, wanting to know if the Captain was watching him like a prosecuting attorney, but saw only a Captain's concern there. "No, sir. All I know is there was an explosion, then the fire."

"Do you have any idea why the fire suppression systems in Forward Engineering didn't work? Did you see anything that might explain that while you were in there?"

"No, sir. DC Central said the systems were out, and later said they'd lost all sensors in the compartment because of the fire, but I didn't hear anything about anyone finding out why the systems didn't work. And I didn't see anything in the compartment, sir. Nothing. The smoke was so thick we couldn't see a thing. Except, um . . ." Paul unsuccessfully tried to avoid a small shudder.

"What?"

"Chief Asher, sir. I think. Some of what was left of him."

Hayes closed his eyes for a moment. "Chief Asher was in Forward Engineering when the explosion happened?"

"He must have been, sir. I don't see how after the explosion he could have run as far inside the compartment as where we found his . . . remains." Paul gulped, fighting down a wave of nausea.

"Okay. Did you sign off on any maintenance activity in Forward Engineering tonight?"

"Sir? No, sir. I hadn't seen Chief Asher since morning quarters."

"No other engineer came by and asked you to sign off on a work chit?"

"No, sir."

Hayes shook his head, his mouth a thin line. "I understand Chief Asher was a good sailor."

"I didn't know him much, sir, but I never heard anything bad about him."

"Asher was by the book? He didn't take shortcuts?"

"As far as I know, Captain. We never had any problems with him during duty days, and nobody ever told me he needed to be watched."

"How'd you end up leading that Damage Control team?"

Paul looked down at his coffee. "Uh, well, sir, Lieutenant Silver and Chief Imari and I were on the quarterdeck, and DC Central told us the team had to go in and knock down the fire, but Chief Asher wasn't there to lead them. Chief Imari had the deck and Lieutenant Silver was command duty officer, so that left me."

"Lieutenant Silver told you to go down there?"

"Um, he, uh, agreed to it, sir." Paul blinked, then looked up again. "Captain, Petty Officer Santiago did a great job.

She really deserves a medal. Petty Officer Yousef, too. The whole Damage Control team did well."

"I'll keep that in mind, Paul. Go ahead and rest for a while." Captain Hayes started to leave, then paused in the hatch. "What about you, Paul?"

"Sir?"

"How'd *you* do?"

Paul's gaze was fixed on his coffee again. He felt a great reluctance to speak, to talk of his time in Forward Engineering. Chief Asher was certainly dead, and offering up any praise for himself felt not only inappropriate but simply wrong. *I don't want any commendation, not one earned by Chief Asher's death.* "I did my job, sir."

Not long afterward, Kris Denaldo came in. "Colleen Kilgary showed up to relieve me and check out Forward Engineering herself. Why isn't Silver doing that?"

Paul shrugged. "I guess because he's Command Duty Officer."

"The Captain, XO, and just about everybody else is back on the ship. Silver doesn't need to worry about running things anymore. What could he be doing that's more important than checking out his gear and trying to confirm what happened to Chief Asher?"

"Do I look like I can read Silver's worthless mind?" Paul glanced up at the resulting silence, seeing Kris watching him. "Sorry. I've been under a little stress."

"That's a given, and you're forgiven for that. But I read some real hostility there."

"I don't like him. Okay? Silver's a no-load."

"I heard he handled the fire okay."

"He was paralyzed! Chief Imari and I were pushing things. I never heard a word from him when I was down there."

"Really. Have you told anyone else this?"

"No." His earlier conversation with Lieutenant Sindh came back. "And I'm not going to. It'd just make me look like I was trying to claim all the credit."

"For heaven's sake, Paul, everyone knows you don't do that sort of thing. Do you really think they'd feel that way?"

"I don't want to find out." A vision from the burning compartment came back to Paul. "And I sure as hell don't want to seem to be trying to hog the spotlight from a tragedy that killed one of our own."

She nodded slowly. "I can understand that. Paul, you really ought to try to sleep."

"Have you got any tranquilizers?"

"I could get some."

"I wasn't serious."

"I was."

Paul shook his head and stood up. "No. I need to handle this without chemicals. I'll go lie down. I guess if anyone needed me, they'd have come by already."

"If they do need you later, I'll make sure you know."

"Thanks."

Before reveille sounded the next morning, Paul stumbled into the wardroom in search of more coffee, his mood unimproved by a short, restless night that had featured only fitful sleep. Commander Sykes, seated in his accustomed place at the wardroom table, raised his coffee mug in greeting. "Good morning, young Sinclair."

"It's morning, sir." Paul got some coffee, took a big slug, then shuddered as the bitter liquid ran into his stomach. "What are you doing up so early, Suppo?"

"Early? I'm wounded. My work ethic is well-known."

Paul managed a small smile. "Yes, sir, Commander. That's why I'm wondering why you're up so early."

"There will be, I assume, much ado today over the need for replacement parts. I prefer to be ahead of that game rather than being pulled along behind the mob." Sykes waved to a chair. "Take a seat."

"Thanks, Suppo, but—"

"Consider it an order, young Sinclair."

Paul frowned, but sat. "What's so important?"

"You are. I feel certain your haggard appearance has little to do with the stress of your firefighting efforts last night."

Paul closed his eyes, trying to breath calmly. "Chief Asher's dead."

"So I understand. I, like everyone else on the ship, regret that deeply. But what's bothering you isn't that kind of regret, is it?"

"Suppo, he was part of my duty section! My responsibility! And he died. So I'm also responsible for that."

Sykes sipped his coffee slowly. "In a moral and professional sense, yes, that's true. In a practical sense, I'm unaware of any action you took that led to that death."

Paul inhaled deeply. "I don't know of any, either."

"Being a limited duty officer, I have little familiarity with the handling of fires and other emergencies, but my understanding is that Chief Asher must have died within seconds of the explosion, if not immediately. Is that true?"

"I'm sure it is."

"Within seconds, then, meaning he died even as the alarm was sounded. What could you have done to save the man, Paul?"

"I . . . don't know."

"Yes, I believe you do." Sykes leaned back, gazing into the distance. "I believe you know there's nothing you or any other human being could have done to save Chief Asher. Since God, or whichever deity you care to cite, did not see fit to intervene, the man's fate was sealed before you even knew he was imperiled."

Paul sat still for a long moment, then shook his head. "I know that. I also feel like there should've been something . . ."

"A word of advice, if I may. Focusing on things you *couldn't* have done will bring you nothing but sorrow."

"What else should I focus on?"

"Things you *can* do. Investigating and determining the cause of the accident. Finding the answer to that may save lives in the future. I understand you spoke highly of the Damage Control team you led into the fire."

Paul smiled again, wider this time, and nodded. "Yeah. They were great, Suppo."

"You can work at seeing such actions are properly rewarded. Drafting and shepherding medal recommendations through the approval process is tedious, but it can both reward the deserving and give you a meaningful sense of accomplishment."

"That's true." Paul leaned back as well, closing his eyes. "Thanks, Suppo. Why *aren't* you a line officer?"

"My dear Mr. Sinclair, since I lack masochistic tendencies, I have no wish to expose myself to the daily miseries endured by line officers."

Paul actually found himself laughing briefly. "You have a point there. Can I ask you something else, Suppo?"

"If it's about spare parts, my office hasn't opened, yet."

"Do you think Commander Herdez would've approved of what I did last night?"

"Hmmm." Sykes took another slow drink. "Many details are not known to me or to her at this time, but she seemed appreciative of your work."

"What? She knows what happened already?"

"The grapevine works at speeds exceeding those of light, although I'm unfamiliar with the physics which permit this. Yes, Commander Herdez and I spoke of the matter not long ago. As I'm sure you can guess, Commander Herdez is reserving judgment on all issues until a thorough investigation has been conducted."

Paul nodded. *Which is exactly what I should have expected. No more, no less.*

"However," Sykes added, "she did state it was 'a good thing Sinclair was on duty.'"

"Really?"

"Or words to that effect. The statement does not bring you comfort?"

"I can't help wondering if I lived up to them. Living up to Commander Herdez's expectations is—"

"Probably impossible." Sykes gave Paul an unusually serious look. "Give yourself due credit for attempting to do so. And listen to the advice of your elders."

"I will, Suppo. Thanks."

The day from that point on seemed almost surreal to Paul. Life and routine continued, but the aftermath of the fire kept appearing. Liberty was canceled for much of the crew on Sunday, as they were needed for the cleanup and as-

sessment of damage to Forward Engineering. The regular
duty section came on, with Lieutenant Kilgary as command
duty officer. Paul overheard part of her turnover with Scott
Silver, in which Kilgary kept pressing Silver for details that
apparently weren't forthcoming. Captain Hayes, Commander Kwan and all the department heads remained on
board. The black cloud of sorrow that seemed to perpetually
follow Commander Destin, the chief engineer, appeared to
have grown into a virtual storm. About noon, a small cara-
van of medical personnel arrived, equipped with isolation
suits, and went down to Forward Engineering. They left a
couple of hours later laden down with a large sealed box
whose proportions made it clear it contained the remains of
Chief Asher. Many of the crew, somehow forewarned of the
sad procession, lined the passageways to see it pass.

Most personnel avoided asking Paul about Saturday
night's fire, something he appreciated. His friends made a
point of having conversations about different issues.

Late in the afternoon, Paul received a page to report to
the executive officer's stateroom. He went there quickly,
afraid it was about the fire, so wishing to confront the meeting as fast as possible. "Lieutenant JG Sinclair, sir."

Commander Kwan looked up from his chair, then passed
Paul a hard-copy printout. "Fleet staff wants a thorough investigation. They've appointed an investigating officer. He's
the Captain of another ship. Find out what he needs from
us."

"Yes, sir. Uh, sir, my actions are also going to be investi-
gated—"

"I know that. That shouldn't prevent you, as ship's legal
officer, from seeing what the man requires for his investigation."

"Yes, sir." Paul headed back from his stateroom, paging
Sheriff Sharpe as he did so. *The ship's master-at-arms needs
to be in on this.* Once in his stateroom, he finally read the
printout.

He was still staring at it when Sharpe arrived. "You asked
to see me, sir?" For once, Sharpe didn't display his usual ir-
reverent attitude.

"Yeah."

"What's the matter, sir? Aside from the obvious, that is."

"They've appointed an officer to conduct a full investigation into the explosion and fire. Captain Shen of the USS *Mahan*."

"Captain Shen? Is he any relation to Lieutenant Shen, sir?"

"He's her father."

"The father of your main squeeze is the guy in charge of raking us over the coals? That's way harsh, sir."

"I was just thinking the same thing."

"And you're one of the prime objects of the investigation."

"Right again, Sheriff. Are you trying to cheer me up?"

Sharpe leaned against the hatch opening, staring contemplatively into space. "This Captain Shen. You ever meet him, sir?"

"Yeah. Once."

"What's he like?"

"He's Ms. Shen's father. What do you think?"

"Ouch. No offense intended to Ms. Shen, sir."

"None taken. She'll be proud to know she's remembered that way on this ship." Paul leaned back and looked upward. "What'd I do? Somebody up there seems awful mad at me."

"You're better off than Vlad Asher, sir."

Paul frowned, looking toward Sharpe again. "He was a friend of yours, wasn't he?"

Sharpe nodded abruptly. "Yessir. A fine man. A fine sailor. I don't know what happened in Forward Engineering, but I can't believe it's his fault."

"Something screwy happened, that's for sure. Not just the explosion, but the fire suppression systems not working. What're the odds of that?"

"Dunno, sir. I'm not a snipe," Sharpe pointed out, using the common slang for engineering personnel.

"Do *you* know why Asher would have been in there at that time?"

Sharpe frowned at the deck. "Sir, with all due respect,

that touches on testimony I might be called upon to give in the investigation. I shouldn't discuss it with you."

Paul nodded. "Or anyone else. I suppose the automated engineering logs will tell us something."

"Uh, no, sir, apparently not."

"What?"

"I have this reliably, sir. The engineering logs are badly damaged. They're not sure how much of them will be recoverable."

"How the *hell* could those logs have been damaged? They're supposed to survive having the ship blown apart."

"Sir, I don't know. There's some guesses about the explosion and the fire."

Paul stared at nothing for a moment, then shook his head rapidly. "That's just weird. But I suppose it's not impossible. I guess that's something the investigation will really have to dig into."

"Yes, sir. I really want answers to this one, sir."

"I understand. We'll get them, if I have anything to say about it. I'm really sorry, Sheriff."

"Thank you, sir. Can you tell me one thing? You saw him, right?"

"Yeah." Paul closed his eyes and tried to control his breathing. The brief, close-up glimpse of Chief Asher's remains kept coming back to him as if burned into his memory.

"Could you tell if he'd suffered any?"

"Honestly, Sheriff, no. There wasn't much left." Paul looked away as Sharpe flinched. "Sorry. I don't know. But I can't believe he lived through that explosion. I don't think he ever knew what hit him."

"Thanks, Mr. Sinclair. I guess Petty Officer Davidas might have some company now."

"Yeah. I guess." Davidas had died over a year earlier in an accident on board. Since then, the crew had attributed any odd happening to Davidas's mischievous ghost. "I haven't heard anyone laying this fire at the feet of Davidas's spirit, though."

"Hell, no, sir, begging your pardon. Fooling around with

people's one thing, but Davidas always looked out for his shipmates. He wouldn't have hurt Chief Asher or anybody else on this ship."

Paul sighed. "Too bad Davidas's ghost wasn't in Forward Engineering on Saturday night."

"Yes, sir."

"Sheriff, I don't know what kind of assistance Captain Shen will ask for, but we're to make sure he gets everything he wants. Let me know if there are any problems, and I'll make sure the CO and XO make 'em right."

"Yes, sir. What if Captain Shen doesn't want me talking to you about the investigation?"

"Notify me, then go straight to the XO after that. I'm the only person between you and the XO in the chain of command, so that's how it'll have to be. I won't have it said that we hindered this investigation in any way."

"Aye, aye, sir." Sharpe nodded slowly. "Chief Asher'd want it that way. And one thing more, sir."

"Yeah, Sheriff?"

"Thanks for going in after him, sir. I know it was risky."

"Somebody had to put out that fire, Sheriff."

"Yes, sir, but it didn't have to be you. Thanks for trying, sir."

Paul looked away, bitterness rising in him. "It didn't make any difference." When no reply came, he looked back to see Sharpe watching him with a surprised expression. "What?"

"Sir, whether it made a difference or not isn't the point. You tried. Everybody's telling me Vlad Asher couldn't have made it no matter what. But you tried, sir. Thank you, sir." Sharpe straightened and saluted Paul.

"Ah, hell, Sheriff." When Sharpe held the salute, Paul stood and returned it, feeling awkward. "Get back to work."

"Yes, sir."

CHAPTER SEVEN

☆　☆　☆　☆　☆

CAPTAIN Shen eyed Paul flatly, nothing about him betraying any evidence he'd ever met Paul before. "Lieutenant Junior Grade Paul Sinclair?"

"Yes, sir." *Well, that makes how to handle this easy. Captain Shen's going to keep it totally impersonal. That's a relief. I think.* As Paul had expected, Captain Shen had completely cut him out of the investigation process as soon as he knew Paul had been on duty the day of the fire. Now, barely three days later, he was seated in the wardroom of the *Michaelson* opposite the man who was Jen's father and would also render judgment on Paul's actions. *I'm still wondering why he didn't recuse himself from the investigation when he found out I was one of the subjects. But how can I formally bring that up without creating the appearance I have something to hide?*

Shen pushed a data pad toward Paul. "Read and sign this."

Paul read quickly, recognizing a standard form for a sworn statement from the Judge Advocate General's Manual. *Do you, Paul Sinclair, Lieutenant Junior Grade, United States Navy, solemnly swear (or affirm) that the evidence you shall give in the matter now under investigation shall be the truth, the whole truth, and nothing but the truth (so help you God)?* He signed quickly and returned the data pad to Captain Shen.

Captain Shen checked the signature, then fixed his eyes on Paul. "On 19 September 2100 you were on duty aboard the USS *Michaelson*?"

"Yes, sir."

"Where were you when the explosion occurred?"

"I'd just left my stateroom and was proceeding toward the quarterdeck, sir."

"What did you do when the explosion occurred?"

"I paused to wonder what it was, then heard the alarm sound and ran to the quarterdeck, sir."

"How much time elapsed while you 'paused'?"

"A second or two, sir. No more than that."

"Who was on the quarterdeck when you arrived?"

"Chief Petty Officer Imari, the officer of the deck in port, and her petty officer of the watch."

"No one else?"

"No, sir."

"How did you end up leading the on-scene damage control team?"

"DC Central informed us Chief Asher, the regular team leader, could not be located."

"You decided to leave the quarterdeck at that point?"

"No, sir. Lieutenant Silver, the command duty officer—"

"So Lieutenant Silver was also on the quarterdeck."

Paul hesitated, taken aback by the statement. "Yes, sir. By then he was. He arrived a couple of minutes after I did."

"And he then ordered you to assume duties as the Damage Control team leader?"

Paul phrased his reply carefully. "Lieutenant Silver was CDO, and Chief Imari had the quarterdeck watch. I was the only one free to assume that duty, so I asked permission of Lieutenant Silver to proceed to the scene."

"You volunteered."

"Yes, sir."

"Didn't you have other duties to attend to?"

Paul swallowed before answering. "There were other things I could have been assigned to do, sir, which is why I requested Lieutenant Silver's permission before going to the scene of the fire."

"And he told you to go."

"Yes, sir."

"His exact words were?"

"Sir, as I recall, all he said was 'okay.' "

"He said 'okay.' And you were certain that constituted orders to proceed to the fire scene?"

Paul nodded firmly. "Yes, sir."

"You assumed command of the Damage Control team and led it into Forward Engineering. Why did you decide the enter the compartment?"

"The fire suppression systems in the compartment weren't working, and DC Central reported the fire temperatures would damage the bulkheads if we let it burn. Since we couldn't drain the fuel tank feeding the fire until the fire was out, we had to put the fire out."

"How much experience did you have at such firefighting?"

"Just my damage control training, sir."

"Specify the extent of that."

"One week damage control training during my Academy time, then another week during specialty training."

"And you felt that qualified you to decide to enter the compartment?"

Hell, he's not just being impersonal. He's digging at me. Why'd he have to ask it that way? "Yes, sir. Before I went down to the scene of the fire, Chief Imari—"

"Why did you decide to use water hoses on full fog?"

"Sir, I asked the lead hose, Petty Officer Santiago, for advice, and she suggested that."

"So lacking experience of your own, you simply did what this petty officer said you should?"

Paul took a moment to answer, fighting down an impulse to respond angrily. "No, sir. I asked Petty Officer Santiago for her advice. I weighed that advice against my own knowledge and training, then made a decision."

"Did you receive authorization to enter Forward Engineering before opening the hatch?"

Paul started to reply, then hesitated. *Did I?* "I don't recall receiving specific authorization, sir. I kept the quarterdeck and DC Central advised of my intentions, and I was not told to take any other course of action."

Captain Shen, his expression hard but unreadable, tapped some information onto his data pad. "You appear to have done a number of things on your own, Lieutenant Sinclair."

"I did what seemed appropriate, sir. I kept everyone informed."

"When you left Forward Engineering, did you know what had happened to Chief Asher?"

"Yes, sir." Paul had finally managed to partially suppress his emotions at the memory. "I'd seen his remains."

"Were you certain they belonged to Chief Asher?"

Paul hesitated again. "Sir, there wasn't much left."

"Then the remains could have been those of someone else?"

"I hadn't been advised anyone else was unaccounted for, sir."

"Did you make any attempt to check the rest of Forward Engineering to see if Chief Asher was present, to see if he'd managed to get into emergency survival gear and was still alive?"

"Sir, we had zero visibility, the team was exhausted from putting out the fire, I had an injured team member, and our suits were warning of impending system failures owing to the heat."

"Then your answer is 'no.' "

Paul felt his jaw tightening. He tried to control his voice as he answered. "Yes, sir."

"When was the last time you were in Forward Engineering prior to the fire?"

"About a week earlier."

"You hadn't checked the compartment that day?"

"No, sir."

"Even though you'd been on duty since that morning?"

Paul's teeth were hurting, now, from the way his jaw muscles were clenching. "No, sir."

"Had you inspected any compartments on the ship that day?"

"Yes, sir, I had." The reply sounded too sharp, too defensive. Paul tried to moderate his tone. "I always conduct a walk-through of the ship on my duty days."

"You check every compartment."

Paul felt his teeth grinding painfully together and forced them to relax. "No, sir, not every compartment."

"Why not?"

How do I answer that? Because the officers who taught me how to stand duty didn't check every compartment? Because I didn't think it was necessary? Maybe because I didn't think. "I . . . No excuse, sir."

Captain Shen kept his eyes on Paul. "This isn't the Academy, Lieutenant. You're expected to provide explanations for your actions. Or your inactions. Why hadn't you inspected Forward Engineering that day?"

Paul felt a stubborn anger rising. "Because officers in the duty section do not routinely check every single compartment. I was going to the quarterdeck where eight o'clock reports were going to be presented. Chief Asher would have informed us of any problems in Engineering spaces at that time."

"So you effectively delegated the responsibility."

"No, sir." Paul almost spat the reply. "I delegated the task. I am well aware that I cannot delegate responsibility."

Captain Shen stared back impassively for a moment, then made some more notations. "When was the last time the fire suppression systems in Forward Engineering had been tested?"

"I don't know, sir."

"Why not?"

"I'm the Combat Information Center officer, sir. I do not work in Engineering. If I need that information I will ask the appropriate officer or enlisted in the Engineering Department."

"You don't think you needed that information the day of the fire?"

"It would've been irrelevant, sir. The fire suppression systems didn't work. Knowing when they were last tested wouldn't have helped me handle the situation or put that fire out."

"If you'd familiarized yourself with the date the systems were last tested, and discovered they were overdue for a test in time to take corrective action, couldn't that have prevented the fire from causing such extensive damage to the compartment?"

Paul stared, momentarily at a loss for words. *They hadn't been tested recently? Nobody's said anything about that.* "I . . . was unaware of that, sir."

"Then you admit your lack of knowledge regarding a critical compartment on this ship could have negatively impacted on the emergency?"

Paul almost snapped out an angry, "Yes, sir," then found himself hesitating again. *Wait a minute. Think before you speak. That's practically a confession of wrongdoing he's asking me to make. Did I fail that badly? How come nobody on the ship has acted like I screwed up and helped make that emergency worse?* "No, sir."

"No." Captain Shen pursed his lips, and made another notation. "Are you sure you don't want to reconsider that answer?"

This time Paul recognized a technique he'd seen Sharpe employ with suspects. Imply you know something you don't really know and let them implicate themselves. *Were those fire suppression systems really overdue for a test? He never said they were, he just implied that. Why's he trying to nail me? Well, it doesn't matter why, because it's not happening.* "No, sir, I do not."

"Very well, Mr. Sinclair. There's no further need for you."

Something inside Paul made him answer in a calm, firm voice. "As a witness, you mean, sir."

"Yes. Send in the next witness."

Paul had intended going back to his stateroom, but found

himself so worked up over the interview that he started roaming the ship to burn off his anger. *Interview? Hell, that was an interrogation. What's he up to?* Reason slowly asserted itself. *Maybe he's doing his job. Which is finding out what happened and why. For all I know every other person going in there is getting the same treatment. Judging by the way the officers on the* Mahan *acted, Captain Shen's always a hard-ass.*

He's Jen's father, for Pete's sake. Jen can be really tough, too, but she's always fair. Why assume the worst?

T HE next several days were frustrating. Paul, used to being on the inside of investigations, could only watch from the sidelines as witnesses disappeared into the wardroom and various specialists came aboard to check the damage and other systems on the ship.

"What're they finding out, Paul?" Mike Bristol asked on Friday.

"Damned if I know."

Randy Diego looked around conspiratorially. "I heard they couldn't get anything out of the engineering logs. They taught us those logs are hardened against all kinds of stuff, so how'd that happen?"

Paul saw everyone was looking at him for an answer. "I don't know! Look, guys, I'm not in on this. I don't know any more about the logs than you do."

"I saw Jill Taylor leaving the wardroom after she'd talked to Captain Shen," Randy continued. Paul nodded. As Electronic Materials officer and a skilled specialist, Ensign Taylor would be a logical person to ask about the condition of the engineering logs. "Boy, did she look mad."

Bristol looked intrigued. "Do you know why?"

"No. She didn't say anything, and I didn't ask. Even I know not to cross Taylor's path when she's that pissed off."

Paul saw them looking at him again. "Captain Shen's questioning is, uh, really aggressive. That's about all I can say."

*   *   *

AFTER two more days of questioning and bringing in people to check over different parts of the *Michaelson,* Captain Shen left, leaving in his wake no clues as to what his conclusions would be. The first couple of days after that, everyone kept checking their messages for reports the investigation had been completed, but after another three days they'd gone back to concentrating on whatever individual crisis of the day had popped up in the areas of responsibility. Which, naturally, was when the text of Captain Shen's report arrived on the ship.

Paul started to read slowly through the report, fighting off a powerful urge to skip directly to the conclusion. But the urge triumphed partway through the dry and detailed description of the fire suppression systems in Forward Engineering. Paging rapidly forward, Paul went straight to the conclusions. *In light of the lack of evidence of other causes, the damage to engineering records must be laid to an unusual combination of shock and effects of the fire . . . Recommendation: Conduct testing to determine if systemic fault exists in log protective mechanisms . . . The initial explosion occurred in the power transfer junction for Forward Engineering. The cause of the explosion cannot be reliably determined because of massive damage to the area . . . Recommendation: Review fault limits on power transfer junctions . . . The state of the engineering logs prevents identification of what Chief Petty Officer Vladimir Asher was doing in Forward Engineering . . . no evidence exists of deliberate misconduct on his part . . . death judged instantaneous . . .*

Paul shivered as he read that finding, breathing a prayer of thanks, then went back to skimming the conclusions.

Reactions of Damage Control personnel were appropriate . . . their response time was within standards set by Damage Control instructions . . . actions of command duty officer were appropriate to the circumstances . . . actions of other officers reflected occasional hesitation in responding . . . inadequate inspection and monitoring of shipboard conditions prior to accident . . . no cause for misconduct finding, but enhanced training and supervision recommended.

Paul stopped reading. *What the hell? He's not naming me, but he's practically blaming me for what happened! I didn't want a commendation out of this, but I didn't expect to get hammered for it!*

He reread the conclusions, searching for a different interpretation. *Damn. Damn! At least he gave the Damage Control party credit for doing their jobs right. Otherwise, it doesn't explain what happened to Chief Asher or why. Just an unavoidable accident, except for "inadequate" actions on my part.*

Paul finally checked the distribution on the report. He'd received a copy as the ship's legal officer, as had the Captain, the Executive Officer, and the Chief Engineer. The investigation and its findings had already been forwarded to the Commodore for his approval. *Even if I wanted to talk to Captain Hayes about it, would it matter? Hayes gets to comment on the findings, but why should he kick? The investigation gives him a clean bill of health.*

"Mr. Sinclair, sir."

Paul looked up, startled, to see Petty Officer Sharpe. "Sorry, Sheriff, I didn't hear you at the hatch."

"I can understand why, sir." Sharpe inclined his head toward the display where Paul had been reading the investigative report.

"How do you know what's in it?"

"Sir, a good cop doesn't divulge the identity of his informants. Suffice to say, I think it sucks."

"Sheriff, it's nice of you to say that—"

"Begging your pardon, sir, but while you didn't come out smelling like a rose, I'm frankly more concerned about the rest of it. It doesn't explain why Chief Asher died."

"No."

"Or how those logs got damaged when they shouldn't have been."

"No."

"Sir, I'm about to ask something. If you don't want to

give me permission, can we assume I never spoke to you
about it?"

Paul eyed Sharpe. "You don't ask that kind of favor too
often, Sheriff. What's on your mind?"

"What if I was to bring on board someone to check those
logs, sir?"

"They've been checked."

"Someone who's an expert, sir."

"I thought . . ." Paul frowned at his display. "I guess I
don't know the qualifications of whoever Captain Shen
brought in."

"Then I have your permission, sir?"

"And if you don't?"

"Then we never talked about it, sir, and you won't know
anything if I bring the guy aboard."

"Sheriff, I don't work that way. There's no legal reason
your expert can't check the logs, too. Captain Shen's finished his examination of them. For God's sake don't let your
expert do any more damage, though."

"No way, sir."

Paul peered closely at Sharpe. "Level with me, Sheriff.
There's something else, isn't there?"

Sharpe pointed toward where the investigation was displayed. "I gave a statement, sir. It's not in there."

"Huh?" Paul looked back and forth from Sharpe to the
display. "Why'd you make a statement?"

"Because I saw Chief Asher that morning. He was really
unhappy, sir."

"About what?"

"I don't know. He was muttering something about 'just
do it' when I came by. I asked him what was up, and he just
shook his head and walked away."

Paul stared at the master-at-arms. "And that's not in
there?" *Okay, assume Captain Shen was gunning for me.
But I still believe he's underneath it all just as ethical as his
daughter, and Jen wouldn't bury some evidence just because
she didn't like it.* "Any idea why?"

"No, sir."

"That's . . . odd. I can't honestly say it'd change the conclusions of the investigation, but it's still odd. Okay, Sheriff. Bring your expert aboard."

"It may take him a day or two to get over here, sir, but I'll let you know when he comes on board."

"Thanks, Sheriff." Paul began reading the report again after Sharpe left, this time with an unpleasant sensation in his gut. He'd felt bad when he read the investigation's conclusions, but this was a different kind of bad, brought on by what Sharpe had said and what Sharpe obviously suspected. *He thinks the investigation missed some important stuff. Important enough to make a difference, to answer questions left unanswered? I guess I'll find out.*

Within a week, the Commodore had approved the investigation's findings, then forwarded them to the Admiral, who'd also approved them. If Captain Hayes had submitted any comments on the investigation, Paul hadn't seen them, but then the Captain wouldn't have been likely to involve Paul in anything that addressed Paul's own performance. Besides, Paul had seen his award recommendations for the members of the Damage Control party receive similarly expedited treatment.

For the awards ceremony, they used the same hall the change of command had been in, of course. The Commodore himself came by to award the medals. One by one, members of the Damage Control party were called forward. Petty Officer Santiago received the Navy Commendation Medal. Petty Officer Yousef received the Navy Achievement Medal. The rest of the enlisted received letters of commendation.

After the last enlisted had been presented with their awards, the Commodore held up a last medal case. "Lieutenant Silver, front and center."

Paul tried to keep his expression fixed as Silver marched up to stand in front of the Commodore, and as the Commodore began reading the medal citation. After lauding Silver's leadership during the crisis, and proclaiming it in the highest traditions of the Naval Service, the Commodore pinned a Navy Commendation Medal on Silver.

Paul somehow kept his face impassive, his eyes front, but

out of the corner of his eye he could see Captain Hayes. The smile Captain Hayes had carried through most of the award ceremony had vanished, and his face seemed to be reddening. Paul didn't know what that meant, nor did he really want to know. At that point, he just wanted the ceremony over.

It ended mercifully a few minutes later. Paul quickly dismissed his division, then headed back for the ship, avoiding contact with anyone else.

But he couldn't hide on the ship. Within a few minutes of his own arrival, a group of his friends arrived at his stateroom. "They gave *Silver* a medal?"

Paul glanced up, keeping his expression flat. "Yeah."

Kris Denaldo was standing in the hatchway, Lieutenant Mike Bristol just behind her along with Ensign Randy Diego. "Why?"

"I don't know. I just work in the Combat Information Center, so I never know anything."

"That's really funny. Why'd they give Silver a medal?"

"You heard the commendation. I didn't really listen. Something about his control of the situation and crap like that."

"Crap is right. He got a medal, and you didn't?"

Paul looked down at his desk, still trying to keep his face rigid. "Yeah."

"Isn't that kind of lame?"

"Look, Kris, what do you want me to do?"

Silence stretched, until Paul looked up to see everyone still standing there. Kris looked around at the others, then scowled. "Nothing, I guess. Do you want to vent?"

"No."

"You've got to be pissed."

"Sort of."

"But there's nothing you can do about it."

"Right."

"Any idea why Hayes did that?"

Another voice answered. "Captain Hayes didn't do it." They all looked to see Commander Sykes leaning against the bulkhead not far away. "The Captain was just as surprised as you, Mr. Sinclair. He is not a happy man. This is, of course, not for attribution."

Bristol was staring at Sykes. "The Commodore did it? Without input from Captain Hayes?"

"Apparently. Our Captain is attempting to run down the source of the medal recommendation. He can't really pull the medal. Not without cause. What damage has been done is done. I believe Paul is wise to attempt to accept this aspect of things."

"Suppo, he got hammered for that accident even though he led the Damage Control team in, and now Silver's getting rewarded even though he didn't do anything."

Sykes looked away. "I can't promise a just resolution to this."

Ensign Diego shook his head. "Paul's just got to live with it?"

"Unless he can find a constructive alternative, yes."

They all looked at Paul, who shrugged. "I don't know."

Mike Bristol grinned humorlessly. "I have an alternative. Liberty call's in fifteen minutes. Let's go have a drink."

That sounded as constructive as anything else.

The next morning, Paul was nursing a mild hangover when Ivan Sharpe called. "Sir, I have someone I believe you'd like to meet."

"Fine, Sheriff. Where?"

"In Combat, sir?"

"See you in a few minutes." Paul gulped a couple more aspirin, then headed toward Combat. Commander Garcia and he passed each other outside the wardroom. Garcia frowned at Paul, then glared in another direction and went on his way. *Is he mad at me or for me? Sometimes you can't tell with Garcia. He's almost always mad about something.*

Sharpe, waiting near Paul's command console in the Combat Information Center, indicated the man standing next to him. "Mr. Sinclair, this is Chief Warrant Officer Rose."

Paul offered his hand, trying not to look too young. Warrants were former enlisted who'd worked their way up the ranks, which meant they were both highly experienced specialists and notoriously underimpressed with typical junior officers.

But Rose smiled politely and accepted Paul's handshake. "Pleased to meet you. Bob Rose. Sharpe here tells me you're okay."

Paul glanced at Sharpe with exaggerated surprise. "He never tells *me* that."

Rose smiled a bit wider. "No, he wouldn't. Where do you want me to work?"

Paul looked around Combat. Two of Paul's sailors were lounging around, watching Paul's group curiously. Then they saw the look on Sharpe's face and hastily went in search of another resting place. Paul indicated his command console. "You should be able to do anything you want to do from here, Warrant."

"Looks good."

"Do you need me to log in?"

"No." Rose grinned at Paul's reaction. "I actually want to see how easy your system is to crack, among other things." Rose sat, poised his hands above the controls, then glanced meaningfully at Paul and Sharpe. "I work best when nobody's leaning over my shoulder, if you know what I mean."

Paul barely bit off a reflexive, "yes, sir" to an officer who was junior to him in the military hierarchy but carried authority and confidence with the ease of someone who knew his job and knew the Navy as only someone with decades of service could. Instead, Paul nodded, and he and Sharpe retreated to the far side of Combat.

Rose worked intently, his eyes never straying from the console display. Paul looked over at Sharpe, made a motion as if to speak, then a questioning gesture. Sharpe responded with an "I don't know" gesture of his own, so they sat silently.

Eventually, Rose straightened, stretched, then looked their way. "It was hacked."

"What?" Somehow, Paul hadn't expected to hear anything like that. "What was hacked?" he asked, even though he already knew the answer.

"The engineering logs."

"The damage was deliberate?"

"Yup. No question."

"Why didn't the investigation find that out? They called in someone to check the logs for the cause of the damage."

"Because the hacker used a real effective program that's been available for a while to anybody who really wants it. It leaves no fingerprints. At least, that's what most folks think. A few of us know it leaves one." Rose pointed at his display. "The designer of the software had as big an ego as anyone. His program takes one line in one shredded file and adds on his initials. In code. Unless you're looking for exactly that, you'll never find it."

"My God." Paul tried to absorb the news, looking neither at Sharpe nor Rose. *Somebody mangled those records on purpose. Which means somebody tried to cover up something. But who? And what?* "You're absolutely positive, Warrant?"

"Absolutely."

"You'd swear to it?"

"Absolutely."

Sharpe leaned forward, his posture that of a hound straining to leap after prey. "Can you tell who did it?"

Rose shook his head, his face unhappy. "No. *That's* impossible. There were about thirty people logged on during that time period, but since it's real easy to use someone else's password and access, that doesn't really narrow it down."

"Then we can't rule out anybody on the ship," Sharpe noted with clear disgust.

"Maybe not. What time was that fire?"

Paul answered, the time burned into his brain. "The alarm sounded at 1922."

"Okay, then, you can rule out one suspect." Rose pointed to his display once more. "The line that contains the hack program designer's name also gets a time stamp put on it. According to that, this database got hacked at 2235 that night."

Sharpe shook his head. "So?"

Paul answered. "That means the database was hacked over three hours after Chief Asher died, right, Warrant?"

"Right. Whatever else that chief did, he sure didn't mess up this data. Somebody else did that. For certain."

Paul didn't want to think about it, didn't want to consider what he'd have to do. *The investigation is completed, the case closed. Nobody got their heads handed to them. Granted, I didn't come out too well for reasons I don't understand, but given that a sailor died and the ship took extensive damage to Forward Engineering, the lack of specific wrongdoing by anyone was a welcome finding to everyone. But now it looks like that finding was wrong. Somebody did do something, something that worried them enough to cause them to hack that database to wipe out anything that might point to them. Did they cause Chief Asher's death? Or did they just make a mistake that contributed to it? And if I bring this up, will* anyone *thank me?*

He remembered something, then, words once spoken to him by Commander Herdez after another shipboard accident had claimed the life of Petty Officer Davidas in Carl Meadows's division. That had been an unavoidable accident, with no one at fault, but Herdez had bluntly told Paul that had Carl been at fault, it would have been their duty to hold Carl accountable because the sailor's sacrifice demanded no less. *And she was right. Still is right, for that matter. Chief Asher's dead. It looks like somebody played enough of a role in that to want to destroy the evidence. Well, Chief, I couldn't help you escape that fire, but I can sure as hell make sure anyone involved in causing it and your death gets brought to account.*

Paul suddenly became aware both Warrant Rose and Ivan Sharpe were watching him intently. "I'm sorry. Did someone ask me something?"

The Warrant shook his head. "No. I think we're just wondering what you're going to do, Lieutenant."

"It's not like I have a choice, Warrant. Make a copy of that evidence, please, and I'd appreciate a formal report from you on what you found."

"Sure. Can I ask what you're going to do with it?"

"Take it to the Captain. He needs to know this."

Rose nodded, smiling grimly. "That he does. I'll write it up here for you. Just give me a few minutes."

"No problem. Hand it to the Sheriff when you're done. I need to check some references in my stateroom."

Paul started out of Combat, pausing as Sharpe held a hand before him. "Thanks again, Mr. Sinclair."

"For what, Sheriff? Like I said, I don't have a choice."

"Yes, you do, sir. And in my book you made the right one."

Less than an hour later, Warrant Officer Rose's report in one hand, Paul waited in the line outside of the Captain's stateroom. A line almost always existed there, as officers waited to get messages approved or to deliver personal reports the Captain had requested, as enlisted brought by other routine reports that still required the Captain's okay, and as those seeking approval or orders waited for their turn to plead or explain their case. Paul tried not to let any nervousness show, his experience on the bridge helping a great deal in that effort. One of the first things he'd learned was the need to project calm and certainty. As long as you sounded like you knew exactly what you were doing, everybody else tended to believe you did as well.

The last supplicant before Paul left through the hatch. "The Captain says to go right in, sir."

"Thanks." Paul stepped through the hatch. "Sir, request permission for a private conference."

Captain Hayes examined Paul closely, then nodded. "Very well. Close the hatch. Take a seat."

Paul did both, sitting as erect as possible, as if he were still at attention even when seated.

Hayes looked at Paul, his eyes sharp. "What private issue brings you here, Mr. Sinclair?"

"Sir, I . . . I . . ."

"Spit it out, mister."

"Sir, I have reason to believe the investigation into the fire on board the USS *Michaelson* missed important information."

Hayes leaned back, his face now questioning. "Is this

some sort of personal appraisal? I think you got a bit of a raw deal in that investigation, Paul, but nobody wanted to go to the mat to change those findings about a junior officer. I did try."

"Thank you, sir. And no, sir. There's evidence involved." Paul let his distress show for a moment. "Serious evidence."

Captain Hayes leaned forward. "Talk to me. What've you got? Any hard evidence, or just speculation about it?"

Paul spoke cautiously, aware of the stakes in what he was saying and how he said it. "I had a computer expert check the engineering maintenance logs. He said they'd been hacked. Not damaged in the accident, but deliberately hacked."

Hayes's eyes narrowed. "The investigation reported they couldn't find any evidence of what'd caused the data loss in those logs. Who's this expert of yours?"

"Chief Warrant Officer Rose, sir."

"Bob Rose? From fleet staff?"

"Yes, sir."

Hayes rubbed his forehead with the fingertips of his right hand. "I know Rose. He's good. Very good. He says the logs were hacked?"

"Yes, sir. He's willing to swear to it." Paul held out the report Rose had prepared. "He gave me this."

Hayes read swiftly, his eyes darting back and forth. "Not just gun-decking to falsify data. Deliberate destruction of data. Damn. What else have you got?"

"The only other thing at this point is Petty Officer Sharpe, sir. He says Asher was mad that morning, and said something about 'just do it.' Sharpe thinks Chief Asher had been told to do something Asher didn't like."

"I don't remember seeing anything like that in the investigation report."

"Sharpe says he turned in a sworn statement, sir. But it's not listed in the attachments to the investigation, and there's no copy of it there."

"You think Captain Shen concealed it?"

"No, sir. That's not my impression of Captain Shen. I think Captain Shen never saw that statement. He didn't call

Sharpe in for an interview, and he surely would've done that if he was aware Sharpe knew something."

"Sharpe's a cocky son of a bitch, but he's also a good sailor." Hayes stood up, pacing back and forth within the small confines of his cabin. "A very good cop, too. He's got good instincts." The Captain stopped pacing and focused on Paul. "And you're not Admiral Spruance, but you're also not a fool. What's the bottom line here, Mr. Sinclair? You're talking about the investigation being deliberately impeded, aren't you? To ensure it wouldn't reach the correct conclusions."

"Yes, sir. I think there's a chance that may have happened."

Hayes stared at the bulkhead above Paul's head. "The investigation results have already been officially approved. That means a lot of heavyweights have signed off on them and attested to their accuracy."

"Yes, sir."

"And you and I are both aware of the personal issues involved regarding Lieutenant Silver. I was informally made aware that Vice Admiral Silver was following events."

"That's . . . that's illegal, sir."

"It is if there's any record of it, Mr. Sinclair. In any event, that investigation gave Lieutenant Silver a clean bill of health."

"Yes, sir."

"But he was also Chief Asher's division officer. The main propulsion assistant. That was Silver's equipment in Forward Engineering. But you don't have any evidence implicating Silver?"

Paul shook his head to emphasize his reply. "No, sir. At this point, it implicates no particular individual. I have no idea who might be involved, either in misleading the investigation or possibly in the original accident."

Hayes nodded, his face pensive. "There are an awful lot of people who would be very unhappy to have the results of that investigation questioned. Even I might suffer if a reinvestigation finds me at fault."

"Yes, sir."

Hayes locked his gaze back on Paul. "But I'm Captain of this ship. One of my sailors died. And, if your suspicions are right, at least one of my crew lied or falsified evidence. I have to be able to trust my crew, Mr. Sinclair." He sat down slowly, then gave Paul a sidelong look. "You and Petty Officer Sharpe keep looking. Quietly. Have you ever gone hunting, Mr. Sinclair?"

"Uh, no, sir. Not really."

"The first rule is not to make a lot of noise or fuss. Because if you do, whatever you're hunting is going to hide. So you don't make a lot of noise, Mr. Sinclair. Keep it quiet. Check out these things that don't add up. If it turns out to be nothing, or nothing you can substantiate, I want you to tell me that as soon as you're comfortable with that conclusion. If you find something more, I want to know that, too."

"And if anyone questions what I'm doing, sir?"

"Refer them to me. That's not a blank check. Act with discretion and forethought. If I hear you're running around like a loose cannon, I'll come down on you like a ton of bricks, and you'll wish you'd never started this. *¿Comprende?*"

"Yes, sir."

"But if you're on the track of something important, I'll back you." Hayes smiled without humor. "Here's your chance to prove the quality of your professional judgment, Mr. Sinclair."

And if I'm wrong, the chance to drop-kick my career out of the nearest airlock. "Yes, sir."

"If you're right, if you find that evidence, then we'll make noise, Mr. Sinclair. We'll flush our prey and nail him or her to the bulkhead." Hayes's face flushed slightly, his mouth a thin, tight line. "Accidents happen. They're an ugly fact of life. But if someone caused this one, and if someone covered up their involvement, I want that someone off my ship and preferably out of the Navy."

Paul simply nodded back, unsure of the proper reply.

Hayes used one hand to indicate the hatch. "If that's all, Mr. Sinclair, we both have plenty of other things to do." He paused, causing Paul to hesitate in midreach for the hatch handle. "Quite frankly, I don't know whether I want you to be right or wrong about this."

"Sir, quite frankly, I don't know which I'd prefer, either."

CHAPTER EIGHT

☆　☆　☆　☆　☆

PAUL hadn't been in Forward Engineering since the night of the fire. It had changed a great deal since then. Once the investigators had gone over it carefully in search of evidence, the repair work had begun. Equipment damaged by the explosion, the fire, or the water used to put out the fire, had all been evaluated for repair or replacement. Wiring, cabling, control panels, ventilation, all the systems that made up the nerves and lungs of that compartment, were pulled or blocked off for replacement. The bulkheads, the deck, and every other surface had been scrubbed clean of debris and tested for damage. During most hours of the day, the compartment resounded with a bedlam of work designed to get the USS *Michaelson* operational again as soon as possible. Right now, late at night, Forward Engineering was temporarily quiet and empty, except for Paul and his companion.

Paul glanced around. Even though the compartment had been cleaned and most of the damaged equipment removed, he still found himself uneasy. Something clattered off to one side, where shipyard workers had been replacing damaged equipment, causing Paul to jerk around nervously. He reached the spot where he'd found Chief Asher's remains and stopped, staring downward.

"What's this about?" Colleen Kilgary asked. "Why'd you want me to meet you down here?"

Paul tore his eyes away from the spot and looked at her. "You were the main propulsion assistant on the ship until Scott Silver took over the job. I was wondering if you could help me with something."

Lieutenant Kilgary shrugged. "I couldn't help the investigation much, not that they asked me."

"Chief Asher's body was here, meaning he probably was working on something not too far away. The investigators reported the explosion occurred in the power transfer junction."

Kilgary pointed to an empty area nearby. "Yeah. That'd be here."

"Could Chief Asher have been working on that?"

"Alone? That wouldn't be like Chief Asher."

"Why not?"

"Because of the interlocks. The only way to work on stuff like the power transfer junction is to use two people, one to monitor the safeties and the other to do the job."

"So it's impossible with one person?"

"It's not impossible. You just have to shut off the interlocks, which shuts down the safety monitors, which shuts down the fire—" Kilgary scowled. "The fire suppression systems."

"Asher could've done that?"

"No! He wasn't like that. But, yes, in theory somebody could've shut off all that stuff in order to work on something like the power transfer junction single-handed." She walked over to the spot the piece of equipment had occupied. "But it didn't need work, Paul. It wasn't on the casualty reporting system."

"You checked?"

"Of course I checked." Kilgary folded her arms, staring around with a stubborn expression. "I leave and within a month the leading chief dies and a major fire occurs. Of course I checked."

"I'm really sorry, Colleen."

"Why should you be sorry? You didn't do it, despite what that damned investigation says."

Paul nodded gratefully. "What would've happened if somebody did shut down all those interlocks? Wouldn't you get an alarm?"

"No." Kilgary gestured toward the general direction of Damage Control Central. "Not if whoever shut it down used the right authorization codes. But it would show up in the engineering logs." She bit her lower lip. "If they weren't damaged."

"I know the bridge logs don't get reviewed very often. Too much data and detail. They just get filed. Is that what happens to the engineering logs?"

"Yeah. Unless something happens." She looked at Paul. "This all adds up in a very strange way. But I don't see why Chief Asher would've done such a thing."

"I don't know why he would've either."

"Do you think he damaged the engineering logs somehow?"

"No. No, that's one thing I'm certain of. He had nothing to do with that." Paul followed as Lieutenant Kilgary led the way out of Forward Engineering. Something pinged behind him, and Paul whirled around quickly to stare into the empty compartment.

Kilgary followed Paul's gaze. "Probably just a loose screw dislodged by the vibration of us walking past. Contractors tend to leave screws lying around."

"Yeah. Probably." But he was grateful when they'd left the compartment behind. *There are too many ghosts on this ship for my comfort.*

And there it sat. A week later, Paul was still trying to put the pieces together. *Who can I talk to about this? Sharpe and I have gone over it time and again and can't find anything else. Jen'd be great, but she won't be back for another two months. And I can't just blab about this to any of the other junior officers. Who's that leave?*

Put that way, the answer was easy.

"Commander Sykes, sir? Can I talk to you in confidence?"

Sykes raised his eyebrows in apparent surprise. "Not just 'Suppo,' eh? I'm 'Commander Sykes.' This must be quite serious."

"I can't talk to you unless you promise to keep it confidential, sir."

"My dear boy, I'd be happy to so promise, but you understand if the talk involves issues of criminal acts, I won't necessarily feel bound by such a promise."

"I understand." Paul sat close to Sykes. "Sir, here's the problem." He outlined events as concisely as he could. "And that's where it sits. Somebody wiped the logs on purpose. Chief Asher could've been working on the power transfer junction, but only if he'd gone against the grain and shut off the interlocks, and there's no indication anything was wrong with the power transfer junction to begin with."

"Hmmm." Sykes sat silent for a few minutes. "This is an ill matter, Mr. Sinclair. Are you thinking someone may have killed Chief Asher deliberately?"

"No, sir. Petty Officer Sharpe says the investigators would've been certain to find any trace of a bomb. They didn't find pieces of anything that didn't belong in Forward Engineering."

"Then apparently he *was* working on that power what's it."

"It wasn't broken, Suppo."

Sykes smiled sadly. "Ah, youth. It wasn't officially broken. But was it actually broken? There's a difference."

Paul let that thought sink in. "Maybe the power transfer junction had gone on the blink, and nobody'd been told?"

"It happens, lad. Equipment casualty reports are regarded by some officers as signs of shame, or more often they hope to get the equipment repaired so quickly they feel no need to file the necessary reports. The result is the same. Officially, it's fine. In practice, it's not."

"But if there had been a problem with that piece of equipment, surely Chief Asher wouldn't be the only one who'd have known."

Sykes gave another sad smile. "That is certainly correct."

"Meaning some of the other engineers aren't talking. But why wouldn't they?"

"Group silence is usually a form of protection."

"Who'd they be protecting, Suppo?"

"Perhaps themselves. Perhaps the dead."

Paul stared at Sykes, mentally upbraiding himself. *Of course. If Chief Asher had done all that stuff, he'd be guilty of criminal misconduct. I don't know if or how that'd affect Navy death benefits for him and his family, and I bet the rest of the engineers don't know either.* "Thanks."

"One more thing, Paul." Sykes rubbed his chin, his brow furrowed in thought. "Something is missing."

"What's that?"

"If our chief was repairing that equipment, where is the replacement part? And where did he get it? And, for that matter, how? My own departmental records would've shown if it'd been drawn from our stocks."

"And they don't?"

"Not to my imperfect knowledge." Sykes sat quiet for a while. "I would recommend, Mr. Sinclair, that you enlist the aid of Mike Bristol in this."

"Sir, Mike's a friend of mine, but he's not nearly as experienced as you are."

"That's precisely the point, Paul. I want Mike to gain such experience, and the only way to do so is to give him opportunities like this one. You can count on him to keep your investigation secret."

"Yes, sir. I'll do that. Thanks for the advice, sir."

"Not at all. Visit my figurative mountaintop whenever you are in need of wisdom."

Paul smiled and left. *I'll find Mike Bristol and—* Commander Garcia came down the passageway, his eyes on Paul, his ill humor readily apparent. *Oh, gawd. What'd I do or not do?*

"Sinclair." Commander Garcia used one finger to almost pin Paul to the bulkhead. "What's this I hear about you asking questions about the fire, Sinclair?"

"Sir, I—"

"Drop it, Sinclair. It's over."

"Sir—"

"Look, I understand you feel like you've been screwed. We've all been there, Sinclair. I've been screwed by the Navy so many times I feel like a cheap hooker in a port town. Trying to stir up things isn't going to make it better. It's just going to keep attracting attention to you. Bad attention. That's no good for you, and it sure as hell isn't good for me. *Drop it.*"

Paul nodded to buy himself time to get a word in. "I understand, sir. Sir, I have orders."

"Yeah, and I gave 'em to you."

"No, sir. The Captain."

Garcia's eyes narrowed. "*He* told you to keep looking into this."

"Yes, sir. He said you should talk to him, sir."

"What's up, Sinclair? What the hell are you doing?"

How do I answer that in a way that won't tell Garcia more than Hayes might want and also keep Garcia from ripping my throat out? "Following orders, sir."

Garcia's face reddened. Paul could almost see the internal struggle going on. On the one hand, Garcia didn't like having secrets kept from him by his subordinates, especially secrets that might cause him trouble. On the other, if Paul had been told by the Captain not to discuss his orders, then any attempt by Garcia to browbeat Paul into talking anyway could get Garcia into big trouble with the Captain.

Commander Garcia took a half step back, his finger still pointed at Paul. "You'd better be telling the truth, Sinclair. Because I'm going to see the Captain."

"Yes, sir." Another searching gaze, then Garcia shook his head with a grimace and stalked off in the direction of the Captain's cabin. Paul watched him leave. *I'll give Garcia credit. He really tried to give me the best advice he could.* Paul started to move on, then stopped and frowned. *Who told Garcia I was asking questions? It was probably Sam Yarrow up to his usual tricks, but what if it was somebody else?*

Mike Bristol reacted to Paul's story with a dropped jaw. "Are you serious?"

"Yeah. How can you help me run down this question of whether or not that power transfer junction was busted?"

"Paul, if Commander Sykes finds out—"

"He's the one who sent me to you."

"Really?" Bristol chuckled. "That old schemer. I guess he wants me to learn the tools of the trade. As he practices it, anyway. Okay, the simplest thing to do is check our own supply records. We'll see if any parts for that equipment got pulled just before the accident." He faced his terminal and typed rapidly. "I can do all that from here." More typing, Paul catching sideways glimpses of data screens flashing by. "Oh. That's interesting."

"What?" Paul craned his head to see, but couldn't interpret the columns of codes.

"This here. That's labeled as a critical part for the power transfer junctions. But we don't carry it on board usually because the failure rate's so low."

"That's crazy, Mike. What happens if it fails anyway while we're out in the middle of nowhere?"

"Ask the snipes. Is that the only power transfer gizmo on the ship?"

Paul thought for a moment. "No. There's one in After Engineering, too."

"That's probably it, then. The ship can probably operate on one of those things. If something's extra expensive or in extrashort supply, we often don't carry it on board as long as the safety margin's okay. That kind of decision is way above my pay grade, of course. Anyway, here's the interesting bit." Mike Bristol's finger pointed to one code element. "This says that Friday, the day before the accident, was the last time someone queried the system about the availability of that part."

"That *is* interesting."

"But, like I said, we don't carry it, so the system told them they'd have to requisition it from the station spare part stocks."

"Did they?"

"No."

Paul peered at the lines of supply system codes as if that would help him understand them. "Why not?"

"Let's see. Ah, estimated delivery date from the station would've been sometime the next week."

"We were due to get underway for drills on that Monday."

"We were, weren't we?"

"Yeah. Having Forward Engineering gutted by the fire made sure that didn't happen. But that means they wouldn't have gotten that part before we got underway, and I'm willing to bet that even though the *Merry Mike* can run on one power transfer junction that there's limits on what we could do. That means they would've had to tell someone the thing was broken. And until we had the part, we probably couldn't have gotten underway."

Mike Bristol looked alarmed. "That's very bad. People get really upset when that happens."

"That's putting it mildly. Could Chief Asher have been trying to repair the busted part?"

"Not according to these records. They say the part is a sealed black box. Fixing something broken inside is beyond anything this ship can do."

Paul leaned back and pressed his hands against his temples. "Then what was Chief Asher doing?"

"Well . . ."

"Tell me, Mike."

"Uh, well, you see, there's official requisitions, and then there's, uh, unofficial requisitions."

"What's that mean?"

"It means somebody might've gotten that part from station stocks. On Friday. They're not open Saturday or Sunday, unless the station authorities authorize an emergency parts draw. And believe me, we'd know if that'd happened."

Paul nodded, trying not to get his hopes too high. "Can we find out? About Friday?"

"We can try." Mike Bristol stood. "Want to take a walk?"

Reaching the station supply office was inconvenient, naturally, and there was a long line of personnel waiting for parts, also naturally. Paul and Mike Bristol waited as the line inched forward and each successive petitioner begged and pleaded with various degrees of success for the part they absolutely, positively had to have at that very moment.

The office was about to close when Mike and Paul finally reached the front of the line. "Hi. Lieutenant Mike Bristol, from the *Michaelson*."

The supply corps lieutenant and petty officer crewing the desk eyed him warily, their gazes finally resting on Bristol's own supply corps insignia before the lieutenant nodded. "Office hours are about over."

"Yeah, I know. I really appreciate you looking into this." Bristol leaned close, speaking in a low voice. "We had a line officer mess up. I'm trying to clean up the mess. You know?" Both supply types nodded sympathetically and gave Paul looks which meant they thought he was the line officer in question. "I just need to know if a part was drawn from here for the ship. Otherwise, my CCAB and HGF will be rejected by the CFSS, and you know what kind of a pain *that* is." Another pair of nods. Mike proffered the part number. "Just a quick check?"

"Okay. We can do that." The lieutenant ran the number quickly, then nodded. "Yeah. That part got drawn by an officer from the USS *Michaelson* on, uh, 18 September."

Paul felt like his heart had stopped. "Do you have the officer's name?"

The supply lieutenant gave Paul an annoyed look. "As if I could forget the guy. Showed up just before closing with a real sob story. I still don't know how he talked me into providing that part." She pointed to her terminal. "The guy's name was Silver. Lieutenant."

Mike Bristol walked silently alongside Paul most of the way back to the *Michaelson*, finally blurting out a question when they were not far from the ship. "What're you going to do?"

"See what I've got."

"It looks like you've got plenty."

"No. It's all circumstantial evidence."

"I've heard that term. What exactly does it mean?"

Paul shrugged, feeling irritated, but knowing he felt that way not because of Mike's questions but because of the obstacles he still faced. "Basically, it means somebody could have done something, but doesn't prove they did do it. Like if a house gets robbed, and I prove you were seen standing outside the house, and that you were wearing shoes that would've left the same footprints in the mud outside the window where the break-in occurred. But I don't have any fingerprints of yours from inside the house, and I haven't found any of the stolen stuff on you."

"Oh." Bristol thought for a moment. "Then everything you have so far just says Silver might have been responsible for what happened, but none of it proves he *was* responsible?"

"Bingo."

"Which makes it what?"

"A judgment call."

"What'll it take to make up your mind on it? To make you sure enough to tell the Captain one way or the other?"

Paul stopped walking just short of the *Michaelson*'s brow. "Maybe just one more thing."

Bristol hastened off to check on his own duties, while Paul went up to Combat to make sure no crisis had suddenly erupted there, then headed back to his stateroom. Partway there, he encountered Commander Garcia again.

Garcia stared at Paul, then shook his head. "You're an idiot. You know that, Sinclair? You should've let it rest."

Not knowing how to reply, Paul stood silently.

Garcia turned away. "Just don't make me look bad. Understand?"

"Yes, sir."

Paul got back to his stateroom, paged Sharpe, and filled him in on the part. "I need you to get to those snipes who worked for Chief Asher. They must have known something about the problem with the power transfer junction. Now that we have something specific to ask about, maybe one of them will spill their guts. And make sure you tell anyone you talk to about something that I checked on. There are no

determinations of misconduct made when a service member
dies in the line of duty."

Sharpe looked happier than Paul had seen him in weeks.
"Will do, sir."

"One other thing. Have you found anybody yet who saw
Lieutenant Silver around the time the engineering logs were
hacked?"

"No, sir. Not any enlisted, anyway. Maybe an officer . . ."

"Do you think anything known to the officers on board
remains unknown in chief's quarters? Get on those snipes,
Sheriff. I want to know what answers they'll give this time."

Paul dodged out of dinner as quickly as he could, wondering if he was just imagining the funny looks he was getting from the other junior officers. *Garcia knew I was doing
something. How many other people heard? I know why Mike
Bristol's acting a little weird, but the others . . .*

Sheriff Ivan Sharpe awaited him outside of his stateroom,
a nasty smile on his face. "I just had a long talk with Petty
Officer Third Class Valyati."

"I take it he's a snipe in Lieutenant Silver's division?"

"Yep. And guess what?"

"At this point I don't dare guess."

"It seems the day after the accident, Lieutenant Silver
had a talk with the sailors in his division. Mr. Silver told
them he was really worried about what might happen to
Chief Asher's family if anybody thought the chief'd done
anything wrong that might've caused the explosion."

Paul held his breath. "That's interesting."

"Isn't it? As best Valyati remembers, Mr. Silver never
told them not to speak freely to the investigators, but he really laid it on about how that could hurt Chief Asher's family. Would you care to guess what the sailors concluded?"

"Not to talk about what really happened. Did they know
there was something wrong with the power transfer junction
in Forward Engineering?"

Sharpe's smile widened, not in humor but like a wolf bar-
ing its teeth. "Yes, sir. Valyati said he'd heard Chief Asher
had wanted to report it with a casualty equipment report, but
Mr. Silver wouldn't let him."

"That's hearsay, Sheriff. Somebody saying they heard someone said something isn't admissible as evidence."

"I know that, sir. But Valyati knows from firsthand knowledge that the junction'd been going bad for a while. They were expecting it to fail."

"So it should've already been replaced. But the casualty reporting system never got notified that a spare was needed. Instead, Lieutenant Silver pays a frantic visit to the station supply depot late Friday afternoon and begs a replacement from them. Saturday, Chief Asher's really unhappy. A few hours later, the power transfer junction blows up, killing Chief Asher. Soon after that, engineering's logs are messed up, during a time period when nobody can specify Lieutenant Silver's whereabouts. The next day, Silver convinces his troops not to talk to the investigators."

"That sums it up, sir."

Paul slammed his fist onto his desktop. "Damn! It's all circumstantial, Sheriff. We don't have one piece of evidence that directly ties Lieutenant Silver to what happened."

"Sir, with all due respect, this is plenty to go on. We can nail this guy."

"No, Sheriff. Look, I know, you're a cop. To you this is open-and-shut. But we don't need to convince a bunch of cops this is good enough."

"Sir, guilty is guilty. When you know a dirtball's done something, you hammer him. Or her. You don't let them get away because you're worried the evidence might not be good enough."

Paul gazed back at Sharpe. *Now, this is hard. I respect Sharpe as a petty officer, and I respect his knowledge as a master-at-arms. And he's been working in law enforcement since I was in high school. But I have to tell him he's wrong.* "Look, Sheriff, you're a damn good master-at-arms, but I've already figured out the attitude that comes with that. If the guy wasn't guilty in the first place, why is he a suspect? Cops tend to identify someone as a suspect, then go after that guy hard. Right? Don't look all offended. You and I both know you're a great cop. But this isn't about what you believe, or what I believe. We need to convince the Captain, then a military judge and maybe a panel of officer members of a court-martial, that the son of Admiral Silver is such a rotten officer he caused the death of one his sailors, then covered it up. I know you know that. Getting Lieutenant Silver charged might sound real great, but it won't mean a thing if the charges get tossed out. We have to be sure we're doing this *right*. So we can get a conviction."

Sharpe made an unhappy face as he thought about Paul's words. "Yes, sir," he finally admitted. "I guess you're right about that. But just because this is all we've found doesn't mean that's all there is. We haven't exactly been able to go whole hog on our little investigation. If it turns formal, a lot more ugly stuff might crawl out of the woodwork. Probably will, if my experience counts for anything."

"I'm sure it does." Paul slumped in his chair, staring at his display. *It's all there. Oh, nothing that says beyond a shadow of a doubt that Chief Asher received orders to do what he did, and nothing that absolutely proves who it was that messed up the engineering records, but it all points in one direction.*

So what do I do? Everything I've got is circumstantial evidence, but I've got a lot of it. The Captain's supposed to make this decision, but Captain Hayes will make up his mind based on what I tell him. I think. In any case, it'll look like sour grapes to some people, especially since Scott Silver's one real talent appears to be trying to make people like him. A lot of those people will just see this as an attempt by me to blame someone else. And the someone else everything seems to point toward isn't just any screwup. He's a son-of-an-admiral screwup, which has apparently gotten him out of every jam up until now. But as far as I know, he's never been implicated in causing the death of a service member before.

Vice Admiral Silver has a good reputation for doing his job. Does that mean he'll look at all kindly on having his son implicated in Asher's death?

The best I can hope for is for my own conclusions to be proven right. Which means Lieutenant Silver gets a court-martial and gets proven guilty. When did I turn into some-

body'd who send another officer to a court-martial based upon evidence even I admit is circumstantial?

Petty Officer Sharpe stayed silent, waiting. Paul screwed his eyes shut. All he could see was the random patterns of light and dark, which didn't hold any more answers than the sight of his display had. *Why does this have to be my decision? It's not just because I was in the duty section. It's because I got stuck with this legal officer job when I reported aboard. As if I know what the hell I'm doing. Thank you, Commander Herdez.* The thought of his former XO brought up more memories. His first days and weeks on board the *Michaelson*, his first Captain's Masts, mistakes he still shied away from remembering, the death of Petty Officer Davidas.

Davidas's death had definitely been an accident. No question. Paul had been vastly relieved, knowing the officer who'd be held to account if it hadn't been an accident would've been Carl Meadows. Herdez had seen that relief, just like she seemed to see everything on board. *What was it she told me then? Our duty requires us to follow our investigations to their conclusions, regardless of how much we dislike those conclusions, because a sailor had died and we couldn't betray that sailor's sacrifice by shirking our duty, no matter how much it hurt us personally. Something like that. I never forgot that, because I knew deep down it was true. Herdez isn't easy to love. She's an ironclad bitch, I guess, but she's sure easy to admire as a professional. So I know what she'd do.*

His eyes opened and strayed to a small portrait fastened on one side of his desk. Jen, caught in a candid photo, laughing during some forgotten celebration in the wardroom. *What would Jen think about me putting my career on the line this way? Dumb question. Jen's a professional, too. If she thought another officer had caused the death of one of his sailors, then tried to cover it up, she'd go after him with a vengeance. For good reason, too, because the next person that officer caused the death of might be Jen or a whole ship's worth of Jens.*

And as for me, I know what I should do. I know what the

heroes I admired growing up would do. Damn the torpedoes, full speed ahead. He who will not risk cannot win. Can I do any less? I'm not even risking my life, like they did. Hell, not *acting risks other people's lives.*

That's three in favor of sticking my neck out.

Paul looked directly at Sharpe.

Sheriff Sharpe looked back. "Sir?" The question Sharpe really wanted to ask was clear enough.

"Don't worry, Sheriff." Paul copied his findings to a data coin. "I took a poll and got three votes for doing the tough thing, and none against."

"Three votes, sir?"

"Yeah. One was mine. The others were two people whose opinions I respect." Paul grinned. "Don't worry, Sheriff, I respect your opinion, too. But I already know how you'd vote."

"You're going to see the Captain now, sir? May I come along?"

Paul hesitated, then shook his head. "This is about an officer, Sheriff. It's better if the Captain and I discuss it without an enlisted sailor present. You understand."

"Yes, sir, I do. And, to be perfectly frank, sir, there's some officers I'd worry about making decisions like that without an enlisted around watching them. But I think you and Captain Hayes will do the right thing."

Assuming Captain Hayes agrees with me on what the right thing happens to be. "I'll let you know, Sheriff."

As usual, a line of personnel trailed away from the hatch of the Captain's cabin. Paul waited patiently as the line inched forward, each officer or sailor getting the signature they needed to get personally or personally delivering the report they needed to personally deliver to the Captain. Even with so much of the ship automated and so many reports sent around via the ship's intranet, Navy traditions and rules kept much of the work on a face-to-face basis. Despite his resolution, Paul felt his stomach knotting up as he neared the hatch. He didn't look forward to delivering his report, and wasn't sure how it'd be received.

Captain Hayes took one look at Paul's face when he entered, then directed him to close the hatch. "What's up, Mr. Sinclair?"

Paul offered the data coin. "Sir, I've completed my investigation into the accident."

"I see." Hayes took the coin, turning it slowly in his hand, then looked sharply at Paul. "What's the bottom line?"

Paul swallowed, partly out of nervousness and partly to clear a throat which felt too tight. "Captain, I believe a preponderance of circumstantial evidence points to the conclusion that Lieutenant Silver ordered Chief Asher to undertake emergency repairs on the power transfer junction in Forward Engineering, and to do so single-handedly in violation of safety procedures. That required Chief Asher to disable the safety interlocks. This is what prevented the fire suppression systems from functioning. The engineering logs would have clearly shown that this activity had taken place, as well as an authorization clearance from Chief Asher and an officer. Therefore, I also believe Lieutenant Silver is responsible for damaging the engineering records to prevent his role in the matter from being discovered. Further, I have a statement from a member of Lieutenant Silver's division that he discouraged them from cooperating with the initial investigation by frightening them with the claim that anything they said would harm Chief Asher's family."

Hayes stared silently at Paul for a long moment. "Are you recommending I court-martial Lieutenant Silver?"

"Sir, I . . . The decision of what action to take is yours, sir."

"I didn't ask you to make the decision, Mr. Sinclair. I asked if that was what you were recommending."

It actually hurt to answer the Captain's blunt question. "Yes, sir, I am so recommending."

Hayes's gaze shifted to the data coin still resting in his hand. "Have a seat."

"Yes, sir." Paul sat, his back stiffly erect, trying not to look anywhere in particular, while Captain Hayes loaded the coin into his data unit and, with painstaking care, reviewed the material Paul had gathered. Paul occasionally stole glances at the clock on one bulkhead, seeing the minutes drag by, wondering what those still in line outside thought about the closed hatch and Paul's long meeting with the Captain.

Hayes finally made an angry snort, then turned back to Paul. "I could wipe this, Mr. Sinclair. Tell you I'd looked into it and disagreed. But I won't. You did a good job."

"Th-thank you, sir."

"I'm not sure I should thank *you*. Have you ever met Admiral Silver?"

"No, sir."

"He's tough. He's professional. He's not going to be happy." Hayes made a fist, as if he were going to slam it into his display. "But I'm not in this job to keep people happy. Not when I see this kind of evidence. Are you sure there's nothing aside from that supply part thing that actually names Lieutenant Silver?"

"There might be, sir, but I couldn't find anything."

"So I'll have to assume there isn't, until or unless I find out otherwise. Which leaves what to do up to my discretion." Hayes rubbed his lower face for a few moments. "Okay. You write me up a charge sheet, Mr. Sinclair. Whatever charges against Lieutenant Silver you feel would be appropriate and provable. No more, no less. Don't talk to anyone about this. Bring the charge sheet to me when you're done."

"Yes, sir."

"I want a clean document, Mr. Sinclair. If I approve of the charges, that charge sheet will serve as justification for convening a court-martial."

"Y-yes, sir."

Hayes rubbed his entire face, looking weary. "Some people think being the Captain of a ship is a great deal. All this authority. You get to do just about anything you want to do. But you also have to do a lot of things you'd rather not do. I hate the idea of court-martialing an officer. But I hate the idea of someone doing this and getting off free even worse."

Paul waited a moment, but after Hayes stayed silent Paul stood up. "I'll get right on it, sir."

"One more thing, Mr. Sinclair. This is *my* decision. Understand? You didn't make it, you don't get blamed for it. It's my job to make decisions and live with the consequences."

"Yes, sir." Paul paused, then blurted out, "Thank you, sir."

Hayes looked cross for a moment. "For what? Get to work on those charges, Paul."

"Yes, sir." Paul exited the hatch, oblivious to the curious stares of those in line, and was halfway back to his stateroom before he realized that the Captain's last word to him had been his first name. At the least, that seemed to signify approval.

Paul delivered the charge sheet to Captain Hayes the next morning. He notified Ivan Sharpe soon afterward, swearing him to secrecy until the Captain took action.

Sharpe bent a concerned look at Paul. "You don't look so good, sir."

Paul snorted and massaged the joints of his jaw to relieve the stress there. "I'm a little strung out, Sheriff. I spent a good part of the night writing up those charges and trying to make sure they're as well chosen and well drafted as I could make them. And every minute I was doing it I couldn't help thinking that the object of my work was to send a fellow officer to a court-martial."

"Sir, that guy's not worth your stress. Not after what he did."

Paul glared at Sharpe. "Lieutenant Silver hasn't been formally charged, and he sure as hell hasn't been convicted."

"Are you telling me you don't think he's guilty, sir?"

Paul looked away, glaring now at a blank spot on the bulkhead. "No. I wouldn't have gone this far if I'd believed that. But, dammit, he's innocent until proven guilty."

"A cop can have trouble thinking that way, Mr. Sinclair."

"I know, Sheriff. That's why cops don't run the courts. Don't get me wrong. I respect the need for a 'find the guilty bastard' attitude. But we can't afford to fall into a mind-set of 'he's accused so he must be guilty.'" The silence made Paul glance up again, to see Sharpe frowning in turn. "Hey, a big part of my job is making sure the Captain doesn't hit any legal rocks and shoals. If I don't do that right because I'm convinced of someone's guilt or for any other reason, I'd be doing what Silver's accused of. Not doing my job right and letting someone else get hurt as a result."

Sharpe nodded. "Fair enough, sir."

"And I need a good cop like you to handle the cop side of things."

"Ah, shucks, sir, you say the nicest things. Did the Captain give you any idea when he'd do something?"

Paul shook his head, looking away again. "No. It might be a few days, at least. He's got to read those charges, decide which he supports, decide if he still wants to go ahead with a court-martial. I'm not sure if there'll be anything public before the court-martial order is issued."

"Maybe not, sir. I don't envy you, sir. I don't have to be around Lieutenant Silver. You're going to have to work with him."

"Thanks for reminding me. Hopefully, it'll only be a couple of days."

ONE week went by. Whenever Paul encountered Captain Hayes, he ached to ask about the charges, but knew he shouldn't, and Hayes didn't volunteer any information. Paul's growing irritability at first worried his fellow junior officers, until Kris Denaldo suggested it was being caused by the extended absence of his girlfriend Jen Shen. The resulting teasing caused Paul a bit more stress, but at least of a different kind.

The second week had almost crawled to a close when Commander Kwan summoned Paul to his stateroom. Paul stood in Kwan's stateroom, wondering as to the reason, while Kwan scanned his terminal with an unreadable expression before looking up at Paul. "Mr. Sinclair. Lieutenant Silver has been referred to a general court-martial by the fleet commander." Kwan stopped speaking for a moment, his face hard. "By order of the Captain, Lieutenant Silver is to be immediately relieved of all his duties. His stateroom is to be sealed off until it can be searched for evidence. Commander Destin is taking care of escorting Lieutenant Silver off the ship. You are to take care of sealing his stateroom."

Paul nodded, trying not to let his reaction to the news show. "Aye, aye, sir. Lieutenant Silver shares a stateroom with Lieutenant Bristol."

"Then Commander Sykes will just have to find a new home for Lieutenant Bristol for a few days!"

"Yes, sir."

"Dismissed. No, wait." Kwan pointed to his screen. "Did you know about this?"

"Yes, sir."

"So did I, Mr. Sinclair. There'll be no celebrating this event on this ship. Is that understood?"

Paul stared at the executive officer. "Yes. Sir." He knew his voice had come out hard and angry at the implications behind Kwan's order, but at the moment didn't care. "There's nothing to celebrate."

"That's right, Mr. Sinclair. I'm heartened to hear that you realize that. Dismissed."

Paul headed for Silver's stateroom, paging Petty Officer Sharpe as he went. He'd need the ship's master-at-arms to formally seal off the stateroom. Reaching the stateroom, he paused, wondering if Silver might still be inside, or if he'd already been escorted off the ship by Commander Destin. As he stood there, Mike Bristol came up and reached for the hatch. Paul held out a hand. "Sorry, Mike. You can't go in there."

Mike gave him a puzzled look. "Okay. And the joke is?"

"No joke. Captain's orders." Sharpe came quickly down the passageway. "Petty Officer Sharpe will be sealing this stateroom pending a search for evidence."

Bristol's jaw dropped as he looked from Paul to Sharpe. "Oh. Where's Silver?"

"Off the ship, I think, and not coming back."

"Geez. It happened? You found what you needed?"

"Yeah."

"Geez." Bristol stepped back automatically as Sharpe went to work, then finally snapped out of his shock. "Hey, all my stuff's in there!"

"Sorry, Mike." Paul let his helplessness show. "I'll loan you stuff. It's only for a few days."

"Thanks. I guess." Bristol stared wide-eyed at the Do Not Enter notification Sharpe was posting. "What's happening to Scott?"

"Court-martial."

"Oh, man." Bristol looked at Paul. "How am I supposed to be feeling?"

"I don't know, Mike."

Sharpe finished his work, then turned to Paul. "Sir, with your permission, I'll contact the Naval Criminal Investigative Service agents attached to fleet staff and see how soon I can get them over here to search this stateroom."

"Permission granted. Let me know when they'll be coming."

"Aye, aye, sir."

Paul watched Sharpe leave and Mike Bristol head in search of Commander Sykes so he could get new temporary living quarters. After a few minutes, Paul realized he was still looking at the seal on the stateroom hatch. He went back to his own stateroom, which happened to be blessedly empty, and sat down, staring at nothing in particular while emotions and thoughts swirled inside him without coalescing into any clear images.

Randy Diego came in, tossed some work on his desk, and glanced curiously at Paul. "Aren't you coming to lunch?"

Paul, startled, checked the time. "Yeah. Let's go."

They passed the sealed stateroom, causing Ensign Diego to do a double take. "What happened here?"

Good old Randy. Always the last to know. "It's a long story."

When Paul entered the wardroom, it was immediately obvious at least part of the story was known to everyone else. They all watched as Paul took his seat, no one saying anything. Finally, Paul looked around irritably. "All right, already. Doesn't anyone feel like talking?"

Mike Bristol forced a smile. "Well, under the circumstances . . . Is Scott Silver really being charged with murder?"

Paul shook his head. "No. Manslaughter."

"What's the difference?"

"Well . . ." Paul thought for a moment. "I'm sure a lawyer would have all sorts of problems with this definition, but basically it's murder when you set out to kill or injure someone, and they die. It's manslaughter if you're not setting out to hurt anyone but someone dies because your actions were so careless and reckless you should've known they'd result in someone's death."

"You mean like if I was, uh, firing a gun randomly and hit somebody it'd be manslaughter?"

"Right. It's the difference between aiming at someone, and pointing a gun in their direction without looking and firing. Except if you deliberately kill someone but do it in the heat of passion. That's manslaughter, too."

Lieutenant Kilgary mimicked surprise. "You can kill somebody when you're having sex, and it's not murder?"

Paul laughed with everyone else, grateful for the diversion. "That's not exactly what the heat of passion is supposed to mean."

Kris Denaldo grinned. "Have *you* ever killed anyone while you were having sex, Colleen?"

Kilgary smiled. "Wouldn't you like to know."

As the next round of laughter died out, Kris aimed her next question at Paul. "Then Silver's not being accused of *trying* to kill Chief Asher?"

Paul nodded. "Right. He's being accused of doing something so reckless he should've known it could cause Chief Asher's death."

Lieutenant Sindh smiled wryly. "I suppose that means a total idiot couldn't be charged with manslaughter."

"Yeah. That gets into stuff like mental competence. Did the accused have the ability to understand what they were doing? Did they know it was wrong? I wouldn't want to get into that."

"Am I correct in assuming such a defense on Lieutenant Silver's part would be counterproductive? Arguing that he was incapable of understanding the recklessness of the acts he's charged with committing?"

Paul snorted a brief laugh. "They could try saying that, yeah, but like you said, arguing that an officer couldn't understand the danger would be a career-killer even if it worked as a defense. I don't expect that, though. I'm not a lawyer, needless to say, but I'd guess the defense will try to say Silver never did any of the things he's charged with."

Sindh smiled again. "That's better, isn't it? I imagine issues of mental competency are raised when guilt is otherwise certain based on evidence."

"Probably."

"Are all of the charges against Silver of that nature?"

"No." Paul looked down, uncomfortable with the questions but understanding why his fellow officers wanted to ask them. "Most of them do require an intent, a decision to do something wrong. Like making a knowingly false official statement. You can't be charged with that if whatever you say is correct to the best of your knowledge, even if what you say isn't actually right. It comes down to intent, like a lot of other crimes. Often, you need to prove an intent to carry out a certain crime. But not in manslaughter. That just needs the fact that it occurred."

"Or like being absent without leave," Colleen Kilgary suggested. "You don't have to intend to be AWOL to miss the deadline for getting back to the ship. You're not back, and that's that."

Commander Sykes finally chimed in. "Not entirely, dear Lieutenant Kilgary. Since most AWOL incidents are handled via Non-Judicial Punishment, anyone who committed the offense is allowed to offer an explanation or excuse. A plausible argument that AWOL was not intended can suffice to limit or prevent any punishment. Call it a case where a lack of intent to commit the offense is important as a mitigating factor."

Everyone looked at Paul. "Suppo's right," Paul agreed.

"Of course Suppo's right," Sykes stated. "You should all practice saying that several times a day. 'Suppo's right.' It's an excellent guiding philosophy."

Mike Bristol nodded with exaggerated enthusiasm. "Suppo's right."

Paul looked down at the table while Bristol tried to fend off various objects hurled at him. *I didn't expect to see horseplay in the wardroom again this quickly. Call it whistling past the graveyard, or just coping with another bad thing. We're getting good at it, I guess.*

"Paul?" Randy Diego leaned closer. "When's the court-martial going to happen?"

"I don't know. There'll be a convening order issued, then time for the lawyers to put together their cases. They can't even issue the convening order until they locate enough officers to serve as members of the court."

"Oh. I thought maybe it'd happen real quick."

"No. I can guarantee it won't be quick. It could easily be months." *Weird. Chief Asher dies in a heartbeat, but everything else takes a long time. Why is a death so fast, and figuring out who caused it so slow? That old poem talked about the mills of the gods turning slowly. Who's going to get ground up by those mills when they finally get moving? Silver? Or maybe me.*

CHAPTER NINE

☆ ☆ ☆ ☆ ☆

C OMMANDER Carr glanced up as Paul knocked on her doorframe. This deep inside Franklin, the compartments were larger, and subdivided into rooms that could've been somewhere on Earth, except for the nagging sense that gravity wasn't quite right. Carr stood in greeting, smiling politely, and offered Paul a handshake. "Lieutenant Junior Grade Sinclair? I'm Alex Carr. I'll be the trial counsel for Silver's court-martial."

Trial counsel was the military term for the prosecutor. Paul tried not to wince from the pressure of her handshake. Commander Carr may have been a bit height-challenged, but what there was of her slim body obviously included plenty of toned muscle. A chin-up bar fastened to one wall offered a hint as to where the muscle came from. "Pleased to meet you, ma'am."

"Have a seat." Carr laughed as she returned to her own chair. "Let me tell you, Mr. Sinclair, no JAG wakes up in the morning wishing she'd get handed the job of prosecuting an admiral's son at a court-martial. Especially Vice Admiral Silver's son. Do you know what Admiral Silver's nickname is among his staff?"

"No, ma'am."

"They refer to him as 'the Neutron Bomb,' because he leaves structures intact but destroys people. And I get to prosecute his son! What do you call that sort of thing in the operational forces?"

"We call it an opportunity to excel, ma'am. Sarcastically, of course."

"Oh, I like that. An opportunity to excel. Or to watch your career head for the nearest waste disposal unit." She grinned again. "Fortunately for this case, I'm in this business for the thrill of battle, so the idea of nailing Admiral Silver's son doesn't make me curl up in a ball."

Paul nodded. *I have the feeling there's not very much that would make Commander Carr curl up in a ball. I'm glad she's not prosecuting me.*

Carr turned toward her display. "It's an interesting case you put together. Interesting because there's strong evidence of misconduct, and an equal lack of evidence directly and unambiguously implicating the individual charged with the offenses."

"I know the case is mostly circumstantial, ma'am."

"*Mostly* circumstantial? Try almost entirely, at this point." Carr's grin faded as she scanned her display, eyeing the information intently. "But still, the evidence does point fairly conclusively in one direction, and hopefully we'll uncover some more. Lieutenant Silver's counsel is going to have to do some real tap-dancing to try to get around some of this." She looked straight at Paul again. "I need to be clear on something going in. Why'd you do all this investigating? What was your motivation?"

Paul tried to keep from frowning. "What does that matter?"

"It might not, and it shouldn't. But it could come up. Why'd the lieutenant junior grade go digging for evidence pointing to malfeasance on the part of the lieutenant?"

"One of our people died, ma'am, and my master-at-arms knew something that hadn't been included in the official investigation. He's a good cop, with good instincts, so I listened to him."

"And what about Lieutenant Silver? Is there anything between you two?"

"Nothing in particular, ma'am. I mean, we serve on the same ship and we're in the same in-port duty section, but we usually don't interact outside business. I don't particularly like him."

"A lot of other people apparently do like him." Carr leaned forward, her eyes locked on Paul's. "Nothing of a romantic nature? No involvements like that?"

"How do you mean, ma'am?"

"You and him. Him and some her. You and some her and him. Whatever combination you like."

Paul's reaction must have shown, as Commander Carr laughed. "Ma'am, I don't swing that way. I have no idea what Silver's idea of fun is, but he's never come on to me, if that's what you're asking."

"Have you got a girlfriend right now?"

"Yes, ma'am."

"Has Silver ever met her?"

"I don't think so. She's on a different ship. Of course," Paul added hastily.

"Of course," Commander Carr replied with a smile. "Since regulations prohibit two officers on the same ship from dating. She's an officer, also of course?"

"Yes, ma'am."

"Have you discussed this case with her?"

"Not yet, ma'am."

"So she's not involved in the case in any way."

Paul hesitated, drawing a raised eyebrow from Commander Carr. "Well . . . there is a connection, ma'am."

"And what would that be?"

"She's Lieutenant Junior Grade Jen Shen, on the USS *Maury*."

"Shen? Where have I seen that name recently?" She glanced at her display. "Didn't a Captain Shen conduct the initial investigation into the accident on your ship?"

"Yes, ma'am. He's her father."

"You're kidding."

"No, ma'am."

"How's he feel about this? About you uncovering evidence his investigation missed?"

"I imagine he's not very happy."

"I bet. Let's just do our best to keep this little domestic drama out of the courtroom, shall we?"

"I'd like nothing better, ma'am."

"I won't put you on my witness list. I don't see where I need to do that. As a matter of fact, I'm sure it'd be a mistake to do that."

"Why, ma'am?"

"Because your motivations and actions are a potent avenue for the defense to question every piece of evidence you uncovered. You didn't come out of the initial investigation covered with glory, and the estimable Lieutenant Silver received a medal for his 'heroic' efforts against the fire while you didn't. The defense might want to discredit you in order to discredit the government's case. If I put you up on that witness stand, I might as well be covering you with steak sauce and dropping you in a shark tank."

Commander Carr leaned back. "The defense might try to call you as a witness, though, to try to make an issue of your motivation and argue that this is all sour grapes, motivated by jealousy and an attempt to spread the blame."

"Ma'am, I swear—"

"You don't have to do that unless you get called as a witness." Carr flashed another smile. "Which we'll avoid at all costs. I expect the defense will start out trying to win this case on its merits. That is, by disputing the evidence and arguing that it doesn't point to Lieutenant Silver in any case. If the defense thinks they're losing that battle, they may try to discredit the case by bringing you and your motivations into it. The court may not allow that, of course, unless there's strong grounds for questioning your professional standing. What's your record look like, aside from this case?"

"Uh . . ." Paul licked his lips. "I was involved with the court-martial of Captain Wakeman."

"Wakeman?" Carr's eyes widened. "I remember . . . Hey. You're *that* Sinclair? You testified for him."

"Yes, ma'am."

"Most line officers go their entire careers without being involved in a general court-martial, Paul. And here you are working on number two already."

"Yes, ma'am."

"Do you harbor aspirations to become a Navy lawyer yourself?"

Paul thought of the smirk he'd see on his hotshot civilian lawyer brother's face if he heard Paul was pursuing a legal degree. "No, ma'am!"

Commander Carr tried to smother another smile. "That's a firm enough reply. All right, Paul, I'm still familiarizing myself with the evidence, but I'll probably have some questions for you later, and I'll want to tour the ship itself."

"Herself." Paul blurted the correction without thinking.

"Herself? I thought ships were officially 'it' nowadays."

"I guess officially they are, ma'am, but to us who serve on them, they're ladies."

Carr grinned yet again. "Then they're exceptionally tough ladies, Mr. Sinclair."

Paul nodded, thinking that Commander Carr, despite her quick smiles and pleasant demeanor, seemed to be exceptionally tough as well.

She offered Paul a data pad. "The convening order hasn't been disseminated, yet, but here's the names of the members of the court. Do you know any of them personally or by reputation?"

Paul read the list carefully. *Captain Michael Mashiko. Line officer. Currently at Space Warfare Officers School. Commander Juanita Juarez, also line, attached to the Joint Space Intelligence Center. Commander Gwen Herdez*—

His reaction must have been apparent to Commander Carr. "I take it you know one of them?"

"Yes, ma'am. Commander Herdez. She was my executive officer until about six months ago."

"Is that good or bad? What's she like?"

Paul pondered how to describe Herdez in a few words. "Very tough, very demanding, very capable, and expects a thousand percent from everyone who works for her. She loves the Navy, I guess. At least, she gives it everything she can and insists everyone else does, too."

"Hmmm. Commander Herdez doesn't sound like the sort of officer who'd look kindly upon an officer accused of grossly neglecting his duties."

"Yes, ma'am, but—" Paul struggled for the right words. "She's very fair. Commander Herdez doesn't let her emotions or preferences decide an issue. She'll have to be convinced."

"Fair enough." Carr made a note on her own data pad. "Convincing her's my job, but I'd appreciate any hints you might think of for what would best serve to do that. What about the rest of the members?"

Paul went back to reading. *Lieutenant Commander Peter Bryko, attached to the Commodore's staff. Lieutenant Commander Susan Goldberg, from the Space Officers School, just like Mashiko.* "No, ma'am. I don't know them. I'll ask around the ship, though. Some of the other officers may have worked with them."

"Okay, but keep it discreet. What's your ship's schedule look like for the next couple of months? Will you be underway much?"

Paul couldn't help a short, bitter laugh. "Sorry, ma'am. No, we won't be underway at all. Forward Engineering was very badly damaged by the fire. They're having to replace, rebuild, and test everything there and check everything in surrounding compartments for damage. The last estimate I saw called for completion of that work in about two and half months."

Commander Carr shook her head. "It'll be a pleasure to nail Silver's hide to the wall." She saw Paul's look. "What's the matter?"

"Well, ma'am, isn't he presumed innocent?"

Alex Carr laughed again. "By the court. By the members. But my job is to presume he's guilty and do everything I can to prove it. I'll always talk about Silver as being guilty. You don't want the prosecution arguing that the accused could be innocent!" She sobered. "Needless to say, that doesn't mean if I found proof of his innocence that I'd disregard it. Okay, the word I have is the court-martial will convene in about two months. The defense counsel and I have both already tentatively agreed that'll be long enough to build our cases. That doesn't rule out a request for a continuance, of course. I'm going to ask your Captain for permission to work directly with you during that period. Will that cause you any problems?"

Paul thought of Commander Kwan, and Commander Garcia. Kwan had been very unhappy with what had happened to Silver already, and Garcia wouldn't like either the chance of negative attention nor any distraction from Paul's regular duties. Then he thought of Chief Asher. "Some of my superiors on the ship might not be thrilled, ma'am, but there won't be any problems I can't handle. I don't think Captain Hayes will have any objections to it."

"Good. Oh, yes, one more thing. I understand the military judge will be Captain David Halstead." Another smile. "Within the JAG Corps he's known as 'Hang 'em Halstead.' He runs a tight court, but he's actually very fair through the trial. It's only if Judge Halstead decides the punishment that his nickname applies. That's it, then. I'll be in touch."

"Thank you, ma'am." Paul left, thinking about two months for him, Scott Silver, and everyone else to spend wondering how the court-martial would come out. Then he realized that time span meant the *Maury* would be back before the court-martial. *At least I'll have Jen around.*

As expected, Captain Hayes approved of Paul working directly with Commander Carr. Also as expected, Commander Kwan and Commander Garcia found ways to let Paul know they weren't happy about it. The agents from the Naval Criminal Investigative Service took apart Lieutenant Silver's former stateroom piece by piece, looking for any evidence of wrongdoing but confiding nothing to the ship's personnel. Their work done, Mike Bristol could finally get to his own shaving kit and bunk again. Alex Carr came aboard one afternoon, touring Forward Engineering with such an exhaustive attention to detail that Paul found himself wondering if she'd learned to conduct inspections at the feet of Commander Herdez.

As for Lieutenant Silver, Paul heard he'd been assigned temporary duty at a desk job somewhere deep within the bowels of Franklin Station. Wherever Silver happened to be working, no one from the *Michaelson* caught any glimpses of him, something that brought Paul great relief. On the ship, Silver had become sort of a nonperson. Everyone was aware Silver was gone, but no one talked about his absence, about the job he'd held, or shared memories about his time on the ship. Conversations dwelled on the upcoming court-martial, but aside from that Silver might never have been assigned to the *Michaelson*.

Lieutenant Commander Bartlet Jones had been assigned to conduct Silver's defense. He also came aboard the *Michaelson*, interviewing crew members and conducting his own inspection of Forward Engineering. He didn't ask to talk to Paul.

And, in due course, the USS *Maury* returned to Franklin. Paul watched her arrival from Combat on the *Michaelson*, as the *Maury* approached closer and closer, until her symbology merged with that of the station. By calling in-port ship status readings, Paul could tell when the *Maury* had finished mating to the station. But there wasn't any sense in heading down to her dock at that point. Even if he hadn't a workday to finish on the *Michaelson*, Paul knew all too well that many jobs had to be closed out before officers and crew could bolt from the ship that had been their sole home for three months.

Liberty call sounded on the *Michaelson*, and Paul finally headed down to the *Maury*'s dock. He waited about fifteen minutes after that, surrounded by a crowd of others greeting the arrival of the ship, before he heard liberty call being passed on board the *Maury*. Within a few minutes, crew members began filing off the *Maury*'s quarterdeck as fast as they could request permission to go ashore.

Paul spotted a familiar figure, waved, then waited until Jen made her way to him. "You came back."

"Yeah. Not that I had a choice. My ship came back, and I was sort of tied to her." Jen looked around. "I don't see any new girlfriends."

"Nope."

"I don't have any new boyfriends."

"That's good."

"You still want me, huh?"

"More than ever."

"Still desperate, I take it."

"Not at all. At the moment I'm feeling incredibly lucky to be with you again."

"Lucky? Like you won me in a lottery?"

"Maybe that's not the best word."

"It's not. Luck has nothing to do with it. Three months away made me sure of one thing. I want to be with you because of who you are, Paul Sinclair."

"And I want to be with you because of who you are. Don't look at me like that. It's true. The last three months have helped me realize how important you are to my life. You're my anchor."

"Your anchor? That's certainly a lovely analogy. Are you saying I'm really heavy and tie you down? That I'm often filthy and snag objects as I drag along the bottom? That you're chained to me and straining to break free?"

Paul grinned. "My spiritual anchor. I'm only chained to you by chains of love."

"Oh, gag me. Good thing I haven't eaten yet."

"I love you, Jen."

She eyed him, smiling slowly. "I love you, too. We're both in uniform, so you'll have to consider yourself mentally hugged and kissed." They started walking. "I heard there was a fire on the *Michaelson*."

"Oh, yeah, there was a fire."

"Has anything else happened since I left?"

"You might say that."

It took Paul a few minutes to outline events, then Jen shook her head. "For heaven's sake, Paul! Can't I leave you alone for more than five minutes without you getting involved in a court-martial?"

"You were gone for three months," Paul pointed out. "That's a lot more than five minutes."

"The principle's the same." She gave him a suspicious look. "You haven't mentioned something, yet. What is it?"

Paul sighed and passed over his data pad. "This is the investigation initially conducted to determine the cause of the accident and where the fault lay."

"I have to read it all?"

"No. Just the summation and the name at the end."

Five minutes later, Jen slammed down the data pad. "Great! My father. And he blamed *you*."

"Not in so many words."

"He didn't have to." Jen shook her head and sagged onto a nearby bench. "When you met my father he joked about my high standards and past boyfriends not lasting long. Remember? That was always my decision, but some of them also ran head-on into my father's standards for me, which frankly seem a lot more restrictive than my own."

"Oh. I'd wondered why he didn't recuse himself from the investigation. Now I'm wondering even more, if he goes after your boyfriends."

"My father should have refused to conduct this investigation because he couldn't be impartial. But he didn't, because sure as hell he honestly believes he was impartial. You just happened not to come out all that well in the investigation. He could swear to the truth of that without hesitation." Jen rubbed her face with both palms. "Now I also have to worry about him getting charged with some kind of dereliction of duty."

"What? You mean for going into the investigation biased? I wouldn't charge him, if that's what you're thinking."

"I don't think you're that big an idiot."

"I love you, too. As for anyone else . . . intent counts a great deal in violations like that. If your father honestly believed he was being impartial, if he thought he had no bias, then he didn't intend conducting an investigation improperly. His personal judgment could be questioned, but he didn't set out to break any laws."

"Good. Not that you're a lawyer or anything, but I appreciate your telling me that." Jen slumped a little more.

"Obviously, you found evidence enough to charge this Silver guy. Is that based upon my father's investigation?"

"Uh, no."

"You found evidence he hadn't uncovered?"

"Yes."

Jen stared at Paul. "Oh, is he going to be pissed."

"That's what I figured."

"You haven't talked to him since the investigation?"

"Would you have in my place?"

"No way." She suddenly looked tired. "I knew Chief Asher. He was good people."

"That's what I hear."

"The first priority is finding out for certain if this Silver killed him through sheer careless stupidity. That's all that matters."

"It's not an open-and-shut case, Jen. A lot of it's circumstantial."

"All the more reason to dig as deeply as we can to find the truth. The *Mahan*'s in port. Let's go over and talk to my father. Don't look like that. We'll work it out. My dad's a reasonable man."

This time the sharply turned-out ensign on the quarterdeck of the *Mahan* looked startled when Jen asked to speak to the Captain. After a call to Captain Shen conducted in whispered tones on the quarterdeck's end, the ensign beckoned to his messenger of the watch. "Escort these two officers to the Captain's cabin."

Paul tried to keep his breathing steady, tried not to think ahead, until they were ushered into the Captain's cabin and faced Kay Shen once again. Captain Shen looked steadily at Jen for a long moment, not offering them a seat.

"I'm disappointed, Jen." Captain Shen shook his head to underscore his words. "You had considerable time to rethink this relationship. I expect better judgment from you."

Jen glared back at him. "What does that mean?"

"It means you'd benefit from my guidance in this situation, young lady."

"Are you under the illusion that I'm some piece of property that belongs to you? That I'm incapable of acting independently?"

"It's no illusion that you're still young and in need of guidance."

"I don't believe this. I'm an officer, Dad. I could've ended up sucking vacuum on my last cruise if a backup seal had failed while we were doing emergency repairs. Repairs *I* was overseeing. I am *not* a child in need of 'guidance' on how to live my life."

"You're disproving that little speech by your own actions, by letting your emotions get in the way of your judgment, Jen."

"Of course I'm deciding this based on emotions! You don't decide to forge a serious relationship with someone else based purely on logic! Or have you forgotten that?"

"I haven't forgotten that this young man has displayed a serious lack of judgment of his own which has no relation to what is going on between you. If he's incapable of carrying out his duties properly, and if he responds to corrective advice by attempting to besmirch the reputations of other officers—"

"*He* is standing right here! If there's something you want to say to Paul, say it to *him!*"

Paul, already upset over the fight he was witnessing, felt his guts tighten as Captain Shen whirled to face him. *Gee, thanks, Jen.* Not wanting to give Captain Shen the initiative, he spoke quickly. "Sir, follow-on investigation revealed—"

"Oh, yes." Captain Shen frowned at Paul. "Follow-on investigation. You didn't want to accept the results of my investigation so you cooked up something that blames someone else."

"That's not true, sir!"

"Now I'm a liar, huh?"

"No, sir! I—"

"Mr. Sinclair, I don't want to see you on my ship again, and I'd thank you to stay away from my daughter from this point forward."

Paul felt his face flushing with anger. "Sir, Jen is the only person who can tell me to stay away from her."

"Wasn't my order clear enough for you?"

"That's not a legal order, sir, as you're well aware. I'm under no obligation to obey it."

"A sea lawyer." Captain Shen faced Jen again. "That's what you want? A damn sea lawyer?"

Jen's eyes were hard. "*I'll* decide what I want, Dad. Let's go, Paul." She came to attention and saluted formally. "By your leave, *sir*."

Captain Shen snapped a fast, angry salute in reply. "I expected better of you."

Not replying, Jen led Paul out of the stateroom and out to the *Mahan*'s quarterdeck, the surprised messenger of the watch hastily following them all the way, then onto the dock. They walked in silence for a few minutes, Jen moving quickly with her face tight, Paul knowing she needed time to deal with the scene they'd just left. Finally, she erupted. "I cannot believe this! Who does he think he is? Who does he think I am? Who does he think you are? Say something, Paul!"

"Which question am I answering?"

"You don't have to answer any of them." Jen's face shifted from pure rage to a mix of anger and sadness. "I can't believe it."

"I'm really sorry, Jen."

"For what? You didn't do anything."

"I've come between you and your dad."

"No, you haven't. Stop it, Paul Sinclair. Right now. Stop thinking what you're thinking."

"What is it I'm supposed to be thinking?"

"I know you. You're thinking you've come between a loving father and his daughter, and maybe you ought to step aside for a while so they can be a happy family again. No, no, no. You did nothing wrong, here."

"Jen—"

"Paul, have I ever hesitated to tell you when I thought you'd screwed up?"

"Uh, no. You're pretty straightforward about that."

"You didn't come between my dad and me. He did. He's

making totally unreasonable demands on my life. Again. He's trying to treat me like his little girl. I'm *not* a little girl."

"I've noticed that."

"Then you've also noticed that I don't let anyone push me around. I do things for you because you don't act like it's some sort of obligation for me to do whatever you want. Like I need a firm guiding hand to keep me from veering from stupid decision to stupid decision. I can't believe my dad actually thinks he can do that! I'm so mad I'm tempted to haul you off to the nearest chaplain and get married as fast as we can, only if we did that it'd just seem like it was confirming my dad's belief that I'm a hormone-addled lovesick loose cannon." She subsided for a moment, then spoke in a quieter tone. "I'm sorry. You shouldn't have had to endure that. I should've known it'd be a disaster."

"That's okay, Jen."

"No, it's not. You're upset, aren't you?"

"Yeah. You might say that."

"You should've slugged him."

"Jen, that really would've been a bad idea."

"I know that! Promise me something, Paul."

"What?"

"Whatever happens with this, we will not let it define our relationship."

"Your dad hates my guts and thinks I'm a lousy officer."

"What does your dad think of me?"

"He's never met you!" Paul mustered a small smile. "Though he's heard a lot of good things about you."

"You're lying to your father?"

"No! Be serious, Jen. In any case, it wouldn't matter what my dad thinks . . ." Paul grinned. "Point noted."

"Good. Let's go get some dinner."

"Okay. You deserve a homecoming celebration better than what you've had so far. But tell me about that stuff you mentioned to your father. Emergency repairs? Sucking vacuum?"

"Oh, that." Jen gave Paul an arch look. "It's kind of like firefighting. It comes with the job sometimes. So when's the court-martial? Will you be there?"

"It starts next week. And, yeah, I'll be there. Captain Hayes wants me in the courtroom as an observer."

Jen laughed. "Garcia's still your department head, isn't he? I bet he's really happy about that."

Paul grinned. "Oh, yeah. It's not as if Chief Imari can't handle everything for a few days, and it's not as if I won't be coming back to the ship after court proceedings are over each day. But I'm the blankety-blank Combat Information Center officer! Not a blankety-blank JAG! It's not my fault I got assigned ship's legal officer duties. Hey, that reminds me, guess who one of the members of the court is?"

She shrugged. "I can't imagine."

"Herdez."

"Herdez? Good God. I was thinking of trying to drop by the courtroom, but now . . ."

"Jen, she liked you."

"She ran me ragged! Don't say it. I know I once told you that was Herdez's way of rewarding people. Give them more to do! But she didn't do it to me as a reward."

"Then why did she?"

"Damned if I know. Here you are, going back to a court-martial, and Herdez will be there. Old home week. Speaking of home, did you get a room for us, yet?"

"Well, sure."

She glanced around to see if they were being watched, snuggled close for a moment, and grinned at him. "Dinner can wait. Let's you and me go celebrate my homecoming right now."

Paul smiled back and nodded. "Sounds good to me." *No wonder they compare the ocean to women. Moods change in a heartbeat, and all you can do is try to keep up. Not that I'm complaining.* It was the next day before Paul realized Jen had avoided telling him anything about the hazardous emergency repairs she'd overseen on the *Maury*.

THE courtroom in which Lieutenant Scott Silver would face a general court-martial wasn't the same as that in which Captain Wakeman, former commanding officer of the

Michaelson, had once also faced a trial. Other than that, though, to Paul it appeared identical to the other courtroom. The judge's bench, set higher than the other seats and tables in the room, rested in the front. A table had been set up on one side of the room, facing the area in front of the judge's bench and draped with a navy blue tablecloth. It had five chairs, one for each member of the court. Two doors in the back of the courtroom were for the judge and the members respectively to use. Facing the judge's bench and to either side were the tables for the defense and the trial counsel. After a gap of a couple meters, rows of chairs for spectators were lined up, with a clear path down the middle for those entering the court through the front door.

Paul hesitated in the entry, memories of Wakeman's court-martial filling his mind.

"Looking for a seat?" someone asked behind him.

Paul simultaneously slid to one side and spun around to offer apologies to whoever had been held up by his blocking the door. One certainty in the life of a lieutenant junior grade, though less so than for an ensign, was that just about anybody in authority you encountered would outrank you. "My apologies, ma'am."

Commander Carr smiled impishly. "Nervous? Don't be. This is my show. I'm glad your Captain agreed to let you be here as an observer. Do me a favor and sit right behind my table. I may have some questions for you as the court-martial progresses."

"Yes, ma'am."

"If any of the testimony makes you think of something you think I should know, tell me at the first opportunity."

"Yes, ma'am."

"Now relax."

"Yes, ma'am."

Alex Carr grinned again and walked up the aisle and over to the trial counsel table. Paul followed, taking a seat where she'd instructed. Lieutenant Commander Jones came in, placing some items on the defense table, then crossing to talk briefly with Commander Carr. He gave Paul a dispassionate glance as he turned to leave the room again.

An enlisted legal assistant bustled around, making sure the members' table and the judge's bench had cold water, data pads for note taking, and were otherwise arranged just right. Spectators began arriving, scattering themselves around the available chairs. Paul glanced around a few times, trying to discern whether the spectators were there to support Silver or in hope of a conviction, but nothing in anyone's bearing gave their desires away. *The one thing I do know is that Vice Admiral Silver won't be making an appearance. That'd be such an obviously prejudicial move, something that would surely influence the members of the court, that he couldn't do it without causing a mistrial. It must be hard, or humbling, for a vice admiral to realize he can't even watch his son's court-martial.*

Lieutenant Commander Jones reentered, this time with Lieutenant Silver. Scott Silver walked without the jauntiness Paul had grown accustomed to seeing on the *Michaelson*, but he still had a hint of smile. *He'd better drop that real fast. A face like that'll make the members vote him guilty the minute they see him.*

The court bailiff came in, taking a position in the front of the court and holding up one hand for attention. "I will announce 'all rise' when the military judge enters, and everyone is to rise. The military judge will instruct everyone to be seated. The judge will direct me to summon the members of the court, at which point everyone should rise again. The military judge will inform you when to be seated after that. Are there any questions?" After waiting a moment, the bailiff went to one of the back doors, opened it a bit, and spoke to someone inside before returning to the area near the judge's bench. "All rise."

Paul came to attention automatically, only his eyes moving as Captain David "Hang 'em" Halstead entered. Halstead paused to examine the courtroom, then walked to the judge's bench and took his seat. "This Article 39 (A) session is called to order. You may be seated."

One thing about a military court, Paul reflected, is that when someone ordered you to stand or sit, everybody did it quickly.

Commander Carr stood, her back erect, somehow look-ing taller than her height should have permitted, and ad-dressed Judge Halstead. "The court-martial is convened by general court-martial convening order 0320, Commander in Chief, United States Space Forces, copies of which have been furnished to the military judge, counsel, and the ac-cused. The charges have been properly referred to the court-martial for trial and were served on the accused on 12 October 2100. The accused and the following persons de-tailed to the court-martial are present: Captain Mashiko, Commander Juarez, Commander Herdez, Lieutenant Com-mander Bryko, Lieutenant Commander Goldberg, Com-mander Carr, Lieutenant Commander Jones."

"Very well. Bailiff, the members of the court-martial may enter."

After passing on the message to those behind the other back door to the room, the bailiff called out, "All rise."

With Captain Mashiko in the lead, the five officers en-tered. Captain Mashiko took the center of the five seats at the members' table, with the other officers taking seats to ei-ther side in decreasing order of seniority. As Commander Herdez took her seat, her eyes swept the court, lingering for just a moment on Paul. A fractional nod acknowledged Paul's presence, then Herdez's attention turned fully toward the judge.

When they were all seated, Captain Mashiko nodded to Judge Halstead. "We're ready, Your Honor."

"Thank you. Everyone may be seated. Trial counsel, con-tinue."

Commander Carr stood again. "I have been detailed to this court-martial by order of the fleet judge advocate gen-eral's office. I am qualified and certified under Article 27(b) and sworn under Article 42(a). I have not acted in any man-ner which might tend to disqualify me in the court-martial."

Lieutenant Commander Jones stood. "I have been de-tailed to this court-martial by order of the fleet judge advo-cate general's office. I am qualified and certified under Article 27(b) and sworn under Article 42(a). I have not acted in any manner which might tend to disqualify me in the court-martial."

Paul listened to the declarations, remembering when he'd last heard them. Much of what the lawyers and judge would say to open the court-martial was written in stone, or at least in the Manual for Courts-Martial, to ensure every legal nicety had been observed. For some reason, this seemed to give the stately formality of the announcements extra weight.

Judge Halstead looked toward the defense table. "Lieutenant Scott Silver, you have the right to be represented in this court-martial by Lieutenant Commander Jones, your detailed defense counsel, or you may be represented by military counsel of your selection, if the counsel you request is reasonably available. If you are represented by military counsel of your own selection, you would lose the right to have Lieutenant Commander Jones, your detailed counsel, continue to help in your defense. Do you understand?"

Lieutenant Silver nodded firmly, his expression now studiously serious. "Yes, sir."

"In addition, you have the right to be represented by civilian counsel, at no expense to the United States. Civilian counsel may represent you alone or along with your military counsel. Do you understand?"

"Yes, sir."

"Do you have any questions about your right to counsel?"

"No, sir."

"Whom do you want to represent you?"

"I wish to be represented by Lieutenant Commander Jones, sir."

"Very well. Counsel for the parties have the necessary qualifications, and have been sworn. I have been detailed to this court by order of the judge advocate general's office of the Commander in Chief, United States Space Forces."

Commander Carr left her table, walking briskly to take up a position where she faced both the judge and the members' table. "The general nature of the charges in this case allege culpable negligence that resulted in the death of an enlisted member of the United States Navy and extensive damage to United States military property, and subsequent criminal acts to cover up responsibility for this death and damage. The charges were preferred by Commander, United States Naval Space Forces, and forwarded with recommendations as to disposition to Commander in Chief, United States Space Forces." Commander Carr faced Judge Halstead. "Your Honor, are you aware of any matter which may be a ground for challenge against you?"

"I'm aware of none."

"The government has no challenge for cause against the military judge."

Commander Jones stood again. "The defense has no challenge for cause against the military judge."

Halstead focused on the defense table. "Lieutenant Silver, do you understand that you have the right to be tried by a court-martial composed of members and that, if you are found guilty of any offense, those members would determine a sentence?"

"Yes, sir."

"Do you also understand that you may request in writing or orally here in the court-martial trial before me alone, and that if I approve such a request, there will be no members and I alone will decide whether you are guilty and, if I find you guilty, determine a sentence?"

"Yes, sir."

"Have you discussed these choices with your counsel?"

"Yes, sir, I have."

"By which type of court-martial do you choose to be tried?"

Lieutenant Silver looked confidently toward the members' table. "By members, sir."

"Very well. The accused will now be arraigned."

Commander Carr held up her data pad. "All parties and the military judge have been furnished a copy of the charges and specifications. Does the accused want them read?"

Jones looked at Lieutenant Silver and whispered something. Silver's lips twitched in a smile, and he nodded. "The accused wishes the charges to be read."

"Very well." Carr positioned her pad where she could easily read it. "Lieutenant Scott Silver is charged with violations of the following articles of the Uniform Code of Military Justice.

"Article 92, Dereliction in the Performance of Duties. In that Lieutenant Scott Silver, United States Navy, who should have known of his duties on board USS *Michaelson*, CLE(S)-3, from about 20 August 2100 to about 19 September 2100 was derelict in the performance of those duties in that he negligently failed to ensure the proper operation and maintenance of equipment under his area of responsibility as Main Propulsion officer.

"Article 107, False Official Statements. In that Lieutenant Scott Silver, United States Navy, did, on board USS *Michaelson* CLE(S)-3, on or about 19 September 2100, with an intent to deceive, make to Captain Richard Hayes, United States Navy, his commanding officer, an official statement, to wit his knowledge of events onboard USS *Michaelson*, CLE(S)-3, the evening of 19 September 2100, which statement was false in that it failed to correctly state Lieutenant Silver's actual knowledge of and role in those events, and was then known by said Lieutenant Silver to be false.

"Article 108, Military Property of the United States—sale, loss, damage, destruction, or wrongful disposition. Specification One. In that Lieutenant Scott Silver, United States Navy, did, on board USS *Michaelson*, CLE(S)-3, on or about 19 September 2100, without proper authority, willfully damage and destroy by ordering actions contrary to established safety procedures and regulations, military property of the United States, to wit all equipment located within the Forward Engineering compartment. Specification Two. In that Lieutenant Scott Silver, United States Navy, did, on board USS *Michaelson*, CLE(S)-3, on or about 19 September 2100, without proper authority, willfully damage and destroy by use of unauthorized software the records contained within the engineering logs of the ship.

"Article 110, Improper Hazarding of a Vessel. In that Lieutenant Scott Silver, United States Navy, did, on or about 19 September 2100, while serving as command duty officer and main propulsion assistant on board USS *Michaelson*, CLE(S)-3, willfully and wrongfully hazard the said vessel by ordering a subordinate to take actions contrary to established safety procedures and regulations.

"Article 119, Manslaughter. In that Lieutenant Scott Silver, United States Navy, did, on board USS *Michaelson*, CLE(S)-3, on or about 19 September 2100, by culpable negligence, unlawfully kill Chief Petty Officer Vladimir Asher by ordering him to undertake single-handedly repairs of the power transfer junction in the Forward Engineering compartment in culpable disregard for the foreseeable consequences to others of that act.

"Article 131, Perjury. In that Lieutenant Scott Silver, United States Navy, did, on board USS *Michaelson*, CLE(S)-3, on or about 23 September 2100, in a statement under penalty of perjury pursuant to section 1746 of title 28, United States Code, willfully and corruptly subscribe a false statement material to the matter of inquiry, to wit the cause of the death of Chief Petty Officer Vladimir Asher and associated explosion and fire in the Forward Engineering compartment, which statement was false in that it did not reveal Lieutenant Silver's knowledge of Chief Asher's purpose in Forward Engineering nor Lieutenant Silver's orders to Chief Asher that directly led to the accident, and which statement he did not then believe to be true.

"The charges are signed by Commander, United States Naval Space Forces, a person subject to the code, as accuser; are properly sworn to before a commissioned officer of the armed forces authorized to administer oaths, and are properly referred to this court-martial for trial by Commander, United States Space Forces, the convening authority."

Paul's eyes had been fixed on Commander Carr as she spoke, but now he swiftly shifted his gaze to the defense table. Lieutenant Silver was standing at attention, his expression that of a man enduring assaults on his character with dignity. *I have to give Silver credit. He's good. I bet that's why he asked the charges to be read, so he could act noble and aggrieved while listening to them.*

Judge Halstead looked at Silver as well. "Lieutenant Silver, how do you plead? Before receiving your pleas, I advise you that any motions to dismiss any charge or grant other relief should be made at this time."

Lieutenant Commander Jones answered instead of Silver. "Your Honor, the defense moves that all charges and specifications be dismissed in light of the lack of evidence directly implicating Lieutenant Silver as being guilty of any of the offenses listed."

"The motion is denied. The purpose of this proceeding is to determine whether the evidence the government has compiled is sufficient to prove the charges brought against Lieutenant Silver. Do you have any further motions?"

"No, Your Honor."

Lieutenant Silver faced the members rather than the judge. "I plead not guilty to all charges and specifications."

Halstead nodded. "Very well. Does the prosecution have an opening statement?"

"Yes, Your Honor." Commander Carr also faced the members. "The prosecution intends to demonstrate that Lieutenant Silver exercised negligence in his duties as Main Propulsion assistant, which caused the failure of a critical piece of equipment in Forward Engineering on the USS *Michaelson*. As a result of this, and in an attempt to conceal his negligence, Lieutenant Silver personally obtained a necessary spare and ordered Chief Petty Officer Asher to install single-handedly that spare on Saturday, 19 September 2100. In order to do so, Lieutenant Silver ordered Chief Asher to disable safety interlocks which further disabled the fire suppression systems in Forward Engineering, assisting Chief Asher in this by providing an officer's authorization. Following the explosion and fire that resulted in Chief Asher's death and extensive damage to the ship, Lieutenant Silver lied to his commanding officer about his knowledge of and role in the events. Lieutenant Silver then used software to destroy the records in the USS *Michaelson*'s engineering logs that would have documented his role in the explosion, fire, and death of Chief Asher, then subsequently swore to a false statement during a formal investigation of the accident. Lieutenant Silver should be found guilty as to all charges and specifications, for his culpable negligence, which led to the death of a sailor under his command, for his lying to his commanding officer, for the destruction of government property engineered by him, and for his perjury during the investigation of the accident.

Commander Carr returned to her seat, as Judge Halstead looked toward Commander Jones. "Does the defense have an opening statement?"

"We do, Your Honor." Commander Jones walked to the same position Commander Carr had occupied. "The defense contends that the government lacks proof of the charges lodged against Lieutenant Silver. There is no evidence Lieutenant Silver engaged in the actions alleged by the prosecution, and if he did not commit those acts, then he did not make a false statement or commit perjury when describing his role in the terrible events on board USS *Michaelson* the evening of 19 September 2100. While the loss of life and property on board USS *Michaelson* is cause for deep regret, scapegoating Lieutenant Silver will not bring back Chief Asher or undo the events of that night. Lieutenant Silver is a dedicated naval officer who has done his duty to the best of his ability. Since the prosecution lacks proof otherwise, he should therefore be found innocent on all charges and specifications."

Commander Jones, his statement completed, returned to his seat. Silence reigned in the court for a brief moment as Judge Halstead seemed to be pondering his own thoughts. Then Halstead gestured to Commander Carr. "You may proceed, Commander."

"Thank you, Your Honor. The United States calls as its first witness Petty Officer First Class Alysha Kulwari."

CHAPTER TEN

☆ ☆ ☆ ☆ ☆

PETTY Officer Kulwari, looking slightly uncomfortable in what appeared to be a new uniform, came down the aisle, her eyes fixed on the witness stand. Commander Carr stood before Kulwari, her posture more relaxed, her expression encouraging. "Do you swear that the evidence you give in the case now in hearing shall be the truth, the whole truth, and nothing but the truth, so help you God?"

"I do, ma'am."

"Are you Petty Officer First Class Alysha Kulwari, United States Navy, assigned to the Engineering Department on the USS *Michaelson*?"

"Yes, ma'am."

"Do you know the accused?"

"Yes, ma'am. Lieutenant Silver's my—Excuse me, Lieutenant Silver was my division officer for about a month."

"In other words, you worked directly for Lieutenant Silver during that period. Is that correct?"

"Uh, well, ma'am, orders would usually come through Chief Asher, but Lieutenant Silver gave him those orders, yes, ma'am."

Commander Carr crossed her arms, her eyes still on Petty Officer Kulwari. "What can you tell us regarding the power transfer junction in Forward Engineering on the USS *Michaelson* during the period when Lieutenant Silver was serving as your division officer?"

Kulwari's eyes flicked around the room, avoiding resting on Scott Silver as they did so. "Ma'am, about a week after Lieutenant Silver took over from Lieutenant Kilgary the junction controller started going bad."

"It *started* going bad. The controller didn't just fail?"

"No, ma'am. They don't do that. You see them start to go bad, and they get worse and worse until they crap out. I'm sorry, ma'am, until they fail."

"How long does it take them to fail?"

"Usually two to three weeks. You can nurse them along and compensate for the problems for that long, but after that they're too bad to use anymore."

"The controller is a critical part of the power transfer junction?"

"Yes, ma'am. That junction won't work without it."

"What happens if the junction doesn't work?"

Petty Officer Kulwari bit her lip as she formulated her reply. "The ship can operate on the other power transfer junction in After Engineering, but she can't do everything. There are a lot of limitations."

"Do you carry a spare controller on board?"

"Sometimes, ma'am."

"Sometimes?"

"Ma'am, I don't know why, but there's not enough spares of that controller to go around, so they get reserved for ships that're going out on long missions. If a ship's operating in the local area, we never carry a spare because we can get home in time if one starts to go bad."

Commander Carr walked back and forth slowly in front of the witness stand. "To summarize, then, the controller in the power transfer junction in Forward Engineering started to fail about one week after Lieutenant Silver took over as your division officer. You had about two to three weeks before the controller would totally fail, and when it did fail the ship's ability to operate would be severely curtailed. Is that correct?"

Petty Officer Kulwari nodded. "Yes, ma'am."

"To your certain knowledge, was Lieutenant Silver informed of the impending failure of the controller?"

"I'm sorry, ma'am. My . . . ?"

"Your certain knowledge. Did you see or hear Lieutenant Silver being informed of the impending failure?"

"Oh, yes, ma'am. I was standing in Forward Engineering maybe a couple meters from Chief Asher when he was talking to Lieutenant Silver about it."

"What did Chief Asher say to Lieutenant Silver?"

"I didn't catch every word, ma'am, but he was saying we needed to get a spare installed."

"And what did Lieutenant Silver say in reply?"

"Uh, something like 'I'm on it, Chief.' Something like that."

"You're certain? Lieutenant Silver discussed the impending failure of the controller with Chief Asher in your hearing, and assured Chief Asher the issue was being addressed?"

"Uh, yes, ma'am."

"Did the controller eventually fail?"

"Yes, ma'am, it did."

"When?"

"Friday, uh, 18 September. About noon, I guess. I came back from lunch, and Petty Officer Lai told me the controller had gone belly-up, and everything was being routed through the power junction in After Engineering. Chief Asher told us he was going to talk to Lieutenant Silver about it."

"Lieutenant Silver wasn't present? Even though a critical piece of equipment he was responsible for had failed?"

"No, ma'am."

"Did Lieutenant Silver come to Forward Engineering at all that afternoon?"

"No, ma'am, not that I saw and not that anybody else told me. But that wasn't unusual."

"It wasn't? The ship's main propulsion assistant not visiting Forward Engineering wasn't unusual?"

"Not with Lieutenant Silver, ma'am. We never saw him much."

"You never saw him much?" Commander Carr paused to let the statement sink in. "Then what happened?"

"We worked on other stuff, ma'am. There wasn't anything we could do about the controller until we got the spare, and it didn't show. When knock-off ship's work was announced I called Chief Asher and asked what we should do about the power junction and he told me Lieutenant Silver was working on it, and we shouldn't bother hanging around."

"How did Chief Asher sound when he told you that?"

"He was real unhappy with somebody, ma'am."

"Are you certain of that?"

Petty Officer Kulwari couldn't suppress a quick smile. "Ma'am, I've been around Chief Asher when he was real unhappy with someone, and believe me, you don't forget what he sounds like." The smile vanished. "Uh, sounded like, I guess I oughta say."

Commander Carr nodded sympathetically. "What time was knock-off ship's work that afternoon?"

"It's almost always 1700 in port. Sometimes 1730 or 1800 if there's an extra lot to do."

"Petty Officer Kulwari, how would the controller be replaced? How many personnel does it require?"

"At least two, ma'am. Two specialists, that is. They gotta know that gear. There's some kinda safety interlocks to keep the junction from overloading and blowing while the controllers are being swapped out."

"Could one person do the job?"

"If'n they were crazy, ma'am. They'd have to shut off the interlocks and work real fast, and if nothing made the junction overload without the controller in, they could do it. You'd have to be real good and a bit lucky."

"So it's not impossible for one person to do it, but it's very unwise."

"Yes, ma'am. I wouldn't do it."

"What if you were *ordered* to do it, Petty Officer Kulwari?"

As Kulwari hesitated, Commander Jones rose. "Objection. The trial counsel is asking the witness to speculate as to what she would have done if faced with a hypothetical situation."

Commander Carr faced Judge Halstead. "Your Honor, Petty Officer Kulwari is an experienced, highly trained specialist. Her answer will shed light on the reaction of such a person to an order of that nature."

Halstead shook his head. "Sorry, Counsel. No matter what the witness's qualifications might be, unless you're willing to argue she did receive such an order, then her response will not be germane. Objection sustained."

If the setback fazed her, Commander Carr gave no indication of it. "Petty Officer Kulwari, how long did you serve with Chief Petty Officer Asher?"

Kulwari furrowed her brow in thought. "About a year and a half, ma'am"

"In all that time, did you ever witness Chief Asher bypassing or circumventing safety procedures?"

"No, ma'am. He always told us to go by the book on that."

"Would you say, from your experience with Chief Asher, that for him to have worked on repairing that junction single-handedly would be out of character?"

"Yes, ma'am. He didn't do that."

Commander Carr turned, walked a couple of steps, then faced the witness again. "Tell me what happened the Monday after the accident in Forward Engineering. Lieutenant Silver spoke to all of you, didn't he?"

"Yes, ma'am, he did." Petty Officer Kulwari's eyes shifted toward the defense table, where Scott Silver was watching her intently, then back to Commander Carr.

"What did he tell you, Petty Officer Kulwari?"

"I don't remember all the words exactly, ma'am, but he told us how terrible it was that Chief Asher'd died, and how it'd be a lot more terrible if anybody thought he'd died doing something wrong, because then his wife and family wouldn't get any benefits."

Carr came closer to the witness. "And what message did you and the other personnel in the division derive from that?"

"Derive, ma'am?"

"What did you all decide based upon what Lieutenant Silver told you?"

"That, uh . . ." Petty Officer Kulwari looked around again, her nervousness visible also in hands that kept twisting around each other. "That we shouldn't tell anybody what Chief Asher'd been doing."

"What do you mean, Petty Officer Kulwari? What did you all believe Chief Asher had been doing?"

"We knew, or figured we knew, that he had to've been replacing that controller, and that'd been what made the power junction blow. And doing that alone meant he'd broken some regulations."

"And Lieutenant Silver led you to believe that if Chief Asher had broken any regulations, Chief Asher's family would receive no death benefits from the Navy?"

"Objection!" Commander Jones waved toward Kulwari. "Trial counsel is leading the witness and attempting to cast her own individual interpretation of Lieutenant Silver's words as both reasonable and unmistakable. Neither position is supported by the testimony of a single witness."

Commander Carr held her data pad aloft. "As defense counsel is aware, I have sworn statements signed by every enlisted member of Lieutenant Silver's division attesting that they reached the same conclusion based upon Lieutenant Silver's words. I'd like to have all those statements entered into the record at this time."

Halstead curved his lips in a momentary, tight-lipped smile. "Objection overruled. All the statements are hereby ordered to be entered into the record. Continue, Commander Carr."

"Thank you, Your Honor. I'll restate the question for the witness. Petty Officer Kulwari, you've stated all the enlisted personnel in Lieutenant Silver's division assumed Chief

Asher had been working on the power transfer junction. None of you disclosed that information, or even the status of the power transfer junction prior to the accident. Why was that?"

Kulwari bit her lip again and looked down. "We didn't want Chief Asher or his family to get into no trouble."

"Because of what you had all been told by Lieutenant Silver?"

Still looking down, Kulwari replied in a strained voice. "Yes, ma'am."

"Thank you, Petty Officer Kulwari. No further questions."

Judge Halstead nodded toward the defense table. "You may cross-examine."

Lieutenant Commander Jones walked slowly toward the witness stand, his face skeptical. "Petty Officer Kulwari, you claim you heard Lieutenant Silver and Chief Asher discussing the problem with the controller. Yet you also said you didn't catch every word. How can you be sure of what you did hear?"

"Sir, I heard enough to be sure of that."

"Could they have just been generally discussing the controller?"

"Sir, they were talking about the controller going bad."

"Are you certain the discussion wasn't theoretical? That Lieutenant Silver might have been asking his chief about that piece of equipment and trying to learn about it?"

Petty Officer Kulwari looked taken aback. "Sir, that part was going bad."

"But are you absolutely certain Chief Asher was telling Lieutenant Silver that? Can you swear the discussion was about what was wrong, or about what *might* go wrong?"

"Um, well, sir, I thought—"

"I'm not asking for your interpretation, Petty Officer Kulwari. I want to know what you heard. Are you certain?"

"Well, sir . . ."

"Isn't it possible that Chief Asher never told Lieutenant Silver what was actually wrong with that power transfer junction?"

"Sir, that may be possible, but—"

"Thank you, Petty Officer Kulwari. Now, as to Lieutenant Silver's presence in Forward Engineering. That's a pretty big compartment, isn't it?"

"For a ship, yes, sir."

"It contains a lot of equipment, too. Is there any point within that compartment from which you can see everyone who's in there?"

Petty Officer Kulwari twisted her face as she thought. "I don't think so, sir."

"So someone could be in that compartment, and you wouldn't know it."

"Uh, yes, sir."

"At any point, did Chief Asher tell you he had orders to replace that controller single-handedly?"

"No, sir, but—"

"This meeting the day after the accident. Can you tell us exactly what it was Lieutenant Silver said to you?"

"Exactly, sir? No, sir."

"Lieutenant Silver expressed concern for Chief Asher's family?"

"Yes, sir, he did."

"Do you find anything inappropriate about that?"

"Uh, no, sir."

"At that meeting, did Lieutenant Silver tell the personnel in your division to lie to the investigators? Did he order anyone to hold back information from the investigators?"

"Not like that, no, sir."

"Not like what, Petty Officer Kulwari? Did or did not Lieutenant Silver order the enlisted personnel in his division to lie to the investigators?"

Kulwari looked around desperately. "N-no, sir. He didn't order us to do that."

"No further questions."

Judge Halstead watched Commander Jones walk back to the defense table, then looked toward Commander Carr "Does trial counsel wish to redirect?"

"Yes, Your Honor." Commander Carr stood before Petty Officer Kulwari again, smiling once more. "You had something to add when you answered the question about whether or not Chief Asher could have failed to inform Lieutenant Silver about the true state of the controller. Would you care to say that now?"

"Yes, ma'am." Kulwari glanced defiantly toward Commander Jones. "I've no doubt Chief Asher told him it was really broken. Why else would the lieutenant have said he was working on it?"

"That's a good question, Petty Officer Kulwari. Now, I understand Forward Engineering is a big compartment with a lot of equipment. But if someone were walking through that compartment, would you miss seeing them?"

"If they were moving around? No, ma'am. I couldn't miss them."

"In your last conversation with Chief Asher, on Friday afternoon, you said he indicated the spare part hadn't been located?"

"Yes, ma'am. That's why he told us to knock off work."

"Would Chief Asher have told you to knock off work and go on liberty if he either had the spare or expected to see it soon?"

"No, ma'am, no way."

"So obviously he couldn't have received orders to install a spare he didn't have at that time, correct?"

"Uh, that's right, ma'am. If he'd had it, he would've held us until we got it switched out."

"Petty Officer Kulwari, how long have you been in the Navy?"

"About ten years, ma'am."

"Then you have a lot of experience listening to officers, don't you?"

"Oh, yes, ma'am." A brief chuckle ran around the courtroom until it was silenced by a hard look from Judge Halstead.

"How many times do officers say 'I order you' to do a task?"

"Not very often, ma'am. Usually, they just say to do it, and you know it's an order."

"Based upon your experience, did you interpret what

Lieutenant Silver told his division the day after the accident as an instruction?"

"I . . . Yes, ma'am. I guess I did. It sure felt like it."

"No further questions."

Halstead nodded. "How about you, Commander Jones?"

"No further questions."

"Captain Mashiko, do you or any of the other members have any questions for the witness?"

Mashiko looked at his fellow officers before replying. "Petty Officer Kulwari, you said you didn't see Lieutenant Silver very often in Forward Engineering. During the month he served as Main Propulsion assistant, how many times do you recall seeing him there?"

Kulwari paused, her face reflecting concentration. "Just a couple of times, sir."

"A couple? One? Two?"

"Two or three, sir. Three maximum for sure."

"What about Lieutenant Silver's predecessor in the job?"

"Lieutenant Kilgary, sir? She was down there just about every day when she was Main Propulsion assistant."

Commander Herdez spoke next. "Petty Officer Kulwari, how often did you speak with Lieutenant Silver?"

"Me, ma'am? Uh, a couple times, I guess."

"A couple of times. About what? Did he ask about your equipment?"

"No, ma'am. Lieutenant Silver just sorta said 'hi, howya doing,' and moved on."

"He never asked you any questions about your job or the equipment in Forward Engineering?"

"No, ma'am. I'd've remembered that, ma'am."

"Thank you, Petty Officer Kulwari. I have no more questions."

Lieutenant Commander Bryko held up some fingers for attention. "Petty Officer Kulwari, you say the division personnel knew the power transfer junction was broken, and that you needed that part to be working for the ship to get underway on Monday. Did you voluntarily stay aboard the ship over the weekend to ensure that task was done?"

"Sir, it wouldn't have mattered if I did. I'm not checked

out on that gear. There's about a half dozen people in the division qualified to do that. Of them, only Chief Asher had duty on Saturday."

"Did any of them speak to you about volunteering?"

"We talked a bit about it, sir."

"But none of you did?"

"No, sir."

"Why not?"

Petty Officer Kulwari shook her head, looking down again. "I wish some of them had, sir, but everybody's attitude was sorta 'the lieutenant don't care, so why should we?'"

"Why did you conclude the lieutenant didn't care?"

"We knew there wasn't any spare on board, and the equipment hadn't been casualty reported even though it'd been going bad for a while, and the lieutenant hadn't been down to Forward Engineering that afternoon to talk to anybody about it. I guess that's why."

Captain Mashiko looked at his fellow members one more time. "There are no further questions from the members."

Judge Halstead nodded. "Very well. Petty Officer Kulwari, you are temporarily excused. Please ensure you are present for the remainder of this court-martial in the event you need to be called again. As long as this trial continues, do not discuss your testimony or knowledge of the case with anyone except counsel. If anyone else tries to talk to you about the case, stop them and report the matter to one of the counsels."

"Yes, sir. No, sir. Uh, I'll do what you said, sir." Petty Officer Kulwari stood up with a stiffness that betrayed the tense way she'd been sitting and left the court with relief clearly visible on her face.

Commander Destin, the *Michaelson*'s chief engineer, was called as the next witness. After swearing her in, Commander Carr indicated the defense table. "Commander, were you ever informed by Lieutenant Silver that the controller on the power junction transfer in Forward Engineering was failing and in need of replacement?"

Destin seemed gloomier than ever. "No. I never received that information."

"Not in writing? Not in an E-mail? Not verbally?"

"No."

"Did Lieutenant Silver ever indicate in any way that he had any equipment problems?"

"I received some status reports from Chief Asher."

"But not directly from Lieutenant Silver?"

"No."

"What was your impression of Lieutenant Silver as an officer?"

Destin looked stubborn as she replied. "He'd just come aboard and was still learning the ropes. I had a favorable impression overall."

"Based upon what factors, Commander?"

"His attitude, his bearing, his general approach."

Alex Carr looked momentarily puzzled. "Pardon me, Commander Destin, but that list lacks specifics. Is there any specific action Lieutenant Silver carried out while working for you that you recall favorably?"

"He'd only been aboard a few weeks."

Paul tried not to let his own reaction to Destin's attitude show. *Great. I break my butt trying to do everything I should, and get chewed out by my department head. Silver coasts through his days, sucking up to his bosses, and they think he's doing great. Like Sonya Sindh said, it's not fair, but there's nothing we can do about that.*

Commander Carr nodded in response to Destin's last statement. "What did Lieutenant Silver tell you about the accident in Forward Engineering?"

"He didn't know any more about it that anyone else."

"That's what he told you."

"Yes, and I believed it. Believe it."

"Even though Lieutenant Silver's enlisted personnel all say Mr. Silver did know something about it?"

"If I have the choice between believing one of my officers or an enlisted sailor, I'm going to make the same choice every time."

"What about *one* of your officers and almost twenty enlisted?"

"Same difference. You either trust your officers, or you don't."

"Then you don't trust the enlisted in Lieutenant Silver's division? Yet you still allow them to run vital equipment?"

Lieutenant Commander Jones stood. "Objection. Trial counsel is harassing the witness."

Halstead gave Carr a sour look. "Sustained. You've made your point, Counsel."

Carr nodded. "Yes, Your Honor. Commander Destin, you returned to the ship on the evening of 19 September after you'd been paged and informed of the fire, correct?"

"Yes."

"About when did you return to the ship?"

"I got back about 2200. I remember because I checked the time just before I reached the area near the quarterdeck."

"Where was Lieutenant Silver at that time?"

Destin frowned. "I don't know."

"When did you first encounter Lieutenant Silver that evening?"

"About . . . maybe 2300. Maybe a little later. We were drafting our report on the accident and needed his input."

Commander Carr assumed her momentary puzzled look again. "Lieutenant Silver was the command duty officer, responsible for events on the ship, and was the Main Propulsion assistant, whose Forward Engineering compartment had just sustained serious damage, and whose leading chief had apparently died. Yet you didn't see him for an hour?"

"I assumed Lieutenant Silver was busy elsewhere. As you just pointed out, he had many responsibilities to deal with."

Carr leaned closer, her attitude now challenging. "Commander Destin, have you met *anyone* who saw Lieutenant Silver during that period? Anyone at all?"

Destin glowered back. "I haven't gone around asking."

"I can help with that, Commander, because I have. No one saw Lieutenant Silver. Not on the quarterdeck, or in the wardroom, or in Damage Control Central, or anywhere near

Forward Engineering. As his immediate superior, how do you explain that?"

"Objection." Commander Jones gestured toward Carr. "Trial counsel is citing matters not previously introduced into evidence."

Halstead cocked an eyebrow toward Carr. "Counsel?"

Alex Carr held up her data pad again. "I have sworn statements from every officer and chief petty officer on the USS *Michaelson* attesting to their inability to account for Lieutenant Silver's presence during the period from about 2200 to about 2300 the night of 19 September. With the court's permission, I'd like to have them entered into the record at this time."

Judge Halstead glanced toward the defense table. "I assume you mean every officer except Lieutenant Silver?"

"Yes, Your Honor. I apologize for the inaccuracy."

"I hereby order the statements entered into the record. Objection overruled. Continue, Counselor."

Carr faced Destin again. "Commander? How do you account for Lieutenant Silver's disappearance during that period of time?"

"I can't. Ask him."

"I'm asking you, Commander, because as his immediate superior you are responsible for his behavior and evaluating his professional performance. Do you, personally, believe a professional officer with those responsibilities should have been unseen and unheard from for an hour's time on the evening of a serious accident and death on the ship?"

Destin stared back, but finally shook her head. "No."

"No, you do not believe this was something a professional officer should've done?"

"No, I do not."

"Do you like Lieutenant Silver, Commander?"

Destin flushed as she spoke through clenched teeth. "What are you implying?"

Commander Carr held up two palms in a calming gesture. "Nothing unprofessional, Commander. Not at all. I'm simply asking whether you, as the department head, liked having Lieutenant Silver as a division officer."

Commander Jones, halfway out of his seat to register another objection, sat back down.

Destin's flush faded a bit. "Yes. Lieutenant Silver has been respectful and demonstrated a pleasing personality. As I noted earlier, I've had no grounds for questioning his professional capabilities."

"Until now, Commander? You just indicated his disappearance for an hour that night was unprofessional in your opinion."

"Yes."

"The night of the accident, the data in the engineering logs was so severely damaged that it was unrecoverable. As chief engineer on the USS *Michaelson*, do you know of any accidental cause that would account for that?"

"The investigation of the accident found the cause of the data loss could not be determined."

"Yes, I know that, Commander. I'm asking for your professional judgment. Aren't those logs designed to survive the complete destruction of the ship?"

Destin made a face. "That depends how the ship's destroyed."

"Conventional explosion? Fire? Decompression?"

"They should be able to survive those."

"Then, again in your professional judgment, should the accident on 19 September have been able to destroy the data in those logs?"

Destin's lips pressed together in a tight line, then she shook her head. "Not to my knowledge."

"What sort of information would those engineering logs have contained?"

"Anything pertaining to the status and operation of the equipment in Forward and After Engineering."

"In other words, they would've told us if someone were working on the power transfer junction in Forward Engineering?"

"Yes."

"And if whoever was working on that equipment had disabled safety interlocks?"

"Yes."

"What does it take to disable those safety interlocks, Commander Destin? Could Chief Asher have done it by himself?"

Destin's mouth worked for a moment. "No."

"Doesn't the engineering system require authorization codes from an officer and an enlisted to disable safety interlocks?"

"Yes."

"Then an officer had to have been involved in assisting Chief Asher if he was working on the power transfer junction, correct? An officer in the Engineering Department?" Destin stared stubbornly past Commander Carr. "Commander Destin. If Chief Asher was working on the power transfer junction single-handedly, doesn't that mean he had to have disabled the safety interlocks, and isn't that only possible with the assistance of an officer from the Engineering Department?"

Commander Jones was on his feet. "Objection. The witness is being asked to describe a situation whose existence has not been proven. Whether or not Chief Asher was working on the equipment remains speculative."

Commander Carr spoke directly to Judge Halstead. "Your Honor, the question pertains to standing procedures and system requirements within the Engineering Department. There is nothing speculative about the nature of those requirements."

Jones shook his head. "Your Honor, the question only matters if the theoretical situation is assumed to exist. Trial counsel cannot simply assume the existence of that condition but must first prove it."

"I disagree, Your Honor. Engineering system requirements are matters of fact. If defense counsel prefers, I could simply introduce the Engineering Department system manuals into evidence in order to establish the same point."

"Your Honor—"

Jones's latest point was cut off as Judge Halstead held up one hand in a warning gesture. "I'd appreciate the chance to get a word in edgewise, Counsels. Trial counsel's question clearly pertains to a matter of fact, though any attempt to subsequently link that fact to events must be regarded as theoretical unless further proof is supplied. Objection overruled. The witness is directed to answer the question."

Commander Destin looked at the judge as if trying to be sure she was the one being addressed, then focused back on Commander Carr. "Yes. The system requires an officer and an enlisted to provide authorization codes."

Commander Carr eyed Commander Destin a moment longer. "Thank you, Commander. No further questions."

Lieutenant Commander Jones came forward to stand a little farther back from Destin than Carr had, his posture less challenging. "Commander Destin, you've already testified to having a general good impression of Lieutenant Silver's work and attitude. While Lieutenant Silver worked for you, were there any specific negative incidents that caused you to question that assessment?"

"No."

"At any time prior to 19 September, were you approached by any personnel who worked for Lieutenant Silver expressing concern over his leadership or the status of the equipment in Forward Engineering?"

"No."

"Ma'am, would you expect a chief petty officer to execute a clearly illegal order if you gave him that order?"

"No, of course not."

"Have you ever had an individual who worked for you die, Commander?"

Destin's face worked for a moment. "Yes."

"After you had carried out all of your immediate responsibilities, Commander, did you find a need to grieve? In private?"

"I . . ."

Destin's voice seemed to choke off, then she swallowed and tried again. "Yes."

"Would you regard that need as a plausible explanation for Lieutenant Silver's inability to be found for a brief period on the evening of 19 September?"

"Yes. Yes, I would."

"Commander Destin, authorization codes are supposed to

be kept confidential. Are any ever disclosed either on purpose or by accident?"

Destin nodded quickly. "Yes. Yes, they are. Everybody knows that."

"Then one person could've had access to two authorization codes?"

"Objection." Commander Carr pointed at Commander Jones. "Counsel for the defense is introducing theoretical situations."

"Your Honor, this is also a matter of fact."

"It is not a matter of fact, Your Honor. No evidence has been provided that authorization codes were in fact compromised. If such evidence existed, I would be surprised by any attempt by counsel for the defense to introduce such evidence knowing it would serve to substantiate the charge of dereliction of duty."

Judge Halstead shook his head, his eyes reflecting annoyance. "These disputes over theoretical issues appear to be a habitual problem. I expect better of professional lawyers. Counsel for the defense, do you in fact have evidence authorization codes were compromised within Lieutenant Silver's division?"

"No, Your Honor. Not at this time."

"Then the objection is sustained."

Commander Jones looked back toward Commander Destin. "No further questions."

Halstead focused back on Commander Carr. "Do you wish to redirect, Counsel?"

"No, Your Honor."

Halstead looked toward the members. "Do the members of the court have any questions for the witness?"

Lieutenant Commander Susan Goldberg spoke up. "I have a question. Commander Destin, you replied to a question about whether or not Chief Asher should be expected to obey an illegal order by saying no. What would you have expected Chief Asher to do, assuming he did receive such an order, ma'am? One requiring him to do something unsafe?"

Commander Destin remained silent for a moment. "Report the matter."

"He should jump the chain of command, ma'am? Bypass his division officer and go straight to you?"

"That's correct."

"But you also testified you'd always take the word of an officer over that of an enlisted. If Chief Asher came to you and said one thing, and Lieutenant Silver said another, you'd believe Lieutenant Silver."

Destin's expression started becoming hostile as she stared at Lieutenant Commander Goldberg. "All other things being equal, yes."

"I repeat, then, what would Chief Asher's alternatives have been, ma'am? Obey an illegal order, or report it to you and be branded a liar by Lieutenant Silver, knowing you would accept Lieutenant Silver's statement?"

Commander Destin looked around the courtroom as if seeking an answer. Lieutenant Commander Jones stood slowly. "Your Honor, I wish to object to the member's question. She is asking the witness to speculate about her response to a theoretical situation."

Judge Halstead tapped one finger on his desk as he thought about the objection. "And here we are *again*. Lieutenant Commander Goldberg, do you require an answer to your last question from the witness?"

Goldberg shook her head. "No, sir. I believe the question has already been answered."

"Trial counsel?"

Commander Carr gestured toward Goldberg. "Trial counsel defers to the member, Your Honor."

"Then I will sustain the objection. Again. Do the members have any further questions?"

Goldberg shook her head again. "I don't, sir."

Commander Destin received her instructions and left the courtroom, her gloom now lighted by a clear flare of anger.

Commander Carr called her next witness. "Petty Officer First Class Ivan Sharpe."

Sharpe strode to the witness stand looking every inch a master-at-arms, took the oath, then waited attentively for the first question from Commander Carr.

"Petty Officer Sharpe, did you encounter Chief Asher at any time on 19 September of this year?"

"Yes, ma'am."

"Describe that encounter, if you please."

"Ma'am, at approximately 1800 I returned to the ship to drop off a few personal purchases before heading out on liberty for the evening. As I headed back toward the quarterdeck, at about 1830, I passed Chief Petty Officer Asher going the other direction. He wasn't really looking at me, just glaring ahead like he was very upset, and he was talking to himself."

"What did you hear Chief Asher say?"

"I heard three words distinctly as Chief Asher came abreast of me, ma'am. They were 'just do it.' "

" 'Just do it'? What was Chief Asher's tone when he said those words?"

"Angry, ma'am."

"What did you do?"

"I said hi, and he didn't react at first, then he looked at me like he was surprised to see me. I said hi again, and asked Chief Asher if he needed anything, if I could help him with anything. He looked at me for a couple of seconds, then shook his head, said 'no,' and headed on down the passageway."

"You didn't follow him?"

"No, ma'am. Chief Asher'd made it real clear he didn't want to share anything with me."

"You had no idea why he was upset?"

"Not then, ma'am, no. Not an exact idea. I do know whenever I hear a fellow enlisted say 'just do it' he or she's repeating something they've been told by an officer."

"Objection." Commander Jones pointed at Sharpe. "The witness is speculating about matters beyond his factual knowledge."

"Sustained." Judge Halstead gave Sharpe a hard look. "The witness is reminded he is to testify to what he saw or heard and is not to speculate as to the meaning of those things."

"Aye, aye, sir."

Despite Sharpe's dispassionate reply, Paul could have sworn he caught a glint of satisfaction on his face. *You did that on purpose, didn't you, Sheriff? You weren't sure it'd come out in questioning, so you went ahead and said it even though you knew you shouldn't. Well, I'm not going to rat on you.*

Commander Carr tapped her data pad. "I have the text of the investigation done on the accident on the USS *Michaelson*. It doesn't contain the information you just provided about Chief Asher. Why isn't that information in the investigation?"

"I don't know, ma'am. I submitted a statement."

"A sworn statement?"

"Yes, ma'am. Witnessed by Senior Chief Kowalski of the USS *Michaelson*."

"What became of that statement?"

"I don't know, ma'am. I submitted it."

"Thank you, Petty Officer Sharpe. No more questions."

Lieutenant Commander Jones approached Sharpe in an almost wary fashion, which somehow made Paul think of a mongoose closing on a cobra. "Petty Officer Sharpe, had you ever seen Chief Asher angry before the evening of 19 September?"

"Of course, sir. Chief Asher was human."

"What sort of things made him angry on those earlier occasions?"

"The usual, sir. Personal problems, problems with enlisted junior to him, problems with equipment, problems with people in other divisions, problems within his duty section, problems with officers." Another low chuckle briefly sounded through the courtroom.

"Then Chief Asher could have been angry for any of those same reasons that evening, couldn't he?"

"No, sir."

"Why not, Petty Officer Sharpe?"

"Chief Asher shared problems like that with me. We were friends. Whatever was bothering him that night wasn't the usual stuff, or he'd have told me."

Jones seemed to have tasted something sour. "No further questions."

Commander Carr smiled at Judge Halstead. "No redirect, Your Honor."

Paul wondered why Carr's smile seemed happy as well as polite. *She sandbagged Jones, didn't she? She could've had Sharpe tell the court that bit about Asher being unhappy for an unusual reason, but she left it out in hope Jones would ask a predictable question that'd let Sharpe say it. Tough and sneaky. I definitely don't want to cross swords with Commander Alex Carr.*

The next witness, Lieutenant Mike Bristol. Commander Carr questioned him about his knowledge of the spare. Yes, the ship's supply system had been asked about the status of a spare controller for the power transfer junctions. No, none had been available on board, but some were available from the station supply depot within three or four working days. "Wasn't your ship due to get underway on Monday, Lieutenant Bristol?"

"Yes, ma'am."

"Then three or four days wouldn't have cut it, would it? Was there any way to get that spare part over the weekend?"

"Yes, ma'am. You can ask the station authorities for an emergency parts draw. That needs the ship's commanding officer's approval for the request, and it needs to go to the station's senior duty officer."

Commander Carr paced back and forth before the witness stand. "Then that spare could've been acquired over the weekend. Officially acquired in time to install it. But to do so Lieutenant Silver would've had to get his commanding officer's approval, and his commanding officer would've had to make an emergency request of the station."

"Yes, ma'am."

"In other words, he would have had to inform his superiors of the situation."

"Yes, ma'am."

"If the court pleases, I have a copy of a revised report from the physical investigation of Forward Engineering following the accident, and will quote from the revised conclusions: 'Initial investigations had focused on searching for unexplained fragments in the debris that might have represented explosive devices or sabotage, and upon analyzing remnants of equipment for evidence of the cause of the explosion. Based upon information supplied by shipboard personnel, fragmentary evidence from the compartment was reanalyzed and confirmed that pieces of *two* controller units for the power transfer junction were present.' This report confirms that by Saturday 19 September a spare *was* on board the USS *Michaelson*." Carr tapped her data pad a few times. "Lieutenant Bristol, I have displayed here a picture of the package for a controller spare. Do you recognize it?"

"Yes, ma'am."

"Why?"

"Because I share, I mean I *shared* a stateroom with Lieutenant Silver. On Friday night, Lieutenant Silver had a package like that under his desk."

"Friday night 18 September?"

"Yes, ma'am."

Paul couldn't hide his surprise. *I never thought of asking Mike about that. But it makes sense. Where else would Silver have kept the part until Saturday?*

"You didn't comment on it?"

"No, ma'am. There's not a lot of storage space on the ship. If parts get drawn but need to be stowed for a few hours, it's not unusual at all for officers to park the parts in their staterooms."

"Lieutenant Silver had the part on Friday night. When did you notice the part gone?"

Mike Bristol twisted the corner of his mouth. "I know it was there when I went to sleep. I'm pretty sure it was there in the morning."

"Then Lieutenant Silver had it overnight before providing it to Chief Asher."

"Yes, ma'am."

"No more questions."

Lieutenant Commander Jones took up position directly in front of Mike Bristol. "Lieutenant, are you certain the box you saw under Lieutenant Silver's desk was that part?"

"Yes, sir."

"You couldn't have been mistaken? It couldn't have been something close to that part's package in appearance?"

Mike Bristol shook his head. "No, sir. I work with spares a lot, and Commander Sykes, he's my boss, he says I need to be able to look at a box and know what's in it. I pay attention to boxes, sir."

"You said you were 'pretty sure' the box was there the next morning. You're not certain?"

"I can't claim to be one hundred percent certain, sir. But I'm 90 percent sure."

"Is being 90 percent sure you have the part needed to fix something the same as being one hundred percent sure?"

Mike Bristol flushed slightly. "No, sir."

"No more questions."

Then came Lieutenant Fung, the officer from the station supply office. Yes, the part had been drawn late on Friday afternoon. Yes, it had definitely been Lieutenant Silver. "He had this big sob story. I really don't remember why I agreed to let him draw the part. He's really persuasive, I guess."

Commander Carr nodded. "Then Lieutenant Silver got the part without requesting an emergency parts draw, which would have required his Captain's signature?"

"That's right, ma'am."

"At what time did Lieutenant Silver receive the spare controller?"

"According to our database, the part was logged out at 1630."

"1630? Then Lieutenant Silver had the part as of 1630 on Friday 18 September?"

"That's right, ma'am."

"Which, as a petty officer from the *Michaelson* previously testified, is at least half an hour prior to knock-off ship's work. Thank you."

Lieutenant Commander Jones shook his head. "No questions."

Judge Halstead consulted his watch. "I'm aware that line officers have a tendency to work through meals, but since this is my courtroom, we will break for lunch. The court-martial is closed and will reconvene at 1300 in this court-room."

"All rise!" Paul and the others in the courtroom came to attention as Judge Halstead and the members filed out through their respective doors. "Carry on. Court will reconvene at 1300."

Commander Carr sank back into her chair, then swiveled in it to look at Paul. "That didn't go too badly."

Paul nodded. "It sure isn't making Silver look very good."

"Ah, but we not only have to make him *look* bad, we have to convince those five officers that he *did* bad."

"Did you deliberately set up Lieutenant Commander Jones to ask that question of Petty Officer Shape?"

Carr grinned. "You caught that, huh? You may have the makings of a lawyer, Mr. Sinclair. Yes. It served two purposes. Having Sharpe say Chief Asher was upset over something out of the normal in response to the defense counsel's question gave the answer more force since no one expected it. It also made Commander Jones a bit gun-shy with the next few witnesses, since he's worried about me ambushing him again."

"How much could Commander Jones have done against Mike Bristol and the other supply lieutenant? Their testimony was pretty straightforward."

Carr's grin turned knowing. "A good lawyer, if that term's not an oxymoron, can make any witness look bad. Exactly what time did it happen? There aren't any other boxes that look exactly like that one? Are you positive Silver is the man who picked up the part? Could it have been Chief Asher? Etc., etc., and so on. Besides, my knowledge of line officers is that they don't place a lot of credence in what supply officers tell them. Right?"

Paul smiled. "I'm afraid so, but that doesn't apply to Mike Bristol."

"Great. But those members of the court don't know Bristol personally. Those two supply officers would have been the easiest witnesses for the defense counsel to discredit on the stand in the eyes of the members of the court. But defense counsel held back because he thought I might have laid another mine in his path."

"It sounds like you're into strategy and tactics as much as line officers are, ma'am."

"Why not? We're both out for the kill. Metaphorically speaking in my case, of course, since the charges against Silver don't merit the death penalty. I'll see you at 1300."

Paul left the courtroom trying to decide where to eat lunch, but to his surprise found someone waiting for him. "Jen? How'd you get off your ship?"

She smiled. "I walked. After I convinced my department head I could really use some time ashore. Interested in lunch?"

"You bet. We've got 'til 1300."

"I've got less than that. I have to be back on the *Sorry Maury* by 1230."

"Okay. Quick lunch. Let's hit some vending machines."

Paul filled Jen in on the events of the morning, then spread his hands. "I wish I knew what the members of the court were thinking."

"I know what *I'd* be thinking. Do you ever get the feeling Silver's been coasting on being an admiral's son?"

"The thought had crossed my mind. I've also been wondering how much being a Navy officer was really his idea in the first place. He sure doesn't act like he wants the job."

"You may be right, especially with a daddy like Vice Admiral Silver, who might've just expected his son to follow in the family footsteps. Or else." Jen looked away, her face troubled. "Speaking of fathers, I do have some news you need to know. My father's been tapped as a defense witness."

"Oh, great." *I'll be sitting there looking at Captain Shen staring at me from the witness stand as he answers questions about whether or not Lieutenant Silver's to blame for that accident.* "And my Captain wants me in that courtroom."

"Captains in front of you and Captains behind you. I'd dodge, if I was you."

Paul laughed briefly. "Immediate evasive maneuvers! Brace for collision!"

"Abandon ship?"

"No, I think I'm supposed to go down with it."

"How do you go down with a spaceship?" Jen asked. "Unless you're in a gravity well."

"I'll let you know. Does this mean you've talked to your father?"

"Uh-uh. Strictly intelligence collection using secondary but reliable sources. Speaking of intelligence collection, how are you and that hot little commander getting along?"

Paul frowned. "You mean Commander Carr? She's way out of my league, Jen, even if I wasn't taken. How would I ask a commander on a date?"

"Oh, you've wondered about how to do that, huh?" Jen giggled. "I'm just teasing. The commander's married, in case you haven't noticed the ring."

"No, I guess I hadn't. I haven't really looked at her that much—"

"Uh-huh. Sure. But I'll pretend to believe you."

Before Paul knew it, Jen had to head back for the *Maury*. He was halfway back to the courtroom himself before he realized Jen's bantering had driven thoughts of the trial from his mind for a while. *Thanks, Jen.*

CHAPTER ELEVEN

☆　☆　☆　☆　☆

THE first prosecution witness called after lunch was the first to be wearing civilian clothes. "Special Agent Sullivan, you are assigned to the staff of the fleet commander as a representative of the Naval Criminal Investigative Service?"

Sullivan nodded as he answered. "Yes, I am."

"Did you conduct a search of the stateroom formerly occupied by Lieutenant Silver on board the USS *Michaelson*?"

"I did, along with Special Agent Connally."

"Can you summarize your findings?"

Sullivan nodded again, then consulted his own data pad. "Most of the material belonging to Lieutenant Silver in that stateroom was of a personal nature. Clothes, toiletries, that sort of thing. We found twenty-two data coins, of which eighteen contained various professional and personal files along with computer games, music, and assorted other software. Four of the coins were totally blank."

"Excuse me, Special Agent Sullivan. Totally blank?"

Another nod. "Yes. Not unused, because then they'd have had all the formatting on them. They'd been scrubbed clean. Nothing was recoverable on them."

"The data on them had been deleted, then."

"No. If it'd been deleted, we could've recovered it. These had been wiped by software designed to render the contents unrecoverable."

"Did you find that particular software?"

"No. It wasn't in the stateroom."

"What else did you find?"

Sullivan consulted his data pad again. "One of the larger drawers assigned to Lieutenant Silver contained a quantity of unopened official mail for the Main Propulsion officer."

"Unopened?"

"Yes. Stuff like software updates for systems, safety advisories, technical manual updates and revisions, that sort of thing."

Paul stole another glance at the members. This time he caught Captain Mashiko's brow lowering in a sign of disapproval. *Let's see Scott Silver explain that.*

"Lieutenant Silver hadn't been opening his official mail and passing on the material in it to his personnel or entering it into the engineering system?"

"No. We found no trace of opened official mail. You know, envelopes that hadn't been discarded, contents of opened mail in the files or drawers, that sort of thing."

"I see. Anything else, Special Agent Sullivan?"

"Lieutenant Silver's data terminal contained numerous pieces of personal software. Mainly games. That's unauthorized, but it's not all that unusual on ships."

"Thank you, Special Agent Sullivan. No more questions."

Lieutenant Commander Jones didn't bother getting up. "No questions."

"I have some questions," Captain Mashiko stated. "Special Agent Sullivan, this unopened mail in Lieutenant Silver's stateroom. It was in a drawer?"

"That's right."

"How was it stored in there? Filed neatly?"

Sullivan twisted his face in thought, then shook his head. "No. It looked like it'd just been tossed in."

"How old was the oldest unopened mail?"

"Let's see." Sullivan checked his data pad. "The oldest date was 22 August."

Mashiko looked as if he were tasting something unpleasant. "According to the charges, Lieutenant Silver assumed duties as the Main Propulsion assistant on the *Michaelson* on 20 August. Is that correct, Commander Carr?"

"Yes, sir."

"Special Agent Sullivan, what sort of games did you find on Lieutenant Silver's terminal?"

Sullivan consulted his data pad again. "I can list them by title if you want. Essentially, they were all action games. Twitch and shoot stuff."

Paul felt like smiling, but repressed it. *Shoot 'em up games are common enough on the ship, but the existence of lots of those games alongside unopened official mail creates a strong image of an officer playing games instead of doing his job. Which matches what I know about Scott Silver. Dammit, I shouldn't be taking any pleasure in this. Besides, even if that convinces Captain Mashiko to vote for conviction on the charge of dereliction in performance of his duties, that still leaves all the other charges against Silver and the rest of the members to convince. If I know anything about Herdez, she's wishing she could get Scott Silver alone for twenty minutes while she reamed him out for not doing his job. But what about the rest?*

Captain Mashiko cast a long look toward the defense table. "The members have no more questions."

Paul knew the next prosecution witness, even though he wasn't from the *Michaelson*.

"If the court pleases," Commander Carr asked, "trial counsel would like to stipulate that Chief Warrant Officer Rose is one of the top software engineers on Franklin Station, and in the Navy as a whole."

Judge Halstead gave Rose a skeptical look. "I might agree to so stipulate if Warrant Rose can fix my case management software so it doesn't lock up almost every time I try to update my files."

Rose looked up at the judge. "Milcourt version 9.5, sir? I can fix that."

"See me after the trial. Does defense counsel have any objection to the stipulation?"

Lieutenant Commander Jones shook his head. "No, Your Honor. Warrant Officer Rose's qualifications are known to me."

"Then the court stipulates that Chief Warrant Officer Rose is an expert software engineer."

Commander Carr nodded to acknowledge the ruling. "Thank you, Your Honor. Warrant Officer Rose, during the evening of 19 September the engineering logs on the USS *Michaelson* were so severely damaged that no data could be recovered from them. Have you examined those logs?"

"Yes, ma'am, I have."

"What was your conclusion?"

"The damage to the logs was caused by a hacking program whose name I've provided to the court but otherwise prefer to keep confidential. It's very hard to detect when this program has been used, but it leaves a couple of markers for those who know where and how to look."

"You're saying the damage to the engineering logs was deliberate."

"Absolutely, ma'am."

Paul glanced over at the members to see how they were taking Rose's testimony. He couldn't decipher the poker faces they were wearing, but they were definitely all paying very close attention. Paul shifted his gaze to defense table, where Lieutenant Silver displayed every appearance of being horrified by the revelation.

"Could you tell the time frame in which the engineering logs were deliberately damaged?"

"Yes, ma'am. The hacking program activated at 2235."

"At 2235 on the evening of 19 September." Carr looked directly at the members. "According to previous testimony, Lieutenant Silver's presence could not be accounted for from about 2200 to about 2300 that evening. Was Lieutenant Silver logged on to the *Michaelson*'s system when the damage occurred?"

"Yes, ma'am."

"Objection." Jones pointed to the witness. "Warrant Officer Rose can only testify to what he knows, which is that someone using Lieutenant Silver's account and password was logged on at that time."

Commander Carr nodded. "Defense counsel is correct. I'll restate the question. Warrant Officer Rose, was someone using Lieutenant Silver's account and password logged onto the *Michaelson*'s system when the damage occurred?"

"Yes, ma'am."

"This hacking program you described. How would someone acquire it?"

"Off the 'net, ma'am. Anyone can find stuff like that if they look for it, which is why I don't want to name the program here."

"Warrant Officer Rose, four data coins in Lieutenant Silver's stateroom had been rendered unreadable. Are you familiar with software that does this?"

Rose shrugged. "Ma'am, there's a number of programs out there that can do that."

"Where would you get them?"

Another shrug. "You can buy them, like the government does. We use that type of software to wipe hard drives or data coins that are being disposed of. But there are a number of versions available free on the 'net as well."

"The ability to render data unreadable, then, while still allowing the coin to be reused in the future, requires software for that purpose."

"Of course."

"Then Lieutenant Silver must have had such software in his possession."

"At one time, yes, ma'am."

"Warrant Officer Rose, you're responsible for updating fleet guidance on software that is allowed on military and government systems. Is software capable of rendering data unreadable authorized?"

"Not unless it's the government's program, and only system administrators are supposed to have that one." Rose shook his head and looked weary. "Let the average user get his or her hands on that stuff, and they'll destroy critical data or wipe their hard drives without knowing what they're doing. Users do enough damage without allowing them to have software *designed* to cause damage."

"Thank you, Warrant Officer Rose. No more questions."

Lieutenant Commander Jones stood up but stayed at the defense table. "Warrant Officer Rose, I'd just like to clarify a few points. Is there any evidence you are aware of directly tying Lieutenant Silver to the destruction of the data in the engineering logs?"

"You mean something with his name on it, sir? No, sir."

"Is there any evidence Lieutenant Silver actually possessed the program that did that damage?"

"I'm not aware that anyone found that program in his possession, no, sir."

"Warrant, do you ever have data on file that you'd prefer no one else ever saw? Personal matters, perhaps?"

Rose grinned. "Everybody does, sir."

"Then even if Lieutenant Silver had somehow used unauthorized software to render the four data coins found in his stateroom unreadable, that doesn't mean whatever information those coins once contained bears on the charges against Lieutenant Silver, does it? Those coins could've contained anything."

"Yes, sir, they could've. We have no way of knowing. Unreadable means unreadable."

"I'd also like you to restate one point, Warrant Officer Rose. If the system shows an individual was logged on at a certain time, that doesn't prove that person was the one who logged in, does it?"

Rose shook his head, looking annoyed. "No, it doesn't. People are too careless with passwords."

Paul tried not to show his dismay. *Jones zeroed right in on the weakness of the case against Silver there. We know someone did it, but we can only infer it was Silver. There's no way to prove it, even though it's easy to speculate one of those unreadable coins once contained the program that allowed Silver to damage the engineering logs.*

"No further questions."

"Does trial counsel wish to redirect?" Judge Halstead asked.

"Yes, Your Honor," Commander Carr stood, though also remaining at her table. "Warrant Officer Rose, we have established that a spare controller for the power transfer junction was present with Chief Asher in Forward Engineering. The chief engineer of the USS *Michaelson* has already testified that it required authorization codes from an officer and an enlisted to disable the safety interlocks on engineering equipment. Would those authorizations, and who entered them, have been recorded in the engineering logs?"

"No question. Yes, ma'am."

"Then by destroying the data in the engineering logs, whoever committed that act ensured we could not identify that officer, the officer within the Engineering Department of the USS *Michaelson*, who provided an authorization to disable the safety interlocks."

"That's correct, ma'am."

"How often are the engineering logs backed up, Warrant Officer Rose?"

"Once a week at midnight, ma'am. The process is automatic."

"Once a week at midnight. They're backed up to a separate storage area?"

"Yes, ma'am."

"Then it's reasonable to conclude that whoever destroyed those records was attempting to conceal something that had occurred within the last few days, isn't it?"

"Yes, ma'am, it is."

"No more questions."

Captain Mashiko leaned forward. "Warrant Rose, is there any other possible explanation for the damage to those logs? You are positive the damage was deliberate and caused by destructive software?"

"Yes, sir, I am."

"Do you know why this deliberate destruction was not detected in the initial investigation?"

Rose looked a bit uncomfortable as he answered. "Sir, not all experts are created equal. I know the sailor who checked for the cause of the data loss for the initial investigation. He's not bad, he's really very good, but he's not as experienced as some other people. Like I said earlier, you need to know exactly what to look for to spot the evidence that this software had been used."

"And the investigation's expert didn't know what to look for."

"He does now, sir."

Captain Mashiko smiled for a moment. "Thank you, Warrant."

Paul watched Rose leave, exchanging brief nods as Rose walked out of the courtroom. *Clever. Carr could've brought out that stuff about the interlock authorization and the recent time period during her first questioning of Rose, but she waited so she'd have something else to toss in front of the members after the defense counsel brought up the lack of evidence proving Silver did the damage.*

Commander Carr stood. "The prosecution has one more witness. Captain Richard Hayes, commanding officer of the USS *Michaelson*."

Paul stared at her, then looked toward the back of the courtroom as Captain Hayes came walking down the aisle. *Why the hell didn't somebody tell* me *my Captain was testifying?*

After Hayes had been sworn in, Commander Carr took her usual position in front of the witness stand. "Captain Hayes, on the night of 19 September 2100, you were paged to return to your ship."

"That's right. I was informed there'd been an explosion and a fire, which was still being fought at that time."

"Who informed you of that, Captain? Who paged you?"

"Chief Petty Officer Imari, the in-port officer of the deck."

"Did you speak with Lieutenant Silver at that time, sir?"

"No. I assumed he was engaged with dealing with the shipboard emergency."

"You then returned to the ship."

"Yes. As fast as possible." Hayes's face had grown progressively grimmer, apparently because of recalling the events of that evening.

"What did you find on the quarterdeck?"

"Chief Petty Officer Imari was fielding calls and information, and relaying those to Lieutenant Silver."

"Then Lieutenant Silver briefed you on the current situation, sir?"

Captain Hayes frowned. "He tried when I told him to, but he didn't seem to have a handle on a lot of things. General impressions, but few details. I finally told Chief Imari to give me a rundown."

"Can you give an example of this lack of detail on Lieutenant Silver's part?"

"Certainly. The, uh, teams sent to assist us from other ships. All Silver could tell me was that some had come aboard. Chief Imari told me what ships they'd come from and what they were doing. She knew the *Midway*'s people were setting up a temporary airlock to assist our own Damage Control team, for example."

"Did Lieutenant Silver tell you the accident had taken place in Forward Engineering?"

"I didn't need him to tell me that. Chief Imari told me when she paged me."

"Did Lieutenant Silver tell you a piece of equipment in Forward Engineering wasn't operating properly?"

"No."

"Did Lieutenant Silver tell you he'd acquired a spare for that piece of equipment and passed it on to Chief Asher?"

"No."

Paul felt like flinching every time Captain Hayes bit off a reply. Each "no" came out harder. *I do not want to be chewed out by this man. I'm sure I will be someday, but now I know it's not going to be any fun.*

"Did Lieutenant Silver then or later tell you that Chief Asher could have been in Forward Engineering, working on that piece of equipment?"

"No."

"Did Lieutenant Silver then or later inform you that he knew of a possible cause or contributing factor to the explosion, and the likely reason for Chief Asher's presence there?"

"No."

"Objection." Jones looked toward Carr. "Trial counsel is covering the same ground repeatedly."

Judge Halstead looked questioningly at Commander Carr. "I tend to agree. Counsel?"

Carr smiled in a professionally courteous way. "I had just finished going over those points, Your Honor."

"The objection is sustained. Get on with it."

"Yes, Your Honor. Captain Hayes, at any point were you approached regarding the need to acquire a spare controller for the power transfer junction in Forward Engineering?"

"No, I was not."

"Sir, were you informed the ship could not get underway as scheduled on the next Monday because of a problem with equipment in Forward Engineering?"

"No."

"When did you first discover that problem existed?"

"In the course of an internal investigation I authorized to resolve some new information regarding the events of 19 September."

"At that time you were informed of the problem by Engineering personnel?"

"No. I was informed of the problem by an officer outside of Engineering."

"Do you, sir, as commanding officer of the USS *Michaelson*, believe you received complete and accurate information from Lieutenant Silver on the evening of 19 September?"

Hayes looked directly at Silver, who looked away quickly. "At this point in time I do not believe I have ever received complete and accurate information from Lieutenant Silver. As for the night of 19 September, I have no doubt that Lieutenant Silver deliberately chose to withhold critical information from me."

"Then Lieutenant Silver no longer has your trust and confidence?"

"I never want him on my ship again. I never want him in any position of responsibility in the U.S. Navy again."

"Thank you, Captain Hayes. No further questions."

Lieutenant Commander Jones had a determined look on

his face as he approached the witness stand, as if he were bracing himself for battle. "Captain Hayes, how long had you been commanding officer of the USS *Michaelson* as of 19 September?"

"About a month."

"Only a month? That's a short time to learn all there is to know about a ship and its crew, isn't it, sir?"

Hayes smiled crookedly. "It's a challenge."

"Are there things you still don't know about the ship?"

"You'll have to clarify that question. If you mean I don't know every single thing there is to know, then of course that's true. If you're asking if there's anything important I haven't learned, I doubt it."

"Is it possible, sir, that you could have been informed about the problem with the power transfer junction in Forward Engineering and, in the midst of so much else to do and to learn, misplaced that information?"

Hayes's eyes narrowed. "No."

"Sir, by your own admission, there are still some things—"

"*No*, Commander. The status of that piece of equipment was critical to my ship being able to accomplish her mission. I would *not* have forgotten it."

Commander Jones eyed Hayes for a moment as if deciding whether to pursue the point or not. His next question revealed he'd decided to try another tack. "Captain Hayes, you earlier indicated you were told about the problem with the power transfer junction by an officer on your ship. Who was that officer?"

Commander Carr was on her feet. "Objection, Your Honor. The question is immaterial."

Jones faced Judge Halstead. "Your Honor, I am attempting to establish possible prejudice."

Halstead raised one eyebrow. "By whom? Captain Hayes?"

"No, sir, by this other officer."

"Your Honor," Commander Carr stated, stepping forward, "the identity of that officer is irrelevant to this trial. We've already established that the information regarding the power transfer junction was factual. Why does it matter who reported it?"

"Your Honor, evidence tainted is evidence that is inadmissible in court."

Judge Halstead bared his teeth in a humorless smile. "Counsel, I'll be the one deciding what is and is not inadmissible."

Jones hesitated as if regretting his last statement. "I'm sorry, Your Honor. That is true, and I did not mean to imply otherwise."

"Thank you, Counsel. Does the counsel for the defense intend offering proof of bias, proof that some evidence introduced is in fact inadmissible?"

Paul watched the argument with an icy feeling in his gut. *They're arguing about me. Am I going to get ripped apart on that witness stand, my motivations and own professionalism subjected to trick questions and negative interpretations? I knew I ran a risk of this. I can handle it if it comes to that. But I really hope Carr wins this argument.*

Jones nodded with every appearance of confidence. "Yes, Your Honor."

Commander Carr let skepticism show. "Your Honor, if counsel for the defense had such proof, why did he wait until now to introduce this line of argument? After trial counsel has entered so much evidence into the trial?"

"Good question, Counsel. Commander Jones?"

Jones looked back at Halstead confidently. "Your Honor, defense actions evolve as the trial proceeds. Surely trial counsel will not dispute that, or the right of the defense to introduce new issues in the course of defending the accused."

"Your Honor, a fishing expedition is not introducing new issues. It is a distraction from the business of the court-martial."

"Your Honor, if trial counsel is so certain of the tactics and questions to be pursued by the defense, I would respectfully have to inquire as to the source of her information."

Paul tried not to openly wince. *That's a real good point.*

Jones is better than I gave him credit for. But Carr's supposed to know him! Keep me off that witness stand, Commander.

Judge Halstead raised the fingers on one hand to halt the argument between the counsels. "You've both brought up legitimate arguments. I will allow defense counsel to pursue his line of questioning, but if defense Counsel attempts to divert this court-martial from its course or engage in a prolonged fishing expedition, I *will* bring it to a halt. Is that clear, Counsel?"

Jones nodded. "Yes, Your Honor."

"Objection overruled. Proceed, Counsel."

Commander Carr returned to her seat, tight-lipped, and gave Paul a passing glance, her eyes conveying regret for a moment.

Commander Jones went back to the witness stand, where Captain Hayes had sat watching the byplay impatiently. "Captain, I repeat, who brought this information to your attention?"

"My collateral duty ship's legal officer."

"And who is that, Captain?"

"Lieutenant Junior Grade Sinclair."

"Thank you, Captain. No further questions."

Paul stared at Jones, then back at Commander Carr, who gave Jones's back a hard, questioning look. *Jones went to all that trouble just to ask my name? There's got to be more to this. I wonder what?*

Captain Mashiko nodded in greeting to Captain Hayes. "Captain, Lieutenant Silver has earned promotions to his current grade, indicating good performance evaluations. How do you reconcile that with your current opinion of Lieutenant Silver's performance?"

Captain Hayes shook his head. "Captain, I don't know what Lieutenant Silver did in his earlier assignments. All I know is what he did on my ship. I regard that as more than sufficient grounds for reaching my conclusions."

"I'm assuming you thought long and hard before reaching these conclusions?"

"Yes, of course I did."

Commander Herdez spoke next. "Captain Hayes, as commanding officer, have you toured every compartment on the USS *Michaelson* since coming aboard?"

"Yes, Commander, I have."

"How many times have you visited Forward Engineering?"

Hayes frowned in thought. "I'd say two or three times, at least."

"Then you have visited that compartment at least as many times as Lieutenant Silver, the officer who holds primary responsibility for it?"

"That seems to be right, Commander."

"Captain Hayes, have you observed Lieutenant Silver performing other professional duties on your ship?"

"Yes, I have."

"Which duties, sir?"

"Officer of the deck underway, command duty officer in port."

"What are your opinions of Lieutenant Silver's performance in those duties?"

Captain Hayes frowned again. "As officer of the deck underway, Lieutenant Silver displayed passivity."

"Can you explain that, sir?"

"Sure. Whenever we had a special evolution, Lieutenant Silver would delegate it to his junior officer of the deck. Whenever he needed detailed information, he'd have to get that information from his junior officer of the deck or another watch stander. And he was habitually late in assuming the watch."

Paul fought down another grin. *I'll be damned. Hayes noticed how Silver was doing his job on the bridge. Just like Carl Meadows said. You don't think he's watching, but he is.*

"And as command duty officer in port, sir?"

Hayes shrugged. "Prior to 19 September, on those few days in which Lieutenant Silver stood CDO, I was unaware of any problems. As I already noted, on 19 September he didn't have a handle on the situation."

Lieutenant Commander Bryko licked his lips before speaking. "Captain Hayes, Lieutenant Silver received a

Navy Commendation Medal for his handling of the events of 19 September. Why did he get recommended for that medal if you had such a negative opinion of his performance?"

Hayes's face reddened slightly, and his voice tightened. "I don't know."

"You didn't recommend or approve the award?"

"The recommendation for that award did not originate on my ship."

Bryko looked surprised. "Did you even know Lieutenant Silver had been recommended for that medal, sir?"

"No, I did not. If I had been aware, I would have done all I could to block it."

"Can I ask exactly why, sir?"

"Given what I knew then, I didn't feel Lieutenant Silver's performance rated an award."

"Thank you, Captain."

Judge Halstead checked his watch after Captain Hayes had been dismissed. "Does trial counsel have further witnesses?"

Commander Carr stood. "No, Your Honor. The prosecution rests."

"Then this court-martial is closed. It will reconvene at 1000 tomorrow morning in this same courtroom for the presentation of evidence by the defense."

Paul stood with the others, stretching muscles he hadn't realized were tense. Commander Carr stood at the trial counsel's table for a moment, both hands resting on the desktop as if she needed the support, then turned to face Paul and smiled. Paul smiled back. "That seemed to go real well."

"It went okay. Not perfect, but you work with what you've got." Commander Carr stretched as well.

Paul, sensitized to Carr's appearance by Jen's teasing, tried not to notice the way her body moved. *As if I need that distraction on top of everything else. And with a superior officer no less.* "Do you think they'll put Silver on the stand tomorrow?"

Carr finished flexing her back muscles and relaxed. "Ah,

now that's a good question. On the one hand, anything Silver says could look bad, like he's making excuses for being such a screwup at his job. On the other hand, good ol' Scott Silver is a consummate actor and may try to charm the members of the court into submission."

"You don't think he'll make a sworn statement, do you?"

Carr snorted. "No chance in hell. The little bastard's guilty, and they know if I get to cross-examine him, I'll tear his entrails out and let the members read the proof of his guilt in them."

"He'd probably take the Fifth—"

"Yeah, yeah, yeah." Carr paused. "Wasn't there a song like that a long time ago? Anyway, you and I know that taking the Fifth Amendment as grounds for refusal to self-incriminate is not ever, no way, supposed to be used as a presumption of guilt. You and I also know that just about everybody thinks anyone taking the Fifth is guilty, no matter what instructions they get from the judge. Otherwise, why do they refuse to talk? Unfair or not, that's the way it is. As defense counsel, I'd know that minefield was waiting for me, and there's no way to sweep it, though if you're really good and really lucky, you can navigate through it without getting your butt blown off. As trial counsel, I think that universally assumed presumption of guilt is great."

"Why do you think Commander Jones went to all that trouble to get my name introduced into evidence, but then didn't do anything with it?"

"Obviously, he's *planning* to do something with it."

Paul felt the ice in his guts again. "Will I get called as a witness?"

"No." Alex Carr shook her head for emphasis. "If Lieutenant Commander Jones had any intention of doing that, he'd have moved to have you excluded from the courtroom. No, I think he'll try to attack you indirectly. Undermine our evidence by raising questions about how it was obtained, about whether someone else could have been motivated to set up Silver. He doesn't have to convince the members you actually did the dirty deeds. All Commander Jones has to do is create sufficient doubt in the members' minds that Silver did it."

"Oh." Paul exhaled heavily. "I hope he doesn't manage that."

"It's my job to make sure he doesn't, and I'm going to bend every effort to ensure Lieutenant Scott Silver's head is mounted on my trophy wall in the very near future."

Paul started to laugh at the image, then sobered. "You really do believe he's guilty?"

"That's *also* my job, Paul. You can be as ambivalent as you want to be, now. The outcome's in the hands of the judge, the members, Commander Jones, and me."

Paul nodded. *Starting a court-martial's a fire-and-forget weapon. Without any recall capability. Set it on the target, watch it go, and hope like hell the target deserves to get hit. What was that saying? "Cry havoc and let slip the dogs of war." You don't control them once you've set them loose. You just get to watch them do their work.* "I'm not ambivalent about his guilt, either, ma'am. I just wish it hadn't come to this."

"If it all-too-often didn't come to this, I'd be out of a job. Unfortunately, I have the best job security in the world."

Captain Hayes was waiting for Paul outside the courtroom. Paul felt another knot form in his gut, wondering how long he'd kept his Captain waiting, but Hayes just indicated Paul should walk with him as they returned to the *Michaelson*. "How'd it go in there today? What can you tell me now?"

"Sir, there's not a lot I can tell you now. Not if you're also a witness."

"Okay. I understand that. Damned nuisance, but it's worth it to make sure Silver gets his."

Paul launched into a general recital of the day's events, speaking carefully to ensure he didn't veer into specifics. When he reached Commander Destin's appearance as a witness, Paul felt an even greater reluctance to talk. *How am I supposed to critically report on the performance of an officer senior to me? You don't do that. At least, you're not supposed to do that.*

Hayes gave him another look. "That's all you can tell me about Commander Destin's testimony? You pretty much just said she showed up."

Paul felt sweat starting under his uniform. "Sir, I'd be commenting on the behavior of a senior to another senior."

"You would, wouldn't you?" Hayes looked forward for a moment, then nodded. "Fair enough. Any idea what the defense is up to?"

"Commander Carr thinks they'll try to discredit the evidence."

"That doesn't take a lawyer to figure out."

"No, sir."

"Any idea why that guy made me name you?"

"Not for sure, sir."

"Keep your guard up."

The *Michaelson*'s quarterdeck loomed ahead. Captain Hayes boarded the ship, returning the officer of the deck's salute as the petty officer of the watch struck the ship's bell four times in two pairs of bongs, then announced over the all-hands circuit "USS *Michaelson*, arriving."

Paul followed Hayes across the brow, saluting the officer of the deck. Ensign Gabriel returned the salute, along with a questioning look. "Can you talk about it?"

"Yes and no."

"Man, if you keep hanging out with lawyers, we'll never get a straight answer out of you."

Paul grinned. "Ouch. That hurt."

"Don't tell Lieutenant Shen about it, then. I hear she's fiercely protective."

The joking statement aroused mixed emotions in Paul. *On the one hand, I like knowing Jen'll defend me. But on the other, I can fight my own battles.* "Hey, I can be pretty fierce, too."

Gabriel unsuccessfully tried to smother a laugh. "Paul, I like working with you. I'm sure I'd like working *for* you. But not because you're fierce."

"I'll take that as a compliment." Paul waved farewell and headed for his stateroom. *First I need to check what came in that I have to deal with, then I'll call Chief Imari for a run-*

down on how things are going on the ship. He turned a corner, squeezing around two sailors working on a piece of equipment that had been helpfully installed in an almost inaccessible spot, and found himself facing Commander Garcia at the other end of the passageway.

Commander Garcia's expression couldn't be made out for certain, but he hooked some fingers toward Paul in a "come here" gesture. *Oh, great. Now what? Chief Imari didn't give me a heads-up on any problems.* "Yes, sir?"

Garcia gave Paul one his usual demanding looks. "You just get back?"

"Yes, sir."

"How's it going over there, Sinclair?"

"You mean in the court, sir?"

"Yeah, I mean in the court. Does it look like he'll get convicted?"

Paul tried to think through his reply. *Does Garcia like Silver? I don't remember Garcia ever talking about him. What answer does Garcia want? I can't even guess, and in any case what else can I tell him but the truth as I see it?* "I'm not sure, sir. The members of the court are hard to read. They've asked some questions that imply they're not happy with what they're hearing about Lieutenant Silver, but I can't tell if they're unhappy enough to vote for conviction on any of the charges."

"What about Commander Herdez?"

"She looks like she always did, sir. Not missing a thing and keeping her thoughts to herself. I wouldn't want her judging me if I was Lieutenant Silver, though."

"Neither would I. That prosecutor. How's she doing?"

"She's very good, sir."

"Good." Garcia seemed to be trying to decide whether or not to say more. "Sinclair, I'm not happy you get involved in distractions like this. You're supposed to be working for me. But if Silver did even half of what he's charged with, then I'm damned glad he's off this ship. And I want I him to pay for what he did to that chief. You and that prosecutor better make damned sure Silver doesn't come back. You understand?"

"We're doing our best, sir."

"That better be good enough." Garcia turned to go, then looked back for a moment. "Thanks, Sinclair."

"Yes, sir." Paul, his mouth hanging open, watched Garcia walk away. The words "thanks, Sinclair" were the closest Garcia had ever come to praising Paul's work.

The rest of the day passed in a blur. Paul normally had about a day and a half's worth of work to do on any given day, so trying to get that all accomplished in a couple of hours made for an even more hectic pace than usual. Knockoff ship's work and then liberty call passed with Paul barely noticing. Jen came aboard to chat, saw how busy he was, and kept her visit very short, but also insisted on dragging him to the wardroom to for-god's-sake eat something for dinner. Paul eyed his meal dubiously, wondering if Suppo had somehow managed to slip another serving of Syrian beef stew past the captain, but managed to eat some of it.

He did take time to walk Jen to the quarterdeck afterward. "See you tomorrow?"

"No can do. I've got duty. It looks like you won't be visiting me, either."

"I think I can catch up. It sort of depends on what happens tomorrow."

"My father's going to be there tomorrow?"

"Yeah. No doubt of that."

"He respects it when you fight back, Paul."

"I'm not going into battle, Jen."

"Yes, you are. Be brave, my warrior." She giggled again. "I can't believe I'm joking about this."

"Me, neither."

"Oh, Paul, you'll comport yourself in the highest traditions of the Naval Service, yada, yada, yada."

"Yada back to you. Good night, Jen."

"I prefer saying that when we're sleeping in the same bed." She looked carefully in all directions, then seeing no witnesses, leaned up and gave Paul a quick kiss. "See you tomorrow, or the day after. Hang in there."

"That I know I can do. Love you, Jen."

"Ah, you say that to all your girlfriends."

Paul watched her leave, then walked slowly back to his stateroom. *Hang in there. I guess that's the secret of life. Only I won't settle for just hanging in there where Silver's concerned. Commander Carr is right. We've got to nail him.* After Paul finally got to bed, he spent a long time twisting and turning restlessly, his mind filled with questions about what Commander Jones might do the next day in defense of Silver.

CHAPTER TWELVE

☆ ☆ ☆ ☆ ☆

"THE defense calls as its first witness Captain Kay Shen, United States Navy, commanding officer of the USS *Mahan*." Captain Shen marched to the witness stand and took the seat as if he were striding to the Captain's chair on the bridge of his ship. He glanced at the members' table, nodded very slightly toward Captain Mashiko, then looked straight ahead. If he took notice of Paul's presence in the courtroom, he didn't acknowledge it in any way.

Lieutenant Commander Jones adopted a similar rigidly correct stance as he stood before Captain Shen, matching the formality of his witness. "Captain Shen, you conducted the official investigation into the explosion and fire in Forward Engineering on the USS *Michaelson* on 19 September 2100. Is that correct?"

Captain Shen nodded once. "That's correct."

"Captain Shen, can you briefly describe your experience with warships that qualified you to conduct this investigation?"

"Certainly." Captain Shen glanced around as if ensuring everyone was paying attention. "I am currently commanding officer of the USS *Mahan*. Prior to that, I served as executive officer of the USS *Midway*. Before that, I was chief engineer on the USS *Rickover*, and Main Propulsion assistant on the USS *Belleau Wood*. I've also served on the staff of Commander Naval Space Forces, the staff of Commander in Chief United States Space Forces, and as an instructor at Space Warfare School."

"Thank you, Captain Shen. Now will you summarize your conclusions from your investigation?"

"Briefly, I found no evidence of misconduct."

"No evidence of misconduct on anyone's part?"

"That's right."

"Including Lieutenant Silver, sir?"

"Correct."

"Did you reach any other conclusions regarding the performance of the officers and crew on the USS *Michaelson*?"

"I found no deliberate or willful failures, but did identify a number of training and procedural deficiencies that may have contributed to the accident."

"Captain, could you establish the physical cause of the explosion and fire?"

A flicker of anger lit Captain Shen's eyes. "No, I could not. The physical damage to Forward Engineering on the USS *Michaelson* was so extensive it had destroyed almost every source of information."

"Including the engineering logs, sir?"

Commander Carr shot to her feet. "Objection. It has already been established by expert witnesses that the damage to the engineer logs could not have been caused by the explosion and fire."

"Sustained." Judge Halstead bent a stern look toward Commander Jones. "Phrase your questions with care, Counsel."

"Yes, Your Honor. Captain Shen, did you conclude that the physical damage to the engineering logs had been caused by the explosion and fire?"

Commander Carr looked unhappy, but said nothing.

Paul understood her concerns. *Captain Shen's conclusions are a matter of fact. Whether or not they were correct, and whether or not the members remember that they were wrong and why, is another problem.*

"You concluded the damage was caused by the explosion and fire. On what basis did you reach that conclusion?"

Captain Shen looked around again before answering. "I called in an expert computer technician to examine the records. He could find no signs of deliberate tampering. That meant the damage had to have been caused incidental to the accident."

Commander Carr stood again. "Objection. The investigation's conclusions have already been disproved by expert witnesses. Restating them will only confuse the issues before the members."

"Your Honor," Jones insisted, "these conclusions are matters of fact."

"They're *erroneous* matters of fact, Your Honor."

A stern look from Halstead silenced Commander Carr and Commander Jones. "I can rule on what's already been stated, thank you very much. If counsel for the defense wishes to discredit previously established facts, he must provide evidence to support his position. Are you prepared to do that, Commander Jones?"

"No, sir."

"Objection sustained. Counsel for the defense is to refrain from bringing up any further items that have previously been disproved in the course of the trial."

"Yes, Your Honor." If Commander Jones was abashed at Judge Halstead's ruling, he didn't show it.

And why should he be? Paul thought. *He's doing what he wants to do, bringing up stuff that will confuse and mislead the members of the court.* He glanced over at Lieutenant Silver, who had adopted a pose of intent interest. *Too bad he never looked that interested in doing his job when I stood bridge watches with him.*

Commander Jones resumed his position before Captain Shen. "Captain, you've already established your experience in the Navy and as an officer on warships. Was your conclusion that the accident was the result of no willful or negligent wrongdoing based upon that experience?"

Paul looked toward Commander Carr, but she made no objection. *Of course. She can't. We never disproved that result directly. It's one of the things the members of the court have to decide.*

Captain Shen nodded. "That's also correct."

"You did not find Lieutenant Silver to have been negligent . . ." Jones drew out his sentence deliberately as Commander Carr tensed. ". . . based upon what you knew at that time."

Commander Carr relaxed slightly, but her eyes watched Commander Jones like a hawk tracking prey.

Captain Shen answered firmly. "No, I did not."

"Did you find that anyone else on the *Michaelson* had shown a lack of professional conduct prior to and during the fire?"

"I did."

"Objection." Commander Carr had sprung up as if she'd been a coiled spring. "Irrelevant and immaterial. Lieutenant Silver is the one on trial here."

Commander Jones faced Judge Halstead. "Your Honor, Lieutenant Silver is indeed the accused. But if he is being accused of negligent behavior, it is relevant to establish how his actions were judged relative to other officers on the *Michaelson*."

Halstead frowned, then nodded. "Objection overruled."

Carr sat down as rapidly as she'd risen.

Jones turned back to Captain Shen. "I'll ask again, sir. Did you find anyone else on the *Michaelson* had shown a lack of professional conduct prior to and during the fire?"

"I did."

"Among them the collateral duty ship's legal officer, whose own subsequent investigation led to the charges being filed against Lieutenant Silver?"

"Objection!"

"Overruled. For now. Counsel for the defense, you are skating dangerously close to the edge in your examination of this witness."

"Yes, Your Honor." Jones began pacing. "Lieutenant Silver's actions during the accident on the USS *Michaelson* were exonerated by your report, by your assessment based upon your years of experience. Lieutenant Silver was subsequently awarded a medal for his actions the night of 19 September. Yet another officer, one whose actions were judged less than adequate in your report, initiated events that led to Lieutenant Silver being court-martialed. Do you regard that as a fair summation of events?"

"I do."

Paul tried not to look away from the witness stand. He kept his eyes firmly on Captain Shen. *I have nothing to hide. Nothing to be ashamed of. There's no way I'm going to act like the guilty one here.* Commander Carr looked back, saw Paul's posture, and nodded with a quick, grim smile. Paul took another look at Lieutenant Silver, who now had an expression of unfairly wounded pride. *How does he do that? Too bad he didn't go into acting instead of being responsible for the lives of others.*

Jones drove his point home again. "Captain Shen, did you conclude Lieutenant Silver had acted negligently?"

"No, I did not."

"No more questions."

Commander Carr rose with a casual ease which startled Paul. Instead of displaying tension, she moved like a leopard stalking a challenging opponent. "Captain Shen, are you aware of the evidence marshaled against Lieutenant Silver in the subsequent investigation?"

"I am partly aware of it."

"Are you aware of the discovery that the engineering logs were deliberately damaged?"

"Yes, I am."

"Are you aware that a major piece of equipment in Forward Engineering was found to be in urgent need of repair, and that Lieutenant Silver made every effort to acquire the necessary spare without informing either his department head or his commanding officer?"

"I have heard that."

"Are you aware, sir, that Captain Hayes, Lieutenant Silver's commanding officer at the time of the accident on 19

September, believes Lieutenant Silver lied to him regarding his knowledge of events?"

"No."

"Were you aware that a statement provided to the investigation by Petty Officer First Class Ivan Sharpe of the USS *Michaelson* never reached you?"

"Of course not!"

"Sir, which officer on the USS *Michaelson* did you assign responsibility to for gathering and forwarding documents to you during your investigation?"

Captain Shen's jaw worked. "Lieutenant Silver."

A slight rustle of motion attracted Paul's attention to the member's table. The officers there were watching Captain Shen with surprise and making notes. *Another direct hit on Lieutenant Silver, courtesy of Commander Alex Carr. So that's what happened to the Sheriff's statement. I wonder how many other stealth weapons Carr has tucked away inside her blouse?*

Commander Carr continued her questioning of Captain Shen as if unaware of the members' reactions. "Because Lieutenant Silver was the command duty officer on the night in question?"

"Yes."

"Do you find it interesting, Captain Shen, how many pieces of evidence regarding the accident on the USS *Michaelson* and the death of Chief Asher appear to have gone missing while Lieutenant Silver was in positions to influence them?"

"Objection." Commander Jones was doing his own imitation of a great cat whose territory was being challenged. "Trial counsel's statement is an attempt to prejudice the members by placing words in the witness's mouth, as well as an attempt to establish in court evidentiary matters still in dispute."

Commander Carr smiled at Jones. "I withdraw the question, Your Honor."

Judge Halstead eyed her narrowly. "Next time, Counsel, ensure you don't ask such inappropriate questions in the first place. The members are instructed to disregard the last question from trial counsel."

Carr looked momentarily contrite. "Yes, Your Honor. Captain Shen, does any of the information we discussed in any way alter your assessment of Lieutenant Silver's actions the night of 19 September?"

Captain Shen stared back at Commander Carr, his expression as hard as granite. "I would need to review all the information in its entirety. I do not make snap judgments based upon partial information."

Commander Carr leaned forward as if ready to spring. "Isn't that your job, sir, as commanding officer of a U.S. Navy warship? To make quick judgments based upon whatever information is available to you?"

Captain Shen's face clouded. "Commander, I do not need lectures from a *lawyer* regarding my duties as a line officer!"

Instead of responding directly, Commander Carr addressed Judge Halstead even as she kept her eyes locked on Captain Shen. "Your Honor, I ask that the court direct the witness to answer the question."

Halstead nodded. "It is so ordered. The witness will answer the question put to him."

"Thank you, Your Honor. Do you need the question repeated, Captain Shen?"

"*No*, I do *not. Commander* Carr, I am fully capable of, and experienced in, making the necessary decisions based upon available information. This situation does not qualify for such snap judgment."

"With all due respect, Captain Shen, that decision is for the court to make. I ask again, does any of the information found since your investigation was completed in any way alter your assessment of Lieutenant Silver's actions the night of 19 September?"

Captain Shen looked toward Judge Halstead, then Commander Jones, who grimaced but shook his head. He focused back upon Commander Carr. "Yes."

"Do you believe your assessment of Lieutenant Silver's actions the night of 19 September would differ if at that time you had available to you the evidence that has since been uncovered?"

"Yes."

"I would like to ask you, sir, as a Navy officer of unquestioned experience, what you would do if you uncovered information that a formal investigation had not been able to discover."

"It would depend upon the information."

"Information such as has been introduced into this court. Information such as we just discussed, Captain Shen. What would you have done? What would you advise another officer to do?"

"Objection. Trial counsel is asking the witness to answer a question regarding a theoretical situation."

Judge Halstead didn't wait for Commander Carr's reply. "Overruled. This is a matter within the witness's area of professional expertise."

Captain Shen's expression had shifted. Anger and contempt had been replaced by the intent expression of a combat officer sparring with a capable enemy. "I would tell that officer to bring the information to the attention of proper authority."

"His commanding officer, sir?"

"That's right, Commander Carr. His commanding officer."

"And that commanding officer would make the final decisions as to what action to take regarding this information?"

"Right again. That's the Captain's responsibility."

"What would you think of an officer who failed to bring such information to the notice of his commanding officer?"

Captain Shen's eyes finally flicked toward Paul, resting upon him for a fraction of a second before moving back to Commander Carr. "I would believe he had failed in his duty."

"Thank you, Captain Shen. No more questions."

Paul let out a breath he hadn't realized he was holding. *Am I free? Did Carr quash Jones's attempt to make me an issue? She sure turned Captain Shen's testimony around.*

Judge Halstead regarded Lieutenant Commander Jones. "Does defense counsel wish to redirect?"

"Yes, Your Honor. Captain Shen, did you make every attempt to determine the cause of the accident on the USS *Michaelson* and the death of Chief Asher?"

"Of course I did."

"Yet much of the information introduced into court was withheld from you, sir."

"Apparently."

"Captain Shen, suppose an officer had such information during your investigation, but did not reveal it until after your investigation was completed?"

"Objection! Counsel for the defense has introduced no evidence to substantiate innuendo that the evidence regarding the accident was available to anyone prior to the completion of Captain Shen's investigation."

"Your Honor—"

Jones's reply was cut off by a glare from Judge Halstead. "Does counsel for the defense plan to introduce evidence that this information was available to someone else during Captain Shen's investigation?"

"Your Honor, trial counsel has already asked the witness numerous questions regarding theoretical situations. This is simply one more such situation."

Halstead looked unhappy, but finally nodded. "Objection overruled. Continue."

Commander Jones couldn't hide a quick look of triumph. "Captain Shen, do I need to restate the question?"

"No. If someone deliberately withheld such information from my investigation, I would regard it as not only unprofessional but also as grounds for disciplinary action against that person."

"And since we're dealing with theoretical cases, Captain Shen, is there any way of knowing whether such a person had uncovered that information after your investigation and promptly passed it on in a professional manner, or unprofessionally withheld it and only gave it to his commanding officer after the results of the investigation proved unfavorable to him?"

"Objection!" If Commander Carr was simulating outrage, she was doing a very good job of it. "Your Honor, counsel for the defense is once again attempting to introduce speculation into evidence. He has provided not one iota of evidence to back up the question he has just put to the witness."

"Your Honor—"

"No." Judge Halstead's glare didn't fade this time. "Save your speculations for closing arguments, Counsel. I remind you once again that it is Lieutenant Silver who is on trial here."

"But Your Honor—"

"I said no. Objection sustained. Counsel for the defense is directed to avoid similar lines of questioning in the future."

Commander Carr seated herself, then made a quick thumbs-up gesture under her table, where only Paul could see it.

Commander Jones pondered Captain Shen for a moment longer, then shook his head. "No more questions."

"Do the members have questions for this witness?"

"Certainly." Captain Mashiko leaned forward, his elbows on the table and his hands clasped under his chin. "Captain Shen, your reputation is well-known to me. I respect your judgment. Given what you know at this time, would you want Lieutenant Silver to serve under you?"

Captain Shen frowned, though with apparent thought this time instead of anger. "I would wish to see more of the evidence before rendering final judgment on an officer."

"Assume what you know is all the information you'll have available. Would you want Lieutenant Silver in your command?"

Captain Shen glanced toward the defense table, where Lieutenant Silver once again wore his wounded-but-proud-professional face. "No. Not if I had a choice."

"But he did impress you favorably during your initial investigation."

"Yes, he did. Lieutenant Silver appears to be very good at impressing his superiors. In light of the factual information

I have since learned, I no longer trust that initial impression."

A rustle ran through the courtroom until it was once again stilled by an angry glare from Judge Halstead. Paul looked at Captain Shen, his own impressions shifting. *He did catch on to Silver. And he's admitting it. He's honest enough to do that. Well, he's Jen's father. He can't be all bad.*

"Thank you, Captain Shen. Do any of the other members have questions?"

Commander Herdez spoke respectfully. "Captain Shen, it appears you no longer stand by the results of your investigation."

"That's correct, Commander." Another rustle in the courtroom followed.

"Because of the information which was developed since you formulated those results, sir?"

"That is also correct."

Commander Jones came to his feet but spoke calmly. "Commander, if there is to be any attempt to impeach Captain Shen's work on that investigation—"

Herdez held up one palm. "No, Commander Jones. I have no intention of drawing such a conclusion."

Captain Mashiko nodded brusquely. "Nor can I imagine anyone attempting to pursue such a course of action against an officer who reached perfectly reasonable conclusions based on all of the information then available to him."

Commander Jones nodded. "I understand that, sir. But you must understand that Captain Shen is testifying for the record, under oath, and that his testimony could be used against him."

Captain Shen frowned at Jones, then at Commander Carr. She rose from her seat. "The government has no intention of pursuing any case against Captain Shen. There is no evidence of misconduct on his part."

Jones smiled tightly. "Thank you, Counselor, but as you're aware, your words now are not binding upon the government."

"Then the government is willing to stipulate as a matter of fact that Captain Shen conducted his investigation in a professional manner with no purposeful or inadvertent misconduct on his part."

"Thank you. I withdraw my objection to the member's line of questioning subject to that stipulation."

Commander Carr settled back in her seat, one hand gesturing Paul to lean forward so she could whisper to him. "We didn't need that kind of distraction clouding the case. If line officers think the JAGs are on a witch-hunt, they'll circle the wagons around each other in a heartbeat."

"Yes, ma'am. And we really don't have any evidence of misconduct on Captain Shen's part."

"Aside from him investigating an officer who's dating his daughter? Never mind. I agree."

Commander Herdez focused back on Captain Shen. "If you had been aware of the information that has since developed, would you have reached the same conclusions, sir?"

"No. I cannot imagine doing so."

"Thank you, Captain Shen."

Lieutenant Commander Goldberg cleared her throat softly. "Captain Shen, sir, why didn't you use the talents of Chief Warrant Officer Rose in your initial investigation?"

"I believed I had employed an expert with all the necessary expertise."

"But that expert wasn't as good as Chief Warrant Officer Rose."

Small spots of red appeared near Captain Shen's cheeks. "No, he was not. How many times must I state I was *wrong?*"

Commander Goldberg looked startled. "My apologies, Captain. My question wasn't meant to—"

Captain Mashiko shut her off with a wave of his hand. "That's all right, Commander Goldberg. Your question was a reasonable one, as was Captain Shen's response. These are not pleasant issues to address. Does anyone have further questions? That's it then."

Captain Shen left the courtroom, his posture militarily perfect, his eyes looking straight ahead. Paul watched him go. *I'm not looking forward to my next meeting with that man, whenever that may be.*

"Counsel for the defense recalls as his next witness Petty Officer First Class Ivan Sharpe."

Paul glanced around in surprise, seeing Sharpe marching down the center aisle of the courtroom until he reached the witness stand and was sworn in. *What's Jones planning to get out of the Sheriff? Talk about a hostile defense witness.*

Commander Jones stood before Ivan Sharpe. "Petty Officer Sharpe, I've reviewed your service record. It's very impressive. Not a blemish on it."

Sharpe watched Jones warily. "Thank you, sir."

"You assisted trial counsel in collecting statements from the crew of the USS *Michaelson* regarding the accident on 19 September, correct?"

"Yes, sir."

"And you earlier assisted Captain Shen in his investigation, once again handling his interactions with the enlisted crew."

"Yes, sir."

"In all those interviews, and in every other attempt to generate evidence against Lieutenant Silver, did you ever find anyone who could swear to having heard Lieutenant Silver order Chief Asher to undertake repairs to the power transfer junction in Forward Engineering?"

Sharpe's eyes shone with frustration, but his voice stayed clear and professional. "No, sir."

"No one? Did you find anyone who could swear to Lieutenant Silver having been the one who damaged the engineering logs?"

"No, sir."

"Was Chief Asher a friend of yours, Petty Officer Sharpe? You've previously testified that he often spoke with you."

"Yes, sir. Chief Asher was a friend of mine. Before he died."

Paul twisted one corner of his mouth upward. *Good one, Sheriff. You made sure nobody forgot that little fact.*

"Then you would have been strongly motivated to fabricate evidence if necessary in order to obtain a conviction?"

"Objection. Defense counsel's question—"

"Ma'am?" Sharpe interrupted Commander Carr even as he eyed Commander Jones. "I'd like to answer that question, ma'am."

Commander Carr made a gesture of acquiescence. "Very well, Petty Officer Sharpe. Objection withdrawn."

Sharpe held his head high as he answered. "Sir, I have never been motivated or tempted or attempted to fabricate evidence in any case I have ever encountered."

"Never, Petty Officer Sharpe?"

"Never, sir."

"Even if you were convinced of the guilt of the suspect?"

"Sir, if the suspect's guilty, they'll make a mistake. I'll find it, and I'll nail them. I'm not going to risk sending miscreants to jail, then having them sprung on appeal because I tried to ensure a guilty verdict. That's not the way I work."

"Then it's both a moral and a practical issue for you?"

"Yes, sir."

"You're to be commended, Petty Officer Sharpe. As I'm sure you're aware, on some occasions law enforcement professionals will attempt such measures."

"Only a few, sir."

"I won't debate that, Petty Officer Sharpe. Then you can confidently swear that the evidence so far presented against Lieutenant Silver in this court is complete, accurate, and truthful to the best of your knowledge?"

"Yes, sir, I can."

"Yet, as you previously confirmed, it does not provide any direct and unambiguous proof of Lieutenant Silver's guilt."

Sharpe paused, his eyes once again wary, then he smiled politely. "Sir, what the evidence proves is up to the members of this court to decide. I just gather it. They decide what it proves."

Commander Carr clasped her hands together in a subdued gesture of triumph as Paul grinned at Sharpe. *Sheriff, I would've fallen into the trap you just avoided, and agreed the evidence didn't prove the charges before I realized what I was doing. One more lesson in law enforcement for me from the master.*

Whatever disappointment Commander Jones felt at having his trap circumvented didn't show. "Thank you, Petty Officer Sharpe. No more questions."

Commander Carr hesitated, and Paul leaned forward to whisper. "Ask him what advice he gave me based on the evidence we had then."

"Thanks, Paul." Commander Carr stood and smiled at Sharpe. "Petty Officer Sharpe, what recommendation did you make to your ship's collateral duty legal officer based on the evidence available to you prior to your Captain's decision to refer Lieutenant Silver to a court-martial?"

Sharpe smiled briefly back at her. "Ma'am, I recommended we charge Lieutenant Silver with multiple violations of the Uniform Code based upon that evidence."

"Then you, as a seasoned law enforcement professional, did believe sufficient evidence existed even then to justify charging Lieutenant Silver."

"Yes, ma'am, I did."

"Has anything uncovered since that time caused you to question that recommendation?"

"No, ma'am."

"Thank you, Petty Officer Sharpe. No more questions."

Judge Halstead looked at Commander Jones. "Redirect, Counsel?"

"No, Your Honor. No further questions."

"Members?"

Captain Mashiko gave Sharpe a long, appraising look. "Petty Officer Sharpe, could you work with Lieutenant Silver?"

"I beg the Captain's pardon, sir?"

"Could you work with Lieutenant Silver? Assume he's exonerated by this court. Assume you end up his subordinate."

Sharpe didn't bother hiding his reaction to the question, but he replied in an unemotional voice. "Sir, I wouldn't be happy, but I'd do my job."

"Even though you believe Lieutenant Silver committed multiple violations of the Uniform Code and caused the death of a friend of yours?"

Sharpe's jaw twitched. "Yes, sir."

"But you'd keep on looking for evidence against him, wouldn't you? Even if he'd been acquitted."

"Sir, if new evidence came to light regarding a violation of the Uniform Code of Military Justice, I would bring it to the attention of proper authority. That's also my job, sir."

Captain Mashiko smiled. "Thank you, Petty Officer Sharpe. No more questions here."

Judge Halstead excused Sharpe, then nodded to Commander Jones. "Counsel for the defense, call your next witness, please."

"The defense rests, Your Honor."

Commander Carr looked toward the defense table, her expression guarded. Paul followed her gaze, seeing Lieutenant Silver sitting erect, his expression conveying calm confidence.

Judge Halstead nodded in acknowledgment. "Lieutenant Commander Jones, will Lieutenant Silver be availing himself of pre- or post-Gadsden trial procedure?"

"Post-Gadsden, Your Honor."

"Very well. The court-martial is closed, and will reconvene at 1300 in this courtroom for Lieutenant Silver's statement, followed by closing arguments."

Everyone came to attention once again as Judge Halstead and the members paraded from the courtroom. After the bailiff called out "carry on," Paul took a step closer to Commander Carr. "I guess Lieutenant Silver's making a statement."

Carr glanced disdainfully toward the defense table. "Apparently so. I'll give you twenty-to-one odds it's an unsworn statement."

"Ma'am, I wouldn't take that bet at two-hundred-to-one odds. Why did the defense call so few witnesses?"

Commander Carr sighed. "Because he managed to make most of his points about the evidence while cross-examining my witnesses. That couldn't be helped. A circumstantial case has some inherent weaknesses, and Commander Jones is smart enough to exploit them. I hope you'll excuse me now. I need to work on my summation."

Paul backed hastily away. "Yes, ma'am. I'm sorry, ma'am."

She smiled again. "Lieutenant Sinclair, I'm not one of your space warfare officers. I don't bite."

"Captain Shen might have a different opinion about that, ma'am."

Her smile widened. "I love it when I nail a defense witness that way. Later, Paul."

"Yes, ma'am."

Paul came out of the courtroom once again expecting to eat alone, but this time Kris Denaldo and Randy Diego were waiting for him. "Mike Bristol wanted to be here, too, but he figured since he's a witness . . ."

Paul nodded. "Yeah. Just as well to avoid any implication of impropriety."

Kris grinned. "You talk more like a lawyer every day."

"That's not funny."

"Have you got time for lunch at Fogarty's?"

Paul checked the time, then nodded. "Yup. Judges take long lunch breaks."

"Nice work if you can get it."

"They also have to work with lawyers every day."

"Good point."

They were seated before Randy Diego spoke. "We watched some of the, uh, testimony this morning."

Paul glanced at him in surprise. "I'm sorry. I didn't notice you'd come into the courtroom."

Kris Denaldo laughed. "Maybe because you're tracking the lawyers as if you were a target acquisition system? You're watching everything up there like a Mark 186 on full-spectrum scan."

"Yeah," Randy Diego agreed. "What was all that stuff? I couldn't figure out what they were doing."

Paul took a drink. "Basically, the defense was trying to imply I was at least partly at fault."

"You? They never said your name."

"They got it yesterday. But my name isn't the issue. The whole point of the defense is to throw up doubt that Scott Silver is solely responsible for what happened, and to point out the limitations of the evidence the prosecution has been able to accumulate."

Kris nodded. "That Captain Shen looks like a real tough bastard. No wonder Jen's got some hard edges."

"Yeah. Hey, that's my lady you're talking about."

"I roomed with her, Mr. Sinclair. Care to stop by and take a look at the dents still in lockers that she punched during fits of frustration?"

"No, thanks." Paul frowned down at his lunch for a moment. "I've been wondering. Jen's dad is hard as nails, but she comes back at him head-to-head. She doesn't surrender. But Silver . . . his dad's Vice Admiral Silver. Everything I've heard about him indicates he's as tough as Captain Shen. Maybe even tougher."

"So?"

"So maybe this acting stuff and responsibility avoidance is how Scott Silver chose to handle his father while he was growing up. Throwing up a false front to make it look like he was doing what his father wanted. Maybe he never wanted to be in the Navy, but he wouldn't confront his dad on the issue. Instead, he went in and didn't exactly dedicate himself to the job. But he made people with authority over him think he was dedicated."

"Like he did with his dad? Maybe that's true. I know some people who went into the service because their parents expected it. But none of them were screwups. They maybe wanted out as soon as their service commitment was up, but they didn't play pretend at being officers."

"You're right."

"You're not trying to say you're sympathetic to Silver, are you?"

Paul laughed. "No way. I'm trying to understand him. Why'd he do what he did? That's not the same as feeling he shouldn't get what he deserves."

Randy Diego swallowed a bite. "Then you're sure Silver's guilty?"

Paul hesitated just a moment. "Yeah. I'm sure. I just hope the members of the court feel the same way when all's said and done."

"What's the worst they can do to him?"

"I think the worst he could get is about ten or fifteen years in prison and dismissal from the service. The suggested punishments for each violation of the Uniform Code aren't hard and fast, though."

"Dismissal from the service?"

"Yeah. That's what they call it for an officer. It's like a bad conduct discharge or dishonorable discharge for an enlisted."

"Wow." Randy Diego contemplated his food for a moment. "Do you think he'll get that?"

"I hope he will."

Kris Denaldo cocked one eyebrow. "Wow. Paul Sinclair, thirsting after blood."

"I don't want revenge, Kris. I want justice."

"Are you sure you know what justice is?"

"In this case? As sure as I've ever been. But it's the responsibility of the members of the court to do their best in figuring that out, and I don't know what their definition of justice will be."

Kris nodded slowly. "I don't envy them."

The crowd of observers in the courtroom had grown a little larger by the time Paul returned from lunch. A lieutenant occupying the seat Paul had been using glared a challenge at him, then hastily vacated the seat as Commander Carr turned her own displeasure his way.

Paul waited, trying not to look nervous. *The worst is over. I'm not being called as a witness. Depending on how long Scott Silver's statement is, and how long summations by the prosecution and defense run, this could be over in less than a hour. Then it'll just depend on how long the members need to make up their minds on a verdict.*

Two days, and one morning, I guess. That seems like such a short time to decide someone's fate. But then, Chief Asher had only a fraction of a second before his fate was decided. Scott Silver has nothing to complain about.

CHAPTER THIRTEEN

☆　☆　☆　☆　☆

"THE court-martial will come to order." Judge Halstead looked toward the defense table. "Lieutenant Silver still desires to make a statement prior to the final arguments?"

Commander Jones stood. "He does, Your Honor."

"Very well. Lieutenant Silver, you have the right to make a statement. Included in your right to present evidence are the rights you have to testify under oath, to make an unsworn statement, or to remain silent. If you testify, you may be cross-examined by the trial counsel or questioned by me and the members. If you decide to make an unsworn statement you may not be cross-examined by trial counsel or questioned by me or the members. You may make an unsworn statement orally or in writing, personally, or through your counsel, or you may use a combination of these ways. If you decide to exercise your right to remain silent, that cannot be held against you in any way. Do you understand your rights?"

Lieutenant Silver stood as well, his movements crisp and professional, his face as determined as that of a model from a recruiting-poster. "Yes, I understand, Your Honor."

"Which of these rights do you want to exercise?"

"To make an unsworn statement, orally, and in person, Your Honor."

"Then, Lieutenant Silver, take the witness stand and proceed."

Lieutenant Silver walked steadily to the witness stand. Before sitting down, he looked from the defense table, to the trial counsel table, to the members' table, his gaze clear and confident. He sat, appeared to gather his thoughts, then began speaking. "Members of the court, Your Honor, I wish to offer a firm denial to every charge made against me."

Silver's jaw jutted slightly as he raised it a bit, his pose now almost heroic. "I admit to some errors in judgment. I was new to my job, new to my ship, in the same sort of situation I know you've found yourselves in many times. I chose to concentrate on learning that ship, learning my professional duties aboard her, before concentrating on my duties as Main Propulsion Assistant. In retrospect, this was a mistake, as it created the false impression that I didn't take my primary duty seriously."

Paul barely avoided showing his reaction to Silver's words. *That incredible slimeball. He wasn't concentrating on any duties, as I knew all too well from having to stand watch with the worthless no-load. But boy does he sound sincere.* Paul looked toward the members' table. None of them were showing any reaction to Lieutenant Silver's speech. *Don't fall for it. Please don't fall for it.*

"Yes, I fell behind in one area of my work as Main Propulsion assistant. One area! With so much else to learn, I put off handling official correspondence for a while. I regret that. But that is not a crime, or else every officer who ever fell behind a little in one aspect of their work is also guilty of such an offense.

"I never heard of the problem with the power transit junction until informed the unit had failed on Friday, 18 September."

Paul took a quick look toward the members again. *Did they notice Silver got the name of the equipment wrong? That's a small but telling error.*

"I was startled and upset. Who wouldn't be? I'd been let down by my leading chief petty officer. It happens sometimes. I knew that. But I hadn't expected it because Chief Asher appeared to be a capable sailor."

Oh, man, it's a good thing Sheriff Sharpe isn't listening to this. Or any chief from the Michaelson. *They'd probably jump the gate and break Silver's jaw.*

"What did I do? I endeavored to solve the problem as quickly as possible. If I'd had to involve my department head and my commanding officer, I would certainly have done so. But by using initiative and acting calmly, I was able to acquire the needed spare in the nick of time." Lieutenant Silver paused, nodding toward everyone in the courtroom. "That's what a good officer is supposed to do. I didn't and don't ask for praise for doing that. I didn't even tell anyone because whoever got credit for fixing that equipment wasn't important. Getting it fixed was what counted. Then I made another mistake."

Silver drew in a deep breath, his expression now bearing a shade of sorrow. "I entrusted the spare to Chief Asher on Saturday morning. How was I to know he'd try to install it single-handedly? I can understand why the chief didn't want his own lapse to be widely known, but I never guessed he'd take that kind of risk."

Paul noticed Commander Carr's hands. They were gripping a light metal rod so tightly the fingers were white, and the rod was slowly bending under the pressure. *You and me both, Commander Carr. Right now I'm wishing the stuff Silver's accused of carried the death penalty.*

Lieutenant Silver shook his head. "Apparently, Chief Asher chose to do so. Don't ask me how he got multiple authorization codes. I'm certain he didn't have mine. If only the engineering logs hadn't been damaged, they'd prove this.

"I agree as well that I should have been more forthcoming with Captain Hayes, but the night of 19 September I had no idea of what Chief Asher had attempted. It never occurred to me to link the problem with the power transformer to the explosion and subsequent fire. Once I began to realize what might have happened, it rattled me. I admit that. My concern for Chief Asher caused me to provide an inadequate report to my commanding officer that night. Not deliberately, but out of distress engendered by concern for my personnel.

"As to the other charges, I took care of my equipment. The equipment losses in Forward Engineering are tragic, but nowhere near as tragic as the loss of Chief Asher. I don't know what drove him to his actions, but I do regret them. To fault me for those actions and their consequences is not only unfair, but would set a dangerous precedent for every other officer whose equipment was damaged or lost due to unforeseen events.

"I did not damage the information in the ship's engineering logs! I don't even possess the necessary software to do that. Did those who searched my stateroom find such software? No. Do they have any evidence I was the one responsible for the damage to those logs? No. Ask them. They know what I say is true.

"Manslaughter? My God. Is every officer who loses a sailor under tragic circumstances to be charged with causing that death? I did not order Chief Asher to repair that piece of equipment contrary to safety regulations. Ask them about that. Do they have any evidence I did so? Could they produce anyone who heard such an order? No, they could not, because it did not happen.

"I admit I committed some errors of omission in my statement to Captain Shen's investigation, but this was an error of the heart. I honestly believed any misconduct on Chief Asher's part would cause the Navy to deny his family the benefits they deserved, as well as besmirching the reputation of a man who could no longer defend himself."

Paul noticed a sharp pain, and looked down to see his hands clenched so tight the nails were digging into his palms.

Lieutenant Silver looked around the courtroom again, his expression confident once more. "Of course I mentioned this concern to my division. Of course I did. I deeply regret that they so misinterpreted my remarks. But none of them,

not one, claims that I ordered them to lie. Because I had
nothing to ask them to lie about.

"I ask that you acquit me of all of these unfair charges. In
the name of justice. In the name of honor. In the name of re-
fusing to scapegoat an officer for an accident he could not
prevent, and a death that will always shadow his own life.
Thank you. Thank you for giving me a chance to defend myself. Thank you for judging me as you would wish to be
judged in my place."

Lieutenant Silver stood and began walking back toward
the defense table. Paul heard a small sound and leaned
closer to Commander Carr. He could barely make out the
words she was muttering under her breath. "Five minutes.
Give me five minutes to cross-examine that contemptible
weasel. Just five minutes."

Paul leaned back again, trying to suppress his own anger.
*But Commander Carr won't get five minutes. Or one minute.
Because Silver's unsworn statement can't be subjected to
cross-examination, or questioning by the members. No one
gets to pick apart his self-serving lies and throw them back
at him. And the worst part is that everything Silver said
sounded so reasonable. Invert the truth, the truth as I believe
the evidence proves it, and it sounds perfectly reasonable.
It's all Chief Asher's fault. The fault of a man who can no
longer defend himself. Chief Asher, I swear, if Lieutenant
Silver somehow beats these charges, I'll keep after him until
I find charges that will stick. I owe that to you. Silver's not
going to walk away from this, no matter how good an actor
he is.*

Judge Halstead had also kept his reaction to Lieutenant
Silver's statement to himself. Now he looked at Commander
Carr. "Is trial counsel prepared for closing argument?"

"Yes, Your Honor." Commander Carr's voice was as
smooth and confident as Lieutenant Silver's had been. She
strode to the center of the court, facing the members. "Captain Mashiko, members of the court, you've all heard the evidence. There's no need for me to restate everything. No
need to go back over Lieutenant Silver's knowingly false
statements to his commanding officer. No need to recite the

many errors he deliberately made in his sworn statement to Captain Shen. No need to point out Lieutenant Silver's inexplicable disappearance from his duties as command duty officer during exactly the time period when the engineering logs of the USS *Michaelson* were damaged. No need to review the quality of Chief Asher's service, which had never been questioned prior to this. Not even any need to point out that in his statement Lieutenant Silver *repeatedly* failed to correctly name the equipment that needed repair in forward engineering. Equipment which was *his* responsibility as Main Propulsion assistant, yet he is so unfamiliar with it *even now* that he cannot identify it properly.

"No, I want you to consider three facts. The first is that Lieutenant Scott Silver's commanding officer, Captain Hayes, no longer has any confidence in Lieutenant Silver. What does it take to convince a commanding officer that one of his officers is untrustworthy? Such a determination, as you all know, is not made at the drop of a hat.

"Secondly, Captain Shen, the officer whose investigative report initially cleared Lieutenant Silver of fault, no longer believes his conclusions were correct. He, too, expressed a lack of confidence in Lieutenant Silver. What does it take to independently convince *two* commanding officers that another officer is untrustworthy? Two officers entrusted with command of warships of the United States Navy, two officers with extensive experience and great responsibilities, and neither of them believes Lieutenant Silver.

"Thirdly . . ." Commander Carr spun around suddenly, her arm rose, and a finger pointed at Lieutenant Silver. "When cornered, what did Lieutenant Silver do? Whom did he blame for everything that went wrong? A dead man." A ragged edge of fury crept into Commander Carr's voice. "A dead chief petty officer. A professional who had demonstrated years of selfless service to his comrades, to his superiors, to the Navy, and to his country. That's who Lieutenant Silver blames. Someone unable to defend himself. Someone no longer able to counter Lieutenant Silver's self-serving and totally false statements. Someone who gave his life in the service of his country. Lieutenant Silver claims he doesn't care who gets the credit, but he doesn't hesitate to attach blame to the dead! And worst of all, Lieutenant Silver didn't even care how his actions and orders endangered Chief Asher, does not even now accept responsibility for his culpable and criminally careless behavior that forced Chief Asher into a situation which caused his death."

Commander Carr's voice grew calmer again as she turned her back on Silver and faced the members again. "I am asking you to find Lieutenant Scott Silver guilty as to all charges and specifications. When someone dons the uniform of an officer of the United States Navy and takes the oath of loyalty to the Constitution, they assume great responsibilities even as they are entrusted with great power over their fellows. Lieutenant Silver manifestly failed in his responsibilities. His commanding officer does not doubt that. The evidence all points in Lieutenant Silver's direction. There is no doubt he lied both to his commanding officer and to Captain Shen. A sailor is dead. A sailor whose life was entrusted to Lieutenant Silver. A warship suffered extensive damage, damage in a compartment full of equipment entrusted to Lieutenant Silver. Is there any reason to believe Lieutenant Silver's accusations against Chief Asher? Is there any reason to doubt the assessment of Lieutenant Silver's commanding officer?

"Members of the court, I ask you to ensure Lieutenant Silver is never again given the opportunity to bring about the death of a sailor, never again given authority over any other member of the service, never again entrusted with any equipment or ship belonging to the United States Navy. I ask you to find him guilty as to all charges and specifications. Not in the name of revenge, not in the name of vengeance, but in the name of justice. Lieutenant Silver has repeatedly betrayed the trust placed in him by the United States. I ask you not to give him a chance to do so again. Thank you."

Commander Carr walked deliberately back to her table, while Paul watched her with wide eyes. *If that performance doesn't convict Silver, I don't know what will.* He looked toward Lieutenant Silver, whose expression seemed less calmly confident now. *Sweat, you bastard. You've run into someone who can spin words just as well as you can, and she wants your hide.*

Judge Halstead, still apparently unaffected by the emotions swirling through the courtroom, looked toward the defense table. "Is counsel for the defense prepared to present closing argument?"

"Yes, Your Honor." Commander Jones walked to the same position Commander Carr had taken to address the members of the court. "Lieutenant Silver has already clearly stated the grounds for acquitting him of all charges. Bluntly, there is no evidence directly linking him to most of the offenses with which he is charged. It is a case built entirely on circumstantial evidence, a house of cards resting on a foundation of speculation and innuendo. How can an officer be charged with giving an order that no one can testify they heard him give? How can an officer be charged with negligence because one of his sailors, acting alone, overrode safety interlocks and attempted a hazardous repair task single-handedly? How can an officer be charged with destroying data in his ship's engineering logs when the only evidence supporting that charge is that Lieutenant Silver was aboard the ship when the destruction allegedly happened? He was aboard the ship on his duty day! This is evidence of wrongdoing?

"Certainly, Lieutenant Silver was not seen by others for a brief period during the evening of 19 September. As his own department head testified, seeking out a small moment for private grief over the death of one of his sailors is not only understandable, but also appropriate.

"Yes, Lieutenant Silver admits to having provided incomplete information to his commanding officer on one occasion. Not out of intent to deceive, but out of shock and horror at what had happened. Yes, he tried to protect Chief Asher's reputation and service benefits during the formal investigation. This was perhaps misguided, but it was an error of the heart.

"Dereliction of duty? Because he failed to open some mail? If Lieutenant Silver's performance was so derelict, why was he not relieved of duty earlier? If Lieutenant Silver couldn't be trusted to carry out his responsibilities, why did he continue to serve in such vitally important positions as officer of the deck underway and command duty officer in port? What commanding officer would risk his or her ship in the hands of an officer they truly did not trust? If they did so, wouldn't they themselves be guilty of dereliction of duty?

"There was a tragedy on the USS *Michaelson*. No one denies that. I ask you not to compound that tragedy by convicting an innocent man, a dedicated and caring officer, because a scapegoat is being sought. A conviction on any charge requires proof that Lieutenant Silver did commit such an act, not just an unsupported assertion that he could have done something improper. Such proof was not presented during the course of this trial because such proof does not exist.

"I ask you to acquit Lieutenant Silver of all charges. He has done his duty in trying circumstances. He does not deserve to be the victim of a process aimed at finding a warm body to blame for a tragedy. No officer deserves that. Thank you."

Commander Jones returned to his seat as the courtroom stayed silent. Paul looked toward the members of the court. *That's it. All the evidence has been presented, all the arguments made. Now it's up to those officers to decide Silver's fate.*

Judge Halstead gazed around the courtroom. "Captain Mashiko, the members may begin their deliberations. The court-martial is closed, and will reconvene tomorrow morning at 1000 in this courtroom."

PAUL stood in the wardroom of the *Michaelson*, hastily gulping down some bitter coffee. Commander Sykes nodded to Paul from his customary seat. "Good luck, Mr. Sinclair."

"Thank you, sir."

"You seem a bit uneasy."

"The coffee sucks, Suppo."

Sykes grinned. "I'm wounded. You're really worried about the verdict, aren't you?"

Kris Denaldo, entering the wardroom at that moment, nodded as well. "That's it, right, Paul?"

"Yeah, that's right. No matter how strongly I believe in Silver's guilt, the evidence is overwhelmingly circumstantial. If we'd had Chief Asher to testify, there wouldn't be any problem. But since Asher's dead, Silver's able to avoid that."

Kris shuddered as she tasted some coffee. "Suppo, this stuff really reeks. That's ironic, isn't it, Paul? If Silver did cause Asher's death, then Asher's death helps protect Silver."

" 'Ironic' isn't the word I'd use."

"Have you heard about the snipes? They say Chief Asher's been playing games with them in Forward Engineering."

Paul felt a sudden chill. "Playing games?"

"Yeah. The snipes claim he's still supervising them."

"I guess Davidas's ghost has some company now." Paul sighed and disposed of his empty coffee container. "Have you seen Gabriel? I've got duty today, but she's standing it for me until I can get back to the ship."

"Oh, yeah. She had a departmental meeting, but she asked me to tell you not to worry. As long as you're back before the end of the day it's no problem. If you're going to be delayed past that, Gabriel wants you to give her a call."

"No problem. Thank her for me." Paul sketched a salute toward Commander Sykes. "By your leave, sir."

Sykes hoisted his own coffee in reply. "I'm certain you will perform ably, Mr. Sinclair."

"It's out of my hands, Suppo. See ya, Kris."

Paul stepped out onto the quarterdeck, adjusting his uniform to ensure he looked his best. Lieutenant Sindh came by and inclined her head gravely. "May justice be done this day."

"So I hope." *There's one of my greatest fears resolved. No one's treating me like an outcast because I helped bring Silver to a court-martial. Well, Smilin' Sam Yarrow's been avoiding me like the plague, but that's not exactly a bad thing from my perspective. No matter what the members of the court decide, the good officers of the Merry Mike think I was right to do what I did. Even Commander Garcia, something I never expected.* Paul saluted Chief Imari, the officer of the deck. "Ensign Gabriel's filling in for me in the duty section until I get back. Let me know if anything—" Paul bit his tongue. He'd been about to say "blows up," using the standard slang for a sudden emergency. In this context, with Chief Imari who'd been on the quarterdeck when something did blow up, it wouldn't sound right at all. "If any emergencies arise. Request permission to go ashore."

"Yes, sir." Chief Imari returned his salute. "Permission granted."

Paul strode across the brow, pausing to turn and salute the national flag aft, then headed for the courtroom.

COMMANDER Carr raised one hand in brief greeting, then focused back on the front of the courtroom, her tension revealed only by one thumb tapping quickly against her index finger. Lieutenant Commander Jones sat with Lieutenant Silver at the defense table, neither one speaking as Jones read something on his data pad, and Silver looked straight ahead.

"All rise." A shuffle of feet as everyone came to attention. Judge Halstead looked around, then seated himself. "Bailiff, please ask the members of the court-martial to enter."

The members entered the courtroom, their faces revealing nothing.

"Captain Mashiko, have the members reached findings?"

Mashiko nodded. "They have."

"Are the findings on Appellate Exhibit Six?"

"Yes."

"Would the trial counsel, without examining it, please bring me Appellate Exhibit Six?" A long minute passed while Judge Halstead studied the exhibit dispassionately. "I have examined Appellate Exhibit Six. It appears to be in proper form. Please return it to the president. Lieutenant Silver, would you and your counsel stand up, please. Captain Mashiko, announce the findings, please."

Captain Mashiko cleared his throat. "Lieutenant Scott Silver, this court-martial finds you guilty of violating Article 92, Dereliction in the Performance of Duties, Article 107, False Official Statements, and Article 131, Perjury. This court-martial finds you not guilty of all other charges and specifications."

Paul bit his lip, looking downward, not wishing to see Lieutenant Silver's expression at the moment. *Triumphant? Stunned? It doesn't matter. Dammit. We nailed him with some heavy offenses, but Silver's getting off on everything directly related to Chief Asher's death. Damn.*

"Does defense counsel wish to present any matters in extenuation or mitigation?"

Lieutenant Commander Jones, his face betraying no emotion, shook his head. "No, Your Honor."

Paul finally looked at Silver, whose face seemed locked into rigidity. But his eyes betrayed confusion. *You finally got caught, didn't you? And you can't figure out why the games didn't work this time.*

"Captain Mashiko, have the members reached a sentence, or do you require further time for deliberations?"

"The members have reached a sentence."

"Captain Mashiko, would you announce the sentence please."

"Lieutenant Silver, this court-martial sentences you to one year in confinement, forfeiture of all pay and allowances, and dismissal from the United States Naval Service."

A hissing sound in the courtroom marked sudden indrawn breaths. Paul's stomach knotted. *Okay. They got him. Maybe it was a trade-off. Agree to convict on enough charges to get Silver out of the Navy. I don't care. He's toast. He'll never kill another sailor.*

Judge Halstead began speaking again, telling Lieutenant Silver of his rights to appeal. The statement droned on, long and exactly as laid out in the Manual for Courts-Martial. Paul looked back to see if any other members of the *Michaelson*'s wardroom had shown up, and was surprised to see Jen sitting in the courtroom. She flicked a smile his way, then her face returned to professional detachment as Judge Halstead finished his statement and gazed around the courtroom one final time. "The court-martial is adjourned."

Paul rubbed his face, feeling tension finally begin to ebb from his body. *Not perfect. No. But we got him for you, Chief Asher. Rest in peace. If you can.* He watched Lieutenant Silver being escorted from the courtroom, Lieutenant Commander Jones at his side, Silver's face now reflecting incomprehension at his fate. *And as for you, Silver, I hope your sleep is haunted every night by what you caused.*

Commander Carr turned to face him just as Jen came to his side. "A partial victory, but we got what we wanted, Mr. Sinclair."

"Yes, ma'am. Thank you. You did a great job."

"I've done better. Thanks for the support from your end." Carr focused on Jen. Paul watched the two women sizing each other up, then Commander Carr smiled at Jen. "Does this gentleman belong to you, Lieutenant . . . ?"

"Shen. Yes, ma'am, he does."

"The famous Lieutenant Shen! Thank goodness that issue didn't come up during the trial. And aren't you the lucky one. But I've a feeling Paul's going to be keeping you busy." Carr extended her hand to Paul. "Good luck. Nice working with you, Lieutenant Sinclair. Maybe we can do it again sometime."

Paul shook her offered hand. "With all due respect, ma'am, I'm hoping to avoid courtrooms for a while."

She laughed. "That's often out of our hands. Look me up if you need advice." With a small wave of farewell, Commander Carr headed out of the courtroom.

Jen gave Paul a hard look. " 'Look me up if you need advice,' " she mimicked.

"Jen."

"Maybe I'll just come along when you do that."

"Jen, she's married, she's a commander, and she's never

acted in any way that implies any personal interest in me! Couldn't you at least get jealous of someone I could reasonably get involved with?"

"Like who?"

"Like—" Paul's words froze in his throat. *Am I totally insane? How can I possibly provide any names in answer to that question without digging myself a hole so deep I'll never climb out?* "Like no one."

"You hesitated."

"I just had to run through everyone I'd ever known or met and realize none of them could ever fall into that category. Except you."

"Very smooth."

They walked out of the courtroom. "Are you actually serious about this, or are you just yanking my chain?" Paul demanded. Jen started to reply, then halted. Paul followed her gaze. "Commander Herdez. Good morning, ma'am."

Herdez nodded in greeting. "Lieutenant Sinclair. Lieutenant Shen. Do you have time to accompany me for a drink, Mr. Sinclair? Ms. Shen is of course invited as well."

Paul looked over at Jen, who was watching Commander Herdez as if she were a cobra who'd just reared up in their path. "Certainly, ma'am. Right, Jen?"

Jen exchanged glances with Paul. "Uh, yes. Yes, ma'am."

Commander Herdez started walking toward the officers' club while Paul and Jen followed a half step behind. Jen looked over at Paul and insistently gestured a question. Paul shook his head and made his own gesture to display a lack of knowledge.

At this early hour, the officers' club had few patrons. The simulated wood paneling and lowered lighting gave the bar an unreal quality, as if it were reached by walking through some sort of portal into an old bar back on Earth. That had been the intent when the bar was designed, of course, but Paul could never decide if the environment reassured or disturbed him.

Commander Herdez took a seat near the end of the bar, gesturing Jen to the seat on her left side, then Paul to the seat on her right. Jen managed another questioning glare at Paul behind Herdez's back. Paul answered with another expression of ignorance.

"What will you two be drinking?" Herdez asked.

Paul waved vaguely toward the *Michaelson*'s berth. "I need to go on duty once I get back to the ship, so I'd better stick to straight Coke, ma'am."

Jen nodded. "Me too."

Herdez beckoned to the bartender, another luxury intended to invoke Earth-bound bars. "Three Cokes." She waited silently until the drinks came. "Mr. Sinclair. Ms. Shen. To a job well finished." They all drank to the toast, then Herdez turned to face Paul. "Do you remember our last conversation here?"

"Yes, ma'am. Every word."

"You've a better memory than I, then." Commander Herdez looked intently toward the back of the bar, as if memorizing the labels displayed there. "How do you feel you did, Mr. Sinclair?"

"I wish I'd been able to get him on all charges, ma'am."

"No doubt. I do, as well. But there was sufficient doubt concerning some of charges. Or insufficient proof, if you prefer."

Paul remembered something Commander Carr had said. "We had to work with what we had."

"That's always true, Mr. Sinclair, regardless of our line of work. The only variation is how much we have. Sometimes, though all too few of them, we have all we want and need. Usually, there is less to work with."

"Yes, ma'am." There was another pause, as Commander Herdez sipped her drink. "Ma'am? You told me something once. You said it was easy to work well for good officers, and hard to work well for bad ones. That was the challenge, you said, to work well despite having a superior who wasn't very good. But that also applies even if you're not actually working for them, doesn't it? Any bad officer makes it hard for everyone his or her actions impact."

Herdez looked at Paul again. "Very good, Mr. Sinclair. You're correct. Bad officers require us to make hard decisions."

"There's always the easy decisions," Jen blurted out.

Commander Herdez turned to look at Jen. "There's always the option of doing nothing, yes, even though that risks more and more damage to the Navy and its personnel. I give both you and Mr. Sinclair the credit of assuming you would not shirk your duties in that manner."

Jen met Herdez's eyes. "You *know* I wouldn't, ma'am."

"Yes. I do. You're a fine officer."

Herdez turned back toward Paul, missing the sight of Jen's jaw dropping. "I imagine you nonetheless felt some qualms about bringing about the court-martial of a fellow junior officer."

"Yes, ma'am, I did."

"But you overcame them."

"Yes, ma'am. Partly because I remembered something else you told me once, about honoring the sacrifices of those who die."

Herdez seemed amused. "I rarely hear myself quoted back to me so often in one conversation. Life is full of advice and experiences, Mr. Sinclair. Some good, some bad. That advice and experience don't directly shape us. It's the lessons we draw from them that do that. And then our own examples help shape others. This was Lieutenant Silver's greatest failing, that he did not realize his responsibility to others."

Paul snorted a brief laugh. "You don't have to tell me that, ma'am."

"Indeed. You handled yourself well." Commander Herdez consulted her watch. "I see time is passing. I'm sure you need to return to your ship soon."

"Yes, ma'am."

Paul and Jen stood as Commander Herdez watched. "You make a good couple."

Jen stared back, rattled again. "Ma'am?"

"Oh, you heard me, Lieutenant Junior Grade Shen. There's nothing wrong with your ears or your mind. As for you, Mr. Sinclair, I'm still keeping an eye on you. I'll be going to another ship when I leave the staff. Your presence on board that vessel would be welcome."

It was Paul's turn to be thrown off-balance. "Ma'am?"

"If circumstances permit, Mr. Sinclair, I'd like you as a subordinate again. Was it clear that time?"

"Y-yes, ma'am." *Working for Herdez again? Oh, that's going to be painful. But how could I turn down her offer?*

"That is all." Commander Herdez checked her watch again. "And I must return to work as well. Until next time, Mr. Sinclair and Ms. Shen." She walked briskly out of the bar, half of her drink still untouched.

Jen watched her go. "Did you hear what she said?"

"You mean about us being a good couple?"

"Oh, please. Since when does Commander Herdez care about the personal lives of her juniors?"

"Jen, she does."

"That woman has had her bitch-switch stuck on battle-override since the day she was born, and she never cared for me. 'Watch that attitude of yours, Ms. Shen.' 'Are you certain, Ms. Shen?' 'Is there a problem, Ms. Shen?'"

"But she said she thinks you're a fine officer."

"Yes. Exactly. What do you suppose she meant by that?"

"That . . . she thinks you're a fine officer?"

"Herdez? Ha!"

"Uh . . . what do you think she meant?"

"I don't know, but I'll find out. Right now, you and I have another call to make."

"Where?"

Jen mustered an artificially bright smile. "USS *Mahan*."

"Jen!"

"I mean it, Paul. There's unfinished business. Trust me on this. You've got to beard the, um, lion in his den."

"I didn't know lions had beards."

"Whatever! Let's go."

"Just what am I supposed to say to a captain who thinks I'm pond scum?"

"Just wait." Jen met Paul's stubborn gaze. "Trust me, Paul Sinclair!"

Paul let his gaze drop and shook his head. "Okay. You're the expert on your father, and I'm sure as hell not going to hide from him for the rest of whatever career I have in the Navy."

"Damn straight."

The lieutenant junior grade standing officer of the deck on the *Mahan* reacted to Jen's presence with a barely concealed sense of panic. When he saw Paul, the panic rose by an order of magnitude. Clearly fearing the worst, the *Mahan*'s officer of the deck called the Captain, listened to the reply, then ordered the petty officer of the watch to escort Paul and Jen to the wardroom.

Captain Shen sat there at a table mirroring that on the *Michaelson* except for a different random pattern of nicks and scratches. Two other officers occupied the wardroom, but after one steely glance from their captain they hastily exited. Captain Shen, as erect as if he were sitting at attention, turned to face Jen. "I gather you're not here to give me an apology."

"I only apologize when I'm wrong. I learned that from a certain senior naval officer."

"That you did." Captain Shen stood, then pivoted to look at Paul, his eyes seeming to bore straight into Paul's brain. "It seems you were declared right by the court-martial, Mr. Sinclair. And I was declared wrong."

"Sir, we both did our duty."

"Don't condescend to me, young man. I screwed up. I failed to determine accurately the causes of that accident on the *Michaelson*. I hope you're not expecting me to thank you for bringing that to public notice."

Paul shook his head. "No, sir."

Captain Shen's glower didn't diminish, but he slowly extended one hand. "But I do thank you for what you did for the Navy. You did a good job, mister."

Paul stared at the hand uncomprehendingly for a moment, then reached out to shake Captain Shen's hand. "Thank you, sir." Shen's grip was so tight Paul almost flinched, but instead he returned the pressure.

Captain Shen's eyes locked on Jen. "My daughter is not a fool."

"No, sir."

"There's a difference between courage and foolhardiness. Do you know that difference?"

"Yes, sir."

"That'd better be correct. I will be keeping an eye on you, Mr. Sinclair. God help you if you harm my daughter or her career."

"I will never do that, sir."

"I'll be watching. Dismissed."

Paul saluted, but Jen suddenly lunged forward and hugged her father. "Thank you, Dad. Sorry we fought."

Captain Shen's face actually revealed a brief, gentle smile. "Me, too."

Jen stepped back, saluted, then followed Paul out the hatch. The messenger escorted them back to the quarterdeck, and they left the USS *Mahan* behind.

Paul strode along, his thoughts focusing on Captain Shen's last words to him. *Great. Commander Herdez is watching supportively from afar to see if I measure up to her impossible standards, and now Captain Shen will be watching antagonistically from afar to see if I measure up to his impossible standards. Maybe I should just dive out an airlock in my gym shorts. That way I'd only be subjected to impossible pressure for a few seconds.*

"A buck for your thoughts," Jen stated with a smile.

"You don't want to know."

"I can imagine. My father isn't going to forgive and forget anytime soon that you made him look real bad."

"Pardon me all to hell. How can such an intelligent man fail to see I was trying to do right by Chief Asher and prevent anyone else suffering because of an officer who failed in his duties?"

"He knows that, Paul. He respects what you did. That's why he shook your hand. He just doesn't like it."

"Is this supposed to be helping me understand?"

"Paul Sinclair, I've spent my entire life trying to understand my father, and I'm a long way from achieving that goal. He's proud and he's smart, too proud and too smart sometimes to realize he can be wrong." Jen sighed. "This all complicates things. I wanted to be able to tell you my answer to your proposal by now."

"Proposal? What proposal?"

"Your *marriage* proposal. Did you forget about it already?"

"Oh." Paul felt his face warming. "I'm sorry, it's just so much has been going on, and I'm still pretty distracted and—"

"Uh-huh. Probably thinking about that sweet little lawyer commander of yours."

"Jen, I swear—"

Jen started laughing. "Anyway, with my father still on the warpath, I don't want him thinking I'm marrying you just to spite him. Believe it or not, I'm hoping to fully mend this rift someday."

"I believe you're hoping, yeah."

"Can you wait a while longer for an answer, Paul?"

He smiled and held her close, unworried about observers for a moment. "Jen, I can wait. No problem."

Her voice was slightly muffled against his shoulder. "What happened to the fear of losing me?"

"I'm not afraid anymore, Jen. You stuck with me through this, and, like you said, you came back."

"Oh, great." Jen pulled back a bit and glared up at him. "So now you're complacent and confident."

"That's not how I meant it."

"Let's see. You've alienated my father, and now you've told me you feel secure in taking me for granted. What's next? Are you going to go for three and ask me if I've gained weight recently?"

"No! I meant—"

"It's not like I've been all that wonderful to begin with."

"Jen, that's not true. You've been fine."

"*Fine?* I've been *fine?*"

"No! That's not what I meant to say. You've been great. Wonderful. The greatest, most wonderful—"

"Too late. That's strike three. If this was a baseball game, you'd be out."

"It's not a baseball game. It's real life. No, it's not real life. It's the Navy. Different rules."

Jen grinned. "Very different rules. When you make admiral, I'm going to take credit."

"I'll never make admiral at the rate I'm going. I'm beginning to wonder about making full lieutenant."

"You'll make it. Just try to stay away from courts-martial from now on." The quarterdeck of the USS *Michaelson* loomed ahead. "I know you need to get back aboard."

"Yeah. Duty calls."

"Does it ever stop calling?" She leaned closer and smiled. "I can't kiss you with the quarterdeck of your ship watching us, but I can tell you I'm proud of you. Like Dad said, you did a good job."

"Thanks, Jen. See you tomorrow?"

"Count on it. And stay out of courts-martial!"

She waved and walked rapidly toward where the USS *Maury* was docked. Paul watched for a moment, then walked toward the quarterdeck of the *Michaelson*. *Stay out of courts-martial? It's not like I've ever sought them out.* He saluted the national flag, saluted the officer of the deck, and requested permission to come aboard.

Kris Denaldo returned the salute. "I'm glad you're back. Ensign Gabriel wants to hand over the duty to you, you've got a message to see the Captain as soon as possible, Lieutenant Kilgary says you've got the quarterdeck watch, and Commander Garcia, Lieutenant Bristol, Chief Imari, and Petty Officer Sharpe are all looking for you."

Paul found himself laughing. *Life in the Space Navy's back to normal. I wonder how long that'll last this time?*

NOW AVAILABLE IN PAPERBACK

A NOVEL OF UNIVERSAL LAW

"HEMRY DELIVERS." —William C. Dietz

A JUST DETERMINATION

John G. Hemry
Author of the *Stark's War* series

ACE
0-441-01052-0